Conversations with Biographical Novelists

Conversations with Biographical Novelists

Truthful Fictions across the Globe

Edited by
Michael Lackey

BLOOMSBURY ACADEMIC
NEW YORK • LONDON • OXFORD • NEW DELHI • SYDNEY

BLOOMSBURY ACADEMIC
Bloomsbury Publishing Inc
1385 Broadway, New York, NY 10018, USA
50 Bedford Square, London, WC1B 3DP, UK

BLOOMSBURY, BLOOMSBURY ACADEMIC and the Diana logo are trademarks of Bloomsbury Publishing Plc

First published in the United States of America 2019

Cover design by Daniel Benneworth-Gray

A catalog record for this book is available from the Library of Congress.

ISBN: HB: 978-1-5013-4146-5
PB: 978-1-5013-4145-8
ePDF: 978-1-5013-4148-9
eBook: 978-1-5013-4147-2

Typeset by Deanta Global Publishing Services, Chennai, India

To find out more about our authors and books visit www.bloomsbury.com and sign up for our newsletters.

For Julie, Anya, and Katya,
With Love and Gratitude

Contents

Acknowledgments

My Bloomsbury editor, Haaris Naqvi, has consistently been an astute critic and an unwavering supporter of my work. Above all others, I want to thank Haaris for all his encouragement and insight over the years. Without him, this project could never have happened.

The University of Minnesota is one of those rare institutions that puts a high premium on humanities scholarship. Doing a book of interviews like this requires much funding for travel and a research assistant, and my university (University of Minnesota, Morris) as well as the University of Minnesota system more generally has supported every request I made in order for this project to happen. Specifically, I would like to thank the director of grants development (Roger Wareham) and the interlibrary loan manager (Sandy Kill) for their support and professionalism. They consistently make my job easier and more enjoyable.

Over the years, I have had the good fortune to have outstanding research assistants. Corinne McCumber was my research assistant for this book, and I can only describe her as the Platonic Ideal of the research assistant. There is no way to adequately express my gratitude for all that she has done on this book project as well as other related projects.

I would like to thank all the interviewers and interviewees. This project has required an enormous amount of labor, and I am so grateful to the interviewers for being patient with all my requests and for the authors, who have given so generously to this project.

Finally, I would like to thank my wife, Julie Eckerle, who is always my most severe critic, my most generous reader, and my greatest inspiration.

Introduction: The Agency Aesthetics of Biofiction in the Age of Postmodern Confusion

Michael Lackey

In 2012, when I first had the idea of interviewing biographical novelists for my *Truthful Fictions* book, I felt like I was embarking on an isolated scholarly journey. At that time, I knew no other scholars who were working on biofiction, and I was unaware of the scattered and little work that had been done about the aesthetic form. But as I interviewed authors and started to write my introduction to the book, I made some unexpected discoveries. John Keener, who entered the University of Kentucky's PhD program around the same time as me, wrote his dissertation about biographical novels. It was published in 2001. In *Biography and the Postmodern Historical Novel*, Keener discusses the work of Guy Davenport, who taught at the University of Kentucky and with whom John and I both studied. In one of my graduate courses, a professor had us read Davenport's "Ithaka," a short story about Ezra Pound, and I wrote a paper about this work. In 2009 and 2011, I published articles about Zora Neale Hurston's biographical novels *Moses, Man of the Mountain* and *Herod the Great*, and in my 2012 book *The Modernist God State*, I did an extensive analysis of David Mamet's *The Old Religion*, a biographical novel about Leo Frank. Put simply, biofiction has been a significant part of my academic life for the last twenty-five years: I have been reading and teaching it, I have been writing about it, and I have even published about it, and yet, I didn't see it as biofiction until I started working on my first book of interviews with biographical novelists.

This issue of simultaneously seeing and not seeing came into sharp focus for me at the 2017 MLA convention in Philadelphia. I was at the International Auto/Biography Association's annual party, where a scholar looked at my nametag and said: "You're the guy who has invented a whole genre of fiction, aren't you?" By this point, Bloomsbury had just released my anthology *Biographical Fiction: A Reader*, so I was able to say that people have been discussing biographical fiction for decades. I then named a few past and present authors who have been writing and thinking about the aesthetic form. Of course, it would be disingenuous and even hypocritical of me to fault or criticize the scholar who told me that I invented the genre, because, like him, I totally failed to see what was right in front of me for nearly twenty years.

This blindness in relation to biofiction has been a problem since the 1930s. The first person to exhibit a significant failure in seeing was Georg Lukács. In *The Historical Novel* (1937), Lukács clarifies when and why the historical novel came into being. While Lukács concedes that there were some historical novels in the seventeenth and eighteenth centuries, he claims that the aesthetic form came to fruition in the early nineteenth century. This certainly makes sense. After the French Revolution, there was concern that such a catastrophe could happen again. Therefore, to understand what led to 1789, there arose in Europe history programs, in which professors used rigorous and scientific methods of analysis to identify and define what caused major historical events. This attempt to systematize history and to establish more reliable methods for doing history explains the rise of the historical novel, an aesthetic form that visualizes the laws and causes of major historical collisions.

To his credit, Lukács was able to see that biographical novels were coming into being in the early part of the twentieth century. He notes the popularity of the biographical novel during the 1930s, and he names some of the most prominent practitioners of the literary form. But Lukács fails to see two separate things. One of the many strengths of *The Historical Novel* is Lukács's ability to identify and define the social, political, and intellectual forces that gave birth to the historical novel. But what he does not see is that different forces gave birth to the biographical novel. This is in part the case because he does not see the literary form as separate and distinct from the historical novel, which is the second failure in vision. For Lukács, the biographical novel is a subgenre or a version of the historical novel, and consequently, he uses historical-novel criteria to analyze and assess it. Within this framework, the biographical novel is an irredeemable aesthetic form, one doomed to literary failure.

Ironically, the biographical novel came into being to counter and correct the limitations and even dangers of the historical novel. The post-Enlightenment rise of positivisms (historical, philosophical, and psychological) and the desire to predict historical collisions made the historical novel appealing and even a seeming necessity for political progress. But there were those who considered the philosophy underwriting the historical novel to be deterministic at best and fatalistic at worst. Henry James captures the essence of this critique in a letter to Sarah Orne Jewett. Jewett sent James a copy of her historical novel *The Tory Lover*. In 1901, James responded, but instead of using the occasion to discuss the quality of *The Tory Lover*, he uses it to reflect on the irredeemable vices of the historical novel. For James, this is an aesthetic form that is characterized by "a fatal cheapness." The historical novelist gives readers a multitude of "little facts that can be got from pictures and documents, relics and prints," but what it lacks is "the real thing," which consists of "the invention, the representation of the old consciousness, the soul, the sense, the horizon, the vision of individuals in whose minds half the things that make ours, that make the modern world." All of these are "non-existent" in the historical novel, an aesthetic form that James calls "humbug." Of crucial importance for James is the mysterious, indefinable, semi-autonomous dimension of human consciousness, which is not just different from but diametrically opposed to the "conditioned"[1] consciousness represented in the historical novel.

In *The Master*, a biographical novel about James, Colm Tóibín strategically references the Jewett letter in order to voice some of the problems with the historical novel. Late in the novel, Henry's brother William expresses concern about Henry's work. He encourages Henry to abandon the novel of manners about the superficial and materialistic English and to turn his attention to a "novel which would deal with our American history," specifically "about the Puritan Fathers." Henry not only rejects William's proposal, but also uses this occasion to express his contempt for the historical novel: "'May I put an end to this conversation,' Henry said, 'by stating clearly to you that I view the historical novel as tainted by a fatal cheapness.'" To punctuate his point, Henry ends the discussion by dismissing William's proposal with a single word, "humbug."[2] The significance of these remarks is staggering. In one of the most celebrated biographical novels, the protagonist denounces the historical novel, which clearly suggests that *The Master* should not be considered a historical novel.

In fact, Tóibín makes this point directly in his interview with Bethany Layne, which is included in this volume. When asked if there is a difference between the historical novel and the biographical novel, Tóibín says that there is. He then provides an example. Tóibín notes that James's apartment in Kensington was wired for electricity in 1896. A historical novelist, Tóibín claims, would incorporate such a detail in his or her work: "If you're writing a historical novel this is a marvelous scene for you where you're actually getting a key moment in history and you're integrating it into lives and you're seeing what the next day will be like." Tóibín does not write such novels, because "it would ruin my novel. It would be the end of the novel." By stark contrast, he writes biographical novels, which means that he "must be in James's mind all the time." This interview with Tóibín explains why he incorporated James's claim to Jewett about the historical novel being "tainted by a fatal cheapness" into *The Master*. For both James and Tóibín, there is a fatalistic dimension to the historical novel, because it underscores how humans are at the mercy of ("conditioned" by) external forces—the wiring of the house will have necessary and discernible consequences on the inner life of characters. James considers the historical novel a cheap literary form because it lacks the richness of creativity—the historical "novel" merely copies what is.

Tóibín is not alone in his critique of and objections to the historical novel. Here are some of the claims of biographical novelists in this volume. The award-winning Spanish writer Javier Cercas told Virginia Rademacher: "Sometimes they [critics] say I write historical novels. I don't really like that label. I write novels in which history has a role, but they are not historical novels." Critically acclaimed Polish writer Olga Tokarczuk says something similar in an interview about her biographical novel on Jacob Frank: "I'm not really a fan of historical novels." She objects to them because they prioritize "historic events," and the popular ones reinforce "conservative schemata." Colum McCann is more forceful and direct. As he says in an interview with Robert Birnbaum, which is not included in this volume: "I hate the term 'historical novel.'"[3] He provides more insight into his reasons why in an interview with Synne Rifbjerg, which is also not included in this collection: "I hate the idea of the term 'the historical novel,' not that I hate history and not that I hate the novel, but I hate the way those two words match each other and plunge themselves down into an aspic, a softness; it almost wears a bodice of sorts."[4] McCann's metaphors (aspic and bodice) suggest that the historical novel contains and straitjackets the human, thus inhibiting expansion, development, and growth.

That such prominent biographical novelists object to and/or distance themselves from the historical novel is not as important as why, and it is through the blindness of a prominent American scholar that we might find some answers. Since the publication of *The Political Unconscious* in 1981, Frederic Jameson has been engaging, challenging, nuancing, and correcting Lukács's work. In his most recent book (*The Antinomies of Realism*), Jameson concludes with a forceful and direct confrontation with the Hungarian Marxist. The historical novel was Lukács's favored literary form, and in his 1937 book, he ends by offering suggestions for renewing and reinvigorating it for his present. Given this fact, Jameson's chapter title seems to implicitly throw down the gauntlet at Lukács's feet: "The Historical Novel Today, or, Is It Still Possible?" While Jameson questions some of Lukács's assertions and conclusions, his chapter ultimately does not mark a break with *The Historical Novel*, because Jameson ends by carrying on Lukács's project through his attempt to clarify how the historical novel must be updated in order to represent what he refers to as "historical futures."[5]

There are many strengths in Jameson's book and chapter, but I want to focus on just a couple of his moments of blindness, because they help identify some of the entrenched scholarly prejudices against the biographical novel. Jameson starts by raising some formal problems about defining the historical novel. After indicating that there are so many varying, divergent, and contradictory forms of the contemporary historical novel, Jameson entertains the possibilities that the genre is impossible or perhaps "not the historical novel at all but rather realism as such."[6] What Jameson does so well in this chapter is to chart transformations in the aesthetic form from Walter Scott through Balzac to Tolstoy and beyond. If Scott gave us an aesthetic form predicated on "the distinction between the world-historical individual and the average hero,"[7] what Tolstoy did was to abolish the agency and power of the world-historical individual and to elevate the general will of the masses. Behind this aesthetic shift is Tolstoy's conviction that freedom is an illusion and therefore history rather than people dictates what happens. So Tolstoy "leaves history intact, with all its cataclysmic events," but he does so by "stripping it of its actors and decision-makers."[8]

After *War and Peace* emerges a new form of the historical novel. Here is how Jameson describes this new iteration: "The next logical and formal possibility will then be that of names without events, and indeed I believe this reduction of the world-historical individuals to little more than their names is what characterizes one of the two distinctive forms of the historical novel today."[9] In a move certainly in the tradition of Lukács, who condemned the "biographical form in the present-day historical novel,"[10] Jameson clearly opposes the biographical turn. Says Jameson about the new form of the biography-focused historical novel: "As we shall see, such historical names, bloated with biography, tend towards an autonomy of their own as the history of which they were once a part becomes spongy."[11] Fascinating here is not so much what Jameson says but what he fails to consider. Is it possible that *War and Peace* symbolized not so much the death of one form of the historical novel and the birth of another but the emergence of a new and different aesthetic form? It is worth noting that Jameson does not even mention the term biographical novel in this chapter, even though he discusses a few as if they were historical novels.

At this point, I will use Jameson's evidence and argument to limn an alternative literary history, one that better articulates the conditions under which the biographical novel came into being. In his chapter, Jameson reads developments in the historical novel in relation to the Annales school, which does "away with narrative actors altogether."[12] Jameson does not specifically engage the work of anyone belonging to the Annales school, but one such scholar wrote about the rise of the biographical novel. In his 1938 essay "History and Psychology," Lucien Febvre discusses "novelistic biographies," of which there has been "such profusion in recent years." Febvre is not approving.

He lists a number of vices, including "repeated blunders, mix-ups and gaffes"; "the systematic plundering and cynical plagiarizing of historians by the busy hacks of historiography"; and the tendency of authors to "project themselves as they are back into the past with their own feelings, their own ideas and their own intellectual and moral prejudices."[13] Novelistic biographies, what we now refer to as biographical novels, are irredeemable aesthetic forms, because the authors misrepresent biography and therewith history.

What Febvre, Lukács, and Jameson fail to see is that biographical novelists do something radically different from historical novelists. Oscar Wilde authored what is perhaps the first theoretical reflection about biofiction. Here is what Wilde's Vivian from "The Decay of Lying" says in the year 1889: "If a novelist is base enough to go to life for his personages he should at least pretend that they are creations, and not boast of them as copies. The justification of a character in a novel is not that other persons are what they are, but that the author is what he is."[14] For the author of biofiction, of utmost importance is the artist and his or her creative vision, and not the historical past or the biographical subject, because, as Wilde says: "Literature always anticipates life. It does not copy it, but moulds it to its purpose."[15] According to this logic, those who write history or biography are not and cannot be artists, because they merely represent (copy) what is or was.

This stance against representational aesthetics does not mean that authors should not write biofiction. Wilde acknowledges that novelists can base a work on a person from the past, but he qualifies this claim by saying that the author, to actually be an artist, should appropriate rather than represent the biographical subject's life, and the author should do this in the service of his or her own creative vision. This is exactly what Wilde did. In the play *Salomé*, Wilde uses the biblical figure to create a more sexually aware and liberated female. This work clarifies Wilde's view of art, which is best expressed in "The Decay of Lying": "A great artist invents a type, and life tries to copy it."[16] The gifted writer does not merely picture the past through a representative protagonist. He or she strategically creates a character, even if it is based on a real person, in advance of the age in order to bring into existence a new reality in the present and for the future, thus making this person a creative artist rather than a mere copyist.

Understanding that the biographical novel does something radically different from the historical novel poses a substantive challenge to the work of Febvre and Jameson. History becomes spongy for those who focus on bloated biography, as Jameson says, and authors of biofiction make repeated blunders, as Febvre claims, but this is not because biographical novelists are ignorant of history, as Jameson and Febvre imply. It is because they are using rather than representing history and biography, which is one of the distinctive features of the biographical novel. Take, for instance, George Moore's *The Brook Kerith*, published in 1916. In this novel about Christ, Jesus does not die on the Cross. Rather, Joseph of Arimathea takes Christ down from the Cross right before he dies and nurses him back to health. Moore's Jesus then renounces some of his former teachings as fanatical. Did Moore just happen to get the details about Christ wrong? Did he fail to read the last chapters of Matthew, Mark, Luke, and John? Or, did he consciously and strategically alter the historical record? And if so, for what purpose?

David Ebershoff's 2000 novel *The Danish Girl* will help clarify one of the standard practices of the biographical novelist. Based on the life of Einar Wegener/Lili Elbe, the first person to undergo sex confirmation surgery, Ebershoff states explicitly that the "reader should not look to this novel for very many biographical details of Einar Wegener's life." Ebershoff found "some important facts about Einar's actual transformation,"[17] and he then used those details in order to craft a narrative that would underscore the degree to which "there is universality to Einar's question of identity."[18] In short, Ebershoff converted Einar/Lili into a symbol. Thus, Ebershoff used Einar/Lili, not to picture the actual life of a real historical figure, but to express his own views about the link between a constructed identity and human agency. Given the emphasis on fiction, authors of biofiction do not pretend to give readers unadulterated historical or biographical truth. To illustrate, here are the reflections of three prominent biographical novelists from three different periods. A friend of Moore's noted that the Christ in one of the early drafts of *The Brook Kerith* was not identical to the one found in the Gospels. Here is Moore's reply: "You must look upon my Jesus as an independent creation, and not as an attempt to discover what the real man was from the Gospels."[19] Gore Vidal has written some outstanding biographical novels, and in a 1974 interview with Gerald Clarke, he said the following about the subject of his biographical novel *Burr*: "My Burr is not the real Burr."[20] Joanna Scott has written two brilliant biographical novels, and in a 2016 essay about biofiction, she says the following about Egon Schiele, who is the protagonist of her biographical novel *Arrogance*: "I was not trying to pretend that my Schiele was the real Schiele. I just wanted him to be real."[21]

To bring into sharper focus one of the key distinctions between the two forms, let me briefly discuss two borderline cases. There are some historical figures about whom so little is known that one must raise the question whether a biographical novel is even possible. For instance, Hannah Kent has published *Burial Rites*, a novel about an Icelandic woman who was executed for murder, and *The Good People*, a novel about an Irish woman who killed a four-year-old boy because she thought he was a changeling. For *The Good People*, Kent acknowledges in her interview for this volume that she only "had two newspaper articles" and "no biographical information." Given the dearth of biographical material, Kent turned to history in order to construct her protagonist, so her main character, named after the actual person, is a logical product and representation of her environment:

> With *The Good People* I again did a lot of research into the outside world or environment. I looked at the lives led by people who resembled these characters or who could be said to. So that, while everything was imagined with *The Good People*, it was nonetheless likely, as likely as possible.

This characterization reveals much about the nature of Kent's aesthetic approach, which sounds more like the method of the historical novelist than a biographical novelist. Instead of referring to her novels as primarily fiction, she calls them "speculative biographies," and as such, they "borrow from or lean on history in that they are research-led and a great amount of research is required." Thus, she concludes that her novels "reinstall historical context as significant and determining."

The Nigerian-Belgian author Chika Unigwe has a much different approach. Unigwe has published a biographical novel about Olaudah Equiano, and she is currently writing one about Equiano's daughter, Joanna, about whom almost nothing is known. In my interview with her, I asked if it is possible to do a biographical novel about someone when there is almost no information. Her response is illuminating.

> In a historical novel, the author is invested in being true to the realities of that time, so there is little space to create characters that transcend their time in a very radical way, which you can do with biofiction. So in that way I think that Joanna is certainly more biofiction than historical fiction. There are things that Joanna does that I doubt that she would have been able to do if I were writing historical fiction. So I think in biofiction you are able to dream a lot more, a lot wider. Your dreams are more expansive, as a writer, than in historical fiction.

Given the differences between the historical and biographical novel, readers come to the works for very different things. As Unigwe concludes: "Readers don't come to biographical fiction for truth. They come to biographical fiction for possibilities." What readers want from the historical novel is an accurate representation of "the realities of that time," but what they want from the biographical novel is a model of a figure that transcends the deterministic forces of history and the environment, and this is something that places the protagonist of the biographical novel in irreconcilable conflict with the protagonist of the historical novel.

In her interview for this volume, Rosa Montero best clarifies what readers get from biographical novels. For Montero, the goal of the biographical novel should not so much be to depict a real life as to use the life "to try to better understand the world in its greater complexity." To illustrate, she asks what Robert Graves achieves in his novel *I, Claudius*. Her answer: "He wasn't telling us the story of Emperor Claudius, but rather making an impressive fresco of the human condition." Montero makes a similar claim about Camilo Sánchez's *The Widow of the Van Goghs* (*La viuda de los Van Gogh*). Montero considers this novel exemplary "in the way that the author uses the life of Van Gogh, the character, to tell a greater story about the nature of existence." She specifies exactly what fiction writers give readers in a discussion about the human "capacity for symbolic understanding." Biography is of crucial importance, because it provides humans with an "existential map," which is a framework about "how to live." In Montero's case, she has authored a biographical novel about Marie Curie. But it would be incorrect to say that her goal with this work was simply to give readers a picture of the famous Polish scientist. Rather, Montero unapologetically says that she "used Marie Curie as an enormous screen on which to project . . . possibilities." Like Unigwe, the biographical subject is a figure that the author uses in order to imagine into existence possible ways of thinking and being for readers in the present and the future. As Ebershoff says in his interview: "Artists are visionaries; they see something that does not yet exist. They can bring into creation something that is not yet there." Here is how Kevin Barry, who has authored a biographical novel about John Lennon, puts the matter in his interview: "There are figures [like Lennon] who introduce something new in terms of their persona and in terms of how they carry themselves." Thus, what we get in Barry's novel is not so much the life story of Lennon but the author's reflections about creating meaning and life through art: "It was a book about how to try and make a piece of art: whether it's a novel, or an album, or a painting, or film. It's about going to the dark place—we don't write, or draw, or make music because we are fine, we do it because we're messed up, because life is meaningless, cruel, often disastrous and ridiculous and there is no fucking shape to it. That's why we make art, as an attempt to put meaning and shape onto our lives." For Sabina Murray, who has authored a biographical novel about Roger Casement, the biographical novelist uses the life of someone to illustrate what it means "to be a person" in the midst of overpowering forces that dehumanize us.

What biographical novelists primarily reject is the governing idea animating the historical novel, which is Karl Marx's claim that it "is not the consciousness of men that determines their being, but, on the contrary, their social being that determines their consciousness."[22] By stark contrast, biographical novelists spotlight the power (albeit limited) of human consciousness to evade determinism and thereby to shape an alternative reality into being. This is a central idea in the biofiction of Emma Donoghue (*Life Mask* and *The Sealed Letter*). In my interview with Donoghue, she notes that she has authored a historical novel, and it functions exactly as Lukács says it should: "My very first historical novel, *Slammerkin*, is probably a bit deterministic in that while I show this girl enjoying certain limited freedoms, by the time she's sixteen, she's executed. So she's been slapped down." Instead of foregrounding the protagonist's ability to counter or transcend the deterministic forces of her culture, she invented a character "mostly to show those social forces at work." But her biographical novels are much different. For instance, Donoghue has recently published *Frog Music* (2014), a wonderful biographical novel about Jenny Bonnet, a cross-dressing, nineteenth-century woman from San Francisco who flagrantly defied unjust laws and paid for her defiance with her life. For Lukács, the best historical novelists never create "eccentric figures" like Bonnet, "figures who fall psychologically outside the atmosphere of" their "age."[23] This only stands to reason, because the ideal character of a historical novel is supposed to symbolically represent the whole place and age. But when I asked Donoghue about her objectives as a biographical novelist, she said that she chooses "characters who don't seem to fit the historical narrative." Thus, her character Bonnet is not "an illustration of nineteenth century social forces crushing somebody." To the contrary, she is a character who "has an almost trans-historical memorability to me," says Donoghue.

This objective of using a biographical subject to provide an "existential map" for semi-autonomous and quasi-meaningful living explains the kind of characters to which biographical novelists are drawn. For example, Rudi Nureyev is the protagonist of McCann's *Dancer*, and he functions as the quintessential biographical subject, which is to say that he is the living refutation of the historical novel. A loyal Soviet, Nureyev's father has adopted Marx's political philosophy, and he tries to indoctrinate his son with that ideology. As the elder Nureyev says to the young Rudi: "Your social existence determines consciousness, son."[24] But this is precisely the philosophy that Rudi and McCann ultimately reject as flawed, limited, debilitating, and unacceptable. McCann brilliantly articulates his view of art's uncanny power to assist readers and viewers in the process of evading determinism and of constructing self through his description of the genesis of *Dancer*. At first blush, it might seem that what motivated McCann to write *Dancer* was his passionate interest in Rudi's life. But actually, it was Nureyev's impact on McCann's friend Jimmy Smallhorne that inspired McCann. In my interview with him, McCann admits that he "wasn't really interested in Rudolf Nureyev." To the contrary, he "was much more interested in the story of Jimmy Smallhorne, a working-class friend of mine from Dublin who was mesmerized when he saw Rudolf Nureyev on television. It was a story like Jimmy's that mattered, and that was my beginning of stepping into the biographical novel." The goal of the biographical novelist is not to accurately represent the life of the biographical subject—McCann admits that his Nureyev is "probably 90 percent imagined." Rather, it is to use the life story of the historical figure to make the reader "come alive in a different body, in a different time." In short, the artist's goal is to "embody us in wakefulness," and this is what Rudi seeks to do through dance and McCann through fiction.

Let me briefly specify how this functions in *Dancer*. As an artist, Rudi does not simply project into being a moment of beauty. He sets into motion a process of endlessly discovering and creating a new reality. Here is how one character in the novel describes Rudi's impact on her: "Rudi had stood upon that stage like an exhausted explorer who had arrived in some unimagined country and, despite the joy of the discovery, was immediately looking for another unimagined place, and I felt perhaps that place was me."[25] Rudi's art mentally transports his viewers into the unimaginable, a psychic space that transcends imagined borders and limitations. In sum, Rudi does what Wilde and Tóibín's 1899 James do, which is to use art in order to set life into motion. As one character notes: "Rudi gathers a group around himself, launching into some diatribe about dance as an experiment, all its impulses going to the creation of an adventure and the end of each adventure being a new impulse towards further creation, *If a dancer, he is good*, says Rudi, *he has to straddle the time! He must drag the old forward into the new!*"[26] Rudi uses dance to introduce his audience to the dynamic power of creating life, and McCann, Ebershoff, Barry, Montero, Unigwe, Donoghue, and Tóibín do the same through their novels. Within this framework, it is McCann's usage of Rudi, Ebershoff's usage of Einar/Lili, Barry's usage of Lennon, Montero's usage of Curie, Unigwe's usage of Joanna, Donoghue's usage of Bonnet, and Tóibín's usage of James that enable them to achieve their aesthetic goals. Biographical and/or historical truth—these are subordinate to the more important goal of liberating the reader into the embodied wakefulness of a creating and creative consciousness, a consciousness that leads to new possibilities in seeing and being.

That biographical novelists do something very different from historical novelists should be clear. But what led them to adopt this approach to the novel? A quick look at a recent collection of essays in the volume *The Biographical Turn* will provide one possible answer. This volume focuses on "the emergence of biographical research as an accepted critical scholarly method of investigation since 1980."[27] For the editors of the volume, of crucial importance for the biographical turn was an "agency perspective,"[28] one that emphasizes not the degree to which individuals fit within the causal network of historical systems from a given time, but one that underscores the role "individual agency"[29] plays in redirecting and reshaping established historical approaches to the past. This same intellectual energy led to the early twentieth-century shift from history to biography and the rise of the biographical novel.

The prominent Bloomsbury writer Lytton Strachey, who revolutionized the biography, provides some compelling insight. Like Jameson, Strachey was cognizant of the historical determinism that dominated the nineteenth century, which is found in the works of Tolstoy and the historical positivists. While Todd Avery does not discuss Lukács, his recent work about Strachey provides us with valuable ways of thinking about what led to the shift away from historical fiction and to the legitimization of biographical fiction. For Avery, one of the major developments of the early twentieth century is the concurrent rejection of history as a science and the rise of history as primarily an art. This would lead to the emergence of corresponding aesthetic forms, and for Avery, it was the Bloomsbury Group that would transmute this intellectual development into "a type of life writing that contains biofiction's DNA."[30] The key figure for Avery is Strachey.

In a 1903 essay, Strachey says that history as a scientific method is extremely limited. While it can provide some insight into the mechanical operations of cultures and societies of the past, "the method by which true conclusions are reached with regard to individual minds of the past cannot be termed a scientific method: it is a totally different method." Therefore, Strachey concludes that "the only possible way of narrating the characteristics of human minds is by the aid of—not the scientific—but the artistic method."[31] Thinking of history more in terms of art than science set Strachey on an aesthetic journey that would move increasingly more toward biofiction, a point that Avery intelligently makes by quoting from the preface of *Eminent Victorians*: "Human beings are too important to be treated as mere symptoms of the past."[32] Strachey would develop this idea further over the course of his career, culminating in the book *Elizabeth and Essex*, which, Avery claims, "Strachey deliberately approached . . . in a biofictional spirit" by "intentionally" manipulating and inventing "historical facts in the service of an intensely personal vision."[33] To support this claim and approach, Avery quotes a 1927 Strachey letter that could be read as one of the key ideas in a biofiction manifesto: "I wish I could write Elizabeth as well. If only she could be reduced to nonsense—that would be perfect. The whole of Art lies there. To pulverize the material and remould it in the shape of one's own particular absurdity."[34]

Lukács, who condemns the biographical novel in a whole section of *The Historical Novel*, and Febvre see the biographical novel, but because they consider it a version of the historical novel, they fail to see that it is its own thing, that it consciously and strategically does something different from and even in conflict with the historical novel. Jameson does not even see the biographical novel, but this is because he is so fixated on how intellectual shifts gave birth to different iterations of the historical novel that he could not see that a countervailing aesthetic form like the biographical novel was coming into being.

This blindness in relation to the biographical novel has staggering consequences, because scholars frequently use unsuitable and inappropriate criteria to analyze and assess the literary form. The scandal surrounding the publication of William Styron's *The Confessions of Nat Turner* (1967) will prove useful at this point. While it is true that much of the controversy revolves around Styron's representation of blacks, a close look at the work of prominent writers suggests that the primary objections were aesthetic in nature. More specifically, scholars believe that Styron failed as a historical novelist. For instance, one year after the novel was published, ten black writers wrote vicious attacks of Styron and *The Confessions*. According to Lerone Bennett, "Instead of following the traditional technique of the historical novelist, who works within the tension of accepted facts, Styron forces history to move within the narrow grooves of his preconceived ideas."[35] Within this framework, novelists are free to fill in the gaps of history by inventing characters or scenes that could logically supplement or illuminate the established facts, but they do not have the freedom to alter the historical record. Based on this approach, John A. Williams says that a writer who focuses on a historical figure "is required to be *both* a novelist and a historian."[36] These criticisms explain why the editor of the volume, John Henrik Clarke, raised the following question in his introduction: "Why did William Styron create *his* Nat Turner and ignore the most important historical facts relating to the real Nat Turner?"[37] Had Bennett, Williams, and Clarke understood some of the conventions of the biographical novel, they would have realized that these critiques are misguided and inapplicable. This is not to say that there can be no critique of Styron and his novel. Rather, it is to say that one should not criticize a biographical novel for failing to be a historical novel, for failing to do what a historical novel does.

We get additional insight into the issues at stake in a famous clash about aesthetics. In 1968, the historian C. Vann Woodward moderated a forum titled "The Uses of History in Fiction" with Robert Penn Warren, Ralph

Ellison, and Styron. What made this event so momentous was a tacit conflict regarding the differences between the historical and the biographical novel and the legitimacy of the biographical novel. By this time, Warren had published *All the King's Men* (1946), a historical novel about 1930s populism in the South. While most readers know that the protagonist is loosely based on the life of the politician Huey Long, Warren changed his name to Willie Stark. This enabled Warren to take many liberties with his character. Styron made a different choice by naming his protagonist after the actual historical figure. This caused considerable outrage. Ellison confronted and criticized Styron, saying that "the moment you put any known figures into the book, then somebody is going to say, 'But he didn't have that mole on that side of his face; it was on *that* side. You said that he had a wife; he didn't have a wife.'" Naming the protagonist after an actual historical figure makes a person vulnerable to criticism, so Ellison advises authors to "lie and disguise a historical figure"[38] by changing the name. Ellison was not the only person at this forum to fault Styron for authoring a biographical novel. During the question and answer session, one audience member, someone clearly critical of Styron, made the following remark: "I want to ask Mr. Warren this: since we all felt that *All the King's Men* had to do with Huey Long, why didn't *he* say Huey Long, or King Fish, or something like that? I wonder what would have happened to *The Confessions of Nat Turner* had it just been called the *Confessions of a Revolt Leader*, or something like that."[39] The implication is that, had Styron authored a historical novel rather than a biographical novel, he would not have found himself under attack in the late 60s.

These criticisms of Styron make sense, but only if one uses historical-novel criteria to assess *The Confessions of Nat Turner*. The exchange between Ellison and Styron brings into sharp focus what distinguishes the two aesthetic forms. For Ellison, naming the protagonist after an actual historical figure binds the author to a specific truth contract, one in which authors are obliged to represent the biographical subject with as much precision and accuracy as possible. With the historical novel, the protagonist is an invented figure, even if it is based on an actual person, so the author can do with the character what he or she wants. But the biographical novel is different, which is why Ellison says: "You don't have the freedom to snatch any and everybody, and completely recreate them."[40] By naming the protagonist after the original, the author has severely restricted him or herself as an artist. Thus, if authors take liberties with the actual historical figure, they do so at their own aesthetic peril, which, Ellison implies, explains the critical response to Styron's novel.

But as a biographical novelist in the tradition of Wilde, Styron has a much different view than Ellison. Specifically, Ellison and Styron differ with regard to the kind of "truths" biographical novelists are obligated to give readers.

Styron, like Wilde, holds that the creative writer's obligation is first and foremost to his or her own creative vision rather than the biographical subject or the historical past. So the "truth" that readers get in a biographical novel is of the author's vision of life rather than the life of the biographical subject. Put more specifically, what readers get in *The Confessions of Nat Turner* is not an accurate picture of the nineteenth-century slave rebel. They get a figure that Styron converted into a metaphor in order to represent his own vision of life. Styron is absolutely clear about this. In response to the critiques of his book, he says that a novel has "its own metaphysics, its own reason for being as an aesthetic object." With regard to *The Confessions*, he claims that, while loosely based on history, it "can at the same time be a metaphorical plan, a metaphorical diagram for a writer's attitude toward human existence." This is the case because, as "a work of literature," the biographical novel has "its own reality, its own power, its own appeal, which derive from factors that don't really relate to history."[41] Styron is not really that interested in history, which is why *The Confessions of Nat Turner* cannot be considered a historical novel. The biographical novelist appropriates the life story of a person from history and then converts that story into a metaphor. As such, Styron does not give readers history or even biography. What he does is to appropriate the biographical figure in order to create a "metaphorical diagram" that readers could then use to illuminate something from both the past and the present. The accent here is on the metaphorical diagram, not the historical past or the biographical subject.

Margaret Atwood has authored a spectacular biographical novel, and she offers us an excellent way to think about the non-historical dimension of biofictional aesthetics. *Alias Grace* (1996) is about the Irish servant Grace Marks, who was convicted in Canada of murdering her employer. In a lecture about the novel, Atwood told her audience that "such stories are not about this or that slice of the past." To the contrary, "they are about human nature," they are "about truth and lies, and disguises and revelations."[42] Imagine for a moment a historian saying that his or her book about a specific historical event or figure was not really about a particular slice of the past. This would most certainly disqualify the work from being considered a historical text. And yet, scholars follow Lukács by treating biofiction as a form of the historical novel, despite the novelists' insistence to the contrary.

For Lukács, Febvre, and Jameson, historical novelists do history, and since they think that biographical novelists are historical novelists, they hold that biographical novelists must be doing a biographical form of history. But as I have been arguing throughout this introduction, it would be more accurate to say that biographical novelists use rather than do history. In an interview with Robert J. Harris and Jane Yolen, who have coauthored two important biographical novels for children, I asked them to explain why they made some egregious changes to the historical and biographical record. Here is Yolen's response: "Never forget that this is fiction. It is not biography or history. It is using biography and history to tell a story."[43] Nuala O'Connor, who has authored biographical novels about Emily Dickinson and Belle Bilton, amplifies on this idea in her interview for this volume: "This is a novel. And I think when it says 'a novel,' that should be enough for the reader to realize this is invention. . . What's true and what's not is not what's important to you as a novelist—story is what's important, narrative pay-off." Biographical novelists identify something of major significance in the life of a person from the past and then they appropriate that life in order to express their own artistic vision.

But there is a rich irony in the biographical novelist's reconfiguration of historical and biographical truth. Many of the biographical novelists in both *Truthful Fictions* and this book acknowledge that postmodernism has played a crucial role in the rise and legitimization of biofiction. To quote Susan Sellers, who has authored a biographical novel about Vanessa Bell and Virginia Woolf: the "proliferation of biographical fiction has its roots in postmodernism, with its twin suspicions of truth and fiction." And yet, many contemporary biographical novelists are critical of postmodernism. Author of biographical novels about Roland Barthes and Reinhard Heydrich, Laurent Binet says: "I think that contending that 'truth does not exist, everything is fiction' is literary dandyism. I do understand that this constitutes a critical trend in literature, but I believe that postmodernism is deeper and more thought provoking than this."

If we understand postmodernism as "incredulity toward metanarratives,"[44] to use Jean-Francois Lyotard's formulation, then the authors in this volume can both explain why literary postmodernism came to be, but also why biographical novelists have some serious reservations about undisciplined versions of postmodernism. The primary reason why contemporary novelists cast a skeptical eye on metanarratives is because they realize that authors can create literary symbols, which function and signify like metanarratives, to do whatever they need or want. As Binet says: "It is too easy to demonstrate something by resorting to fiction. If we can invent any situation, any event, and place any character in any fictitious situation, then we can demonstrate anything we want about this character." Since the protagonist of a biographical novel is based on an actual historical figure, this grounds the narrative more firmly in the concrete and puts some limits on the authors' freedom to construct whatever they want. As David Lodge, author of biographical novels about Henry James and H. G. Wells, says: "If you say at the beginning that all the letters are real letters, then there is a documentary element in the novel, which persuades the reader to trust the story. If your priority was not to create this illusion of fact, of factually reporting this life, then you wouldn't do it and you would be free to use your imagination and make your characters do whatever you feel you want them to do." Anchoring the imagination in the concrete, to use Tóibín's terminology from his interview in this volume, limits the author, but it does so in order to ground the imagination and to produce a more plausible and less ideological narrative, which explains in part why the biographical novel has flourished in our postmodern age.

This shift to the concrete does not mean that contemporary biographical novelists reject postmodernism. It just means that these writers have a nuanced approach to and inject more gravitas into postmodernism. The traditional postmodernist approach, endlessly deconstructing arbitrary borders of meaning, frivolously engaging in a semantic game of perpetual play, must give way to a more serious intellectual enterprise, which is the knowing construction of a cultural framework in the name of political advancement and social justice. In his interview with Willemien Froneman, Stephanus Muller, who has authored a biographical novel about the composer Arnold van Wyk, explains how postcolonial theory altered his relationship to postmodernism: "I *am transformed* by the postcolonial condition into this existential form of self-reflection. And literature and the sensibility of postmodern fiction responds to this transformation, which, as you say, pushes beyond mere play, mere intellectualism, mere narcissism. Ever since my 'discovery' of various strands of postcolonial discourse in the nineties, I was struck by the political direction it added to the postmodern sensibility." This has led Muller to think about the need for literature that "takes seriously the act of writing as a political act." Cercas, who simultaneously embraces and rejects postmodernism, puts the matter clearly in his interview when he discusses the limitations of David Foster Wallace's fiction: Wallace "realized postmodernism saw literature as just a game. And for me, post-postmodernism would be literature as a game, but as an absolutely serious game, a game where everything is at stake."

As a scholar of biofiction, postmodernism has been for me a source of much frustration, even though I consider myself a postmodernist and have argued that postmodernism in part has made biofiction possible. I have now edited four special journal issues about biofiction, and one of the most irritating types of submission I receive follows a consistent pattern: the scholar submits an essay that does not discuss a single work of biofiction scholarship but uses postmodern theory to make the obvious claim that there is much overlap between genres. Based on this overlap, the scholar concludes that the historical novel is like a biographical novel, the biographical novel like a roman-a-clef, the roman-a-clef like biography, biography like autobiography, and autobiography like fiction. Therefore, the historical novel is a biographical novel, the biographical novel is a roman-a-clef, the roman-a-clef is a biography, a biography is an autobiography, and autobiography is fiction. What differentiates many contemporary biographical novelists is their yearning for clarity and precision and their insistence that what they are doing is distinct. Tóibín, McCann, Donoghue, and Unigwe distinguish the biographical novel from the historical novel, and Tóibín goes so far as to say that were he to do a historical novel, this would be the end of his work. Many contemporary biographical novelists are different from the many undisciplined postmodern scholars because they make careful distinctions, but they are still postmodernists because they realize that these distinctions are sociocultural constructions rather than ontological realities.

For many biographical novelists, what is behind their frustration with non-rigorous forms of postmodernism is their belief in the power of literature to expose political, cultural, and intellectual ailments and to offer healthier and more life-promoting ways of seeing and being. Since many postmodernists spend their time blending and blurring distinctions, they overlook the precise kinds of critiques and possibilities contained in many first-rate works of literature. Anchee Min is one of those biographical novelists who offers an incisive critique of a specific cultural, intellectual, and political way of thinking and being. When discussing *Becoming Madame Mao*, a biographical novel about Jiang Ching, Min claims that "biofiction can contribute to diagnosing cultural ailments," and she specifically examines in her novel how Ching contributed significantly to China's Cultural Revolution, which led to the oppression and death of millions. For Min, the virtue of biofiction is that readers can see through the "existential map" of Ching's life how contemporary political leaders and media outlets in the United States use similar structures and systems to institute "its own Cultural Revolution."

But merely exposing a cultural sickness is not enough. Many of the best biographical novelists offer an alternative way of seeing and being that promotes a healthier and more socially just polity. For instance, Barbara Chase-Riboud published *Sally Hemings* in 1979, and this work has contributed to new ways of thinking and experiencing Thomas Jefferson, American race relations in the past and the present, and America's founding stories and documents. When it was first released, Jefferson scholars dismissed *Sally Hemings* as a naïve romantic fantasy. Surely, no white man of Jefferson's stature would have had a long-term intimate relationship with a black slave like Hemings, as is depicted in *Sally Hemings*. But Chase-Riboud's novel had such an enormous impact that it in part led to Eugene A. Foster's DNA testing, which confirmed that Hemings's descendants are related to Jefferson, made plausible the idea that Jefferson did have an extended relationship with Hemings, and has since forced Monticello to include Hemings as an important part of the story of Jefferson's estate. In a very literal and material sense, Chase-Riboud has brought into existence a new conceptual and physical reality through her biographical novel, as should be clear from her interview in this volume.[45]

Conversations with Biographical Novelists differs significantly from *Truthful Fictions*. In the 2014 book, I conducted all the interviews, and this had some unfortunate consequences: there is some redundancy in the interviews, my blind spots inevitably appear, and there is a singular perspective in the way the material is framed. To avoid and counter some of those limitations with this volume, I issued a Call For Interviews (CFI), and the response was overwhelming. Unfortunately, there were many fine interviews that I could not include. But the ones in this volume have the virtue of broadening our understanding of biofiction and exposing some differences in approaches to the literary form. In short, not all the interviewers or novelists in this volume agree with each other about the definitions of biofiction. But this lack of consensus is one of the strengths of this book. Some of the interviewers asked questions that would never have occurred to other interviewers, and in the process, these interviews open new pathways for thinking about the aesthetic form.

And evidence suggests there is a hunger for more studies about biofiction. Before 2016, there was no special journal issue devoted to the study of biofiction, but over the last three years, academic publications such as *a/b: Auto/Biography Studies* (2016), *Éire-Ireland: An Interdisciplinary Journal of Irish Studies* (2018), the *American Book Review* (2018), and the *Virginia Woolf Miscellany* (2018) have published special issues devoted to the aesthetic form. Before 2015, there had been no major academic events about biofiction, but in the 2016–17 academic year, there were four: Julia Novak hosted a public roundtable forum titled "The Ethics of Biofiction" at King's College London, England; Bethany Layne hosted a one-day conference titled "Postmodernist Biofiction" at the University of Reading in England; Catherine Padmore and Kelly Gardiner hosted a symposium on "Reading and Writing Australasian Historical Biofictions" at La Trobe University in Australia; and Bénédicte Ledent and Daria Tunca hosted a symposium titled "Illuminating Lives: The Biographical Impulse in Postcolonial Literatures" at the Centre for Teaching and Research in Postcolonial Studies at the Université de Liège in Belgium. Before 2015, there had never been an MLA panel about biofiction, but in 2018, there were three: Hispanic Biofiction, Biofiction and the Antipodes, and Postcolonial Biofiction. In other words, the study of biofiction has not just become a legitimate area of scholarly inquiry, but it has also become a major field of study throughout the world. This current collection thus responds to a burgeoning scholarly interest and need within the academic and intellectual community, while it contributes significantly to the direction that the study of the field will take.

Notes

1 James (1955), Letter to Sarah Orne Jewett, October 5, 1901, in *The Selected Letters of Henry James*. Ed. Leon Edel. New York: Farrar, Straus and Cudahy: 202–03.
2 Tóibín (2004), *The Master: A Novel*. New York: Picador: 317.
3 McCann (2017), Interview with Robert Birnbaum, in *Conversations with Colum McCann*. Jackson: University of Mississippi Press: 71.
4 McCann (2017), "Do What Is Most Difficult," in *Conversations with Colum McCann*: 181.
5 Jameson (2015), "The Historical Novel Today, or, Is It Still Possible?" in *The Antinomies of Realism*. London and New York: Verso: 313.
6 Jameson (2015): 262.
7 Ibid.: 263.
8 Ibid.: 284.
9 Ibid.: 288.
10 Lukács (1983), *The Historical Novel*. Lincoln and London: University of Nebraska Press: 300.
11 Jameson (2015): 288.
12 Ibid.: 263.
13 Febvre (1973), "History and Psychology," in *A New Kind of History: From the Writings of Febvre*. Ed. Peter Burke. Trans. K. Folca. New York, Evanston, San Francisco: Harper & Row Publishers: 7.
14 Wilde (1997), "The Decay of Lying," in *Collected Works of Oscar Wilde*. Ware, Hertfordshire: Wordsworth Editions: 925–6.
15 Wilde (1997): 934.
16 Ibid.: 933.
17 Ebershoff (2001), "Author's Note," in *The Danish Girl*. New York: Penguin Books: 271.
18 Ebershoff (2001), "A Conversation with David Ebershoff," in *The Danish Girl*. New York: Penguin Books: 8.
19 Moore (1942), Letter to John Eglinton, December 18, 1915, in *Letters of George Moore*. Bournemouth, England: Sydenham & Co: 29.
20 Vidal (2005), "The Art of Fiction L: Gore Vidal," in *Conversations with Gore Vidal*. Jackson: University Press of Mississippi: 54.
21 Scott (2017), "On Hoaxes, Humbugs, and Fictional Portraiture," in *Biographical Fiction: A Reader*. Ed. Michael Lackey. New York and London: Bloomsbury: 32.

22 Marx (1977), "Preface" to A Critique of Political Economy in *Karl Marx: Selected Writings*. Ed. David McLellan. Oxford: Oxford University Press: 389.
23 Lukács (1983): 60.
24 McCann (2003), *Dancer*. London: Phoenix: 41.
25 McCann (2003): 148.
26 Ibid.: 245–46.
27 Hans Renders (2017), "Introduction: The Biographical Turn," in *The Biographical Turn: Lives in History*. London and New York: Routledge: 3.
28 Renders (2017): 4.
29 Ibid.: 10.
30 Avery (2018), "Lytton Strachey and the Biographical Roots of Biofiction," *Virginia Woolf Miscellany*, Forthcoming in the Spring Issue.
31 Strachey (2011), "The Historian of the Future," in *Unpublished Works of Lytton Strachey: Early Papers*. Ed. Todd Avery. London: Pickering & Chatto: 63.
32 Strachey (1969), "Preface," in *Eminent Victorians*. San Diego: A Harvest Book: viii.
33 Avery (2018): Forthcoming.
34 Qtd in Avery (2018): Forthcoming.
35 Bennett (1968), "Nat's Last White Man," in *William Styron's Nat Turner: Ten Black Writers Respond*. Ed. John Henrik Clarke. Boston: Beacon Press: 4–5.
36 Williams (1968), "The Manipulation of History and of Fact: An Ex-Southerner's Apologist Tract for Slavery and the Life of Nat Turner; or, William Styron's Faked Confessions," in *William Styron's Nat Turner: Ten Black Writers Respond*. Ed. John Henrik Clarke. Boston: Beacon Press, 46.
37 Clarke (1968), "Introduction," in *William Styron's Nat Turner: Ten Black Writers Respond*. Ed. John Henrik Clarke. Boston: Beacon Press: vii.
38 Woodward (2017), "The Uses of History in Fiction," in *Biographical Fiction: A Reader*. Ed. Michael Lackey. New York and London: Bloomsbury: 145.
39 Woodward (2017): 155.
40 Ibid.: 145.
41 Ibid.: 143.
42 Atwood (1998), "In Search of *Alias Grace*: On Writing Canadian Historical Fiction," in *The American Historical Review*. 103(5) (December): 1516.
43 Michael Lackey and Katya Lackey (2018), "The Ethical Benefits and Challenges of Biofiction for Children," in *a/b: Auto/Biography Studies*. 33(1) (Winter): 19.
44 Lyotard (1991), *The Postmodern Condition: A Report of Knowledge*. Trans Brian Massumi. Minneapolis: University of Minnesota Press: xxiv.
45 For a brief discussion of the impact of Chase-Riboud's novel, see my essay (2017) "The Futures of Biofiction Studies," in *a/b: Auto/Biography Studies*. 32(2) (Spring): 343–46.

1

Positive Contamination in the Biographical Novel

Kevin Barry, interviewed by Stuart Kane

Kane: Let me begin by telling you about this project. The objective is to try and define the nature of the biographical novel. It is also to clarify why this genre of fiction has become so popular in recent years. May I ask why you chose to write about John Lennon specifically?

Barry: Place is always the first thing when it comes to my writing. I'd moved to County Sligo about ten years ago, and in the early summer I'd been going out on my bike a lot around Clew Bay in County Mayo. And here we're going to go straight into fairly esoteric country. I often think that as writers, artists, or musicians, whatever our form is, what we're doing is trying to tune into the energies and reverberations that linger in places. I believe that human feeling escapes from humans and settles into our places. And every time I went cycling around Clew Bay I was getting this haunted feeling from the place. I was thinking a lot, whenever I was cycling around the place, about what Saul Bellow used to call "my significant dead," or my family dead, or close friends I had lost. So there was the atmosphere of this austerely beautiful landscape mixed with this haunted feeling, and I knew that this was the atmosphere for a novel.

I had this before John Lennon came into it at all. But a little pop cultural factoid I had about Clew Bay was that John Lennon used to own an island out there. It was a familiar enough story in Ireland in the 1970s and 1980s but was long since forgotten. But I started to research it a little, or research might be a grand term for it really—I started to google a bit and found out the basics of this little story about John Lennon buying Dorinish Island in 1968. And the story lodged in my brain and just buzzed away horribly, like a bluebottle or wasp. I tried in various ways to get it out of my head. I wrote a little essay for the radio about it, for *RTE*. But it kept coming back, and I referred to it in a short story called "Dark Lies the Island." John's island is just mentioned in passing in the story and also there's a reference to a Beatles' track, "For No One." I thought this would surely take care of this particular trapped wasp in my brain, but it kept coming back, again and again, along with the haunted feeling whenever I went around Clew Bay on my bike. And I remember sitting up suddenly one day, just a couple of months before *City of Bohane* came out in 2011. I suppose, subconsciously, I was shopping around in my brain for another novel to write. So with a start, I realized that I was going to write a novel about John Lennon.

In late 2011 I started, and it was weird. In the first few weeks, I was in this mood of glee; I thought it was a fantastic idea for a novel. Then after that first few weeks, I was in a flap and I realized how difficult it would be to get away with it.

Kane: Yes, it must have been quite a challenge to take on a character of John Lennon's magnitude. I recently read an interview where you said that you listened to the audio of John Lennon's voice from the 1970s to get into a rhythm for writing it. How specifically did you approach the writing of his voice?

Barry: I realized that a lot of readers were going to have an expectation, before they even got to page one, of what the character should sound like. So a lot of the first year was spent looking at YouTube, especially long interviews on the Dick Cavett Show from the 1970s, where a lot of the time Lennon is just ranting off about his visa difficulties. I transcribed sentences from his speech, directly, just to get a feel for it. And he's especially difficult to get on the page because his tone is very capricious. He can go from being really quite charming, fluffy, and light, to being quite dark and paranoid, and all this inside the beat of a sentence. After about a year or so, the voice, just in places, was starting to sound like I might get away with it. For a long time, the story was written in the first person: I am John, but it was just too risky, even for a chancer as brazen as I am. When I moved it to the third person, it felt like the character was motoring. Then the character of Cornelius turned up, initially as a minor figure, but he began to elbow his way into the picture more and more. And it was when I made Lennon part of a double act again, with Cornelius, I think that's when things really started to stand up on the desk for me. I could hear John Lennon's voice very well in relief against Cornelius's West of Ireland voice, this strange mixture of innocence and knowingness, or whatever it is he's got going on. I could do Cornelius's voice at will because I know many Cornelius O'Gradys. Once I got him talking, it was quite easy to have John chipping in.

So after about a year and a half, I knew that I had something, but actually that felt like a dangerous moment for the project—I knew at that point I could do a kind of standard, almost biopic version. I had a character on my desk who sounded like John Lennon, and I could now do a sort of classic buddy movie with fucking you know, character development and lovely neat arcs, but I thought this would be untrue to the spirit of the subject. I had to do something that was a bit looser, wilder, and dottier really. I do think that if you can get the voice right, you can get almost everything else following on from that. If you can get their voice, you can get their soul.

Interestingly, one of the things that gave me the confidence to attempt such an outlandish project as this was the fact that I had spent more than two years living in Liverpool in the mid-noughties. With the Liverpudlian accent, there's kind of an easy way in for an Irish writer, because the two accents are very closely related. I was also very interested in looking at what happens when Irish sentimentality, and pathos, and singing-in-pubs, all that kind of business, what happens when that migrates to the cold cities of the North of England. What do you get when those two worlds collide? And what you get is The Beatles, coming out of that whole music-hall world.

Kane: I understand that you were very selective in your research of John Lennon, but may I ask why?

Barry: I was very wary that I had to limit my research because if you open the closet on a figure of John Lennon's standing, the whole world will fall out on top of you and smother the project. It actually became quite a superstitious thing for me not to read anything, or look at anything on TV, or film, because it would just spoil my version of him. I did listen to the music. I listened to the *White Album* a lot and the *John Lennon/Plastic Ono Band*.

Kane: What do you perceive as the purpose of the biographical novel?

Barry: I think with a question like that it would have to be done on a case-by-case basis. With *Beatlebone*, I wanted the experience of reading the novel to feel like you were being lowered down into a deep fat fryer! I wanted the reader to be lowered down into this bubbling cauldron, which is this great artist's brain at the time of creative strife.

This is where I allowed a little bit of the real-life biography to come in because we do know that around 1978, he was creatively blocked; he wasn't getting the songs as he had done before. The sense that you get from reading biographical stuff about John Lennon, from that time, is that he thought that the problem was that he was too happy. A lot of the issues in his life had been sorted out: his marriage was back on track, his visa difficulties had ended, he had a new baby. He was in this kind of house-husband phase but, of course, he had no songs. So then it was nice to say, well okay, I can now send him to the West of Ireland, so that he can get into trouble and try and make some work out of that. I wanted this to be a very intense experience for the reader.

I thought Lennon was obviously a very interesting character in terms of pop culture history. There are figures that come along who seem to be hinge figures, or cusp figures, who introduce something new in terms of their persona and in terms of how they carry themselves. I was really interested in how his take on masculinity seemed ahead of its time. He wasn't the world's most masculine rock star; he was very much in touch with his feminine side, so he seemed to be a figure ahead of his time.

Kane: What can you as a novelist give readers of John Lennon that they couldn't get in a traditional biography? What kind of human interior does the author of biographical fiction give readers?

Barry: The traditional biography is hemmed in by the facts. I'm a reader of biographies, I love them, but where they can't really go is inside. There is a place where only fiction can go and it's into the nerve endings of a character, into a sense of them as pure consciousness. I think fiction is the only thing that can get you there. I think as well that you can go into narrower places than a traditional biography. The truth of the biography is the broad sweep of the life and the big events, but with fiction, you can go into the tiny moments. But then in a loose biographical fiction, such as this one, where I am making an awful lot of stuff up out of thin air, you have to imagine from nothing what it would be like for John Lennon to be eating some black pudding with a farmer in 1978. When I am writing a scene like that, all I'm thinking is if it's true to the character at some kind of spiritual level: is this how he would react?

The only thing that my two novels have in common is that they are about being unable to escape from the shadows of the past and characters not being able to step forward because they're constantly being dragged back. And how we have to develop some momentum in life, which is what he's trying to do. Biographical fiction can go into the minutiae, and you can bring the character down into very small moments that hopefully can open out, and illuminate in some way their personality.

Kane: Jay Parini (critic, biographer, fictional novelist) states, "When possible, a writer of fiction should behave like a professional historian, seeking the facts where possible." Would you agree with Parini's statement, or do you think this is not the remit of a writer of fiction?

Barry: I think that is a perfectly legitimate remit for some writers and there is nothing in that statement that would suggest you can't write a terrific novel in that way. Pragmatically, my difficulty with such an approach is that I am not a researcher; I skimp on the research, always, no matter what the project is, because for me research always equates to procrastination. If I'm doing research, it means I don't want to write. So I tend to make it all happen on the desk and invent it out of the ether. What I tend to do with research is do a little bit after the fact. After I've written a bit of fiction, I will then look stuff up to see if that holds. In the case of *Beatlebone*, it certainly felt like I was skating on thin ice in some regards, because I was inventing events out of thin air for an actual historical figure. And it felt to me like I was going into elements of the most unfashionable literary genre of all, which is fan fiction! But I just kept saying to myself that if I stay true to the character, then I could get away with it. It was nice, toward the end of the process, when I was confident enough to open a book or two about Lennon, and I was reading a piece by a photographer who was quite friendly with Lennon, at that time, late 70s, and it talks about how he went off to Japan and booked himself into a hotel for the first time, and he'd started to go off on these little solo trips. So it sort of qualified the book for me, retrospectively. I thought that it was absolutely possible that he could go off on such a madcap expedition around this time in his life. It felt in keeping with something that he might have done.

Kane: Do you think it is misguided to see the goal of biographical fiction as an attempt to get to the biographical subject's "true" or "authentic" self?

Barry: I think, again, this is something you'd have to take on a novel-by-novel basis, but in *Beatlebone* that's exactly what I was trying to do. I was trying to give the real, pared-back essence of John Lennon and trying to get down to the very tips of his nerves and trying to expand out from there and show who I thought he was at this point in his life. It became quickly apparent that as I was writing this, with this particular goal in mind, that it was a book about making something. It was a book about how to try and make a piece of art: whether it's a novel, or an album, or a painting, or film. It's about going to the dark places—we don't write, or draw, or make music because we are fine, we do it because we're messed up, because life is meaningless, cruel, often disastrous and ridiculous and there is no fucking shape to it. That's why we make art, as an attempt to put meaning and shape onto our lives. I guess that's what I was trying to do with *Beatlebone*.

Kane: When writing about John Lennon, in *Beatlebone*, was there an internal censor at work in your mind as you were writing? What kind of ethical responsibility does an author have to the actual biographical subject?

Barry: It's an interesting question, and it was absolutely on my mind from the start of the book. Do I have any right to do this? I think it felt to me that it was just about decorous because of the time span. The 1970s were getting to a point where they were moving into the realm of historical fiction. But no matter what I'm writing, I always think you should ask yourself the question: what gives me the right to do this? And I felt what gave me the right, with *Beatlebone*, is the fact that I was prepared to spend four years of my life in a shed in County Sligo using absolutely every ounce of ability that I could muster to do as good a job as I could on it. The fact of your ability and the fact that you're prepared to do the slog, the thousands of hours it's going to take to get something like this through to the finish. I guess those things gave me the sense that I was allowed to do it. Also the sense that I was going to keep a fidelity with the character in a way that felt right. It goes back to what I was saying earlier, that the book had to be nutty, loose, and wild. It had to be loose and wild enough so that no one would take it as something that actually happened in John Lennon's life. And I felt that once I have him talking to a seal in a cave, nobody can take it as any kind of realism. This is going to be a nutty, surreal take. An awful lot of my work begins at a point where it looks broadly realistic, then very quickly moves out to the edges of believability, or likelihood.

Kane: In some biographical novels, there is a prefatory disclaimer that the characters are fictional, but you actually go much further in *Beatlebone* by providing the reader with details about your research methods and your writing processes in a first-person story-cum-essay. Was this because you felt that as a writer of biographical fiction you owed the reader an explanation, or were there other reasons?

Barry: It goes back to the point we were discussing earlier, about this being a book about making something and a book about the nature of artistic creation and how it works. There is nothing new in fiction, and it is as old as time to break the wall in this way. Laurence Sterne was doing it hundreds of years ago. I think in Victorian times they used to call it "baring the device" when the author intruded and appeared in the story. I thought it felt right for me to make an appearance and an awful lot of the time, when you're writing fiction, it's at that kind of gut level, day by day—does this feel right? Is this adding to the portrait, is this deepening the experience and intensifying it for the reader? Because I had another one of those dangerous moments when Cornelius and John had got on the road as a double act. I could see that page by page, it was great fun, and it was really working as that kind of story, and I thought I can just follow this through and give them lots of madcap adventures. But again I wanted to intensify from that point and just bring it up another level, or down another level, or deeper in. So it felt right to go with the baring of the device and showing how I went about it.

Kane: So the essay which appears in *Beatlebone* gives the reader an insight into not just the research methods you used but also brings to light some of the biographical and historical facts surrounding the back story of John Lennon and his purchase of Dorinish Island. It also provides a portrait of the wild West Coast of Ireland and its colorful social history and brings you into the story on a deeply personal level. I am really intrigued by all of this. Can you tell me how this essay came to be such an integral part of *Beatlebone*?

Barry: It initially came about by accident. I had notes written in various little notebooks and on the backs of beer mats, and backs of envelopes. I'd just bought a fancy new notebook to gather all my notes in one place. I was just writing down some of the basic facts of the story, about John buying the island and how much he'd paid for it, and as I did so I found very effortless paragraphs forming, and nothing in the process of writing this book had been effortless, up until this point. And you pay attention when the hand is suddenly moving so effortlessly across the page. That essay wrote itself in not much more than a week. I kind of knew at once that it was the heart of the book, the center of the book, because it clarified for me what I was doing really: I was creating a portrait of the artist, and of course to make a portrait of the artist you bring everything that you have yourself to the table to try and make it believable. So I tried to find correspondences between his life and my life, and we'd both lost a mother at a young age, and I knew this was strong material, that I could use it to give a kind of weight of feeling. It was very interesting for me, it was the first time I'd written directly about my mother's death, when I was a child, and to find myself doing so during the course of writing my John Lennon novel was a great surprise, but it absolutely felt like the heart of the book. I worked with two editors on the book, one in New York and one in Edinburgh, and they both recognized that this was the heart of the book, but of course there were conversations about whether it should really be a postscript at the end of the book. I felt absolutely not, that it had to go bang center because I felt all of the novel fed into it and fed out from it. But it is a serious technical challenge to set yourself which is: can I walk out of my novel for nine-thousand words and then hop back in again? I did think that the trick of the book for a reader was if they went along with the essay, they would go along with the whole thing really, and that seems to have been the common experience.

Kane: Even though your work is acknowledged to be a novel, is it not possible that it infringes upon the rights of the subject under consideration? Please, can you also explain the kind of liberties that you feel justified in taking with the facts? For instance, John's fixer, the wonderful fictional character of Cornelius O'Grady. Can you also specify the kind of liberties you wouldn't take with such a story?

Barry: What I probably wouldn't do is take real-life events and try and do a fictional iteration of them. I love it when that is done in some fictions. One of my favorite pieces of biographical fiction is *Libra* by Don DeLillo, where he does Lee Harvey Oswald, and there must be a lot in that book that is based on actual research. For example, that Oswald worked in a radio factory in Minsk when he lived in the Soviet Union for a while, so we get DeLillo writing about Oswald's working day at the factory. But then there is a lot that DeLillo couldn't possibly have taken from real life where he goes deep into the character and does the internal portrait. But with *Beatlebone*, I was determined to keep the real-life facts of the story at a distance, and just use it as a very basic frame. I was starting from the very basic fact that John Lennon owned an island in the West of Ireland that he had visited twice. I thought if I imagine a third visit that never happened that means that I can be free to invent within the parameters of that, as long as it's wild enough that nobody is going to imagine that this was actually the case: that he met a seal and talked to a seal, and that time itself became unfixed and loose. I was thinking about Lennon's own taste as a reader, as a musician, and what he was into. I thought it was a vaguely surreal, strange, intense kind of world that he would have wanted in a work of fiction. I guess at some level I had at the back of my brain a very particular reader for this book: the man himself. What would he think of this? Would he enjoy it? I convinced myself, with my bionic powers of self-delusion, that he would be into this. This is nutty enough for him.

Kane: As someone who has written a biographical novel, how much does John Lennon represent your views in *Beatlebone*? And is there ever a danger of contamination between a writer's feelings and ideals, and those of the subject?

Barry: I'm sure there is, is the short answer to that. Again, it comes back to the very difficult-to-grasp area of spirit. Is the spirit of the book right? This is going to be a very different question when applied to different biographical novels, case-by-case. I wonder if it is possible to use a term here like positive contamination. In terms of trying to create a portrait of the artist you are trying to bring as much as you can that feels real and genuine into the portrait, and you take what you can from your own life. So an element that I felt I could share with the character was having experienced the early death of a parent, which is common in a lot of writers' and artists' lives. You discover as you read biographies it seems to produce some sort of urge to create in the child when that happens. Something else that I could bring, that I had in common, was some experience of Liverpool and the surrounding language as a force. I could also bring that feeling you get when creative work isn't working out, when it's not going well, and you're really wriggling on the hook with it every day! Those really were the three critical things I brought, I think, from my own life. I tried then to make these bring the portrait to life.

Kane: Would you say that the postmodern construct of truth has contributed to the rise of biographical fiction?

Barry: Absolutely! All I can say on that is that there are different measures of truth that you can achieve on the page. It is a flat phrase, but what I was going for was a kind of psychological truth in *Beatlebone*—I was saying this is how John Lennon may have felt in such circumstances, at such a time, and in such a place.

2

Reflections on Truth, Veracity, Fictionalization, and Falsification

Laurent Binet, interviewed by Monica Latham

Latham: What do you think about authors who, like you, use literary or historical figures as characters? As a practitioner of this genre, what is your opinion about the different forms and the dynamism of biographical and historical fiction today?

Binet: It depends, of course, on how well it is done and on the knowledge the author has of his or her subject. For instance, I am reading Carlos Fuentes's *The Orange Tree* and the first short story is about one of Cortés's lieutenants, who is recounting the conquest of Mexico. I am right at the point when Marina (La Malinche), Cortés's lover and translator, appears in the story. I am extremely excited to see how this famous woman, with her biographical background, is injected into the historical account that I am reading. So I am eager to read the rest of the story but, at the same time, if I sense it is not well done, or if the historical figure is somehow betrayed, this can easily put me off. How do I judge whether an author has betrayed a historical figure? Well, this is highly subjective. For example, I remember that in *HHhH* there was a chapter that I deleted eventually where I was commenting on reading an interview with Gore Vidal, who criticized Margueritte Yourcenar because he deemed that her *Memoirs of Hadrian* were fabricated and artificial, that she made the Roman emperor speak exactly like her, a French bourgeoise from the 50s. This interview had such a profound impact on me that I never wanted to read these *Memoirs*, because I had this presumption at the back of my mind. Maybe I personally would not have sensed this when reading the book, but Gore Vidal ruined it for me.

Anyway, it is always appealing for me to know that a real or historical figure is present in a novel. I am purposely not saying "fiction" (the Americans have this concept of "non-fiction novel" that I find very relevant, maybe even more than the one I personally tried to forge in *HHhH*, "*infra-roman*" ["infra-novel"]). This issue is perfectly well illustrated in Tolstoy's *War and Peace*. The most appealing moments for me are when the characters of Kutuzov, Marshal Murat, Tsar Alexander, or Napoleon appear in the story. The advocates of historical relativism would argue that there is no such thing as the "true" Napoleon: Tolstoy's Napoleon has nothing to do with the real Napoleon, and anyway there is no one true Napoleon; since everything is filtered by the prism of our subjectivity, one can never apprehend reality. I personally do not agree with this and I think Tolstoy gives us his own vision of Napoleon. He never met Napoleon, but I know that his vision is well informed, that he did an excellent, serious job, that he read Armand Augustin Louis de Caulaincourt's memoirs and all the testimonies he could find on the French Invasion of Russia, and that the majority of scenes in which Napoleon appears in *War and Peace* are based on reports by direct witnesses (with the exception, of course, of the scenes where a historical figure meets a fictional character, and these encounters are extremely interesting). I find it captivating to read about Napoleon meeting Prince Andrei on the battlefield, and although this does not correspond to any historical truth, as Prince Andrei did not exist, it is a fascinating encounter that illustrates the question I am interested in myself, that is to say the confrontation or clash between fiction and history.

Latham: Your point of view seems to be reception-oriented, as you mostly speak about your experience as a reader. You seem to therefore understand the readers' interest for this genre, but their frustration as well, especially when the encounter between history and fiction produces artificial prose. As a writer, how do you approach biographical and historical gaps? Do you feel liberated and relieved, as you can give free rein to your imagination, or, on the contrary, do you feel constrained by these blanks, as you feel you must do further research in order to find the missing information?

Binet: You are right to say that I put myself in the reader's shoes. I always write books that I would be interested to read as a reader: it is an obvious assumption. As a writer, I am a fervent advocate for doing research, and I think that filling in the blanks is ultimately the method we use when writing historical novels, like Alexandre Dumas did in *The Three Musketeers*. On the other hand, too often and for so many authors, it is the easy option: I don't know, therefore I invent. It is an easy solution that they think they can take glory in: I invent, therefore I can claim the status of a writer who writes literature. Nowadays, people confuse the concepts of literature, fiction, and novel, which are not at all interchangeable. I think that more often than not (although not always, sometimes one can surprisingly produce excellent novels) filling historical blanks with pure invention is convenient and lazy. For me, it is much more interesting to dig deeper, even though this drives you crazy because you cannot find the information you need. This was my problem with the parachutists in *HHhH*: I had much more information on Heydrich than on them and it was very, very frustrating. This was also one of the challenges of my book. I wanted to write a thrilling, extraordinary, fabulous, exciting novel, to the best of my ability without simply settling for filling the gaps.

Latham: In *HHhH*, you clearly wanted to delimit reality and fiction as well as to limit the use of fiction, so as not to contaminate the real story. Why, in the particular case of this novel, does the mixture between the historical account and fiction seem irreconcilable?

Binet: Nothing is irreconcilable. However, what interested me most was Heydrich's true story, in particular the assassination attempt on him by the Czechoslovakian parachutists, not what a contemporary writer could fantasize about the event. This story already had the "added value of the real." I wanted to know more, to dig deeper and to make known to the public a fantastic, exceptionally fabulous story, which was little known in Western Europe. I wanted to adhere as closely as possible to a historical truth that I thought was really mind-blowing, all the more so as it was proven to be true. In a film, or in a novel, a member of the Resistance who kills three Germans, you can just picture Bruce Willis, but to know that this really happened gives weight to the event and it is simply much more impressive. My story was fabulous enough for me not to want or feel the need to romanticize it. The kinship and the difference between "romanticized" and "*Romanesque*" is quite enlightening for *HHhH*. Romanticizing is the process of fictionalization, whereas "*Romanesque*" is the potential for an adventure novel that lies in an event. And that potential was there. And so, in order not to lose the added value of the real, I wanted to stick as closely as possible to historic veracity. I prefer to say "veracity" instead of "truth" because in "truth" there is always a metaphysical connotation that I find a little bit nebulous.

Latham: You said that the story is too extraordinary in itself to be contaminated by fiction, which would take some of its power away, would falsify the truth—and the truth must be exposed as it really is. Is imagination therefore synonymous with fantasy, and does it have a negative connotation for you?

Binet: In some cases, yes, it does. It is precisely what Charlotte Lacoste criticizes about Jonathan Littell's *The Kindly Ones* and Yannick Haenel's *The Messenger: A Novel*, and I quite agree with her. Lacoste says that there comes a point where fictionalization becomes falsification. And this is dangerous because we leave the realm of playful fictional representation to reach that of political or philosophical demonstration: we basically call this a *roman à thèse* (thesis novel) in French. And this is exactly what I said in one of my chapters: it is too easy to demonstrate something by resorting to fiction. If we can invent any situation, any event, and place any character in any fictitious situation, then we can demonstrate anything we want about this character.

Latham: But fiction is nevertheless useful for several reasons. First, to soften the raw historical facts, otherwise the novel would be a history textbook. It is also useful because the historical truth is contained in a novelistic envelope and is governed by the principles of the thriller; and it is thanks to these mechanisms that the reader is carried away in the vortex of the plot. Fiction also helps you to transmit and popularize history, which is thus made more readable and accessible to the public. In *HHhH* you said that for history to get imprinted on one's memory, you must first turn it into fiction.

Binet: As a matter of fact, I have never said that fiction is useful. It was Gustave Flaubert who, while composing *Salammbô*, said that if it becomes as boring as a textbook, then it is no good. But I strongly disagree with this: there are some fascinating history books and textbooks. You see, you confuse "fiction" with "literature." The exact statement in *HHhH* is, "For anything to have a lasting imprint on people's memory, I would have to turn it into *literature*," not into "*fiction*." For me, there is no equivalence between literature and fiction. So I would say that fiction is not useful or necessary. It is true that in my book I succumb to the temptation of using fiction. Why so? Why do I preserve the chapters where I make things up and by doing so, undermine my project and breach the reading contract I establish at the beginning? Because the chapters in which I fictionalize are always signaled as such at some point, and they purposefully serve as illustrations to the dialogues or debates I wanted to have with the reader on the very question of how to tell a true story. And sometimes they have a double use: they are practical for the story and they give me satisfaction as a writer. For example, during Operation Barbarossa, Heydrich's plane was shot down above Soviet lines. I do not know exactly how this attack unfolded and this was an enormous frustration for me, and fiction came to appease this frustration. At the same time, if I wanted to remain true to my logic, I should have written this episode only for me and not included it in the final version of my book, as the ultimate aim was to adhere as closely as possible to the historical truth. But I tried a double strike, that is to say I wanted to have my cake and eat it, as it were. What I mean is that I liked this scene, so I kept it in my novel, but for it not to betray the reading contract I established with my reader, it became the subject of a meta-creative comment: a few chapters later, I deconstruct it and I admit that I resorted to fiction. And, of course, this is against my creative project and reading contract, so I use this chapter to illustrate the relationship between fiction and history. So it is true that in my book I insert chapters that are purely fictional, but I offer them to my reader as such and I signal their fictitiousness. I believe that my book would have held up well even without these kinds of chapters, I mean they are perhaps useful, they certainly enrich the book, but they are not absolutely necessary.

Latham: In *HHhH* you say: "I just hope that however bright and blinding the veneer of fiction that covers this Fabulous story, you will still be able to see through it to the historical reality that lies behind" (Chapter 1). The layer of fiction the writer applies to his or her story is more or less thick, more or less opaque. It is quite thin and transparent in *HHhH*, whereas in *The Seventh Function of Language* it is thicker and more far-fetched. Was it easier to "skirt around the historical truth" in *The Seventh Function of Language*? Why and how did you decide to take more liberties with history? Was it the genre and the story (the assassination of Roland Barthes) that allowed you to do so? You seem to take great pleasure in yielding to the temptation of making up stories—the same temptation that you had vigorously rejected in *HHhH*.

Binet: For me, the two novels are situated at opposite ends of the spectrum. They are both concerned with the complicated relationship between reality and fiction: the working angle of *HHhH* was the fanatical search for historical truth, while *The Seventh Function of Language* was a more playful approach, which consisted in pulling and twisting the rope of reality until it broke. I found this practice amusing, especially since after ten years of writing *HHhH* I heard the call of fiction. I am fully aware that these are opposite approaches, but they are also complementary. They are two sides of the same coin.

Latham: In *HHhH*, you regularly insert meta-creative interrogations on how to respect historical and biographical fact, on how "healthy" or "dangerous" your thirst for documentation is, as well as on the dosage of the right amount of fiction in the bulk of available information. Do you think that the biographer's and the historian's ultimate obsession is to possess the whole truth about the life of his or her subject? Does the novelist have the same kind of obsession?

Binet: Yes, I think that the biographer's fantasy is to know absolutely everything about his or her subject. The biographer who is writing, for instance, Napoleon's biography wants to know all the details about his socks.

On the other hand, and by definition, this is not necessarily the novelist's fantasy, as he takes liberties with biographical or historical facts and is not utterly obsessed with possessing the whole truth. But personally, I really am. And this is the case even in *The Seventh Function of Language*, where I had carte blanche to invent anything: I could kill people who were not dead and I could resurrect people who were actually dead. As I chose to write a counterfactual story, a uchronia, I had total freedom, but nevertheless—and this is a question of temperament—I had the fantasy of possessing all the facts, which is illusory of course. I was aware that I would never know all the details about Roland Barthes's life, and yet, I still wanted to find out more about him. There was also an additional difficulty: as my characters were all intellectuals, I wanted to know everything about their lives as well as about their works. I admit that I had this frenzy of finding out more and more, and there was the same danger as in *HHhH* of drowning in details as I kept reading, one book leading to another, and so on. At some point I had to select and focus on specific aspects from my characters' lives and oeuvres (what I would call "vectorization"). The most enlightening example in my novel is Derrida: I cannot possibly pretend to have read everything—nor, for that matter, understood everything—he wrote. However, when I read about the disagreement between Derrida and Searle, which constitutes the core of my novel—that is to say the seventh function of language and its power as a performative tool—I knew I had something there, and I wanted to dig deeper into this controversy. So I obsessively read and reread everything in order to know the tiniest details. But a novelist must regulate his ambitions. Knowing everything is a fantasy, and fantasies can never be fulfilled.

Latham: Speaking about the obsession of possessing the whole truth, postmodernism has taught us that it is impossible to apprehend the absolute truth. Instead, we are offered versions, subjective reconstructions, simulacra, and a multiplicity of truths. Do you consider yourself a postmodernist author, or do you prefer to avoid such labels?

Binet: *The Seventh Function of Language* has not come out in English yet and I am curious to see how it will be received. But Anglo-American critics often talk about *HHhH* as a postmodernist novel. I am not sure that I understand everything the concept implies, but I am flattered that my novels are considered postmodernist works. However, I do not quite like the concept of "truth." Instead, I prefer to talk about "veracity": it is more modest. "Truth" is a big word with too many meanings. Everybody can access some form of truth: the truth of literature, the truth of feelings, the truth of art, and so on. I personally call the truth of facts "veracity," and I do believe there is such a thing. With or without Tolstoy, Napoleon won the Battle of Austerlitz and was defeated at Waterloo: it is a historical fact. I am not too keen on this relativism that consists of saying that there is no absolute historical truth. That's something that literary critics say, I think, but it is a dangerous area. Think of the Second World War, for instance: if there is no historical truth, what do you make of Auschwitz? This opens the door to an extremely slippery position. Jewish people in Auschwitz truly lived through this historical truth. So I think that contending that "truth does not exist, everything is fiction" is literary dandyism. I do understand that this constitutes a critical trend in literature, but I believe postmodernism is deeper and more thought provoking than this.

Latham: You define *HHhH* as an "infra-novel" ("*infra-roman*"). What exactly is an infra-novel? Is it a novelistic account stripped of its fictional dimension as much as possible? Is it a novel that resorts to the techniques and mechanisms of fiction, but remains nonfictional?

Binet: Yes, it is exactly that. I usually say that it is a novel that uses all the tools offered by literature, except for the main one: fiction. I mean all the stylistic choices, suspense, compositional methods, ending effects, but not fiction. It is as if I were dangerously approaching the edge of the cliff of fiction, but at the last moment I decide not to jump, not to make the final leap that would tip me over toward fiction.

Latham: Within your novel you play the role and adopt the voice of a literary critic who discusses how other writers deal with, manipulate or shape the genre. You comment on the difference between terms such as "true" and "plausible," between "people" and "characters." Throughout the text of your novel, you reflect on the reconstruction of history from researched facts and clues which you come across. You show the reader the unfolding of your investigation and how the novelistic mechanisms work. You clearly draw the reader's attention to the "strings controlling the puppets" (Chapter 15). Is writing and analyzing your production at the same time part of your signature? Is the fiction that you insert in your novel always accompanied by its modus operandi?

Binet: This is actually a good definition of the modern novel. It is the very signature of modernity, which can be traced back to *Don Quixote*. In the second volume of his adventures, the character of Don Quixote discovers Volume One of his adventures and reads it. The signature of modernity is reflexivity. Whenever the novel (and any other form of artistic expression) questions the conditions of its own functioning, one can find reflexivity. This is also the case when there is a *mise en abyme* in a play, like in Luigi Pirandello's plays, for instance. I am specifically interested in his process of deconstructing a literary work. And I do not know if this constitutes my own signature, but knowing my creative temperament, I cannot imagine ever writing a novel that does not somehow include this dimension. In *The Seventh Function of Language*, this reflexive aspect is presented in a different way: commentary does not come from the author who is omnisciently hovering over the story, but it is inserted within the story itself, and comes directly from a character who gradually develops a paranoid suspicion that he is stuck in a novel. And this is quite Pirandellian: my character questions his ontological status as a real person or fictitious character. Although in *The Seventh Function of Language* I used a more playful approach, it was actually aimed at achieving the same result, that is to point out the novel's reflexivity or self-interrogation.

Latham: In *The Seventh Function of Language* you stage the death of the author of "The Death of the Author." I suppose this is not a coincidence either, in a novel where you put into practice and popularize Barthes's theories and those of other authors of his time. It is quite similar to what Michael Cunningham does in *The Hours*, where he creates the character of Virginia Woolf and at the same time he uses and popularizes her style and critical theories on fiction.

Binet: Of course, since I was manipulating characters who were based on real authors, I wanted to play with and get maximal benefit from intertextuality. This is the reason why, for instance, I wanted the section that takes place in Bologna to refer to Deleuze, who was a real icon there. I enjoyed writing a sex scene *à la* Deleuze, inserting some mysterious Japanese characters into the plot as an allusion to Barthes's love for Japan, and especially borrowing semiology from Barthes to make it the driving force of my novel. Semiology is Sherlock Holmes's science as well. Sherlock Holmes is also an indirect allusion to Umberto Eco, through his character William Baskerville from *The Name of the Rose*. I liked the idea of the migration of characters and the circularity of all these authors' theories, and I wanted my novel to bubble with ingenuity and for exciting things to happen based on their ideas. The book is actually the novelistic representation of these ideas. And yes, for sure, I found it amusing to stage the death of the author of "The Death of the Author," as you so well put it.

Latham: You use facts attested by history to fabricate a truthful story which is promised to the reader from the very beginning. You say: "I want to tell you what really happened" (Chapter 1). The creation of a simulacrum of truth and filling in the blanks of history with invented material requires prior research into biographical information and historical, cultural, and political events, like the 1981 French presidential campaign. What kind of historical documents did you read, besides the primary sources (critical theories) that you knew and used as a teacher?

Binet: I read all the biographies of Barthes available at that time. I used some biographies of Michel Foucault written by his close friends, Didier Eribon, whom I also met, and Paul Veyne. I read all the testimonies provided by François Mitterrand's political entourage, by all his close collaborators who wrote their memoirs. Serge Moati was an invaluable source to find out how the televisual political debate between François Mitterrand and Valéry Giscard d'Estaing was organized. I also read and met Jack Lang. He was the one who organized the lunch meeting between Mitterrand and Barthes. I read Giscard's and Mitterrand's books, too. Eighty percent of what Mitterrand says in my book are actual quotes. Concerning the debate that took place between the two rounds of the 1981 presidential election, all the sentences spoken by the characters-candidates in my book are taken from the real debate. It was quite amusing for me to take real sentences that had actually been said and to reinterpret them in the light of my novelistic hypothesis, that is to say that the seventh function of language was in somebody's secret possession, and it could overturn the course of the debate. In accordance with this hypothesis, I could orient the interpretation of this debate that was based on totally true, authentic material.

Latham: It is interesting that this authentic material comes out of your characters' mouths. You explain in other interviews that these quotes are "first decontextualized and then recontextualized." You skillfully select, arrange and piece them together: this process is quite similar to what Raymond Federman has called "plagiarism." Do you have to take into account legal considerations of copyright when you quote so many writers and politicians and fabricate dialogues out of their theories or discourses?

Binet: Yes, there are legal restrictions: one cannot quote whole pages. In general, my quotes do not exceed more than a few lines, so it was legally authorized. Plus, I felt morally authorized to quote them because I did not have the impression that I was betraying people's ideas. I never make them say something that is contradictory to what they meant, as far as I could understand. On the contrary, my aim was to introduce the reader to their ideas that fascinated me personally and popularize these ideas. Besides quotations, there is also the problem of killing people who were not dead, assassinating them or making them commit suicide. There is a culprit, somebody who killed Barthes in my novel, but as long as fiction openly displays its fictitiousness, then there cannot be falsification—here again I am using Charlotte Lacoste's words. I mean, I am absolutely not trying to make anybody believe that Barthes was really assassinated and that the character of the killer is really a killer in real life. For the credibility of the character, I borrowed true facts, but at no moment do I pass my fiction off as reality.

Latham: Speaking of this moral dimension, as a writer, are there limits that you do not dare or authorize yourself to cross?

Binet: Yes, of course. The limit is when fiction becomes falsification, when one is slipping into a kind of revisionism, then there is a problem. This is immediately obvious when you deal with the Second World War and Holocaust denial. But, more generally, you cannot infringe on people's personal privacy or slander them, or say that they collaborated with the Nazis, for instance. I am thinking of this example because I saw Abel Ferrara's film *Welcome to New York*. In the film, which is openly inspired by the Dominique Strauss-Kahn case, the characters who represent Anne Sinclair's grandfather and father are respectively an art dealer who made his fortune under the Nazi occupation and a collaborator. In reality, Anne Sinclair's grandfather fled from the Nazis and was stripped of his French nationality by the Vichy government that ruled France during the Nazi occupation, and her father was a Jewish resistance fighter. So these portrayals are absolutely disgusting. I imagine that the motivations behind this were to make this story even more sordid than it really was, but for me this is absolutely loathsome. As far as my novel *The Seventh Function of Language* is concerned, I am not denying that I wanted Philippe Sollers to appear as a clown, but it is difficult to prove that he was not. And anyway, almost everything he says in my novel is taken from his oeuvre. In France, after the release of my book, the debate focused mainly on Sollers, but I frankly do not have the impression that I betrayed the reality of Sollers.

Latham: In an interview you stated that in *The Seventh Function of Language* you "smashed the link between fiction and reality: although 75 percent of the characters' dialogues are real quotes (and it goes up to 90% for Sollers), what happens to them is totally implausible." You clearly handle fiction differently in this novel. Was this creative exercise more liberating for you as a writer?

Binet: Yes, it was a different matter. I was probably less neurotically obsessed with historical truth, but at the same time it was quite frightening because of the total freedom conferred by fiction and the counterfactual. For instance, in *The Three Musketeers*, Alexandre Dumas does not kill Louis XIII before he actually dies. *The Three Musketeers* is a historical novel, but not counterfactual fiction. Dumas infiltrates the historical gaps but he does not change the grand historical narrative, something which I occasionally do in my novel. So it was a vertiginous freedom, which was part of the challenge of writing this book.

Latham: In *The Seventh Function of Language* you make up dialogues, you penetrate your characters' memories, you explore Barthes's "comatose sleep" and his last thoughts before dying. Often you signal it when specific scenes come straight from your imagination: "This is how, *maybe*, Barthes dies, thinking of. . ." With these kinds of signals, you constantly interrupt the illusion of the reality you are creating and the reader's suspension of disbelief. You thus lift or rip the veil of fiction to show us its operating mechanisms. Why is it important in your novels to create and at the same time destroy this illusion?

Binet: This is perhaps my playful side: I like to play with the reader and this involves taking risks. One of them is destroying the suspension of disbelief. I like to give myself a real fright, which is challenging: I first try to attract the reader, to hook him, to get him involved in the story, and every now and then wake him up, at the risk of breaking the spell. It can very well fail, but this is really what I want to do: attract the reader to me and then free him, only to attract him back afterward. I think this challenges my writer's vanity, but it is also linked to my professional nature as a teacher. I was a teacher for ten years and I like analyzing or deconstructing other writers' literary texts—and I surely enjoy deconstructing mine. I am a structuralist as well and I like showing what is hidden under the car's bonnet, as it were, and show how it works. This is in fact the job of a professor of literature. And so I like doing this within my very novels. It actually fits the nature of *The Seventh Function of Language*, because in a way it is based on a deconstruction approach that is quite similar to Derrida's project, that is to say it undermines the presuppositions of what we think we know on any given subject. This is precisely what I love about Bret Easton Ellis's novels, *Lunar Park* or *Glamorama*: the way his narration dismantles itself. Because his characters are never sure of what they have seen, the reader is not sure either of how to tackle, and to what extent to trust, the story he is reading. It is a sort of *mise en abyme* of the novelistic illusion where we realize that the whole narration is built on sand. This is exactly what Thomas Pynchon and Philip Roth do, too. It is a very American novelistic approach.

Latham: Characters like Simon Herzog interpret, translate, or explain various critical theories and give biographical information, in small doses, about the linguists or critics mentioned in the novel (Todorov, Jakobson, Eco) that Jacques Bayard—and perhaps many readers—had never heard of. Are Simon's courses and discourses based on your own experience as a teacher and do they have an autobiographical dimension?

Binet: Yes, absolutely, I have drawn on my teaching experience. I have given classes on semiology. But I also have a very practical side: *docere et placere*. I try to teach things in a ludic way. The course on James Bond, for example, alludes to Umberto Eco's article. I did not teach that specific course, but I could have. In fact, I wrote it in ten minutes, and I wrote it as I would have written a class preparation. Also, at some point in my novel I had to explain Jakobson's functions of language, in a synthetic and efficient way so as not to bore my reader. Lastly, I had to explain what semiology is, and my approach was that semiology is Sherlock Holmes's science. And so, I wanted to carry out my demonstration in a scene *à la* Sherlock Homes to explain what semiology implies both to the character Jacques Bayard and to the reader. I tried to combine my pedagogical skills—those of a teacher—and my playful talents—those of a novel writer, which can actually overlap.

Latham: In *The Seventh Function of Language* you bring together several types of characters: those who have a counterpart in the real world (Barthes, Derrida, Foucault, Kristeva, Sollers), those who originally come from other fictional universes (for instance, Morris Zapp from *Changing Places* by David Lodge), and characters created specifically for the needs of your story, "supernumeraries" (Umberto Eco's term), like Simon, who questions his ontological status as he feels "trapped in a fucking novel" (Chapter 72). How did you manage to make all these characters from various ontological horizons cohabit so harmoniously and interact so naturally in your novel?

Binet: Maybe by treating them in the same way. Even the characters that Eco calls supernumeraries originally come from somewhere. Simon Herzog shares Sherlock Holmes's initials and my own academic and professional career; he is a mixture of Sherlock Holmes and myself. Jacques Bayard is also a mixture of Inspector Maigret and Jack Bauer from whom he borrows the name, Jacques Bayard being the French equivalent of Jack Bauer. Morris Zapp is an example that perfectly illustrates the circularity between fictional universes—what Eco calls possible worlds—and this specific, real world. My idea was to treat these fictional levels in the same way, and Morris Zapp was the best material to embody this idea, as he was inspired by a real person, Stanley Fish, a famous American professor, who was David Lodge's friend, I think. So it was quite amusing for me to put in Morris Zapp's mouth the words actually pronounced by Stanley Fish, the real person who inspired this fictional character that I borrowed from my fellow writer David Lodge and inserted in my own fictional world. Playing with the intertextuality of both possible fictional worlds and the real world was quite fun. Another high point in my book is when I put in Foucault's tribute speech to Derrida the very discourse that Derrida wrote in homage to Barthes. This game of displacement was also great fun. And nobody has noticed that, except my German translator. I had chosen with great care this passage in which Derrida speaks about power and it could very well be taken for Foucault's own philosophy. For me, this was the zenith of the game of displacement between fiction and reality. I believe that displacements are what sum up best my novelistic project in *The Seventh Function of Language*.

Latham: You said that *The Seventh Function of Language* is more playful than *HHhH*. Did you consciously use a more varied array of postmodernist tricks?

Binet: Yes, of course. Compared to *The Seventh Function of Language*, *HHhH* was really simple: a combination of the unfolding of the historical account and my personal narration of how I fabricated the novel. *The Seventh Function of Language* is much more ambitious and sophisticated. I wracked my brains to create complex fictional effects based on intertextuality. You can find so many mechanisms at work within the novel: sometimes only simple references, but more often than not very elaborate structures. It was more of a novelist's work.

Latham: Concerning this ambitious and sophisticated novel, have you ever wondered what happens when the reception mechanism gets stuck, that is to say that the readers cannot decode all your intertextual, hypertextual and architextual references?

Binet: No, because if they cannot, that's fine. Baudelaire said about metaphor that it must function first and foremost as literal meaning and must hold up even without its metaphorical connotation. So I think—and I hope—that one can read my novel as a simple detective novel in which, at the same time, one will learn interesting things about a few intellectuals that lived in the 80s. I am absolutely convinced that no reader—even my German translator, even the most erudite reader—will grasp all the intertextual allusions in the book. The biggest specialist in linguistics, who can identify all the echoes to Eco's work, may not notice that I reversed the result of the Roland Garros tennis match. And that's alright. And the reader who notices that I reversed the tennis score may probably not see that one of the songs on the playlist at the party on the Cornell campus is anachronistic: Kim Wilde's song "Kids in America" was released in 1981, whereas the action in my book takes place in 1980. If you miss this, it does not really matter, but each time I distil such an anachronism (or some dysfunctional detail that deviates from historical reality) in the unfolding of my story, it has some kind of repercussion. And it is always Simon, my spokesman for these matters, who senses there is something wrong and is bothered by it. So you can have the pleasure of spotting all kinds of intertextual allusions, but if you cannot do so, it does not matter because what I wanted to do was to communicate to the reader my character's malaise: he senses something but he cannot really put his finger on it because he is stuck in a novel. But anyway, about which novel can we say that nothing has escaped us?

Latham: So there are several levels and layers of meaning, which makes this novel accessible to a wide audience. And each reader, according to their literary capital, decodes as much as they can.

Binet: Exactly. The greatest academic will never be able to decode everything because I am also immersed in popular culture, sports, American TV series, and televisual entertainment in general. And maybe David Lodge, for instance, if he does me the honor of reading my book, will miss these hints.

Latham: You started your career with an autobiographical account (*La Vie professionnelle de Laurent B*), then you wrote a biographical novel (*HHhH*) and more recently, in *The Seventh Function of Language*, you rely even more on fiction and imagination. Do you think that one day you will explore even further the depths of imagination and resort to magic realism, for instance? Are you tempted by a kind of fiction that leaves (auto)biographical and historical truth far behind? Or else, do you think, like Virginia Woolf in *A Room of One's Own* that fiction must be attached to reality: "Fiction is like a spider's web, attached ever so lightly perhaps, but still attached to life at all four corners?"

Binet: It is not an obligation, but it is necessarily the case. Even the most imaginative science fiction novel is based on elements of our own reality. It is an illusion to believe that our imagination can give birth to pure fiction; fiction is always set against reality: it adheres closely to it or deviates far from it. And magic realism is a good example. One of my favorite books by Gabriel García Márquez is *The General in His Labyrinth*. It is extremely poetic, it is the most exemplary form of magic realism, but it is also about Bolívar's last days. One learns a lot about the history of Latin America from this novel. The same goes for another novelist I have discovered recently, Eduardo

Galeano. He uses an absolutely fantastic kind of magic realism but at the same time he writes about the history of Latin America. Another example is Carlos Fuentes whom I am reading right now. I am totally absorbed by the stories of Hernán Cortés and Moctezuma II. In all these examples, there are very solid historical foundations. Anyway, I know that it is impossible not to draw on reality. In my novels I use great historical figures, and although there is certainly a counterfactual dimension, I did not alter historical facts or the grand narrative. I did not change the end of the Second World War, for example, like Philip K. Dick or Philip Roth.

But if you mean fiction in terms of deviation from historical truth, yes, it is possible that I deviate even further. However, my aim is not to create bigger and bigger gaps with history. I know that one way or another I will find a third form, after *HHhH* and *The Seventh Function of Language*. The issue of keeping in check fiction and reality will be present in my next novel, I can assure you.

Latham: Among the international authors who write novels to be found at the crossroads of (biographical and historical) reality and fiction, what is your French specificity?

Binet: I do not know if there is a French specificity. I quite like Milan Kundera's idea that novelists form a sort of chain that transcends borders. Most of the books I quoted during this interview have not been written by French writers. Even *The Kindly Ones*, which was originally written in French, is the work of an American writer, Jonathan Littell. I like it when there are multiple, unexpected sources of inspiration and models. For instance, even if Bret Easton Ellis's influence on my work is not immediately obvious because our approaches are not similar, there is nevertheless a common point in that we both like the idea of the novel dismantling itself. Plus, all the party scenes in *The Seventh Function of Language* are inspired by Bret Easton Ellis's universe and techniques. So I like borrowing from diverse models that are not directly recognizable. For instance, I do not want Vasily Grossman's *Life and Fate* to be the primary, obvious reference for *HHhH*, or Philip K. Dick and other writers who wrote uchronia to be the obvious reference for *The Seventh Function of Language*. Besides, I like the idea that novelistic work is first and foremost a question of technique. I always use tennis metaphors: I like to observe Roger Federer's forehand stroke; in the same way, I like to observe how Bret Easton Ellis writes his dialogues—even though his universe of degenerate Californians does not have anything to do with my themes. I also like reading interviews with authors in *The Paris Review* which focus on their technique and practice. And I will read this volume with great pleasure.

Latham: Do you think that the genres of biographical and historical fiction can be constantly renewed, can always offer original ramifications with each writer and his literary and cultural heritage, or do you think it is a literary phenomenon which will soon reach its limits?

Binet: I believe that the novel in general has infinite capacities to permanently renew and reinvent itself. The novel is protean and hybrid by nature, and this constitutes its greatest strength. Hybridity guarantees its endurance. Biographical and historical novels are as strong as ever and have fine days ahead of them.

Interview conducted in and translated from French by Monica Latham.

3

Resisting the "Dictatorship of the Present" in the Biographical Novel

Javier Cercas, interviewed by Virginia Rademacher

Rademacher: While the biographical novel has long existed, beginning in the 1980s, this genre suddenly became very popular with a growing number of well-regarded authors and their readers. I am interested in better understanding why there is this "boom" in the biographical novel, and why now? What about the current moment has drawn so many writers to this mode, and to what extent does this literary trend comment on the experience of contemporary life?

The editor of this collection of interviews, Michael Lackey, has observed that the biographical novel surged at the same time as interest waned in the historical novel. He notes, for example, that a number of influential authors rejected the historical novel's overemphasis on the influence of social forces in determining identity and its simultaneous neglect of the importance of individual decisions.

In your books, you also place great emphasis on private moments and individual decisions in forming what we understand as history. Do you believe this context of individualism, of fragmentation, of the powerful role of uncertainty, and of the contingent in our lives are influencing this literary shift? Feel free to speak purely from the perspective of your own work.

Cercas: I'm not sure that I agree that the biographical novel has overtaken the historical novel. At least in Spain (but not only in Spain) the historical novel remains highly popular, although maybe less ambitious in terms of literature. We would also have to discuss what is meant by a historical novel. Sometimes they say I write historical novels. I don't really like that label. I write novels in which history has a role, but they are not historical novels. My novels often center on the past; that's true. But the past appears as a dimension of the present. To me, the past on its own doesn't interest me at all. I'm interested in the past that invades memory, that bears witness to this past but is not yet past. I am interested in this expanded present that encompasses, in some form, the past. Because I think that we live in a dictatorship of the present.

Rademacher: Can you describe what you mean?

Cercas: Since *Soldiers of Salamis* (2001), all of my books are really about this ongoing dialogue between past and present. Before that, my books only lived in the immediate present. That's why I believe I used to be a postmodern writer and maybe now I'm a post-postmodern writer. In terms of the dictatorship of the present . . . well, my impression is that, naturally, all of us tend to think that the past doesn't have anything to do with us, with our real lives and current interests, but is instead something distant and archival, and as a result, our interest in the past (this "history") emerges from intellectual curiosity rather than out of any authentic, essential need. And it's true that the tendency to ignore the past has become stronger in a society like ours, dominated by the power of social, and other mediated forms of communication. These, in actuality, don't only reflect reality, but define, and in some cases even create it. But the speed and immediacy of communication, which has its benefits, also means that examining the past becomes a kind of luxury for which few of us have time (because what happened yesterday is already history, and what happened last week, essentially prehistory). The result of this compression is to intensify the dominion of the present; that is to say, the illusion that the present alone can explain itself.

This is completely false: this illusion that I call the dictatorship of the present. Rather, the past—as recorded by memories and witnesses, these differing versions that inform my books—also forms part of the present. It is a piece and a dimension of this reality, without which the present would be incomplete and incomprehensible. The past is never fully past because it is here, acting on the present, forming part of it, inhabiting us. To live the present without the past is to live a damaged present. And, as I stated, beginning with *Soldiers of Salamis*, my books took on a battle with this impoverished present and in support of one that is more complete, complex, and that draws more fully from the past.

And to answer your other question, yes—I think that chance, that individual decisions, at times risky ones that depend largely on chance, are absolutely crucial in our lives. They're not myths in my novels; they're essential realities of people's lives. We are determined by fate, by decisions that at times even we ourselves don't know why we've made, choices that sometimes we instinctively make. I think these contingent moments are such a central part of my books because they are so important in life. It's possible that recent history, through any number of circumstances, has given a great deal of importance to social, collective phenomena, and has overlooked the importance of individual decisions.

And maybe that has something to do with what we're talking about here. I mean, for example, to try to explain the Spanish transition from dictatorship to democracy, all of its complexity and moving pieces, there is a very important factor: the main characters' personalities. Do you know why, Jenny? In my opinion, the more consolidated a democracy is, the less important the individual players, because there is a system that protects, organizes, guides; there are laws, structures. But, during the transition, individual personalities were crucial. The personality of Adolfo Suárez and of Santiago Carrillo, just to mention two examples. They were essential because they made very important decisions, but also because they had so little reason to trust one another. For example, the secret meeting of Suárez with Carrillo, just before the Communist Party was legalized. Picture it: the president of a country that is still a dictatorship going to a clandestine meeting with someone that was virtually the devil to the people that had governed that dictatorship for forty years, and for a lot of people. This is an intensely personal version of history—the fact that they both were able to understand each other and to get along: Suárez, who was in fact a young Francoist leading the country into democracy, and Carrillo, an old Communist who'd fought the war.

Rademacher: I read an article recently—it may have been in the *New Yorker*—about people who've had terrible accidents in which a split-second moment had tragic consequences that impacted their lives tremendously. And it is something that doesn't get talked about much, how guided we are by chance. We think about these events because they happened, because a child crossed the street at the wrong moment and someone else was distracted at just that same time, or couldn't stop soon enough, or it could have been even something that was not at all their fault, simply because. But what happens is that we don't think about all of the tons of things that *didn't* happen, even though they could have. I think Rosa Montero calls these the "what-ifs," these other possible realities in the sense of Borges, perhaps.

Cercas: But Jenny, fate rules our lives. We were born because of chance. One day my mother and my father were getting along well and fate left room for one sperm. It might never have happened and I would not be here. Everything is chance. So, why wouldn't literature pay attention to this important factor in our lives? Literature that doesn't acknowledge the role of chance in lives is false literature, don't you think?

Rademacher: Building off this idea of a false literature, of imposture . . . among others, Jesus Bolaño has written about the end of postmodernism, the reign of irony, and of a new period of sincerity in writing. He refers to David Foster Wallace as one of the first authors to expose the holes of relativity and ambiguity, the absence of real connection, and in turn the desire to recover a lost referentiality and essentialism, not only in literature but more broadly. What are your thoughts about this shift in paradigm, and where do you locate your work? Do you think we are in a post-postmodern world, within which the biographical novel plays an integral part?

Cercas: There is a short book of mine, an essay, called *The Blind Spot.* There I collect and rewrite a series of lectures I delivered at Oxford some time ago, and in one of the conferences I talk about this, and specifically about Foster Wallace. In any case, it's complicated, but I would say I consider myself a postmodern writer up to, let's say, the third part of *Soldiers of Salamis.* That is to say, I was a writer who had been educated in postmodernism. And well, the immediate forerunner is Borges, for me the creator of postmodernism; and the remote predecessor is the second part of *El Quijote.* That's how I see the origins of postmodernism, and how I educated myself as a postmodern writer. My models were Borges, Kafka, Calvino, some other American postmodern writers, etc. And for me, my first books—*The Motive, The Tenant, The Belly of the Whale*—are postmodern books. Books where the past didn't exist, where there was no collective or political dimension, metaliterary books, profoundly ironic, humorous books, sometimes fantastic literature, books that would play with literary genres, etc., etc., etc. A whole panoply of characteristic features.

Starting with *Soldiers of Salamis*, it's not that I abandon postmodernism. What happens is that there are new things that maybe were only germinating in my previous books. And these new things come to light. For instance, the past as a dimension of the present. Or the collective as a dimension of the individual. And there appears, let's say, a strong moral inquiry that was there before, but was more subdued, much less evident. In other words, a series of new tools and interest come to light. And I think this has to do with what Bolaño talks about, whom I don't know, and even more so with what Foster Wallace says. In my opinion, Foster Wallace is quite right in terms of diagnosis, but he's wrong when it comes to the solution. And this is very interesting.

Rademacher: Wrong in what way?

Cercas: Foster Wallace is very intelligent. I believe he's one of the brightest writers of my generation. But in my opinion, his work is unfulfilling. I think

Infinite Jest is a grand book, but not actually a great book in the sense that he wanted it to be. He realizes the limits of postmodernism, and how much it depends on sarcasm. For example, he is a very good essayist and, in an essay about Dostoevsky, he says that today Dostoevsky would be considered a corny writer, sentimental. Because postmodernism is only sarcasm, only irony, according to Foster Wallace; so he proposes returning to a literature that is almost pedagogical. This is a serious mistake. In essence, with Foster Wallace there is a huge contradiction between what he wrote, which was full of pop culture, of sarcasm, of irony, etc. and what he wanted to write, which was Dostoevsky. And I think there was in Foster Wallace, whom I respect very much, an enormous frustration, a frustration only exacerbated by his success, because, of course, he was famous for something that deep inside he didn't really appreciate. And Foster Wallace's essential confusion is the following one: it's the fact that he confuses irony with sarcasm.

In *The Blind Spot*, I try to explain how irony is the essence of the novel. In fact, the way of acquiring knowledge in the novel consists of irony, understood as Schlegel would conceptualize it—as the shaping of paradox. I mean, what's irony? This is Cervantes' great invention, one of his most impressive creations. Don Quijote is completely mad. But at the same time, he's incredibly intelligent, lucid, capable of carrying on with absolute clarity about the more complex questions . . . That's irony: illuminating contradictions. "King of the hidalgos, lord of the sad," as Rubén Darío would say. That essential contradiction is the crux of the novel as a genre, and the novel can't . . . it mustn't leave it aside because then it would be reduced to pedagogy. Because then it turns into monolithic knowledge, into propaganda.

So, Foster Wallace was at the crossroads of postmodernism. That is to say, he wasn't able to find a path forward or to produce literature capable of expressing feelings, emotion, morality, without being pedagogical. Yet, that's what great figures in literature do; that's what Cervantes does, what Shakespeare does; that's what great writers do. And that is what he wanted. He realized postmodernism saw literature as just a game. And for me, post-postmodernism would be literature as a game, but as an absolutely serious game, a game where everything is at stake.

Rademacher: Elaborating further on what you have said about irony, I am thinking of *Soldiers of Salamis* when the fictionalized Roberto Bolaño tells Cercas, the narrator, that he'll just have to invent Miralles—make up the interview with him. That was a powerfully ironic anecdote but also an essential part of the story that makes one think a lot about how to access another life, and the relationship of truth in that process.

Cercas: Definitely.

Rademacher: I'm thinking about this issue you posed earlier about precursors and what continues to resonate, or to be questioned. If modernism was the awareness of fragmentation and postmodernism takes a more playful approach to this collapse of truth and meaning, then I wonder to what extent the biographical novel occupies this space of saying that, however incomplete and unsatisfactory, even the fictionalized truth of a life has to be more than just a game. It has to get at something else more meaningful.

Cercas: It's a game where you risk everything. Because writing is a type of game—ludic, ironic, at times even humorous; but it's also a highly serious game: as serious as life itself. The most humorous novel I know, *El Quijote*, is also the most serious one, and it shows that there is nothing more serious than humor.

Rademacher: To continue along that line, since we've already talked a little bit about critics who perceive the exhaustion of postmodernism, these same critics have contended we're much better positioned to build literature that addresses honestly the real problems of the world. And your most recent book, *The Monarch of the Shadows*, especially given what has been going on in Catalonia, is a very contemporary novel—one that manages to speak to the past and the present. And this could be because we are experiencing a simultaneously more authoritarian world and at the same time one that is profoundly more diffuse, in the sense that there's a profusion of information and images that we don't know how to process. The Libyan writer Hisham Matar has argued that dictatorships and writers are natural opponents because dictatorships are interested in a single narrative, while writers are interested in multiple truths. Is there something in the current context, in the confusion of our world, that compels us to look for a "tangible" reality, that encourages us toward a biofictional (rather than purely fictional) approach?

Cercas: These are several questions. First of all, my books always talk about the present, as I've already suggested. They never talk about the past on its own. So, in *The Monarch of the Shadows*, it's very clear that half of the book happens in the present. This book doesn't focus on Spain's civil war, or maybe I should say it does not talk only about it, but also about the inheritance of violence, about what we do with the past, especially the worst past. And you were right, the fact that this book speaks to the present is very evident, because the problems of the thirties are the problems of the present in a clearer way than it has ever been. When I talk about fascist ideologies and the fanaticism that seduced, or "abducted" Manuel Mena, those are actually the ideologies we have today, in a new disguise. We have returned to epic, emotional politics, haven't we? Mass politics, the use of lies in massive doses, charismatic leaders, all those things. Certainly, Manuel Mena is a symbol of all young people that go to war because adults send them.

But he is also a symbol of the ease with which people can be misled. And particularly nowadays, that is a lot easier, because, you have talked about the media, right? Nowadays, lies have a really greater power than ever before. We've seen that with Trump; we have seen it with Brexit; we see it with what is happening in Catalonia. Isn't that true? Tons of lies being said without penalty, thanks to Vladimir Putin, among other things.

The internet and social media are fabulous tools for the expansion of lies that co-opt people with promises of paradise: Trump's America, an England free of Europe, independent Catalonia, right? A France without immigrants . . . illusions of artificial ideals that create a type of hell. This is exactly what happened to Manuel Mena, a young boy abducted by the ideals of fascism. So, obviously this book talks about the present. I was especially aware because I saw these same debates resurface while I was writing the book. There's a speech by José Antonio Primo de Rivera that talks about Falangism, about Spanish fascism that could have been given today.

And there's a struggle between literature and power, as Hisham Matar says, which is evident. The less authoritarian or the more democratic power is, there is more competition over meaning; there are different stories about the past and the present. But with more authoritarian power, as in Franco's Spain, there was only one truth. So, what literature does, one of the things literature does, is to fight against the story imposed by power. It's trying to tell the truths that power is concealing. And it also aims at showing there is no one truth, that there are polyvalent truths.

It's very interesting because, nowadays, I have the feeling that telling the truth is scandalous.

Rademacher: Also, the idea that there are always multiple truths does not mean that they are interchangeable. If there are always truth alternatives, what authorizes any one version as more true, more credible?

Cercas: Factual truths are one thing, and moral truths are something else, and these are multifaceted. Literary truth is not journalistic or historical truth. You and me, we are here. This is true. Today is Monday; this is true. We are in Barcelona, that is also a fact. Here, there is no risk of competing truths. But with moral truths, which are novelesque, those are indeed multiple. This is a very important difference. In other words, you can be a wonderful person, but you can also be the opposite, depending on the circumstances. And you're the same person. The same goes for me. Don't you think? These are the truths of literature.

Rademacher: This is a key facet that biofiction explores.

Cercas: In this sense, Suárez was a Francoist social climber and also a hero. He became a democratic hero. Both things are true. Those are moral truths, the most complicated truths, aren't they? What we call post-truth is something completely different: it has to do with factual truth, journalistic truth, the truth of history, not of literature. Pay attention to the incredible ease with which Donald Trump, for example, tells lies. We should all read *Mein Kampf*, because there are a lot of similarities with Trump. Hitler said, "little lies don't matter": lies need to be really big because the petit bourgeoisie, or rather most of us, say that it can't be a lie—that's impossible! It has to be true, right? That is how Trump works, he tells enormous lies and nothing happens. And people believe them. Now we are stuck in the midst of an avalanche of lies.

Rademacher: The loss of connection with truth.

Cercas: It's extraordinary. If you lose your connection with the truth, you are lost.

Rademacher: Turning to a question that's maybe more practical but that has to do with navigating uncertainty. . . I'm interested in how the process of imagining a character very loosely based on reality, like Miralles, differs from creating the internal life of a real person you knew, like your great uncle, Manuel Mena in *The Monarch of the Shadows.*

Cercas: It's completely different because Miralles is an invented character, while Manuel Mena is a real character. I mean, the case of Manuel Mena is completely different because I wanted to be extremely faithful to the facts, to a real person that existed, to tell his real life and to do that with the greatest possible precision. *The Monarch of the Shadows* has two narrators. One that is called Javier Cercas and that is myself or somebody very close to myself, somebody that exposes the process of writing the novel itself—something that is as important as the story of Manuel Mena and my family and my little town, the story of the past—somebody that has a certain freedom to invent, at least in part. But, on the other hand, there is another narrator, a historian who even talks about me in the third person: he's the one who tells the story of Manuel Mena and my family and my little town, someone who wants to reconstruct the past of Manuel Mena and my family with the greatest possible accuracy or precision; he even corrects me. I needed that second narrator. I had this need not to invent anything about Manuel Mena and my family. What I tell there is what I know. I can imagine things, I can say "maybe he felt like that, maybe he felt in some other way." I can use imagination, but not fantasy.

That's the difference. Imagination is something historians and scientists also use. It's the capacity to make unexpected connections. Fantasy is something else. It's what I use to invent Miralles. Miralles is an invented character, very remotely based on a real person. But it has nothing to do with that person. I make it all up. That's where fantasy and invention differ. For instance, with Adolfo Suárez or Santiago Carrillo, two historical characters, I imagine things as a historian, a little bit more freely than a historian, but I don't invent anything. There's no fantasy there. Instead, with Miralles or el Zarco in *The Laws of the Frontier*, for instance, everything is fantasy.

I believe this difference between imagination and fantasy is fundamental and very often people don't understand it. They don't get it. Historians and scientists use imagination, but they can't use fantasy. Even journalists use it or can use it in some way, under certain circumstances. But they can't use fantasy, no. Fantasy is reserved for novelists.

Rademacher: I'm wondering about this blending of biographical truth and fiction that we see in the biographical novel. Noting that the German author, Takis Würger felt the necessity to write "This story is not true" in the prologue of one of his novels, José Ovejero observes that "perhaps we've arrived at a point in which the relationship between fiction and reality has become more confusing than ever. The recent proliferation of biographies and stories based on real events reveals a desire for reality that seems new in literature and film." Similarly, Rosa Montero has said that before there seemed to be a clearer frontier between reality and fiction. But now that border is more blurred. Accordingly, fiction and reality are so interconnected that there is a lot of infection between both. I'm wondering what your opinion is. With the surge in the biographical novel, are we seeing a new type of realism that incorporates uncertainty as an unavoidable facet of our lives?

Cercas: I don't know that I agree. All novels, all fictions, all books want to appear real. In other words, they want the reader to experience it as if it were real. So what changes are strategies. Strategies change because the reader grasps the way writers want to seduce them, somehow deceive them or make them believe that what they are reading is real. So, those ways become exhausted and new ways must be created. But the writer has always wanted to bewitch the reader, seduce him, in a certain sense cheat on him. He has always wanted to convince the reader of the fact that what he's telling is real. It's the strategies that change.

I'll give you an example. When *Soldiers of Salamis* was published, many people thought it was true, which is wonderful. Why? Because the prose was too plain, too different from the affected, serious prose that was the style in Spain at that time. It looked like a chronicle, and in addition to that, the narrator held my name and apparently was like me. That's fantastic. It's what we look for as writers.

With regards to the confusion between fiction and reality, I'm not convinced that this is true now more than before, maybe even the opposite. One of the basic principles of postmodernism is Nietzsche's phrase, as you know, "there are no facts, only interpretations." But that's false. There are facts, and there are interpretations of those facts. You and I are here and that's a fact. But you can go home and narrate this interview and I can go home and narrate this interview and our stories will be completely different because our interpretations will be different. However, we can still be faithful to reality, to facts. I mean, both things exist, and it is false to pretend otherwise.

Rademacher: But I think that distance that Ovejero and Montero were talking about is rather the space between invented reality and fiction, as you mentioned before, not fact and fiction.

Cercas: That's different.

Rademacher: It's between those things, as we said, that people become confused, and that writers and others are experimenting. . . Between what's being introduced as reality but is actually fiction, and fiction that is intentionally playing with that dichotomy.

Cercas: Literature can delude, it can tell things that are not true, but journalism can't do that. Sometimes people have said to me, not very intelligent people actually, "Cercas deceives the reader in his books." Of course I do, or at least I try.

Rademacher: That's part of being a novelist.

Cercas: Exactly! In literature you can invent, use fantasy, combine fiction and reality, you can do it all, because that is literature, especially the novel as I see it: complete freedom. That's where novels come from. In journalism, you can't. Something that is true, Jenny, is that now, as we were saying before, the capacity of lies, the capacity of spreading those lies is enormous. That is true. Because the media has more power than ever before. As I mentioned before, they do not only reflect reality, they also create it: anything that doesn't appear in the media doesn't exist; we have no knowledge of it. So yes, lies have an extraordinary power, an extraordinary capacity for diffusion. But that doesn't mean saying that confusion is legitimate. We must fight against it. But in literature, the mixture of fiction and reality is essential.

Rademacher: Yes. But the intention with biofiction is not to pretend to journalistic truth, but to very conscientiously, overtly draw attention to the creation of a fiction—as you do. For example, José Ovejero has talked about a nostalgia for the real, and that it would be easy to minimize or to ridicule this nostalgia. But at the same time he says that nostalgia should not be devalued, that it is always the testimony of a lack, as a ghost pain reminds us we've lost a necessary element in our lives.

I'm thinking about this in terms of what you said in another interview, that perhaps you began to write in this way—employing biofiction, in my words—out of a lack of satisfaction with pure fiction. That is to say, the mix of fiction and reality in your works distances itself from postmodern play, and rather reflects the desire to anchor to something real. Do you think there is a type of absence in our lives that reveals itself in a desire for a new type of realism that incorporates conjecture and speculation as essential parts of our lives? Walter Benjamin, as you've mentioned elsewhere, talks about the "crisis of fiction," of how to convince people that something we know is fiction is real.

Cercas: We always want what we read to seem real, that it is experienced as if it were real. People read *Madame Bovary*, and thought that it was true. And this is what we want, even despite the pact that we create with the reader that it is fiction. This is not new to me. Strategies change; how to get people to believe that something is real, or that it affects them as if it were real. That is the question.

Rademacher: But, for you, what is the place of fiction in the novels of "no-fiction" as you've termed them? I read, for example, Emmanuel Carrère's *The Adversary*, a story similar to your novel, *The Imposter*. But for me, the fact that Carrère tried to write it as a pure biography limited the story, something that didn't happen for me with *The Imposter*. I'd like you to explain why you chose the strategy of writing *The Imposter* as biofiction, or why you included biofiction as an essential part of the book.

Cercas: In the case of *The Imposter*, why did I chose to "saturate it with fiction"? Why? Very easy. Because as I was working, I felt Marco not only had invented his time in the Nazi concentration camp of Flossenbürg, but had also invented his whole life. In other words, Marco was a truly mobile fiction. He had invented everything, from beginning to end. So I considered it senseless to construct a fiction about another fiction. And what meant something, or could mean something, was to create a struggle to the death between fiction and reality in this book. I mean, between the lies that Marco had told, his fictions, and the truth hidden behind those fictions. I thought that was potentially the center, the most interesting part of the book. So, the book is largely a struggle between fiction and reality. In that sense it is a biofiction. The reader ends up knowing about Enric Marco's true life, but also about his fictional life. And in Marco's fictional life there's a part that is true. Because what we invent about our own life, what we fantasize about our own life is also part of what we are. My imaginations, my dreams, my desires, those things are also part of who I am.

Rademacher: I'm particularly thinking of the chapter where there's an invented dialogue between the narrator Cercas and Enric Marco.

Cercas: To me, this dialogue is the most important part of the book. I'm going to make a confession: that's the first thing I wrote. When the news burst about Marco's case and I was pondering the story, the first thing I started writing was that dialogue.

And some years after that, I resumed my work on it because I felt there was something important there. In fact, the book is a struggle between fiction and reality, but it's also a struggle between Marco and me. I mean, between two imposters. It's just that the writer is authorized to be an impostor and regular people are not. I don't know if I've explained myself?

Rademacher: Definitely.

Cercas: So, that chapter is the most important one. It's the perfect example of what I call irony, because it's open to many interpretations. I needed to invent a version of myself. At the beginning of the chapter, I say "I fantasized." Do you remember? That is, I tell the reader, "This is fiction." I needed Marco to relive things with me, to fight with me. I needed Marco to say: "You are like me." In other words, it's kind of self-irony.

It's a way of laughing at myself, because the best humor starts with oneself. I don't think a person is able to speak ironically about anything if he or she is not able to speak ironically about himself or herself. I don't think the book could exist without that chapter. Many people were surprised by it, of course. It's an essentially humoristic chapter, in the most serious sense of the word.

Rademacher: For me that was what *The Adversary* was missing, because it didn't have that irony.

Cercas: It's just that, actually *The Adversary* is a book that is only similar to mine in the theme. Everything else is immensely different. When people, sometimes journalists, asked me, "Was this inspired by *The Adversary*," I'd think: "You haven't read *The Adversary*." Because Carrère, who I respect a lot, his idea for the novel is completely different from mine. To me, *The Adversary* is a type of chronicle. Instead, my book is a novel and has this multiple thing that my novels have; they contain many literary genres: there's essay, there's history, biography, autobiography. . .

Rademacher: I'd like to talk more about what you've said about this style of your novels, that they have many genres, many components. Carlo Ginzburg has talked about the circumstantial paradigm, where following the traces or remains of a life, things that in isolation don't build to coherence or explanation, give us hints and provocations to perceive another life. Do you think that by means of the abundance of images and information, the profusion of the contemporary context, the world has become more circumstantial, more dependent on these vestiges? That is, are we are living in a circumstantial world in which it is almost impossible to see a coherent narrative and we have to constantly convince ourselves of connections among seemingly random pieces? What might this have to do with the growth in biofiction, as a "strategy" of writing, if you will, that incorporates this cacophonous amalgam we call reality?

Cercas: I would say there is a human need to impose order in our experience, order on our biographies. But deep inside, it's an illusion. Life has no order. It's chaotic and we perceive it in fragments. And we impose order or an illusion of order on it. That's what literature does. That's what we all do with our lives. But I don't think our experience of reality is more fragmentary than in the past. I think the human experience is basically the same. Our way of telling or giving meaning to it is different. For instance, a person in the Middle Ages obviously had a fundamental tool to give essence to his life: religion. And in many cases, we don't have that anymore. Some people do, but many don't. But that doesn't mean that the way of living in the Middle Ages was different from ours, nor that our perception of reality is different. There's a desperate desire to construct meaning. What's changed is the way of constructing that meaning. But the core of the issue is the same, isn't it? Why is the world more fragmented today? Yes, we've lost, let's say, it's true, we've lost the great systems that gave meaning to everything, right?

Rademacher: That's postmodernity, but I'm thinking more of. . .

Cercas: Yes—that's postmodernity. That's true. But is our perception of the world more fragmented due to that? Twitter, Facebook, do they change the way we perceive the world? In essence, I don't think so. These are tools. But the essential problems we have today are still the same. Besides, there are people that still have those totalizing perspectives.

In my opinion, that doesn't mean the way we perceive the world is different. The different thing is the way we express ourselves. And that's what literature does, that's what art hopefully does—allows us to perceive continuity before difference. I believe what links us to our ancestors is much more important. Yes, much more than what separates us.

Rademacher: I'm wondering about what drives the process of searching in the biographical novel. In *Soldiers of Salamis*, as well as in other books you've written, there's a lot of attention to the historical record, to tangible documentary evidence that can be rescued: pictures, documents and journals, and also to what goes missing, what has been destroyed, lost or falsified, as we've talked about, these fragments. And I'm thinking of Nancy Miller's book, *Pieces of a Jewish Past,* where she talked about "splines," which is a dual metaphor referring to both the frame of a window and also, in science, to imagined connections between different points. These *splines* seam together the documentary material that forms the scaffolding of a biographical narrative—through these imagined associations—constructing and making visible the complex connection among evidence, memory, and narration. And she talks about the way in which the need for finding those splines, for using them to connect these circumstantial details of a life, helps to recover the fragments and to bind those memories into some kind of coherence. I was really interested in that aspect of your books.

Cercas: It's true. For example, in *The Monarch of the Shadows,* what we have is a past that is virtually erased, a past that has almost disappeared, the story of a very young boy, an anonymous boy, almost all of the documentation surrounding his life has been destroyed. So, there is a desperate attempt to reconstruct that story based on little fragments: a conversation with a witness, a paper that resurfaces at just the right time and provides a sort of background story. So, it's a combination of all of these things. Do you know what *pecios* are? These are like the remains of a great shipwreck. So, when you have these remains from the shipwreck of time, of the past that erases everything, what narration does it to gather all of these remains from the wreck to give them meaning, to search for what they might mean.

The past goes away; it disappears. People disappear. In his *Confessions*, Saint Augustine has a wonderful passage that talks about that, about the way in which the past consumes everything and nothing is left. Very few things are left of most people's lives. So, what we have in *The Monarch of the Shadows* is an effort to salvage something of a life, at the last moment, when everything is about to disappear, and give these things meaning. Don't you think? With these fragments, we try to reconstruct the past of a person that used to exist. Maybe in the future we'll discover more traces. I don't know.

That was one of the great struggles of this book. Collecting all the remains of a shipwrecked life. I hadn't thought about it before, about putting it that way. But that's how it is. An anonymous life. There were things that were hard to discover about Adolfo Suárez, and he was president. But about a boy, a seventeen-year-old kid that went to war and died, whose family destroyed everything and nothing was left, that was a great struggle.

Rademacher: That's important. Because to me, that struggle was not as much a part of postmodernity.

Cercas: Do you think so? Why?

Rademacher: Maybe in part because of what you said before, for example—of focusing that much on the present. There's a loss of connecting this present to something greater, something more substantial. So I think there's a desire to connect all of these multiple truths to something provable, tangible, because we lack certainties and we miss them.

Cercas: Maybe. I can say that in my books that's true. I mean, that past didn't exist in my postmodern books. But, it does exist in my post-postmodern books. But bear one thing in mind, I started talking about the past when I was thirty-nine years old.

Rademacher: Until then, you were only thinking of the future.

Cercas: Yes, up until that moment I was only thinking of the future, maybe because I had no past; probably that's what happens to almost everybody. Does it have to do with postmodernism? Well, probably it does, with post-postmodernism, probably it does. But I can't tell in what way.

Rademacher: I want to talk about another strategy that is very characteristic of your work: you use metafiction in a very interesting and particular way. Many times metafiction can be seen as a postmodern tool simply exposing the construction of story, as we've already talked about. But, at the same time as the critic Alison Gibbs has written in another context, it can be more than self-reflexive—a way of showing the hermeneutic function of stories in our memories, in our relationships with others.

Cercas: This is something my postmodern and post-postmodern books have always maintained. I love metafiction as a hermeneutic element, as a tool of knowledge. It's not just a game in which literature looks at itself. It looks at itself to observe reality. To bring up political, moral, and real problems. I'm not interested in metafiction on its own. But the process of exposing the narrative process is essential. Sometimes it's more important than the story itself. And I do it for one purpose. I tell the reader, "Look, this is fiction. This is how it works. I'll show you my doubts, my questions. I'll show you everything. I'll play with this. I won't hide anything from you."

Not long ago, I read a letter by Italo Calvino. He's a paradigmatic postmodern writer, and to me he was very important at the time. He says: "In some books, showing the process of shaping the story is almost a moral duty." You don't hide anything from the reader, and it's a moral duty because you're showing your cards to the reader. And maybe you take the story in a different direction. But you don't do it for the game itself. That game has a meaning. Consider, for instance, in *The Monarch of the Shadows*, I talk about how I go to see someone who I believe is the last witness of Manuel Mena's life and I tell how I go there with my friend David Trueba and all that. But in my conversations with David Trueba, the most important problems of the book become clear; my relationship with my Francoist family, the idea of war, all of these fundamental problems are communicated through metafiction. So, it's not just a game. It's not even just an act of honesty to bare the mechanisms of the book and show them to the reader. It's also a tool to set out the central problems of life. I really like how Gibbons categorizes this use of metafiction as hermeneutics.

Rademacher: What are the ethical issues of inserting yourself into the biography of someone else? For instance, in *The Imposter*, you observe the complexity of gaining the trust of someone that had horribly lied to many people and telling his story without being an accomplice or a judge. In the chapter we touched upon earlier where you create the fictional conversation or interview between Cercas as narrator and Enric Marco, you call into question many of the motivations for writing the book. You play, for example, with the criticisms of having benefited from historical memory in *Soldiers of Salamis*, while in *The Imposter* the narrator Cercas challenges the ambitions of the historical memory law. How did readers or critics react to this?

Cercas: There were diverse reactions, of course. Obviously, *The Imposter*, here in Spain, it's a book with a critical treatment of Spanish reality, of the way of managing the past. So, many people got angry. And the fact that, in Spain, people might feel defensive is normal. That was the purpose.

That the writer that got his start with historical memory is the one that later criticizes it. . . Of course, people got irritated. That's all good. It's my most award-winning book outside of Spain. But, I would have been thrilled to have more of a dialogue here. And I think what I was ultimately saying in the book was "We've done it wrong. What we've done is incomplete." That's it. What people interpreted is that I was against the Law of Historical Memory. Of course, that was false. Though on the whole, the book was well-accepted, for sure.

And the ethical question you asked about, it's different in every case. In that chapter, as you rightly said, it's the most important question: I set out my doubts. But I'll simply tell you that when I approach a book about a real character, with real characters, I always make an agreement with these people. For instance, with Marco, he wanted me to rehabilitate him, to say what he had done was okay. And I told him, "Look, I'll tell the truth." Facts are facts and interpretations are interpretations. And before publishing the book, I gave him the manuscript for him to tell me his opinion. He didn't like it.

Rademacher: Of course.

Cercas: If he had liked it, I would have worried about that because this wasn't a revisionist story. So, that's the relationship I had with him and the relationship I had with the people appearing in my books; David Trueba, for instance, who appears as a character, I gave him the manuscript of this book. The characters that appear in my books receive the manuscript and I correct it, etc. However, the relationship you have with a real character is always complicated because we all want to look good in pictures. Biofiction, as you've denoted it, is very dangerous. You take a lot of risks. But a writer that doesn't take risks is not a writer; he's a scribe. Writing is about taking risks. As a person, I can be reasonably cowardly, but I can't be like that as a writer. If I am, then I've misunderstood my profession. It's like a cowardly bullfighter. Risks are normal because you're working with real people, right?

Rademacher: And the risk can be deepened when there is a concerted mix in a biographical novel between the real and the fictive. . . . So, you include those parts in which the fiction tells a truth. But this fiction can be misunderstood for fact.

Cercas: There are always people that misread your texts, or read what they want to read. I create half the book; the reader contributes the other part. I'll give you a perfect example. All of the characters in *Soldiers of Salamis* were real, except Conchi, the girlfriend of the narrator and the fortune-teller of a local TV station. She was the only wholly invented character. But the fortune-teller of the local TV station in Girona took me to court, because she said she was Conchi. She said she was that character because she had bleached hair, was a fortune-teller on the local TV station, wore a miniskirt… so she said she was Conchi. And of course, the judge asked her in the trial, "Hey, but do you know Cercas?" "No, I don't." "So, how could you be that character?"

Rademacher: Talking about the trajectory of your books, I think many of your characters appear lost—from Sánchez Mazas, who not only loses his physical way in the wilderness but also metaphysically due to his lack of belief in the ideals he has fought for and defended, up to Enric Marco, who loses himself completely appropriating the lives of others. Is there a reason you are so interested in all of these lost individuals?

Cercas: If you're asking me whether I identify myself with them, the answer is yes. Maybe I write to see whether I can find myself through them. None of us is quite sure about where we are. Maybe that's the essential condition of what we are: lost people. People looking for their place and not finding it.

Rademacher: To add further, in your interview for *Page Two*, the interviewer mentioned how the trajectory of your works demonstrates something in common, and that is that all of them are somewhat detective novels and your characters try to find a hidden truth. I'm interested in knowing whether what you are looking for through those stories has changed over time.

Cercas: It's just that I don't know what I'm expecting to find. I think it's true, my novels are in some way detective novels, strange detective novels. I'll tell you that, in a sense, my favorite novels are like that. Well, I would say they are more anti-detective novels. Because in detective novels, there's usually a specific question: whodunit? Who killed the lady? So, the whole novel is an attempt to find out who did it. And in the end, we learn it was the butler, or somebody, don't we? That's not how my novels are. In my novels there's a question, but in the end it is an unanswerable question.

I mean, why didn't the soldier kill Sánchez Mazas? Why did Adolfo Suárez stay where he was? Who denounced Zarco's gang? Who was Manuel Mena? And the whole novel is an attempt to explore that question. It's just that, in the end of the novel, what's the answer? The answer is there's no answer. The answer is the search for an answer. Or, if you want to put that another way, Jenny, the conclusion is never clear, defined, limited and unambiguous as in detective novels; it's always rather ambiguous, contradictory, polyvalent and essentially ironic. In other words, the answer is the search for an answer, the question itself, the novel itself. And this is what happens in the novels I like. It's also what I talk about in *The Blind Spot*. But I'm never searching for something concrete; I don't search, as Picasso would say; I find. And what I find is always surprising. That's the whole point of writing.

Anyway, probably the questions that I posed at the beginning of my career, let's say, in my first books, those questions are different. Of course they are. But . . . let me put it a different way. It's not the writer who chooses the topics; it's the topics that choose the writer. For instance in *The Anatomy of a Moment*, in the midst of Tejero's attempt at a coup, following Spain's transition to democracy, why did Adolfo Suárez, Manuel Gutiérrez, and Santiago Carrillo stand their ground and refuse to go along? That was an image that millions of people had seen a million times. But, why did it so capture my attention? I don't know. There was something important there, and I wrote the book to figure it out. That's why I think a writer's first duty is—to be faithful to their own obsessions. If you care deeply about something, follow it. That's the first duty. Whatever it is, it doesn't matter. Even if it's the fact that a man wakes up in the morning finding himself transformed into an insect. If you're Kafka, there's something important there.

Rademacher: So that leads us to the last question. Finally, I want to note that your books are often focused on stories particularly related to the history of Spain. However, your books have been produced in multiple languages and have been read worldwide. Why do you think these stories of individual lives, often lives of Spaniards, have managed to express such universal messages?

Cercas: Well, that's easy. Making literature. Because literature turns the particular into the universal. That's what happens to me and what happens to everyone, isn't it? A guy that loses his mind in La Mancha speaks to all of us. A woman in France that dreams of living a romantic life speaks to all of us. "Paint your village and you'll paint the world," Tolstoy says. Jorge Manrique, in probably the most famous poem in Spanish, talks about the death of his father. But when he does that, he talks about everyone. That's what good literature does, more than anything else.

Interview conducted in and translated from Spanish by Virginia Rademacher.

4

Sally Hemings's Staircase: On Biofiction's Afterlives

Barbara Chase-Riboud, interviewed by Melanie Masterton Sherazi

Sherazi: Over the course of our conversation, I'd like to foreground two of your biographical novels, *Sally Hemings* (1979) and *The President's Daughter* (1994), in terms of their compelling publication histories, your creative process, and the novels' respective content, form, and style.

Sally Hemings is a classic, pathfinder work of biofiction. It is unique in the sense that, not only did you have to generate and articulate your title character's motivations and inner life, you had the daunting task of defining a historical figure who had long been deemed a nonentity by critical consensus in order to preserve Thomas Jefferson's hallowed persona as a founding father. Needless to say, from the time of its publication, *Sally Hemings* has been a controversial text. You write candidly of your experiences in your "Afterword" to the thirtieth Anniversary edition of *Sally Hemings*, after DNA testing in 1998 by Dr. Eugene Foster corroborated what you had written about in your novel. With the advent of these DNA results, your imagined Sally Hemings became a historical figure. In what ways has your biofictional project become both a public and political project, with Sally Hemings at its center?

Chase-Riboud: Sally Hemings was deemed a figment of yellow journalistic perversity. So I had not only to invent a historical character but to convince an ignorant public that Sally Hemings really existed in time and space. I had to make the Americans believe in her. Sally Hemings, despite barefaced denials from the Keepers of American History, was true and believable.

Sherazi: I am very curious about how you first came across historian Fawn Brodie's study *Thomas Jefferson: An Intimate History* (1974), which discusses Thomas Jefferson's sexual relationship with Sally Hemings?

Chase-Riboud: I was interested in Sally Hemings because I was a poet and sculptor and was married to a Frenchman, Marc Riboud, living in Paris. I knew about the Sally Hemings story long before I began working on the novel, but Brodie's book was the only mainstream Jefferson biography that ever mentioned Sally Hemings except as a canard and journalistic lie. She mentions her only as a possibility and as a kind of legend that had passed down through two hundred years of American history. In Brodie's biography, which is six hundred pages long, there are only a handful of pages about Sally Hemings, *period*, which, nevertheless, got Brodie into a lot of trouble with the "Jeffersonians," his biographers. Since there was no basis for a biography of Sally Hemings, or for any kind of study, it was simply out there, again, as a kind of legend. So once I read Brodie's book, I had this idea to tell the story of a young slave girl in prerevolutionary France, because I was there, and I could walk every street, and the atmosphere was all there, the buildings were all there, and the French had documents. I knew where Jefferson and Hemings had lived. I was living the same life, in a way, as an *étranger* from America who was considered black. Well, that's a lot to imagine, so my idea was to do what I do best, which is write epic poetry, to do an epic poem about Sally Hemings.

I had sold my first collection of poems, *From Memphis and Peking* (1974), to Random House. Well, there was only one black editor at Random House at the time, Toni Morrison, of course, and she published my poetry. I told her what I wanted to do, and Toni told Random House, who said, "We're not interested in slave girls in Paris. If she wants to write a historical novel, then we're ready to talk," and that's when I balked and said, "Look, I'm a sprinter, not a long distance runner—a historical novel that is going to run into four or five hundred pages?"

Finally, Toni said, "Look, Barbara, you've been talking about this book for two years now, why don't you just write it?" "I can't do it," I said, "why don't you do it?" And she said, "I have books to write, Barbara. I cannot do this book. I don't want to do this book. Why don't you just write it yourself? How long will it take you to do? Come on. Three months of your life, four months of your life?" She did not say, "Don't be afraid, I'll help you."

It took me three years of research and writing.

The genesis of my decision to write about Sally Hemings after Random House had declined is the extraordinary story of former first lady Jacqueline Onassis becoming, in a way, the Godmother of the story of Jefferson's enslaved mistress. In the summer of 1975, I was invited to spend the weekend on Skorpios, Onassis' Greek island. Once I arrived, I decided it was a great opportunity to talk to the only person on earth that I knew who would know something about American Presidents, power, backstairs intrigues, public figures, ambition, politics, the press, and the politics of scandal. So sitting on the beach, with an army of sailors tending the *Christina* and paparazzi in shark-like boats circling the island, I spent the next three days explaining Sally Hemings: the history, the controversy, and my instincts and research that proved its veracity to Jacqueline Bouvier Kennedy Onassis, who listened without comment until I had unburdened all my fears and doubts and then she said quietly in her inimitable voice, "You've got to write this book, Barbara."

By the time I had the first chapters written, Onassis had died, Jacqueline had gone to work for Viking Press as therapy for her grief, and my book became her first novelistic acquisition. She called my agent every single day inquiring about my progress, and when I finally had something to show her, she convinced Viking Press to allow her to make a preemptory bid and block the rights by anyone else. To this day, I wonder what the fate of this book would have been if it had circulated. There may never have been a *Sally Hemings* publication in any language. In this way, the story of Sally Hemings was clothed in secrecy and provincially protected until the last moment—protected from censorship until Sally Hemings was introduced to the general public, who took her to their hearts, which made Mrs. Kennedy Onassis her Godmother, so to speak.

The surprise element was stupendous. It was a *NY Times* best seller in all the major markets of the world. Jacqueline and I remained friends and communicated until her demise. What happened to *Sally Hemings* and what could have happened with *Sally Hemings* remains a publishing mystery that continues to this day.

Sherazi: What was your creative practice like as you started working with archival documents and writing the novel?

Chase-Riboud: I realize now that the six hundred letters I wrote to my mother in Philadelphia from Europe, beginning in 1957, were really letters of a writer—that I was already a writer, and a historical one, except that I didn't know it at that time. As soon as I started researching *Sally Hemings* in the 1970s, I realized that I loved it and that I was willing to go all the way. The research and the writing were in tandem. One piece of evidence led to another as I found what I needed to advance the story. I found material at the Bibliothèque Nationale in Paris and in London. Then, of course, I went to Virginia. Finding things like the "Bill of Sale" of Sally Hemings's family, that was the first time I really cried. I really broke down and thought this sheet of paper is all I need to write this story. Then there is the point where you have to take the big leap, the poetic leap, and you've got to say, "Yes, I believe it. I believe her, I believe who she was, and this is what happened."

When you knew where to look, the University of Virginia archives had a lot of documents that were very useful, but I also found a lot of material in the Library of Congress and then at Monticello itself. I went to Monticello as a French woman. I wrote to them, and I told them what I was doing. But I walked into a situation and to the Southern mentality, which was completely foreign to me. I knew nothing about the South—my mother's Canadian, I grew up in Philadelphia until the age of seventeen, eighteen, and then I was in Rome, and then I lived in Paris for years, so I had grown up as a European. I didn't even know how to talk to these Virginians at Monticello.

When I went to Monticello for the first time, there was a tiny staircase leading to this mysterious little room over top of Jefferson's bed, which was fascinating to me because their explanation for its purpose was so stupid and so silly. This became the famous "Hemings room" that tourists asked to see and led to the staircase being torn out. I thought to myself, there's got to be another reason. It was simply because, as an architect and as a graduate of Yale's architectural school, I know something about building, and I know something about structure, and I know something about where things go. This was not pure speculation on my part, as there is a photo of a black butler standing in the doorway of the stairwell and a caption speculating on the reason for the staircase in an issue of *National Geographic* magazine from the early 1930s.

When I returned incognito to Monticello after the publication of the book, I took the guided tour through the buildings, and when we got to Jefferson's bedroom, I said, "Where is Sally Hemings's room?" There was dead silence, and this poor Virginian lady of a certain age was desperately trying to hide the little doorway, which was open. The staircase was only a gaping hole, and so I asked, "Well, where is the staircase that was there?" She said, "What staircase?" and I said, "The staircase that was *there*, that I *saw* on my last visit." She said, "I don't know anything about any staircases." So I stormed into the curator's office, and I said, "What have you guys done to the staircase?" They said, "Oh, Barbara, it has nothing to do with you. It was not authentic. We found Victorian tools under the staircase." I said, "Well, why were you looking under the staircase? You were obviously not tearing the staircase out to find tools underneath, but to get rid of it."

That was my first encounter with total obstruction. There was no logic, there was no plan, there was no discussion, there was no, "Well, Barbara, you see, blah, blah, blah." There was just, "I don't know anything about this." I thought, this is amazing. From that time until this day, I am persona non grata at Monticello. I do not exist. My book does not exist—it is not in the bookstore. Nobody speaks to me, and it is not so much because of the book, it was because of the movie project. Because they could see this situation getting totally out of hand if suddenly the public found out, or was speculating about it, then they couldn't hide Sally Hemings any longer.

After the book was published, it was an enormous success. It won the Janet Heidinger Kafka Prize, it was translated into nine different languages, including Japanese, and then, of course, the movies came. It went through eleven options with Hollywood studios, like Warner Brothers, and CBS. The Jeffersonians threatened to unleash a letter-writing campaign of Virginia schoolchildren against Bill Paley, the chairman of the board. I was talking about an American psychosis. This is what I came up against, finally. Every movie project was squashed. Total Trump-like ignorance, but ignorance that goes beyond simply not knowing anything—it was a kind of willful ignorance that I brushed up against. But since I was so amazed at the gall of these people, it was sort of a crash course in stereotyping, and in racism, in Trumpism. There was no getting around these people, and there was no way to reason with these people, because the Sally Hemings situation was intolerable and had to be constrained at any cost. Lying, blackmail, obfuscation were merely the means to an end.

There was a whole book that was written against myself and Fawn Brodie. I personally think that they hounded Brodie to an early grave. I am the only one standing and the only one who can contradict their new fantasy that they are suddenly "discovering" Sally Hemings after all this time. In 2000, the Thomas Jefferson Memorial Foundation released its "white paper," confirming the DNA evidence that Jefferson was the father of Sally Hemings's son Eston Hemings and likely of all six of her children. Somehow it was as if the whole Barbara Chase-Riboud scandal had never happened. In addition, in July 2017, Monticello announced that they had discovered Sally Hemings's "room," which is the most ridiculous fantasy I've ever heard.

They announced in *The Washington Post* that they have "found" Sally Hemings's room through archaeological excavations, and where have they located it? Smack in the middle of the Monticello kitchens! The most public place in the house! The silliest and most cynical lie of all for a woman who was not even supposed to exist and who had been noisily denied through thirty-eight years of controversy. Instead of the mysterious and subversive Sally Hemings, she is once again shoved into the kitchen with all the other Hemingses. It is sort of like drowning her. . . .

This is part of the plan for the new virginity: a denial of their original denial of Sally Hemings and their complicity with covering up Jefferson's relations with Hemings, this whole part of Jefferson's biography, for more than two hundred years.

Sherazi: I'd like to discuss *The President's Daughter* in dialogue with *Sally Hemings* and what it meant for you at that particular point in time to go back to the story of Sally Hemings—this time telling the story through her daughter Harriet Hemings's eyes. As a *Los Angeles Times* critic observes, "It is as if the often maligned slave had somehow reached through the ether and latched onto the novelist, refusing to let go until her claim to legitimacy was acknowledged." In what ways do you consider *The President's Daughter* a work of biofiction, given the lack of historical evidence about Harriet Hemings?

Chase-Riboud: Although *The President's Daughter* has a historical setting, there is little evidence of who Harriet Hemings was as a person. I had to imagine everything based on the few things that her brother Madison Hemings had written in his memoirs about life at Monticello, which were published in a newspaper in 1873—other than that, there was nothing. My Harriet is pure fiction but her situation as a fugitive slave passing for white was supremely historical and open to myriad investigations and suppositions for a poet. The setting of course is totally historical, but the only things I could draw from were the few documents from Monticello and the newspaper piece that says she ran away, that she was allowed to run away, that she went to Philadelphia, that she married well, and that she passed for white. That was more or less it.

Sherazi: How did the dearth of historical evidence about Harriet Hemings's life afford you greater creative freedom?

Chase-Riboud: I was much freer with Harriet, because she, evidently, was educated and in the situation of a free woman. Free, not only physically, but mentally, and I assume that her husband, or her husbands, were liberal and non-prejudiced. I took great liberty with the characters Thor and Thance Wellington, but that's life. That's *War and Peace*, okay. There's no reason, for instance, for them to be liberal and non-prejudiced, since that doesn't come into the situation—I believe she never told her family about her past, and they never asked. She was taken on different grounds than racial identity. I could have written a whole story about how she finally "confesses" and loses everything, making this a tragedy, but I don't think that's what happened. I don't think she would have confessed, and I don't think any eighteenth- or nineteenth-century woman would have, especially since she had had the choice to stay in the black community if she wanted to, as did her brothers.

It was a decision on her part, not only to go north but to pass for white, and I think it was a decision that really hurt her mother and caused a kind of break between them. Because, of course, by passing for white, she condemned her mother. Harriet complains in the novel to her mother that her mother had not done the same and had chosen to remain enslaved. There's this gulf between them when Harriet leaves, which I don't think that Jefferson really understood, or really cared about. Jefferson was a total egoistic aristocrat of a certain century. If he ever thought about Sally Hemings or Harriet in any way, at all, it would have been in the form of what he did: he allowed Harriet to run away. He didn't free her, just like he didn't free Sally Hemings.

Sherazi: What is Philadelphia's role in *The President's Daughter*? The North is often taken to be a utopic space, the "free" North, during slavery. Why was it important to show the reader a very different view of the North—one structured by racism and class oppression, in which Harriet Hemings passes as a white woman of means?

Chase-Riboud: One of the few things that we know about Harriet Hemings is that she ended up in Philadelphia. Philadelphia is the most Southern of the Northern cities. It's where, now we know, because of what has happened in the past year or so, that the remnants of Jim Crow are as strong in Philadelphia as they are in Atlanta. What I liked about setting much of *The President's Daughter* in Philadelphia was that, at that moment, it was the national city; it was America. This was the Centennial, and people were celebrating this new country, and there Harriet Hemings was, with all those contradictions, and all that history. She represented every single contradiction of American race, gender, class, capitalism, slavery, racism, civil war, and historical amnesia, with the Centennial's purposeful suppression of the United States' violence as a slave nation, born and bred in slavery, and its handmaiden, racism. There is an old Chinese saying, "I have wronged you, therefore, I hate you." All that history is dragging behind her. There was all this cumulative hatred symbolized by the Civil War and its aftermath. Philadelphia symbolized all of this.

Sherazi: There is a great deal of formal experimentation in these biographical novels, which use tropes from passing literature and gothic fiction, as well as multiple voices, as you move from chapter to chapter between historical personages including John and Abigail Adams, Aaron Burr, John Trumbull, Maria Cosway, Maria and Martha Jefferson, and incorporate citations as epigraphs to open chapters, such as from Jefferson's *Notes on the State of Virginia*. I'm curious as to whether you feel your practice as a sculptor has something to do with the architecture, or the many-layered formal qualities of these books?

Chase-Riboud: I think of literature as a kind of form of architecture, so a book has to have a foundation, it has to have walls, it has to have windows, it has to have a roof, and if it doesn't, then it's not a good novel. I was very careful when I constructed both books, actually. I was using what I knew from writing poetry to do something I had never done, because writing poetry is something else. Writing poetry is like making sculpture, which is making objects. Writing a historical novel is like building a city. Especially *The President's Daughter*, owing to the lack of historical documentation, but even with *Sally Hemings*, I had to be very careful. The perimeters were so narrow, because she had to be real, and Jefferson had to be real, and Jefferson could not step out of the perimeters of his known biography. I could do what I wanted with Hemings, but I could not do just anything with him, except in his own words, and there was no condemnation that I could make of him without using his own words, with which the novel's chapters begin. Also important are the affidavits in *The President's Daughter* at the end of the chapters, in which all of the major characters illuminate their role in a sworn statement.

Sherazi: In *The President's Daughter*, William Wells Brown's 1853 novel *Clotel: Or, The President's Daughter* circulates in the hands of the female publisher Sarah Hale, who presents Harriet Hemings with a copy. Here we have historical personages and an actual text, which bears the same name of and some shared content with your own novel, being woven into the novel's texture. What is at work in those levels of textuality and narration, perhaps as another type of this biofictional architecture we're talking about, of formal layering?

Chase-Riboud: That's exactly the way I do my sculptures. There are wax sheets that are folded into forms, and then superimposed one over the other, and then excavated from the inside: the affidavits are the excavations, one level at a time, one event at a time. Exactly the same. That's the only way I know how to write novels, because I had to use all my skills as a poet and all of my skills as a historian to compensate for a form which was foreign to me, and which I had never thought I would work in. Harriet emerges from the Centennial, from Gettysburg, from the abolitionist movement in England, from the American Revolution, from the French Revolution, from her double or triple life as a legal document, and from miscegenation, which remained a crime in many states until 1967 and beyond.

Sherazi: In your acts of creating a biofictional world there is such careful attention to detail, almost an inventorying of objects to create a material world, whether it's in your descriptions of goods, or clothing, or décor. Would you say more about this in terms of your practice as a visual artist and as you are seeing these worlds in your mind's eye?

Chase-Riboud: The material world as I see it is necessary documentation for the imaginary world—it is that combination which produces the contours of reality. That is the easy part. I love to do that, and I love, visually, to create a whole world. That's the best part of writing historical novels. If you don't do that, what do you do? Trying to create not a new world but trying to create an old world.

I think that *The President's Daughter* is a better book than *Sally Hemings*. It had a great success, and I'm very fond of it as a philosophical musing on the meaning of racial identity. Harriet Hemings has no fingerprints—she loses this "identity" in an accident in her husband's laboratory. At the end of the book, she tells her granddaughter who she is, a mixed race woman, but her granddaughter doesn't believe her. Her granddaughter is a white woman who thinks that her grandmother has gone off her rocker, and that is how I ended the book—I left it open because maybe, in the end, the granddaughter will realize, somehow, who her grandmother really was. But Harriet dies without a real identity, because without her old identity, she can't possess a new one. It's more about identity than it is about race. Of course it's a matter of her American identity; I take Harriet to Gettysburg in the novel, and I leave her there among the ruins of American identity, with Jefferson's Declaration and Lincoln's Address as background music in her head as she contemplates the wreckage of the United States.

Sherazi: *The President's Daughter* has a transnational quality, as does *Sally Hemings*—with Harriet going to England, France, and Italy. There is a scene, for instance, in Italy, in which Maria Cosway gifts Harriet Hemings with a locket containing Jefferson's portrait, painted by John Trumbull, the same one that her mother wears around her neck. Cosway says to Hemings, "This is part of your biography." There's a great deal of layering going on here, as you, the author, are conjuring Harriet Hemings's biography for the reader, and, simultaneously, these two historical figures are sharing their life stories with each other. Why did you set Harriet on this journey?

Chase-Riboud: This is another visual technique that comes from my sculpture, which is everything that goes around comes around: all that rises must converge, so to speak. Everything is connected, not only visually, but sequentially in time, which is continually evolving and is never-changing, like the thread skirts in my *Malcolm X* sculptures. It is only visually logical that Harriet ends up meeting Maria Cosway, her father's lover, and is given the visual timepiece of the book: the locket which closes the circle. She is as much Cosway's daughter, as Sally Hemings's neither white nor black ambiguous figure.

Harriet's visit to see Maria Cosway is not historical, or at least not yet. Cosway is a historical figure and everything that she does in the book is accurate. She ended up in a convent in Lodi. Nobody knows why, and nobody knows what really went on between Jefferson and Cosway when they were together in Paris. As far as feminists go, Cosway was a real feminist. She believed in free love, but she also held on to her husband. Free love is okay, but who's going to pay the rent? She was a good painter, and an excellent draftsman, and she persisted in what she did. She was a better artist than her husband. As a miniaturist, she was really superb.

Sherazi: In *The President's Daughter*, Harriet often interrogates her mother during her extended inner monologues. How did you conceive of the relationship between this biofictional character and her mother, Sally Hemings?

Chase-Riboud: That, I imagined. There are no letters. There's no evidence of what she thought. We don't even know whether she deliberately crossed the racial barrier, or whether it just happened because she went north with Jefferson's valet, Adrien Petit, and Petit was French, and so that meant that she was French, and the men who met her saw a French woman. They did not see an escaped slave. I could do what I wanted to with Harriet, because there was no barrier. There were a lot of historical barriers around Sally Hemings, intellectually, practically, and historically. I couldn't do what I wanted with her, because she didn't do it. She didn't stay in France. She came back to Virginia. This was a question that I had to ask myself over, and over again, why didn't she stay where she was in France?

Sherazi: You are very attentive in *Sally Hemings* to Sally Hemings's return from France, where she could have lived as a free woman, to Virginia, as an enslaved woman. You represent a romantic bond in the novel between Jefferson and Hemings. In your 2009 "Afterword" you state that Hemings "dares not call Jefferson 'Thomas' until they are equal in love" and that Hemings "clings to the only thing she can claim as her own: her love and allegiance to her 'master,' her half-sister's husband, and her father figure, Thomas Jefferson." Many would say, however, that love was not possible between Jefferson and Hemings, given slavery's structure and logic of ownership.

Chase-Riboud: I took everything into consideration, as well as the basic consideration that people are contradictory. That they have feelings and thoughts that are totally opposed, one to the other, and they live their lives this way, and they live through whatever it is, the constraints, so you cannot say that it was logical or illogical. Human beings are not logical. Number one. Even love is full of hate. It's full of contradictions, and it's full of all kinds of escapes and rationalizations and delusions. I mean, "love" is a very big word. It takes place in all kinds of ridiculous situations, and so I counted on the fact that I could not make Sally Hemings into a feminist. I could not make her into an abolitionist. I could not make her into an intellectual, because that can't be done.

Sherazi: What other models of historical or biographical fiction were important or influential to you while you were working on these novels?

Chase-Riboud: At a certain point in time, I was an avid reader of historical fiction. Books like E. L. Doctorow's *Ragtime* thrilled me. Gore Vidal's *Lincoln* and his *Burr* are superb. He wrote in the copy of *Sally Hemings* that I gave him, "I wish I had written *Sally Hemings.*" It was so funny and a great compliment. And then the great nineteenth-century novels, all of them. The great Dumas's, the great Tolstoy's, the great Hugo's and Pushkin's. Ever since I was a child, I devoured historical novels, but I never expected to write one. I never expected to write, period.

When I came to writing historical literature, it was really because of Sally Hemings herself, because of the story. I never would have written about another woman, or another situation. I realize that now, but after I had done it once, I had the feeling that I could do it again, and then with Harriet Hemings, I wanted to do it again, because there were things that I wanted to say, that I hadn't said, and situations, ambiguous situations, which I wanted to explore. Also, I wanted to create a new genre of historical fiction, which was all about the details in the documents that I found. We are now approaching the fortieth Anniversary of *Sally Hemings*'s publication, with plans for a reprint of the French first edition, *La Virginienne*, in the works.

Sherazi: To return to Monticello, let's revisit Sally Hemings's staircase: it is still there, in some sense, preserved by your novel, and not there at the same time. You write, "Yet the tiny stairwell still exists at the foot of Jefferson's bed. A corresponding staircase, I contend, should be restored as part of this national monument."

Chase-Riboud: The last time I saw the stairwell, there was an unplastered, gaping hole, witness to the violence and contempt with which it had been destroyed. Even if this symbolic staircase was not the way Sally Hemings got in and out of Jefferson's bedroom without being seen in the public hallways, certainly it is a better guess than the public kitchens, as this latest "discovery" claims! Moreover, Monticello had already lied to my Japanese translator of *Sally Hemings* by showing her dozens of rooms at Monticello, back staircases, and dilapidated structures, any of which they claimed could have been Sally Hemings's room. Why the public kitchens, when her existence was not only a secret but also an aberration that was refuted for two hundred years? They lied ever since the appearance of *Sally Hemings*, a novel. And when they couldn't lie anymore, they appropriated it in order to cover their cover up. …

I've got my own Monticello, a dollhouse that I built for my granddaughter Mathilde. It's really beautiful, and I can visit it every single day. It sits in my loft in Rome in a sixteenth-century historical palace, Palazzo Ricci. I can move the furniture around. I can change the décor. I can put Sally Hemings's bed where I want it. Actually, I even changed it a little bit, the architecture, because when I realized that Jefferson had put a column in front of a window, I thought, "That's architecture?" A column a little bit to the left, a little bit to the right, but not in front of a window. So it's not a pure replica of Monticello, but it *is* Monticello. Because, actually, I could have built a little room over top of his bed, but I didn't. I didn't do it. We'll see about Sally Hemings's room. When they tell me where it is, I will let them know if I believe them. As Voltaire said, "There is no history, only fictions of various plausibility."

5

Voicing the Nobodies in the Biographical Novel

Emma Donoghue, interviewed by Michael Lackey

Lackey: In the past, writers frequently based their novels on actual historical figures, but they changed the name in order to give themselves more creative freedom. The biographical novel is different because it names its protagonist after a specific person. Georg Lukács said that this is a huge mistake.

Donoghue: I think those of us who've written about real people have always run into people over the years who say, "Big mistake, you shouldn't use the actual name." In fact, they often say that it is a big mistake to write anything historical, because some people think anything but writing about the present day is a failure to live up to your responsibility to speak for your moment.

Lackey: Given this resistance, why do you think that the biographical novel came into being? And what are the benefits and drawbacks of doing a biographical novel?

Donoghue: I think the reason I use a specific, real, named protagonist is because my original impulse was very much to represent the ones who'd been left out, like the nobodies, women, slaves, people in freak shows, servants, the ones who are not powerful. I felt an obligation: if I was going to write about them at all, I wanted to give them their little moment in the sun. To name them, even if they were incredibly obscure figures.

When I've written short stories, for instance, they've been about people so obscure that we only know maybe two facts, a name and a fact. But still I try and get the details I know about the person right. But if you're writing about Henry VIII, he doesn't need any more fame, so you can make him into King Ludwig if you prefer. But if I am writing about this girl who got executed in the 1760s, and if I know that her name was Mary Saunders, then that's the name I should stick to. So it was a feeling of loyalty or wanting to represent them, and not just to represent categories or classes, but the actual individuals.

And in terms of the pros and cons of it as a literary choice, I find with a historical figure, readers absolutely love to know about the tiny little bit that is real. And it's not like they want the whole thing to be factual. They want an enjoyable fiction, but they just love that tiny little hook that holds onto the real. But, I suppose, the bigger question is why I choose real individuals at all. I often wonder why am I doing this complicated double job of all the historical research into the real guy, where he was in 1820. And then the fiction as well, because, of course, researching the facts doesn't actually save you any work with the fiction. You still have to make up so much because their inner life below must be a mystery. So it's a double job, it's a complicated one, and all I can say is that the double job appeals to me or attracts me. I like how different those two obligations are: the obligation to find out what really happened and then the obligation to make it all up. I find that exciting.

Lackey: Let me press you on this notion of historical accuracy. You express an interpretation about what prompted the killer to gun down Jenny Bonnet in *Frog Music*. Let's say, hypothetically, that somebody finds a journal, and we know for certain that the one you finger for the crime in your fictional version did not do it. Could your novel still be true? And if so, in what sense would it still be true?

Donoghue: I think I tried to be true to the character. When I deviate from facts, inasmuch as I can find them, it's usually not at the level of character. It's at the level of practical matters like timing. So I will often take factual events and squish them together. Those are the kind of changes I usually make. In *Frog Music*, I remember telescoping time, making it all happen faster and in a more intense way. But I usually try not to deviate from character. I know, of course, the facts and the timing do affect the character, but still I'm always fumbling toward what feels to me like the real person. So yes, even if it turns out that the one I blame couldn't have killed Jenny, I like to think I got Jenny right. That's certainly what I'm aiming for. And it shouldn't matter anyway. Fictional characters are just as satisfying to read. And I enjoy writing fictional characters too. So why I get so possessed by one particular dead nobody, I don't know. It's just like falling in love.

Lackey: Oscar Wilde is an important figure for the study of biofiction, because he said: if you name your protagonist after an actual historical figure, don't pretend that you are trying to represent that person's life. Rather, use that person's life to express your own vision. How would you respond to that?

Donoghue: Of course, that's what we all do. Even by who we choose. It is no accident that in the 1990s I started writing about servant girls and slaves. That was my historical moment to make that choice. Anyone could have written a novel about Jenny Bonnet at any time, but it's no accident that I wrote about it when I did. Her particular qualities and "perversities" are exactly what appeal to us right now.

Lackey: Perversities with quotation marks, right?

Donoghue: Indeed. She was delightfully self-destructive. She'd get arrested for cross-dressing and then she'd get in a bar fight and be arrested for that. So a general perversity. You are of your time in who you choose and of what you choose to say about them, and how you choose to judge them. In a previous era, Jenny Bonnet might have shown up as a figure of complete depravity, whereas I'm clearly very sympathetic to her. I feel warm toward many aspects of her—not just the cross-dressing and the queerness. I decided quite early on that she would be a character with ADHD before the label. I wanted to give her traits like banging a stick off her fence as she passes it to show her restlessness. So I'm making her a figure of our era in all those small ways to try and make sense of the historical record of how she behaved.

Lackey: It is interesting that you say that you try to make sense of the historical record, because it seems that biographical novels are as much about the present as they are about the past. For instance, in the years 2003 and 2004, three Irish authors published biographical novels: Colum McCann published *Dancer*, Colm Tóibín published *The Master*, and you published *Life Mask*. All three of these novels portray the gay lifestyle in a sympathetic manner, and about ten years later, Ireland would legalize gay marriage. Can you reflect on why that happened?

Donoghue: I'm not sure; I think there was a moment when a lot of Irish writers turned to historical fiction. I did it relatively early. I don't think it was a particularly Irish thing, especially as I've been out of the country since 1990. But I did notice a lot of other Irish writers turning to the past, like Joe O'Connor and Anne Enright.

Lackey: Let me clarify my question. According to Georg Lukács, the goal of the historical novelist is to picture the past with as much precision as possible in order to clarify how we came to be in the present. While Lukács extolled the historical novel, he condemned the biographical novel. Oscar Wilde takes a much different approach than Lukács. He would say that an artist is not interested in portraying the past or clarifying how it shaped and determined us in the present. For him, the artist appropriates a figure from the past in order to bring into existence a new reality in the present and for the future. And your biographical novels actually do this. And what I find so fascinating is that a number of you Irish writers did all of this in the early twenty-first century with regard to homosexuality, and gay marriage was subsequently legalized in Ireland. I think there's a connection there.

Donoghue: We all do our little part. I think it's crucial for us to know about queer life before now. If we only seem to exist now, then we look like a shallow phase. We look like a meme, something that's just gone viral. Establishing a history that was not very visible before makes you feel like a grownup. So I think finding out a psychic prehistory for contemporary queer life is a key part of that impulse that drives me to write biographical stories. And naming the individuals and allowing them to be very individual. Not like a typical lesbian of the 1850s but one particular one, whatever she may be like. And one thing I've really enjoyed in writing about people involved in same sex relationships in the past is that because the labels were not being applied in any clear and hard and fast way, they could be really genuinely odd. Take Horace Walpole, for instance. He is a figure I found fascinating to write about because we read him so much as gay, with his taste for antiques and his little "faggy" manners. But there he was, passionately in love with this young woman in his own odd way. So I really like the fact that you could get away from what struck me as the deadening labels of gay or straight in the 1990s. And you could find models of love and of self that just don't correspond to the label. So for me, in some ways, it can be an escape from the present in order to make the present better. In order to make the models of how we live less reductive. So for me there is a restless impulse, and I'm going back to the past because things were truly queerer then.

Lackey: There seems to be two very different approaches to the biographical novel, and I want to see if you locate your work within one tradition more than the other. William Styron wrote a wonderful biographical novel about Nat Turner. But many complained because his Turner had a homosexual experience. Many said that there is no evidence for this, and they criticized him for including this in the novel. But Styron retorted: "Look, I am not doing biography. I am not doing history." He went on to say, "I'm not even that interested in history. I'm interested in creating a symbol and a metaphor that we can use to illuminate something that happened in 1831, namely, the structures that are used to oppress blacks, which happen to be the same structures used to oppress gays in 1967." So he was trying to give us a symbol or a metaphor that would be applicable to both time periods. Oscar Wilde had a different approach. He said, "Look, I'm not really interested in trying to illuminate. I'm actually trying to bring into existence a new reality." And so he used the New Testament figure of Salomé in order to bring into existence a sexually liberated female, which stood in stark contrast to the representations of women at that time. So if someone said to Wilde: "Do you get Salomé right?" he would say, "Who cares? As an artist my goal is to create reality, not to represent it." I'm curious. When you think of biofiction, are you in this tradition of Styron, trying to create a symbol or a metaphor that would enable us to see two time periods in unique and original ways? Or, are you in the Wilde tradition, trying to create new ways of being in the present and for the future?

Donoghue: I'm not sure I can pick one. It doesn't feel like I'm creating symbols, but it feels to me like I'm creating people. But of course those people are made up of my twenty-first-century concerns and interests just as much as they are made up of the raw facts I find. So I suppose I see every biographical novel I write as having tree roots. Those roots are reaching toward that past historical moment but of course they are reaching from right here. And it affects both ends. You could almost say that you are using contemporary insights to make sense of somebody like Jenny Bonnet in a way that she didn't seem to make sense to many people in her day. So it's almost like a rescue mission. I certainly don't feel that it is distorting or spoiling the 1870s moment by me bringing my modern ideas to it.

Lackey: Styron wouldn't care if his novel destroyed the past moment through his anachronistic approach to the past. He would say: "Yes, my novel distorts the past, but that is done by design." Let's take an example from your work. In *Life Mask*, you refer to weapons of mass destruction, clearly a reference to President Bush and the Iraq War. Some critics were critical of you for that anachronism, but for a biographical novelist like Styron, your anachronism is perfect, because it enables you to draw parallels between what happened in the eighteenth century and the twenty-first century. In short, Styron is not doing history. He is using history to get to a different kind of truth. I'm trying to figure out the nature of that truth.

Donoghue: I suppose I am trying to make two periods resonate through this person. It's almost like the character I'm focusing on is a time traveler. There is a connection between the past and the present. And yes, I want readers to be thinking: "Oh yes, these anti-terrorist measures are so scary! Weapons of mass destruction!" I want them to feel that this is now and yet there are enough factual details about then that they also feel like it's then and not now.

I like the discomfort for readers, those moments when they are feeling so close to the protagonist and then suddenly they feel like, "Whoa, these people are very different from me." I don't think it is a comforting or cozy genre. At its best, I find that the biographical novel makes people uncomfortable. They will easily and strongly identify with the main character for some things, and then they will suddenly have—after a remark about class or slavery—the opposite response: "Whoa, these people are aliens to me; they thought so differently." So I really enjoy that game of pulling them close and pushing them farther away. So, yes, I certainly don't feel that I'm just grabbing bits I like from history to make something that's purely about now. I think a lot about the past moment but a lot about my present moment too, and I suppose I'm interested in making the two resonate.

Lackey: Let me pose a more specific question. In *Life Mask*, you examine the way language can and frequently does enslave. For example, you indicate how the word Tommies becomes a weapon to use against gay people. And when you reference weapons of mass destruction, this certainly brings to mind American strategies to demonize the Muslim world. Can you talk about the role of the novel in advancing social justice.

Donoghue: I often think as a reader, why would I read this book? And it's not that you want it to be simpleminded escapism, but I do think that if you're going to harrow the reader, then you owe it to them to give them enough pleasure as well. It's like a date; if you're taking someone out on a date, and you're going to talk about Trump for half an hour, there's got to be some good food as well. You can't just make it a "I'm going to destroy this reader!" I am deadly serious about a lot of what I'm writing about. I care a lot who killed Jenny Bonnet and why. I feel this ethical commitment to these long dead people that makes me go to a lot of trouble to write about them when you could just make them up. But there's something about that attachment to these real long dead people that makes me keep writing. It pulls the cords tightly, and it's one more thing that gets you to your desk. I'm not saying that they have to be real. I've written about fictional people, but I have to say in many of my books that the fact that these are real people I'm writing about, it makes a relationship between me and them. It's something like, "Come on, Emma, write about us, get it right." I know I'm just imagining that they are seriously concerned about their reputations at this point; I do know that. It's a helpful fiction.

Lackey: Lance Olsen has done a couple really important biographical novels. One of them is about Nietzsche—it's a spectacular novel. He said in an interview that every genre of fiction comes into being for a reason, that each genre can do something that other forms cannot. What is it that *Life Mask* and *Frog Music* can do that, let's say, another form of fiction cannot?

Donoghue: Good question. I suppose a lot of readers feel a bit torn between biographies and histories which satisfy them very much in terms of this craving for the real. But you are not quite relaxing into it the way you are with a fictional story. When you are being told a story, you are in a wonderfully kind of childlike state of "What happens next? Tell me the story!" It's all being shaped for you, whether by the oral tradition or by a novelist. And in a way, I suppose biographical fiction is trying to do those two things at once. It's trying to say, "Look, I am going to be committed to the real, no matter how messy it is. But I'm also going to take the trouble to shape it into a story that will satisfy you as listeners." So I'm almost curating; I'm taking the whole messy mass of detail about the past, and I'm choosing which ones to include. So, for instance, people often say, "Oh you've got to do so much research for your novels." But it's really fun research because I'm not having to work out what the average day was like for a servant in 1760; I can afford to make it a non-average day. So I get to immerse myself in so many historical sources and in other people's history books, and then pluck out the one really interesting detail I like which is that they cleaned the carpets with wet tea leaves. I love that detail, the idea of the kind of recycling and the grunginess of it. So I can just pluck a detail and use that and make it a turning fictional scene. I suppose I feel I'm selectively choosing the interesting facts to include. It does matter to me that they be in some sense true, that they are not just invented facts, but nor do I feel I have to make the story solidly representative of everybody's life then. I suppose my focus on the oddballs, the marginalized people means that I can afford to make the peculiar individuals as well. They don't even have to be purely representative of their type. They can afford to be odd individuals. So that's one thing that, for me, biographical fiction does marvelously, is that it includes the really peculiar detail, the detail that doesn't seem to fit. It makes for characters who are more rounded and three dimensional than highly consistent invented ones often are. Of course there are exceptions. You can have truly invented characters who seem just as real.

Lackey: One of the objections to the historical novel is that it seems to be too deterministic, almost fatalistic. Lukács wants us to understand how social and economic forces shape and determine character. And it seems to me that a number of biographical novelists emphasize the mystery, the irreducibility of character. Shifting the focus from history to character and/or consciousness seems to entail a privileging of mystery and irreducibility. I feel like many biographical novelists are saying to Lukács, whether they were in dialogue with him or not: "Your whole philosophy about the historical novel falls apart once we shift to the interiority of character." There seems to be a consistency among biographical novelists to reject the reductive ways of thinking that we see in the historical novel.

Donoghue: Oh, that's interesting. And yes, I would agree. My very first historical novel, *Slammerkin*, is probably a bit deterministic in that while I show this girl enjoying certain limited freedoms, by the time she's sixteen, she's executed. So she's been slapped down. And I did invent almost everything about her because all I knew were a handful of facts. And so you could say that she's a character I've invented mostly to show those social forces at work. I tried to give her a three dimensional quality as a character, but I still do show her pretty much destroyed by social forces by the end. But I'd say since then, I've probably chosen characters who don't seem to fit the historical narrative quite so neatly. Yes, Jenny Bonnet ends up dead. But throughout the novel, she is a playful figure even though she's dead on page one. She haunts the narrative, so it doesn't feel to me as if she's an illustration of nineteenth century social forces crushing somebody. She has an almost transhistorical memorability to me.

Lackey: And Jenny is the one who creates an awakening for Blanche. Blanche, in many ways, is the typical historical novel character because she is totally determined by her environment until Jenny comes in and starts raising questions. Jenny forces her to interrogate not just certain things about her own personal life but why it's structured the way it is.

Donoghue: Why do you hand all the money to the guys? Why do you put your baby in a baby farm? Yes. All these peculiar little norms within their circle.

Lackey: But Jenny and Anne Damer are different, because there is something that makes them resistant to these deterministic forces, something that makes them more unpredictable, mysterious, and autonomous.

Donoghue: I suppose that's why we chose those particular people to write about. It's the selection process that's most revealing of who the writer is. It's not just what you do with them, it's having chosen those people in the first place. I suppose I'm more interested in women who did something peculiar of their own rather than the helpmeet of a famous man.

Lackey: One of the questions we are trying to answer is this: why has there been this major surge in biofiction. There was a minor boom in the 1930s, with biographical novels from Thomas Mann, Heinrich Mann, Arna Bontemps, Robert Graves, Irving Stone, and Zora Neale Hurston, just to mention a few. But from the 1990s to the present, biofiction has become a dominant literary form. Why did this happen? And which biographical novels do you like? Are you a fan of Hilary Mantel, who has written some excellent ones?

Donoghue: Mantel's are remarkably well written. I've read quite a lot of biographical novels, and there's just nothing formulaic about hers. And what I don't understand is how she's managed to achieve this with such familiar material. Everyone knows about Henry VIII and his marriages, and yet she makes you hang on every detail. So I actually think her victory is a stylistic one and also a revisionist one. I think she is very good at looking with a fresh eye at the circumstances at court and figuring out how the behind-the-scenes guy, the lowborn, uncool butcher's son could actually, at moments, be the really key powerful figure and not all the lords. So in a way, she satisfies our wish for it not to have been always the aristocrats who were running things. The idea of meritocracy is one thing that makes her protagonist attractive. But then also he's a bit of a Tony Soprano in that we often see him torturing people, killing people, and yet we are loyal to him at that point. We've seen his daughters and his wife die, so we are with him to the end even though we see him make some very cold blooded decisions. So I think her choice in protagonist was crucial—who she chose to write about is what makes all the Henry VIII material new.

Lackey: I wonder if you can talk about a contemporary issue in a biographical novel about a nineteenth-century figure. Here I'm thinking of *Frog Music*, the Jenny Bonnet story. Obviously, transgender is something worth thinking about in relation to Jenny Bonnet.

Donoghue: I don't label her, but I am exploring her. I'm very interested in what trousers would have meant to her, what they offered her. And also the fact that she wasn't actually passing. Because we've looked a lot at stories of people who are fully disguised as the other, and I liked the fact that she was dancing right on that line. I quite often like to look at when things first got started, so I am very interested in something like transgender as a movement, when people were fresh and naive in their reactions to it. In *Life Mask*, I really enjoyed looking at ideas of feminism and democracy in their very early, nuanced form. When you could still discuss them so frankly at dinner parties with no fearing of offending anybody. You'd have somebody at the dinner party saying "I think women can be anything," and another one saying, "Women don't have minds." The span of opinion is very wide there. I like tracing ideas back to the first time somebody put their hand up and said, "Hey you know what? I'd like to wear trousers."

Lackey: Where do you see biofiction going now?

Donoghue: I suppose I've already said that I don't like when it's formulaic. I also want these characters to stay different from us. Of course, we are choosing them because they are more like us than their peers were. We are going for the ones that we can relate to or who strike a spark with us. But we still shouldn't make them sound as if they are from now. We should keep that uncomfortable difference.

Lackey: Why?

Donoghue: Because otherwise I think we are just writing characters from now but putting them in the clothes of the previous era. For a biographical fiction to retain its ability to actually change things and make us think and provoke us, I think the characters have to keep this odd hybrid quality. So in Hilary Mantel novels, I like the fact that of course we like this protagonist, and we mostly find his decisions very satisfiable. But then you find yourself with him overseeing the torture of somebody, and you are like: "Ah! How did I go with him to this point?" This sixteenth-century guy lured me into this activity. But then, of course, that makes you feel the parallels to the contemporary US military: "How did we end up waterboarding?" So biographical fiction, it is often packaged as if it is very cozy and desirable and an escape into another era, but actually I think it should make us uncomfortable. It should provoke us. If it is done smartly, then it should have a slightly prickly and uncomfortable quality.

Lackey: Let me ask a question about *Life Mask*. Derby is talking to his son Edward about cock fighting, and the boy says: "Why do we have to have game cocks, and why do they have to do this?" Is that based on something real?

Donoghue: Not at all. I knew nothing about young Edward except that he grew up—and, to be honest, it's been a while, so I'd have to check, but my guess is I may have known that when the boy grew up, he had a menagerie at Knowsley. That sounds like the kind of thing I would have found as a fact. I probably knew nothing else about that man. And so I might have thought, "Okay, there's a slight contrast there between having a menagerie and being into game cocks, so I'll give them a conversation about it." But I easily might have made it up. The same applies to Derby's friend Bunbury. I knew almost nothing about Bunbury, so I decided to make him a plain spoken pal who would tease him over a few beers. So much is invented. I use the facts in a way as a stimuli. I like the oddity of them. For instance, I didn't know that much about Anne Damer's father, but I knew that the people of Jersey gave him a set of standing stones and he brought them all back to Oxfordshire with him. And that he had them inscribed with a verse. I found that a very revealing detail, a kind of oddity that I mightn't have thought to make up. So facts stimulate me into fiction, but most of it is fiction. A biographical novel is clearly not a biography, and as soon as it is fiction, most of it, ninety percent, is invented. It doesn't matter how you stimulate yourself into doing the invention.

Lackey: Scholars make a distinction between fictional biography and biographical fiction. Truman Capote's *In Cold Blood* would be considered a fictional biography, because he insists that he made no changes to the person's life. He merely used fictional devices and techniques to render the life with as much accuracy as possible. Fiction is different because the authors are less focused on the biography and more interested in their own vision, so they are using rather than representing the biographical subject. How do you respond to this distinction?

Donoghue: I suppose I see the biographical novel as a personal taste of mine, that I get turned on by the real. Specifically by real lives that are obscure. I don't want to write another biography or another novel about Shakespeare. If they're too famous, I'm cut off because I feel that there isn't enough room for me to come up with my own version. Now maybe I'm wrong because clearly someone can respond to Emily Dickinson and write a very new kind of book. But I just tend to feel there's more psychic room for me. I don't feel overshadowed if the people I'm writing about are pretty obscure. So that just tends to be what rings my bell. It hasn't felt so much like a methodology. It is more just a personal whim of mine. And really it would be way simpler to make the people up. As a writer, you just learn to work with the brain you've got. But readers really do care about facts. When I was doing my first collection of fact-inspired short stories, I felt a little sheepish about the fact that I thought I was really being a fussy academic. And I said to my publisher at Virago, "You know, they all happened to have some real origins, but let's put all that at the back notes, just for the academics. Only the academics will care." And she was like, "Are you kidding? Everybody will care, people will be desperate to know exactly how much was made up." So she insisted I put the note to each story right at the story. In fact, she wanted it to be that the story would end there and the note would start there, and I was always like, "Oh, hang on, no, let the fiction be the fiction. Kind of at least let me have a space. And then on the next page we can put the notes." But she was right. The reviews all said: "Oh, we were so glad to have the notes!" So I think everybody is attracted to this little bit of the real or is intrigued by the play between the real and the fictional. And I always try and give my sources because I don't want to own these historical instances, especially if they're really obscure ones. I'm happy for someone else to go back and read all the Jenny Bonnet material and go "Actually, I don't agree," you know, "I want to do a different version of her." That's great. For me, it's almost a Wiki approach. Let's all pool our ideas about things like what it meant to crossdress in the 1870s. So yes, it's not that I'm trying to establish some new solid version of the truth, it's more me saying "This is my version, can you give a more plausible one?"

6

The Biographical Novel as Life Art

David Ebershoff, interviewed by Michael Lackey

Lackey: In the past, authors based novels on actual historical figures, but they changed the name in order to give themselves more creative license. Can you explain why you decided to name Einar Wegener/Lili Elbe after the actual historical figure, and can you explain the potential benefits and drawbacks of doing that?

Ebershoff: I knew right away I would call her Lili and use the name that she was given at birth, Einar Wegener. And it was a very practical reason. When I first came across the story in the 1990s, she was not well known, and history had partially lost her. She was not as known as she deserved to be as a transgender pioneer and as someone significant in LGBT history. In fact, when I first came across her name, it was in an academic book on gender studies and identity in literature, and it said that she was the first person to have what was then called a sex change but what we now call gender reassignment or gender confirmation surgery. And my reaction to this was: "Wait a minute, I thought Christine Jorgenson was the first." Jorgenson was an American who transitioned in the early 1950s, and I think in popular culture, many people believe she was the first person to have gender confirmation surgery. Why that was the case I do not know, nor do I know if she ever said that, but many, many people believe that she was the first. And so when I came across Lili's name, I was struck that she was somebody who transitioned roughly two decades before Christine Jorgenson and yet didn't have her proper recognition as a pioneer. And so I knew that to write about her, even though I was writing fiction and I would be using the tools of fiction to write about her, I was going to call her by the name she chose for herself—Lili Elbe—and follow the outline of her life and especially her transition. One of the efforts of *The Danish Girl* is to pull her story and her life out of the obscurity that it was in at the time. I don't want to suggest that she was completely unknown; certainly some academics knew of her, some activists. But she did not have, in my opinion, her proper place in LGBT history, and so to not use her name would be a kind of erasure that I didn't want, that didn't have any sort of role in what I was doing. So I always thought of her as Lili.

Lackey: Are there any potential drawbacks of using the actual name?

Ebershoff: Yes, people might assume that *The Danish Girl* is a biography. This is about Lili Elbe, a very significant person in LGBT history, a transgender pioneer. So why is this not a biography? Why is this a novel? Why are some details different than what I might read online? These questions are legitimate; I certainly don't want to dismiss them. But they are some of the potential drawbacks of using her name.

Lackey: You make an important distinction between biography and biofiction. Biographers seek to tell the story of an actual person with as much precision and accuracy as possible, but fiction writers deal with symbols and metaphors in order to make their characters more universal, which explains why they alter facts about their biographical subject. Can you talk about some of the strategies you used in order to convert Einar/Lili into a symbol that has universal significance?

Ebershoff: I agree with you that in fiction, often, the characters can become symbolic and represent something larger than what they are in the book. But I also believe that as a writer, I cannot think of a character as a symbol, because then the character becomes flat, and I could lose the contradictions that any interesting character has. So I never thought of Lili as a symbol while I was writing the book. I certainly understand her as one now. When writing, I asked myself: What are the responsibilities of writing about such an important figure in transgender history? And what responsibilities do I have to transgender readers, to the transgender community, and how do I represent a larger experience than her own? Some people might look to the character as a representation of "the transgender experience." This is a big burden for any writer to feel, and in fact it's an impossible burden because no human can represent fully a community of people who have very diverse individual experiences. And it was only by backing away from that responsibility of representing a community as a whole or an experience of many people and acknowledging that my job was to represent Lili's experience and represent this particular character that I could actually write freely. By focusing on the details of her life and her inner life, perhaps she could become universal. To get back to your question. Only by making her very individual does she perhaps become universal. So I've had over the years many responses from transgender men and women and spouses of transgender men and women, and they have written me different things about their response to the book and to Lili's story. But one thing that often comes up in these letters is they will tell me something that Lili did or felt that was similar to their own experiences in one way or another. And so it seems like there were portions of her life that do represent some part of some transgender people's experience.

Lackey: It seems that your novel challenges readers to think about transgender experience in a broader and more comprehensive way. For instance, when I teach *The Danish Girl*, I spend a lot of time talking about Greta. The original Gerda was Danish, but you made your Greta an American who is uncomfortable with her identity as a wealthy American. In short, your Greta, like Einar, inherited an identity with which she is not comfortable. Your novel explores the idea that many are born into identities that they are not comfortable with, so even if we are not transgender, we can still identify with the transgender community because many of us have gone through this experience of being born into an identity with which we are not comfortable. And what you are looking at in this novel is this whole process of constructing an identity, whether it is a new national or gender identity. Would you agree with that interpretation of your novel?

Ebershoff: I absolutely agree with that. Questions of identity: Who am I? Who do I want to be? Who do I want others to see? Who among us hasn't asked those questions? And who among us hasn't looked in the mirror, at least once, and questioned the reflection in one way or another? It could be a literal reflection or a metaphorical reflection. And part of growing up and part of becoming ourselves is to stare down those questions of identity and answer them honestly and truthfully. For some people, that is not a particularly difficult exercise. They are comfortable in their identity; it is natural to them. And for many others, it is a much more difficult struggle, and it's one that many people continue to struggle with their entire lives. And I know that for LGBT people, this is a huge part of coming into themselves, whether it's coming out or, for a transgender person, transitioning. It is answering those questions: who am I? And who do I want to be? And who do I want the world to see? And how do I reconcile the differences between who the world sees and who I know I am? When there's a discrepancy between who you know who you are and who the world sees, many people sit uncomfortably in their lives, and they're constantly in struggle. That struggle can ebb and flow, but it is a continuous inner struggle, and it can really take up a great deal of one's life and inner life. And it's hard; you can't become yourself until you resolve that struggle to a certain degree. And so you are right that the character Greta, she's rejecting her identity. She's an heiress. She's from a world that expects her to be a certain kind of young woman, marry a certain kind of man. And she's rejecting that as a woman, as an artist, as a wife. So part of her story is becoming her own individual woman and coming up with her own definition of what it means to be a woman of her day. And one of the things that I was always fascinated by is how Lili, as she progresses in her transition, becomes increasingly stereotypical, her understanding of what it means to be a woman, her understanding of femininity. She's drawn to things that stereotypically have been the female realm.

Lackey: She has internalized simple binaries about masculinity and femininity.

Ebershoff: Yes, that's a very good way of saying it. There's not a lot of complexity to her understanding of what a woman can do. And I always found this really remarkable because she lived with such an unconventional woman and a woman who really defined herself, defined what a woman can or can't or will or won't do. And that Lili didn't look to her spouse for a source of inspiration for her own identity really interested me. There are multiple reasons for that, and often when I write fiction, I try to lay out the questions and lay out the story and allow the reader to answer those questions. I don't want to fully answer them. What in part accounts for Lili's simplistic understanding of the masculine and the feminine, and her failure to look to Greta for an example of female complexity, is because what she was doing was so new, and she had no real role models to look to, very few examples of what her life could be. She was really creating her own path. And so, in some ways, she had to rely on some familiar tropes while she created that path.

Lackey: This raises an important question about the value of biofiction. Do you see *The Danish Girl* primarily as creating empathy or inciting action? Let me be more specific. When I teach the novel, my students have more empathy for Einar/Lili, but many come to that experience through Greta. After I show students how Greta transitions from being an American woman to a Danish woman, students realize that identity transformation happens in multiple ways. Therefore, my non-transgender students feel more connection with and compassion for Lili. But if we focus on Lili's transgender experience as a metaphor, then it provides students with a framework for taking that bold step of transitioning from one identity to another. Many people are afraid to take that courageous step into the unknown. Would you say that your novel provides us with a framework for understanding agency, that power to take control of one's own life? Did you see that at all as you were writing the novel? That your novel could impact people, more than just the transgender community? In essence, the transgender community could become a symbol that inspires and empowers people who are not transgender. Do you know what I'm saying?

Ebershoff: I do. One of the wonderful aspects of the last several years as transgender issues have become better understood and more transgender men and women have told their stories is the idea that the world is not binary and that there is a fluidity to many people's gender and to their gender identity, and that it's wrong to assume that the world breaks down in a simple black and white, male and female way. Many cis people see themselves as male and many cis people see themselves as female. But there is a legitimate space in between; not every cis gender man is the same as every other cis gender man and not every cis gender woman is the same as every other cis gender woman. Many people feel like they possess both the masculine and feminine in them, and that is absolutely natural in human history and we have many examples of it. I think that in the last decade or so, as more transgender stories have been told by artists and by individuals, we have a much better understanding of how that applies to all of us. So there's that aspect of what Lili's story means, and I think that goes beyond the book itself.

Lackey: This fluid approach to gender explains one of Lili's mistakes. Near the end of the novel, she wants to get rid of her paintings, because she wants to distance herself from all things Einar and all things male. But Greta responds differently. At first, she wants to cast off all things Waud, which is her wealthy family, and all things American. But by the end of the novel, she accepts both her family and her Americanness, even though she has transitioned to being Danish. By stark contrast, Einar wants to get rid of the paintings. This is one of the mistakes that Einar makes after transitioning to Lili. Was this contrast strategically done on your part?

Ebershoff: Yes, I was always drawn to this particular detail of Lili's story, that when she expressed herself as Lili, even very early in her transitioning, that she rejected painting. And she said specifically that painting belonged to Einar, that the paintings were done by Einar. This is part of the historical record.

Lackey: And women didn't even paint. She, the real Lili as well as your character, says that in the journals.

Ebershoff: That's right, she saw them as the work of someone else. This is a very strong demarcation between her life before she transitioned and her life after transitioning. This is probably not so representative of the experiences of transgender men and women today, but Lili didn't have examples of how to do what she was doing. So I can understand how psychologically she needed to establish very distinct markers for her to make sense of what she was creating of her life. For her to truly believe in herself, to proceed with her transition, she had to break from her past. And so part of her biographical story is that she did not paint and she wasn't interested in painting. And yet there are so many ironies here because it was through painting, not her own but Gerda's, that she could begin to express herself. We have the paintings Gerda did of Lili, and these are representations of an ideal version of Lili and what she wanted to be and how she wanted to be seen. And, so, for Lili to reject painting, even though painting had helped her realize herself in many ways, intrigued me on so many levels.

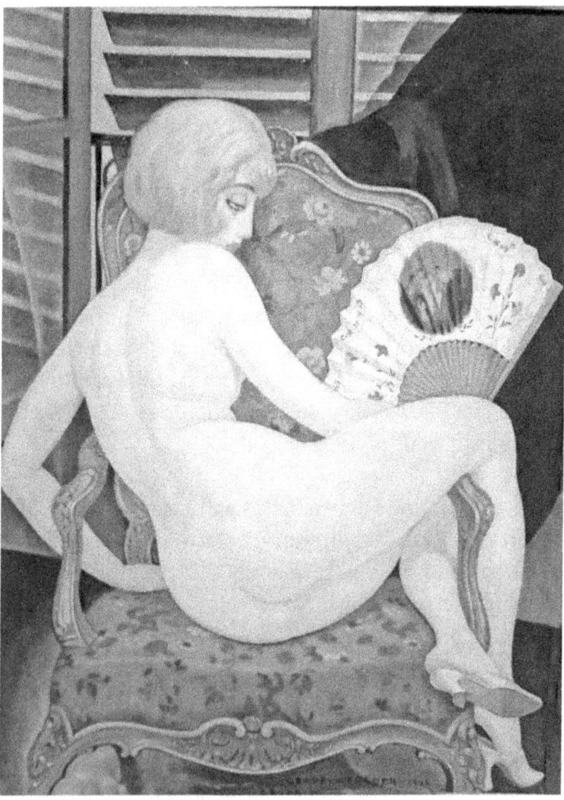

Figure 1 Gerda Wegener, "Lili, Hot Summer," 1924. https://curiator.com/art/gerda-wegener/lili-hot-summer.

Lackey: Can you talk briefly about the way a fictional character, and I'm taking Greta as a fictional character, functions to illuminate the biographical subject that you've chosen? Greta is clearly much more fictional than Lili. And can you talk more generally about the role of the fictional character in relationship to the biographical subject and the biographical novel?

Ebershoff: In *The Danish Girl*, I had a very strategic vision of how to tell the story because I was fictionalizing it. Let me focus on the paintings, because this will enable me to answer your questions. Lili rejected painting and insisted that she wasn't an artist and that she didn't know how to paint. All those skills and impulses belong to Einar, not her, she said. However, I disagree because I believe that she was a great artist, even after she transitioned, and her greatest creation was herself. Artists are visionaries; they see something that does not yet exist. They can bring into creation something that is not yet there. And in many ways this is what Lili is doing: she is envisioning her future self, she is seeing a version of herself that is not yet there, and she is creating it. And this is perhaps greater and more significant than any painting she could have done or did do when she lived as Einar. And so she never saw herself as this great artist, but I do. And so this helped me understand how to write the novel. When I began to think about Lili Elbe and writing a novel about her, I began to think of the story through two important lenses. The first is that she was a transgender pioneer. This cannot be underestimated and I am not underestimating it when I say what I'm about to say. But when I first encountered her, her name was sort of all she was—a sort of footnote in LGBT history. The complexity and contradictions of her life were not present in what I viewed and saw and read about her. But it was through Greta's paintings of Lili that I began to see the depths and layers of her character.

Lackey: Can you give me an example to illustrate?

Ebershoff: Here is a painting of Lili: it's Lili naked, sitting in a beautiful red chair with her back to us holding a fan (see Figure 1). This is an intricate painting. I imagine it must have taken weeks, if not months, to paint this. Think about how long Lili had to sit there, exposed, naked to her spouse. Lili was tacitly saying, "This is how I want you to see me, this is how I want to be seen, this is who I *really* am." Now think about the painter, the real life Gerda or Greta in my book, looking at her spouse this way, carefully, intimately. Imagine the trust and respect of this marriage, for the two of them to create a painting like this. This painting and others like it showed me something about their marriage that I didn't know when I first started reading about

Lili. It showed me that they had a kind of faith in each other that is rare and extraordinary, that they could be with each other as their true selves. It's very hard in life to ever find somebody that you can truly expose yourself to. And then Greta felt so much love and understanding that she could create Lili through her art. This finally gets to your question. I saw this first as a story of Lili Elbe, the transgender pioneer, but there's much more to it, as there's much more to any of us. Nobody's life can be reduced to one sentence. So it's also a story of love and marriage and trust, and it's a story of art. This explains how I decided to write *The Danish Girl*. I would use the lenses of marriage and love, and the lenses of art and creation. That gets me to Greta and why she is much more fictionalized than Lili. I wanted the novel to take the reader into those emotional spaces that led to the creation of that painting. In the book, Einar and Greta thought of their marriage as a cove, a place that's protected just for the two of them, or a dark cave where their intimacy could live and breathe and feel safe. I wanted to take the reader to those spaces that can exist in marriages and may exist in marriages, or relationships. I wanted the reader to know that place that was so intimate between the two of them, but that doesn't wholly exist in the historical record. They were often together, so they weren't writing letters to each other. They were not like John and Abigail Adams, who were separated and wrote these incredible letters that tell us through language the nature of their relationship. That doesn't exist with these two. But the paintings express what was there. I could sense the space that existed between them, this intimate space of marriage. But what was in it, the specificity of what was in it wasn't there, and that's a big part of what I was inventing. So I said to myself: I'm going to call Lili Lili for the reasons I said earlier, but I'm going to do more invention with the wife as a signal both to me as I write the book and to the reader that this is where fiction is coming in even more so. And to change the name from Gerda to Greta was part of that thinking. I do believe that if you were to read *The Danish Girl*, although there are many biographical details about the character Greta that are different from the historical person Gerda, I do believe that you will have an accurate sense of the emotional journey she went on with her spouse as Lili became Lili Elbe.

Lackey: Earlier you said, "Artists are visionaries who bring into existence something that is not yet there." There are two separate ways of thinking about artists as visionaries. Let me give you two examples. William Styron published *The Confessions of Nat Turner* in 1967, and he altered many facts about the actual historical Turner. In his novel, Turner has a homosexual experience, which infuriated many people, because there is no evidence that this ever happened. Styron knew this was not true, but he included it anyway. Why? He said that his novel is not biography and it is not history. What readers get is a "metaphorical diagram," which readers could use to illuminate events that occurred in both the past and the present. So he included the gay scene in order to illustrate how the structures and conditions of oppression that were used against blacks in 1831 are the same structures and conditions of oppression that are used against gays and lesbians in 1967. As an artist, what Styron gives is a new way of thinking about oppression from two separate time periods. Oscar Wilde goes one step further. As an artist, he wanted to create new ways of thinking and being, specifically about homosexuality. Talk about your vision as an artist. Are you, like Styron, giving us a metaphorical diagram for understanding? Or, are you, like Wilde, trying to create something new through your work?

Ebershoff: I'd probably agree with both in some ways. With *The Danish Girl*, I knew that I had to understand her story and then understand it in my way. Lili's life resonated with me, as a gay man, in many profound ways. This idea of struggling to know who you are, ignoring who you really are, coming to terms with it in isolation, and eventually telling more people, and then just accepting yourself and either having the world accept that or reject that—that all resonated with me, significantly. Her courage resonated with me, significantly. But at the same time, every writer will see a story or a life or a place through his or her eyes, based on their own experiences, their worldview. And for me, I needed to understand that. I don't at all think of her as my subject. I never would think of her that way, and I don't think of *The Danish Girl* as the first and last book about her. This is my way of thinking about her life, and I think that's what Oscar Wilde was saying. An artist creates something that can only be created by that individual artist. And anyone else would do it differently just by the nature of the individuality of the artist and their impulses. At the same time, I don't think I can ignore what Styron is saying in that her life does represent something bigger than her life. She was a pioneer and she showed the world a life that few thought was possible. But there is a danger of reducing her to a one sentence description, that she was a transgender pioneer, the first to have gender reassignment surgery. That's such a simple quotation about her life and it eliminates the role of the people around her. And I knew that others were a very significant part of her story. If her spouse had not been a part of her life, her transition would have been fundamentally different. I'm not saying she would not have transitioned, but it would have been a different transition. And I think this is one of the things I wanted to show, how there is a very intimate experience of recognizing who you are and becoming yourself, and that we do this with others. So *The Danish Girl* is a metaphor. I think both Styron and Wilde are right, and I can't be too rigid about it in my thinking. But I do definitely lean toward Wilde in that writers show us the story through their point of view.

Lackey: Russell Banks has given us a useful way of thinking about different genres. In an interview, he says that writers establish different truth contracts with readers. So if a person authors a biography, the reader expects fidelity to the facts. *Cloudsplitter* is Banks's biographical novel about Owen Brown, the son of John Brown. The actual Owen dies in the nineteenth century, but Banks had him live into the twentieth century. I asked him why he did that, and he said: In the novel, I'm examining the terrorist mindset, and I wanted to show how this way of thinking persists into the present. He went on to say: "Of course, if I was writing a biography, I couldn't do that." But he says, "I expect my readers to understand that I have a different truth contract with readers than a biographer." Can you talk about this whole notion of truth contracts?

Ebershoff: I agree with what he's saying. I think that every book teaches a reader how to read it. It will give clues to the reader of what it is, what it's trying to be, and what it isn't, and what it's not trying to be. There are signals. This is going to be *this* kind of book, and you can expect this format from this book. And if the book defies it, it defies it purposely. And so part of that is the truth contract that Banks talks about. In *The Danish Girl*, Lili Elbe is called Lili Elbe, while the character Gerda is called Greta. Those signals are my truth contract, where that story is going to move a little bit further away from the known or unknown facts of this historical person. And part of the truth contract is point of view. The novel switches; it's third person, but it switches from Einar's point of view, then Greta's point of view, then Einar and Lili's point of view, and Greta's point of view. Each chapter goes back and forth, and it's very much part of the signal I give my readers. You're going to see the story from the close point of view of two individuals; no others; and no sort of larger omniscient third person point of view. So with any limited point of view, there's a signal to the reader that this is how these characters perceive these experiences, and that's part of the truth contract.

Lackey: This is precisely why Banks's idea of the truth contract is so important. So many criticized Styron's *The Confessions of Nat Turner* because he took liberties with historical fact and the biographical record. But Styron retorted: I'm not giving you history or biography. I have written a novel, which gives you a metaphor for thinking about history and biography. People criticized the novel because they expected it to do something that Styron had no intention of doing. Does this describe what you did in *The Danish Girl*?

Ebershoff: His answer resonates with me, but it's not the answer I would give if the question is posed about *The Danish Girl*. I felt that the tools of fiction, and especially fiction's ability to mine a character's inner life, could show a reader who Lili was, what she thought and felt, and what her life means. I wanted to bore down to her core because her story is very much about her looking deep within herself to discover herself. Fiction allowed me to do this. Although I was writing fiction I was always aiming for an emotional truth.

Lackey: I have noticed a tension in the writings of biographical novelists. The biographical novel first became popular in the 1930s: Robert Graves, Irving Stone, Arna Bontemps, Thomas and Heinrich Mann, and Zora Neale Hurston published biographical novels in that decade. At that same time, writers were casting a skeptical eye on truth, so most biographical novelists are not moralists. And yet, you all seem to have a deep commitment to social justice. So I wonder if you could talk about the novel as educating readers. Here I do not mean education in a conventional sense, like I'm giving you a universal truth. Rather, education in the sense that you are giving readers ways of seeing that are vastly different from what we get in the moralist novels of nineteenth century.

Ebershoff: A novel can have a profound effect in showing people new ideas, new lives, inspiring them in their own lives. And many of us want that out of a book. But I don't think I can go into writing a book with those goals because I'll be aiming toward them as opposed to aiming toward the truth of my characters. Those goals may be achieved through the truth of my characters. If I'm writing a book to try to inspire people, to try to educate people about LGBT lives and issues, or other issues, I may miss the mark in creating complex, compelling, even contradictory characters. By focusing on my characters, and finding the language to represent their experiences honestly, perhaps the book will have something to say about social justice and inspire people in their own lives. I never start with theme. I start with characters, story, narrative, and language. So social justice is in some ways an after effect of a book, albeit a significant one.

Lackey: Margaret Atwood said something similar. When discussing Grace Marks, the protagonist in her novel *Alias Grace*, she started with a resonant symbol, which was based on Grace's life. But as she began to flesh out that character, the themes started to emerge. She didn't begin with a bulky idea or agenda. Rather, she thought about a character and its symbolic possibilities, and then something powerful emanated from that.

Ebershoff: I have to say I didn't fully understand *The Danish Girl* until I'd written it. I don't want to imply I am just wholly ignorant of subject and the characters because that sounds idiotic. But all the themes and all the symbols in it I didn't have a full command of until it was on the page. And even then, there's plenty that readers point out to me. That's the mystery of fiction writing. And if the mystery is not there, if it doesn't surprise me, it won't surprise the reader. So one of the challenges of the work is to maintain the mystery and the wonder as I write while not being totally lost and just going any which way.

Lackey: Can you talk about that mystery in relation to the character's evolution? It seems that biographical novelists focus on a character who is blind at some point, but through an unexpected transformation, starts to see things in a new and startling way.

Ebershoff: When I look back at what I've written, I see a pattern, and maybe I've seen it because other people pointed it out to me. But I tend to write about people, and Lili Elbe is the first example of this in my work, who have a journey/evolution ahead of them. The first phase of that is always internal. Understanding themselves and having to break out of a society and step out of a comfortable world into the unknown to realize themselves. This is a pattern that I've done in other books as well. And that to me is evolution and transformation. And that kind of story is something I'm always drawn to. We're following an individual through and creating his or her own history. It's sort of personal history. That is what the biographical novel is. It's the creation of one's own history.

7

Fictions of Women

Hannah Kent, interviewed by Kelly Gardiner

Gardiner: In 2014 Bloomsbury published *Truthful Fictions*, Michael Lackey's collection of interviews with American biographical novelists. Now we are undertaking a follow-up about biographical novelists from all over the world. It's an interesting time, because we've been looking at the definitions of biofiction, and the intersections between the biographical and the imagined. Our working definition of biofiction is fiction that takes the name of a real person for its protagonist.

But I've heard you say that you define your biofictional novel *Burial Rites*, in particular, as a work of speculative biography?

Kent: That's true, yes. This was particularly so years ago while I was working out how I was going to approach this project that I knew I wanted to write. I was trying to work out how it might fit within that vast spectrum of novels that take biographical stories but also seek to represent history. Speculative biography was a term that has been used before, sometimes self-consciously, by writers. But I sought to claim it as a way to categorize what it was that I was hoping to do. So, it's a subgenre of biofiction.

I also looked at other novels which might be deemed speculative biography. I specifically focused on representations of historical murdering women, so my scope of study was quite small. But nonetheless I found it fascinating. It was really interesting examining authorial intent behind it as well.

Jill Dawson's *Fred and Edie*, her account of the life and death of Edith Thompson, is a very good example, as is F. Tennyson Jesse's *A Pin to See the Peep Show*, which also looks at Thompson. Certainly, Margaret Atwood's *Alias Grace* and *Fred and Edie* were two novels that I really focused on when considering a methodology for writing *Burial Rites*. Possibly because I had quite a lot of information not only about the books' reception, but also about what the authors were intending to do with them.

Gardiner: And what was the methodology that you came up with?

Kent: For me it was not simply writers taking a biographical life and fictionalizing it. It was much more specific. I thought that in order to separate speculative biography from documentary fiction or fictionalized biography, it needed certain criteria. Keep in mind this is some time ago and some of my thoughts about this have changed. But I thought that speculative biography would largely be composed out of a research-led practice, thus differentiating itself from fiction "inspired" by facts.

It would apply and incorporate critical historical and cultural knowledge and require rigorous primary research. Rather than having practice-led research where you progress from unknown to known, the research practice would direct that creative work until the knowledge base was exhausted. The fiction would take a secondary role.

I thought it might be good to differentiate speculative biography from other novels which were being produced, particularly works about women who had committed crimes—and I'm thinking specifically of the many which have been produced about Lizzie Borden. The inclusion of fiction would never be to create dramatic interest or augment poor research, follow literary whims or just make the narrative a little bit more salacious for entertainment purposes. I thought it seemed to have a deeper intent. That largely, I thought at the time, was to challenge previous perceptions of the historical figures that they were seeking to represent.

I thought that, in some ways, speculative biographies borrow from or lean on history in that they are research-led and a great amount of research is required. But at the same time, they interrogate history. They reinstall historical context as significant and determining, but, in doing so, examine the concept of historical "knowledge."

Gardiner: In both of your novels the historical knowledge is blurry, isn't it? It's blurred by Icelandic legend in the case of Agnes Magnusdottir in *Burial Rites*, and Irish fairy law in *The Good People*, and what's written and what's spoken. Agnes is famous as the last woman executed in Iceland and there's so much misinformation about her as well. So, are you writing back to historical interpretations, and to other imagined stories about these people?

Kent: There was so little that was known about Agnes Magnusdottir, while at the same time there was a glut of information about the case. I say that because most of the sources that looked at the murders of 1828, and the consequent executions in 1830, were largely concentrated on the stories of the men involved. This is true for both nonfictional and fictional accounts.

So, for instance, there were quite a few accounts that focused on the decision and the experience of the bailiff, the district commissioner at the time. And I would say about 80 percent of the sources focused on Natan Ketilsson, one of the murdered men. He was very famous in his lifetime and an interesting man. He was a thief and womanizer, but he was a very well-known doctor and he healed a lot of people. He swindled a lot of people, but at the same time he was incredibly charming.

In all of these representations and retellings, Agnes was there, but only ever as a stereotype. She was only ever the wicked woman, even in fictional representations. There was a play called *Dauðua Natans Ketilssonar* (The Death of Natan Ketilsson), and directions for the actress included: "She smiles like a devil." So it was this constant reiteration of Agnes as monstrous. When that wasn't there, there was no other information. She was either entirely absent or mentioned only as evil.

It was that which I wanted to not necessarily remedy—that's the wrong word—but I wanted to *address* in writing *Burial Rites*. I didn't want to attest or protest her murder conviction; it wasn't to try to make her seem like a good person. I simply wanted to give her the same complexity and ambiguity that I saw in representations of Natan Ketilsson and other male characters. So that was where I started.

A lot of my initial sources were secondary. The research process therefore required going to Iceland and accessing parish records and census material and all that primary source material and finding out as much as I could about Agnes's life. But it was also a matter of looking at what Agnes's life might have resembled outside of a context of crime. You would know this as a historical novelist yourself. It was necessary to do a lot of research into the social climate, cultural climate, political climate of Agnes's time, and, in doing so, trying to work out what sort of life she might have led and how her environment might have led her to make decisions she did, and whether she thought they were the only ones available to her.

I wanted to look at the sources about the murder that were available and contest them. But in the same sense, I wanted to widen a rather narrow parameter of representation and show the world that Agnes existed in. That was a lot easier to do. There's a lot of factual information available about what it was like to live in Iceland as a peasant, and even as a woman, and also as essentially an orphan in the nineteenth century. Knowledge of that time gave me a unique lens with which to regard the biographical information that I would later discover about Agnes.

Gardiner: You often use the word "ambiguous" about both novels, and talk about wanting to create ambiguity. Why is that important? Is that part of the speculation?

Kent: I think so. I like the word "speculative" because it's conjectural. You are not trying to replace—you are trying to interrogate the idea of a single truth. You are trying to interrogate even the idea of authenticity. By providing something that's speculative or conjectural, what you are doing is opening up the possibility of heterogeneous or multiple "truths" and, in doing so, you are suggesting that there might be many other valid, but diverse biographical stories about the one subject. That is particularly true of *Burial Rites*. You are trying to create discussion, and you are trying to alert people to the impossibility of ever having a singular kind of story—that from various points of view history looks very, very different. That is something that I think fiction can do incredibly well. It can contribute to that conversation and can contribute to that awareness.

But *The Good People* doesn't have that skeleton of verified biographical information under it as *Burial Rites* has.

Gardiner: It could still be considered a work of biofiction, although I understand you couldn't follow the same methodology because you didn't have much information to go on?

Kent: No. I was drawn to this story after encountering a newspaper article about the trial of a woman called Nance Roche, accused of the willful murder of a four-year-old "cripple" whom she believed to be a changeling. I had two newspaper articles in that case and no biographical information. I began writing knowing only the ending, this bizarre, crazy ending in which three women are charged for drowning a boy in a river because they thought he was a fairy. I did try to find more sources and biographical information. I went to Ireland, I tried to find as much as I could about the women and found nothing.

So my creative process began with thinking: how do I take this ending and create a narrative that begins at a place of normality? How do I portray these women and their slow, crazy descent to appalling behavior in a way that is nonetheless colored by historical likelihood?

Likelihood. I think that's probably another word I lean on a lot. With *The Good People* I again did a lot of research into the outside world or environment. I looked at the lives led by people who resembled these characters or who could be said to. So that, while everything was imagined with *The Good People*, it was nonetheless likely, as likely as possible. In that way it was research-directed, but nowhere near in the same amount as *Burial Rites*.

Gardiner: So even though you're using Nance's real name, you just couldn't find out anything about her—for obvious reasons?

Kent: Nothing. It was frustrating, but I guess I learned a lot more as a novelist by needing greater recourse to my own imagination—with *Burial Rites* it was sometimes a bit like a dot-to-dot. I had all these events that I knew happened and it was a matter of incorporating the fiction to get to the next point.

With *The Good People*, I had, in some sense, a lot more freedom. That gave me a lot more difficulty, I think, in the end.

Gardiner: I like that term that you use, a "fictional likelihood." Emma Donoghue says, "A story is a different kind of true" and I know that you've talked about trying for emotional truth for the characters. So how do you go about getting yourself and your readers inside these characters?

Kent: I don't think I could do it without the research. That's not just because I need to fill my mind with facts and figures and statistics and know what the place where they lived looked like. For me it's about spending time in the world of these characters so that when I do sit down to write I feel I understand them.

And when I do sit down to write, I put away all my research. I don't refer to books when I do it. That's a technique I use to avoid putting in a superfluous amount of additional information. But for me, spending two or three years reading about the world that these people lived in, reading about their culture, and, in the case of *The Good People*, about folklore and folk stories and folk rituals, women's experiences, allows me to more easily access characters from a place of empathy.

I think that's a word that can be overused, but certainly it's the one that I keep falling back on. For me, empathy comes from a place of familiarization, which comes from research. Initially I feel like I don't necessarily know these characters, because knowing a character comes from the process of writing and drafting. But I feel I can more easily access that which is universal and probably most akin to my own experience, which is inevitably emotional experience, and use that as a starting point.

For example, we all know what it's like to grieve, no matter when in time we might live. Grief is incredibly individual and never uniform, but there are common emotional experiences we share. We know what it's like to feel happiness, we know what it's like to love someone. That stuff doesn't change. When writing I try to explore those emotions, things that I'm very familiar with, while also incorporating an attained familiarization with my characters' time and place and the circumstances of their life.

Gardiner: We don't all know what it's like to be about to be executed, though, as you had to imagine for Agnes. And I'm thinking particularly of *The Good*

People, of trying to think your way into the worldview of somebody who sees the landscape and the good folk as part of everybody's existence. How do you find out how people felt in the past and how they thought about the world, particularly people who didn't record their own thoughts?

Kent: It was a big challenge with *The Good People*. In the newspaper article about Nance Roche, the journalist referred to her with the kind of language you would expect: as a woman of advanced age, as being "superannuated from this world," as ignorant, as a peasant, as superstitious. I probably regarded her as something similar when first reading that article. I certainly initially used the words "superstition" and "superstitious behavior" when talking about the case.

I realized, however, quite early on, that to portray Nance with empathy—not with sympathy, which is easier and less effective—and to really inhabit her world and her way of thinking, as you put it, I needed to discard my contemporary attitudes toward what might be deemed "superstition," my inclination toward a certain kind of rationality. So for me it involved reading as much as I could about folklore, about Irish folk ways. It was also through encountering the stories of people who did everything from faith healing to herbalism and encountering people during my travels for whom these beliefs were still very real, that I was able to understand folk belief and its power, complexity, and wisdom. I soon understood how attractive folklore was to people who were completely disempowered, as Nance was, due to the combination of her gender and her poverty and her age. I started to see the rationality and the logic that is present in a lot of these folk beliefs.

It is incredibly alien and very different to the rationality or the logic we might prefer in our scientifically minded world, but nonetheless I recognized it. That came from a deeper understanding of "sympathetic magic," which lies at the heart of a lot of these beliefs. It is the idea that the world is in secret sympathy with itself and everything is connected.

I discovered and then appreciated a lot of the wisdom that was contained in this folkloric logic. As soon as I had that respect I was able to respect my character and portray her as something other than superstitious.

Gardiner: What a gorgeous idea, the world being in secret sympathy with itself. And so with that incredible amount of detail, even with something like *The Good People* where you don't have information about that particular woman's life, and that framework of the worldview, you are able to create a credible fictional life for her?

Kent: That's always the intention. It's a desire for credibility, something within the realm of the likely. Not the absolute by any means, not the definitive, but the likely. The aim is to have a purity of intention. By that, I mean to write for the sake of exploring these characters or these people's humanity, not to write a thrilling crime story about child murder. To write with the intention of emendation rather than exploitation or appropriation. But ultimately, I think an author's success can only be determined by readers' responses.

Gardiner: Indeed, and that's one of the things we're wondering: why has biographical fiction become so popular with writers and readers since the 1990s? Over the past few years we've had biographical novels winning Booker Prizes, like *Wolf Hall* and *Bring up the Bodies*, and Pulitzers with *The Hours*. Very different approaches, very different styles, critical successes and also best sellers. And you haven't done too badly either.

Kent: No, it's been wonderful, I've had very positive reader responses. It's been great.

Gardiner: So why do you think people are so fascinated by biofictions, both as writers and readers?

Kent: I can only really respond as a reader to this. Because having written only two books and having very different processes at the heart of them, I always felt that my decisions to write the books that I have, all two of them, have been largely through coincidence rather than design. I haven't necessarily thought, okay I'm going to be a writer who takes the neglected or misrepresented lives of others and seeks to correct that by supplying another representation which incorporates fiction.

As a reader, though, I think it's a contemporary concern. In recent times we have seen increasing social awareness of history as a construct. We're aware more than ever that a human hand has pushed the pen. I think this, in turn, has perhaps heightened reader—and writer—attraction to that which has not been said, not been recorded. I think we recognize that omissions exist, with this contemporary understanding. We want to address the silences. We want alternate suggestions.

For example, as a feminist, I really want to read more about women in the past, particularly women who were poor or illiterate or who were clearly misrepresented by the people who did have the literacy, power, time or access to materials to write their stories down. As a reader, I want to have writers provide that which I believe historians have neglected or omitted or misrepresented due to prevailing colonial, patriarchal, or classist ideologies.

It's really exciting. We want to see ourselves in literature. I know as a reader and as a feminist reader, that's what I want. I want more stories of women. I feel like there's not enough. That's probably why I picked up a book like *Alias Grace* in the first place. I was fascinated by it. I didn't want to just encounter another story of a woman as an angel or as the devil. I wanted complexity and ambiguity. That's what's interesting. You want the human.

Gardiner: And the ambiguity?

Kent: We want to muddy the waters a little bit now.

Gardiner: Hence the lack of concrete answers in your novels? They're not so much whodunnits, although some critics have defined them as crime fiction. But as with *Alias Grace* it's: did she or did she not, and how do you feel about this person? Is *Burial Rites* more about digging into why she did what she did, how did she get to that point?

Kent: Exactly. It's never satisfying to hear that someone did what she did because she was evil and that was all there was to it. I think we, these days, recognize that most crimes eventuate through a whole series of events and choices which are largely shaped by the wider world and the external circumstances of anyone's life. That's something that I thought Atwood did so beautifully in *Alias Grace*. But I also think that a lot of these books, in providing a slightly more multidimensional representation, also take up that categorical understanding of woman as devil or angel and dismantle it within the text.

That's something I loved in *Alias Grace*. I think Atwood really plays with the understanding that hitherto Grace has been represented as either an angel or a devil. Grace herself is aware that this is what's been said about her. She comments on what a ridiculous thing it is.

Gardiner: And in fiction we can also move between points of view. *Burial Rites* moves between Agnes's first-person narrative voice, through other people's points of view in third person. What does that approach allow you to do?

Kent: I intentionally chose that approach for quite a specific reason. That was to allow space within this representation of Agnes as something other than a demon (largely done via first-person narration), to nonetheless show that that is the way that she's regarded by those around her (illustrated in the sections of third person). I wanted to include newspaper articles and letters and things like that to show that people regarded her in this one-dimensional light, and then to directly contrast that with her own self-perception as complex.

I was really interested, when I started writing *Burial Rites*, in using language in new ways, particularly when representing women who were not allowed a voice or were not permitted to write or tell their own story in their own lifetime—to use language in ways that showed that they were outside language. I wanted Agnes's voice to be richly lyrical, to give her a voice that was highly poetic. To show not just how she saw herself, but also to indicate that that voice, that story, never had a place in the public rhetorical forms.

Gardiner: That's an anti-authenticity approach really, in terms of voice, isn't it?

Kent: Yeah, totally. All I have of Agnes's voice is two poems, only one of which I know for sure that she wrote and they're both four lines long. I have nothing of her voice. I have accounts of her character which did color the way that I wrote her voice. But it was certainly not based on anything factual. Agnes's voice came out of the blue for me. It was very organic, it was there, and it didn't change throughout the writing process. But I was aware while I was writing her voice that this was the most fictional aspect of the book. Because it was untethered to any source material.

Gardiner: In her essay "In Search of *Alias Grace*: Writing Canadian historical fiction," Margaret Atwood talked about the idea of an audience for the story within the story. In *Alias Grace*, Grace has her audience of one—the doctor. Agnes has the priest, and *Burial Rites* switches from her point of view to his. I wondered if you specifically chose to do that at the end where it would be too harrowing to be in her point of view for those scenes?

Kent: That's true. I borrowed Atwood's methodology initially, where she said that if she could verify something, she had to adhere to it and honor that. She couldn't just change things for her own sake. If she had two contradictory sources, she had to use her wider research to pick the most likely. It was only in outright absences that she could invent. I knew that I always had to include this priest because that was something which I was able to verify, that Agnes Magnusdottir had asked for this particular priest. But in those last scenes, no, I don't think I could have written them from her perspective, because how would you even articulate impending death to yourself as you were experiencing it? I don't think you could. So I reverted back to the priest's perspective—which also I suppose is a way of pointing out that the authorities and their power remain when Agnes is finally silenced.

Gardiner: For all of them, there are spectators in their lives, and in the texts: close-knit communities watching everything they do, and authorities that are watching, or think they're watching, everything they do.

Kent: It's interesting, you have to include those. It's something I do struggle with and I know lots of people have responded, saying, "Oh there's always a villain, it's always the judge or the doctor or the priest"—this "dark trio" as I think Atwood calls them. But that's necessarily so because these people had a huge amount of power. Generally, when you're writing events that include crime and murder and trials, one of these three is going to have a lot of power and they're probably not going to be sympathetically regarded by the people who suffer because of it.

Gardiner: Both books are set at a similar time, touching on that nineteenth-century moment of change, with modernity up against ancient knowledge. In *The Good People* it's the church in Ireland, medicine, and government versus fairy law and the way things have always been done on the land. They're really quite specific moments in both of those countries' histories.

Kent: That was unintentional. But it was a time of change, you're absolutely right. There was this fracture between urban centers and the rural.

Gardiner: And both of those stories found you in a way, didn't they?

Kent: Absolutely. Sometimes a statement like that sounds really naff.

Gardiner: Well, let's just go with it.

Kent: Okay, yeah, they found me. They find you, but they stick with you because of your own interests, whether you are conscious of them or not.

Gardiner: How does it feel when a story takes hold of you like that?

Kent: I think you don't realize it's taken hold of you until it's too late.

Gardiner: These stories have a lot in common, too, being about terrible things happening in cold, compelling places, stories about women alone. Is that coincidence?

Kent: They are similar in setting and landscape. Again, that was by coincidence. I say, jokingly, that I write bleak stories about bleak things happening to miserable people. But, being honest, I don't actually regard my books like that. I don't think of *Burial Rites* as a bleak book in any way. I think it's a sad book. I think it's a tragedy. But in terms of the cold places, Iceland's a beautiful place and a lot of the story takes place in high summer. One of the reasons I wanted to write that book was because I was homesick for this country where I'd lived as a teenager.

It's a place I return to time and time again. It's a beautiful place and I wanted to try to distill that beauty into prose. That was a big incentive for me. In terms of Ireland, when I wrote the second book I wanted to make it a little bit more uplifting. I don't know, looking back, why I thought I could do that, seeing it involves a severely disabled child and the murder of said child. I think with novels, you lead them a little way along, then they lead you. I wrote about 50,000 words of a first draft of *The Good People* where the characters were much nicer and it was dead in the water, pardon the terrible pun. But there was just nothing—there was no heartbeat.

Originally Nora was a lovely, lovely woman and it wasn't working. I knew it wasn't. I think you have these gut instincts about early work particularly. I changed her. So the book, in that case, led me to a darker place that I didn't necessarily want to go, but was what gave it its pulse.

But I'm certainly not averse to writing something slightly more cheerful. I'm also keen to move away from murder as well. I want to challenge myself in different ways as a writer. But it's been really interesting writing two books and looking back and seeing how they've been similar. The writing process has been very different, so I tend to regard them as probably more different than it would appear to readers.

Gardiner: I was conscious of your writing about the weather in *The Good People*, after researching on the coast of Mayo in winter. It was so cold, so, so cold. But it was important for me to feel it.

Kent: Absolutely, I'm with you there. That was really powerful for me because I already knew that my characters didn't wear shoes, for instance. There I am with freezing feet, but wearing boots. What must it have been like for my characters? You can't not include those details. Certain readers of mine have picked up on details like that and think, oh god, misery upon misery. But this is significant, especially when you're talking about the options available to these women and how their choices are curtailed by their poverty. We still have to acknowledge that.

Gardiner: And the psychological impact of the weather, almost like a character in your work?

Kent: It has to be. I think we're dislocated now from the weather. If you live a life which is largely agrarian, of course it's going to have a larger impact. Not only on your state of mind and the circumstances of your day, but also ultimately, eventually, your fortune and your health and all these sorts of things. You have to include it. I like to include it because I love writing about landscape. It's one of the reasons I love Thomas Hardy. I love the presence that the landscape has in Hardy.

Gardiner: You were on a student exchange in Iceland and found out about Agnes's story when you were there. But had you been to Ireland or spent much time in Ireland before the research process for *The Good People*?

Kent: I had been there, but I hadn't spent very much time there. So it was different from my excursions in Iceland. Part of my trip to Ireland was really just spending a lot of time in the landscape. Having done all my research and having an understanding of these people's lives, I wanted to look at the way the landscape and the weather would have influenced their lives and shaped their days and all those sorts of things.

I had spent probably about ten years of my adolescence and teenage years being in a traditional Irish folk band. I'd grown up loving and accessing Irish culture through the jigs and the reels and the ballads and the music. So it never really felt like a foreign place to me. It didn't seem as alien as it might have otherwise been. When I did go to Ireland, it felt familiar to me. It was beautiful.

Gardiner: But you're writing these stories from the other side of the world. There are many Australian authors who do that, especially writing about people from British, Irish, or European history. Do you think that there are different perspectives or challenges at play in that process?

Kent: Yes, I do. I think the more common ones tend to be problems of research and the time that it can sometimes take to access the material that you need. That was certainly true with Iceland for me. But of course, at the same time, libraries these days are increasingly digitizing their collections and it's amazing what you can access. I've noticed a massive difference in what's now available, even in the past five years.

So you have smaller problems like that which tend to be about the practicalities. Things like seeing what the weather's like and the landscape. It's one thing to look at a lot of photos or go on Google Maps or Google Earth. It's another to stand there yourself and live in a place like that.

Other things that I found challenging include the language. Both my books are written in English, but in *The Good People*, for example, my characters would have been speaking Gaelic. Even though I was rendering it into English, it still needed to have a Hiberno-Anglo sort of quality, a particular syntax, a different kind of rhythm. I tried to absorb as much as I could by reading a lot of fiction, especially Irish fiction heavy in dialogue. But it wasn't really until I was sitting in Ireland and eavesdropping like crazy that I got a real sense of it and felt that I could confidently write within that dialect or with those particular intonations and rhythms and proverbs and sayings.

But I think it's actually a wonderful thing to be an outsider writing about a culture and a country and a history that are not your own. Because you ask questions of it that people who are more familiar with it don't. I think that can serve a novelist really well. Probably not a biographer as well, but certainly a novelist. Especially a novelist who perhaps is seeking to amend what they would perceive as a misrepresentation, in the case of Agnes Magnusdottir, or simply wants to come at something from a new angle.

I think of all the stories that I know, Australian stories. I don't think I'd ever be able to supply another representation of those or another incarnation of them, because I don't think I have sufficient distance—my view is not good, I'm not on the outside looking in. It's something that I've absorbed growing up. I would be ill-equipped to interrogate it.

So the most difficult things are those practical aspects of writing a book and researching it and getting your facts right and being able to corroborate sources and check things. But ultimately I don't think it's a hindrance because I think it does offer some new perspectives. I think it allows you interesting entryways into familiar stories.

Gardiner: Are there any dangers in writing about real people from the past? Are there any areas that you're conscious of avoiding?

Kent: I'm very aware that I'm writing about cultures that are not my own, a history that's not my own. There are stories that I wouldn't try to tell because I don't think I have a right to. In saying that, what I mean is that I don't think that I am the best person to tell that story. This is true also of Australian stories.

This is one of the reasons why I spend a lot of time doing my research. Because I don't want to have readers in Iceland or in Ireland contacting me saying, this isn't an accurate portrayal of not only these events but also the way that we live and the way we are. I don't want to offend anyone. Offence is always a risk. So that's why I try to be rigorous in my research and try to understand what it is that I'm writing about and why these things happened. I ask myself those questions. Am I the right person to tell this story? Should it be told by someone else? Am I doing everything I can to ensure that I'm not exploiting these people's lives and that my representation is as likely and as accurate as possible given the sources available to me?

I think that every writer who borrows from real life or even takes someone's name, from the smallest extent to the largest, has ethical obligations. I really do believe that. I know lots of writers do not, but I certainly feel them.

8

The Bionovel as a Hybrid Genre

David Lodge, interviewed by Bethany Layne

Layne: In the last volume of interviews, Michael Lackey noted the need to define "what the biographical novel is uniquely capable of doing." What opportunities does the biographical novel offer, in contrast to traditional history or biography?

Lodge: I haven't read these interviews, and I only found out about the existence of this book from your quotation from it. It did open up a huge area of biographical novels I wasn't aware of. Biographical fiction is different from biography. Respectable biographers regard modern biography as an evidence-based discourse. Everything has to be verifiable, and consciousness, thought, is one thing that is not available, except for the few traces that are left in people's letters, documents, and so on. What people are thinking in time, moment to moment, is not known. I don't know what you're thinking now. Perhaps you know what I'm thinking because I'm speaking it, but that's a special dedicated kind of discourse. So the point of writing a biographical novel is to use the techniques of fiction, particularly those developed in the novel of the nineteenth and twentieth centuries, particularly the device of free indirect style. This is where the narrator's grammar reports what happened to the central character in the third person, but the language imitates the consciousness of that character. Take the case of Henry James: a biographer cannot speculate about what Henry James thought in any particular situation unless James wrote a report of it in a letter or somewhere like that, and this places severe limitations on the biographer. While biographers are often extremely good writers—Michael Holroyd, for instance, is extremely readable, extremely witty and amusing—it's the biographer's voice you're hearing all the time, unless he's quoting from some dialogue that happened to be recorded, or from a letter. And of course the further you go back in time, the less record there is of what people actually said, particularly before the days of tape recorders and similar devices. So the novel is, as I think Susan Sellers said, the supreme form of art for representing consciousness because it can go into the heads of characters. What it offers is interiority. If a novel is about a real person, it can use the clues that are available, the information that is available, to try and recreate what that person's consciousness was perceiving in any given situation. So that's the point of doing it; that's, I would say, the main justification for writing biofiction. It hasn't got the same function as biography, which is informational, basically, and you trust that information. If a text is called "a novel" on the title page, you know an element of imagination has been imported by the novelist who is speculating, guessing, using data that's available to imagine what the person was thinking at any given time.

Layne: As we know, people have written novels based on actual people for centuries, but biofiction offers greater explicitness. So what do you think made novelists feel they had the right to use their subjects' actual names?

Lodge: I think Sellers touched on this, the greater freedom with people's private lives in our culture of exposure. There is also a very noticeable trend toward writing fiction that has a factual basis, not only in the biographical novel, but also in historical novels or novels about current events. There is a book written about this called *Reality Hunger* by David Shields, a kind of manifesto for fact-based writing in which he actually downgrades the novel. It's quite worth reading, but very provocative and overstated, I think. I certainly don't reject the fictional novel, but I think Shields has identified an appetite for fiction that has the imaginative and emotional power of the traditional novel, but also has a guaranteed factual basis, which gives it an extra appeal. I think that this is partly to do with the media, which bombard us with news from all directions twenty-four hours a day. We've to come to rely on fact for truth, rather than the ideal truth or virtual truth of fictional writing, which has to convince by its own integrity and power. It's very noticeable in the last twenty or thirty years that the proportion of fact-based novels, plays, and films has hugely increased, and that must say something about this phase of our culture.

Layne: Keeping with this idea of fact, you provide very extensive notes to your biofictions, *Author, Author* and *A Man of Parts*, where you delineate your diversions from fact quite explicitly. I just wondered if you could say something about where you see the limits of biofiction: does it have the freedom to make things up, essentially?

Lodge: Well, the war historian Anthony Beevor is very opposed to the biographical novel, and has written and given a lecture about it, against it. As a historian, he regards it as muddying the record, by importing speculation that belongs to the novelist into what purports to be a report of a life and thus confusing people. And there is some possibility of that happening, one has to admit, but I don't think you can just resist this by appealing to empirical factuality as the only criterion of legitimate narrative.

Layne: So where would you draw the line?

Lodge: Well, I'll give you an example. I wrote a novel about H. G. Wells, which was a sort of bookend to *Author, Author*. The two books are, in some sense, twins: both are about novelists, about friends, in a way, men with something in common despite the great differences between them. In the case of H. G. Wells, this is a man who had a huge number of sexual affairs, whereas Henry James I don't think had any in a physical sense, though that's a subject of controversy. There's a sequence in H. G. Wells's life when he fell out with a mistress after a long affair. This was Elizabeth von Arnim, who wrote a once-famous book called *Elizabeth and her German Garden*, and had been married to a German aristocrat. She built a house in Switzerland where Wells used to visit her, and toward the end of their relationship, he was being pursued by Rebecca West, a highly intelligent, gifted young journalist. He had kept Rebecca at arm's length, but then he fell out with Elizabeth, partly because of her jealousy. So he left Elizabeth and came back to London, and we know that not long after that he began a relationship with Rebecca West, which was of enormous importance and consequence in his life. We don't know how that actually came about, but we know that it happened. We know that, at some point, they had sex and we know—it's extraordinary how we can know these things—that he couldn't use a contraceptive because there was a housekeeper in the house so he couldn't take her to his bedroom where he kept them. They were necking in his drawing room, and this developed into full sex, which impregnated her and that was how that affair started. If you're writing a narrative, you have to provide a bridge between him leaving Elizabeth and his setting up with Rebecca West. So I had to invent a scene, which has no factual basis, and I did. I imagined a scene when Rebecca West comes out of the Royal Academy just as Wells comes out of Hatchards and he sees her across Piccadilly, through the gaps in the passing traffic. He dashes across the road, greets her enthusiastically, takes her to Fortnum's for tea, chats her up, says, "I've just leased a new flat in Westminster, you must come and see it," and off they go. And that's how it starts—well, I invented that. But I think it's legitimate. If you're writing a novel: you can't just suddenly say "and so, they were already together"; you've got to provide some kind of link. So there's a conversation over tea, in which he can tell that she is interested and that something will come of this. So that's one example, and I imagine that other biographical novelists have done the same kind of thing. But I invent whole scenes like that rather reluctantly, and not if it can be avoided. I like some kind of hook that's in the documents, that I can legitimately connect to.

Layne: Speaking of that integrity, how does your practice as a critic inform your writing of biofiction? Because in *The Year of Henry James* you say that you used to alternate between criticism and novels, and then, of course, in *Author, Author*, you found a way to fuse the two. How does your own history as an academic inform your writing of biofiction?

Lodge: Well, I think that it was extremely useful. I would probably never have thought about writing a novel about Henry James if I hadn't been an academic and studied his work and written about it, and taught it and so on. When I first got the idea, I thought it was a book that I could do as I had some knowledge of nineteenth-century literature, and of Henry James in particular. As you say, I actually alternated these two modes right up until recently, so one feeds the other. I see them as symbiotic; they don't conflict as far as I'm concerned. I think being a critic helps me to solve problems in writing novels. And having written novels makes me a better teacher and critic.

Layne: Do you feel a particular responsibility? Do you think readers are perhaps more inclined to trust the authority of your fiction because of your own status?

Lodge: Perhaps my record as a critic and scholar gives the book a certain guarantee of reliability, but I am sure readers are also sometimes thinking "Where did he get that from? Is that true?" etc. That's why I felt it was necessary to state in the Acknowledgements, etc. at the end of *Author, Author* what the limits of my research were, and I relied a lot on letters because letters are real documents and they are the voices of the people that wrote them. Fortunately, in the case of James, although he burned all the letters he received, a lot of his letters survived, and they're wonderful, very eloquent, well worth including in the story. They give direct access to James's consciousness in particular situations.

Layne: In *The Year of Henry James*, you discuss the particular attention that writers have attracted as subjects of biofiction, and of course both of your subjects are writers ...

Lodge: Very often you have a novelist who is in middle age, or getting toward late middle age, and beginning to wonder if he's got it in him to write another novel, which was my case in a way. When you're young, you're full of the discovery of life and you're having new experiences which go on to middle age: you may get married, have children, all those phases of life. But then there comes a point when you realize that life is beginning to be the same thing for you now, and you don't have the same challenge and stimulus of a new phase of life, and so then you start to look around for somebody else's life that you can write about, or some other subject. You start to research novels more, or I certainly did. And I think that's one reason why you've got this tendency for quite well-known novelists who've never written anything but fiction turning to that form. Julian Barnes is a good example, I think. Not only in his latest novel, which is about the composer Shostakovich, but also the earlier one about Conan Doyle, *Arthur and George*.

Layne: In the case of the two subjects that you've written about, James and Wells, what were the unique challenges? How did they differ?

Lodge: Well, I think the main challenge of writing any biographical novel is actually how you treat the subject's sexual life, because that's the most private part of a person's life: how do you venture to describe that and render it in any kind of detail? The two people I've chosen are two who you could attempt to do that with. I think that Henry James never had a physical sex life, and that he was a celibate homosexually inclined man, which most of his biographers think, although some people, particularly in the queer theory area, contest that. But it's a plausible interpretation, let's put it that way. Wells, on the contrary, had huge numbers of sexual relationships, and he left a lot of traces behind, a lot of passionate letters to Rebecca West, for instance, which give you a very good idea of what his sex life was like. So I felt quite happy to do those two novels, and to touch on that side of the subjects' lives. I don't know that there's any other novelist I would feel bold enough to try and do that with, because it gets rather prurient to invent sexual experiences for real people in a biographical novel. But those two writers I felt I could treat in that way.

Layne: There's a claim by Benjamin Markovitz, that it would be impossible, as he puts it, "to 'do' late James," and I wonder how far that's true?

Lodge: James is fairly easy to parody or pastiche, actually, but it would be disastrous to do so in a novel. I reread *A Man of Parts* in preparation for this event, and I must say I was laughing so much at James's letters, at his critical comments to Wells, the way he would write to a writer-friend in the most elaborate syntax, apparently praising him, but in fact more or less indicating what a mess he thought their book was. I think Henry James is, in that way, a comic character, as well as a tragic one.

In *Author, Author*, the technique I used was free indirect style. It's third-person narrative, so there is a narrator, but it's very much through Henry James's eyes. There are some deviations from James's practice, which was usually to have a single center of consciousness: the chapter about the first night of *Guy Domville*, for instance, and in the first and last "Parts" of the book we see the action through the eyes of his servants at times. But the novel as a whole is focalized mainly through Henry James's consciousness. So what I've aimed at is a style compatible with James's fiction, without being as elaborately wrought as his prose is, particularly in his later work. It would sound incredibly mannered to do that; it would be totally counterproductive. And I don't think that people, that writers, think as they write. You write in a much more formally polished way because, usually, you read and revise what you write about ten times for every sentence, whereas in speech, you're constantly not finishing sentences like I'm doing right now and hesitating, and including "ums" and "errs" and so on. People don't speak in perfectly formed sentences. So that's the explanation, I think: that there is a difference between the language in which one thinks, or speaks, and the language in which one writes. One writes in a more economical and formal and hopefully graceful and eloquent way than one speaks, than one thinks. I aimed at somewhere between the total incoherence of private thought, its wavering nature, and the highly polished, complicated syntax of James's prose.

Layne: My students come to these texts with a fairly limited knowledge of the subjects' works. So I wonder, how do you see your texts working differently for readers with greater or lesser knowledge of the subjects?

Lodge: James has a reputation as being a very formidable writer. The man who edits me at Penguin—his own wife and daughter said they would never have read *Author, Author* if he hadn't been the editor of it, because what they knew about Henry James made him sound so stuffy and difficult that they wouldn't even venture. There is great reader resistance at a popular level to James, so I was pleased that a number of people wrote to me after reading the novel and said "well, I didn't think I would ever read James, but now I'm sort of interested—can you suggest what I should start with?" I always say *Daisy Miller*, and generally point toward the earlier work, because I think if you start with, for instance, *The Wings of the Dove* first off, you may never attempt another of his books. It reminds me of what happened to me. My English teacher at school said "read some Henry James," and I went to the library and pulled out the thinnest book there was in the Henry James shelf, which was *The Sacred Fount*, which is notorious among James scholars for being absolutely incomprehensible, totally perverse in every way as a piece of fiction. So I never read any Henry James until I went to university later. And, in fact, it took me quite a long time to get a taste for James. I think he is a mature taste.

Layne: You speak of the popular resistance to James, and I wonder if the 1990s film adaptations did anything to combat that?

Lodge: Well, it's interesting: James has been very popular with cinema, with filmmakers, and the people who would never dream of reading his novels have gone to see the films and perhaps they have bought the novels and perhaps they've been totally turned off. Why Henry James is so often adapted is very simple: his stories are perfect for film because they're about love and money, and they don't have too many characters, and they don't have too much complication. Really, in most films based on novels the filmmakers can't cope with the amount of plot, and there's not a huge amount of plot in a novel by Henry James; it's just the exploration of a few simple situations. It deals with these issues of love, marriage, money, which are the very stuff of popular literature, popular film, though of course they are done with extraordinary subtlety and complication.

Layne: The very first conference I spoke at was about the literary biopic, and my paper was all about the idea that James's life was "unfilmable," as I called it. I wonder, could you imagine a Henry James biopic, or is the novel the only form that could fictionalize James's life?

Lodge: I think it would be difficult, because it was a life that stretched over a huge tract of time and many different places. So you might possibly try and do a serial of it on television, but it would be difficult to do in a feature film. It was his sensibility that makes his fiction of enduring interest and value; his novels were about consciousness, and because James's consciousness is him, because it's not visible, you can't film it. You can film the circumstances in which people are having emotions but you can't actually film the emotions. Actors can do things with expression and you can do things with music and voice-over. But there are limitations on how much voice-over you can have in a movie before it becomes tiresome. Film places severe limitations on the representation of consciousness.

Layne: I'm interested in the idea that biofiction says something not just about the subject's life, but also about our own historical period, about the contemporary. I wonder what you thought James and Wells had to say about the present, if anything?

Lodge: Well of course Wells is younger and of a later generation; he lived until 1946, so he is more contemporary. James is historically removed from us and belongs to a totally different world, really. He died in the middle of the Great War, and the Great War changed everything, so his life, his sensibility, what he was thinking about, what he was writing about, really belongs to the historical past. Wells was a different kind of writer; he liked to get his hands dirty and he did affect the way society was developing. He was into politics in a very big way, and he was a remarkable thinker who anticipated so many things, including the internet. I think you can still read Wells, even though many of his books are not very well written, and find interesting things in them which are still relevant to us, to our lives now.

Layne: As a final question, could I invite you to speculate about what James and Wells might have thought about biofiction, and particularly their own appearance in it?

Lodge: Well, we know what James thought! He hated any kind of intrusion into his private life; he never gave interviews except once when he gave an interview to the *New York Times* in order to support the British war effort, which he threw himself into and identified with. It was designed to be propaganda, but he insisted on seeing the text of the journalist as a condition of doing the interview, and he probably rewrote the whole thing. He uttered Shakespeare's curse against biographers: "Don't disturb my bones." And he burned all his letters to prevent them from doing so. James's autobiographies are about his early life and only give a glimpse of his life at the time when he was writing. One of the reasons that justify trying to reconstruct his mature life in a novel is that we don't have any real traces of what he felt in that period, except from his letters. Whereas Wells wrote his autobiography, and I don't think would have objected at all to my writing a biographical novel about him, James I'm sure would have objected very strongly. And *Author, Author* was, in a sense, a very unlucky book. I'm sure you know that another writer, Colm Tóibín, was writing a novel about Henry James, which overlapped with mine in terms of the material, something I discovered three weeks after I'd delivered my novel to the publishers. It was lucky that I didn't know this before or I might have given mine up in despair. But it came out six months before mine and I'm afraid there's a kind of law in entertainment and the arts generally that if there are two things that are almost identical the first one will take all the attention, and that happened in my case. So I thought it was an unlucky book in that way, and there were times when I thought that maybe James's curse was actually being thrown my way. But then I thought "Colm Tóibín did alright out of it, so it can't be that!"

[Floor opened for questions]

Questioner A: I haven't heard any mention today of autobiofiction. I'll give you an example: V. S. Naipaul's novel, *The Enigma of Arrival*. He calls it "a novel," and it's about the only thing in the text that would make the naïve reader think so. Is autobiographical fiction something that you yourself recognize and attempt to write?

Lodge: I'm writing autobiography myself, and I see this as a wholly factual kind of discourse. I mean, that's what it should be. Of course, there is an element of construction and editing and self-presentation in all autobiography; we know that it is a kind of fiction. No autobiography can be a totally honest, unbiased, objective portrait: I don't think anybody's capable of doing that about themselves, actually. Even if you set out to be perfectly honest, as I think Wells did. He called his work an experiment in autobiography, and I think the experiment was—by contemporary standards—to let it all hang out. But of course he didn't, particularly his sexual life. Although he did write a postscript, which he left to be published when he was dead and all the women in it were dead. Very honorable of him!

I think that autobiography is different from the biographical novel. Of course there are various ways of doing it; some people write their autobiographies in the third person, which give them a novelistic quality. Salman Rushdie wrote about his experience with the fatwa in the third person, under a pseudonym, which was the one he used to lie low. Coetzee has written several autobiographical novels in the third person. These are marginal experiments, hybrid forms, but the biographical novel is a hybrid itself, that's the point of it. In my biographical novels, I aimed at a seamless marriage of imagination and documented fact, so that the reader should have reason to trust the discourse, but will be taken into areas of the subject's life where the strictly empirical biographer can't go.

Questioner B: E. L. Doctorow wrote a novel called *The Book of Daniel*, very strongly based on the life and trial of Ethel Rosenberg. It's a fictionalized version of what would happen to children whose parents were executed by the US government for espionage. In that case, one of the things I always wondered is: "Why didn't Doctorow actually name the Rosenbergs? Why did he have to invent these children?" And that question leads me to a broader question. What do you think the novelist loses by not claiming his or her sources? The writer always has the option of making it all up. Instead of writing about Henry James, writing about an invented novelist; instead of writing about a specific historical figure, using an invented historical figure. So, what is gained by naming someone? What is lost by making all of it up?

Lodge: I think it depends on what the writer wants to do. If you choose a historical figure, then, in some ways, the problem of getting the reader to believe in the story is partly solved, because if you use your sources accurately then the context you're providing reassures the reader, as it were. If you say at the beginning that all the letters are real letters, then there is a documentary element in the novel, which persuades the reader to trust the story. If your priority was not to create this illusion of fact, of factually reporting this life, then you wouldn't do it and you would be free to use your imagination and make your characters do whatever you feel you want them to do, whatever seems interesting. A novel like that is a kind of thought experiment, you just develop a situation, the characters build up, and the story begins to grow organically by its own impulse. The types of novel, of fictional discourse, are innumerable, so the choice depends entirely on what kind of effect you want to have.

Questioner C: You drew the distinction between Henry James as a seemingly asexual subject and H. G. Wells as a comparatively sexually promiscuous subject. Beyond that appeal to write about someone completely different in that respect, what was it that drew you to H. G. Wells as your next writer and subject, rather than somebody else?

Lodge: The idea of writing a novel about H. G. Wells arose through writing an introduction to his novel *Kipps* for Penguin Classics, and my research into Wells and his life at that time. I had enjoyed writing *Author, Author* so much—though not publishing it—and I liked the form, which seemed to suit my time of life, when I was running out of ideas for fiction. So I looked into Wells's life and learned more about it than I knew before, and found it a terrific story. I discovered the existence of his relationship with Edith Nesbit and her husband: what an extraordinary scene that was, this batch of Fabians and all the affairs they were having. Edith Nesbit is generally thought of as being the kind of middle-class respectable person that she was writing for the children of. But in fact, she was married to a very promiscuous man, and had brought up a child that he fathered on their housekeeper. It was a bohemian life, in other words, and it was also one that took place very near Eltham, a place near where I grew up in South East London. I knew already that James and Wells knew each other, but the more I looked into that the more interested I became in their relationship. Wells wrote one of the kinder reviews of the first night of *Guy Domville*, when he was just starting as a journalist and had only been to two plays in his life. As a result, when he moved to the south coast, near Rye, he met James and they formed a friendship. James rather enjoyed being a sort of patron. He regarded Wells almost as his protégé, being younger, and of course that produced tensions later on as Wells became more successful in a public way than James. So, I began to think, "well golly, this is really good material!" It's material that is similar to that which inspired me to do *Author, Author*, which was being asked to do a television adaptation of *Trilby*. I read *Trilby* for the first time and thought it was absolutely terrible; I couldn't imagine how I could turn this into a television show to please a modern audience. But I found out that Du Maurier offered the story of *Trilby* to James, and it became the best-selling novel of the nineteenth century, at a time when James was struggling to sell even a few copies of his novels. *Trilby* was also put on successfully as a play, whereas James was booed off the stage after five years of trying to make a career as a playwright, and gave up the theatre in despair. During the same time period, his friend Constance Fenimore Woolson, with whom he had a complicated relationship, probably committed suicide, in Venice. All of this came together; it just fell into my hands. It seemed to me it was an irresistible subject. Wells turned out to be more difficult because his life was longer—I couldn't give it the same unity as I did with James by using the *Guy Domville* night as a hub to the whole novel. And so the Wells novel is more of "a loose baggy monster" as James would call it, almost perforce. The unity I gave it was to follow a series of women in his life, five key women and the relationships he had with them, and how he bounced from one to the other, which gives you a panorama of British social and political life for about half a century. I enjoyed writing both novels immensely, and I'm very happy with them.

This interview was conducted as the final plenary event of the Postmodernist Biofictions conference at the University of Reading on March 25, 2017.

9

Contested Realities in the Biographical Novel

Colum McCann, interviewed by Michael Lackey

Lackey: The biographical novel first became popular in the 1930s. But it was only in the 1990s that it had become a dominant literary form. With regard to the biographical novel, the Irish are particularly important, as Oscar Wilde was one of the first to author a theoretical reflection about it. The aesthetic objective is not to accurately reflect the life of the biographical subject. Rather, it is to use the life of the actual historical figure in order to project into being the author's view of the world. Can you talk about your biographical novel in relation to Wilde's reflection about the form?

McCann: First, I want to dispute the idea of a biographical novel. For me, as Clifford Geertz has said, the real is the imagined and the imagined is real. James Joyce's Leopold Bloom is as real a figure to me as, say, my great-grandfather, who was what we might call "a biographical figure." For me, Bloom becomes a biographical figure by reading him into being. I don't see a big distinction between what is created in the imagination and what actually, historically, supposedly occurred. My grandfather was alive on June 6, 1904. He would have been six or seven years old. I only met him once—in a nursing home in London in the 1970s. But I got to "know" him in a profound way by engaging imaginatively with the language of Ulysses. And through this act of literary creation, through Leopold Bloom, I also get to know myself. So you have to question: how imagined was Leopold Bloom, and how real was he at the same time? And it's not just the idea of the biographical that I struggle with—I have problems with the words "fiction" and "nonfiction." What is fiction? Fiction means to shape, but nonfiction also means to shape. To my mind, the journalist and the biographer are shaping things as much as what the fiction writer is doing.

Lackey: But they have different truth contracts, don't they?

McCann: What does that mean?

Lackey: The biographer makes a tacit contract with the reader. The biographer basically says: "I am going to try to give you a picture of this person's life with as much precision as possible. I am not going to strategically or consciously alter facts about this person's life, and I am not going to convert this person's life into a symbol or metaphor." Given this contract, we would never say to a biographer: your biography fails because you didn't portray the subject's life in a way that would enable me to better understand my grandfather's life. Novelists are different. They unapologetically change facts about an actual historical figure and they usually convert their biographical subject into a symbol with which readers can connect. To give you an example, Russell Banks said to me in an interview, "In my novel *Cloudsplitter*, Owen Brown narrates his story in the year 1903, but in real life, he died in 1889." I asked him why he made that change, and he said, "My novel's about the mind of the terrorist, and I wanted to show that that mindset is still alive in the twentieth century. In order to convert Brown into a symbol, I changed some facts." We would get really angry with a biographer for making such a change, and we never critique a biographer for failing to convert the biographical subject into a symbol. But with biographical novelists, we expect them to do something very different, something metaphorical or symbolic. You certainly did that with your Rudi Nureyev, who you claim was a symbol of the Soviet Union. Your biographical subject was supposed to be symbolic, something that could be used to connect with and represent other figures. So how would you respond to these different truth contracts?

McCann: The truth contract is an interesting notion. Let me try to answer your question by talking about Julie Kavanagh's biography, *Nureyev*. Julie, who had been working for years on her biography, was very generous about my novel. In fact, she told me she envied me because of the sheer latitude I had. Whereas she had to follow the absolute logic and facts of his life, I made some wild shotgun leaps. I could spend forty pages on a single night in a New York nightclub, for instance. At the same time I could leave out four years in one fell swoop. That section of the novel was an exploration of language, dance, rhythm, sound, sex, celebrity, and much more. She envied me my freedom to engage on such an intimate, microscopic level. I don't want this to sound disparaging to Julie's book, which was wonderful, but the friends of Rudi, who knew him very well, and who had been interviewed by Julie and read her biography, felt that the novel captured the character of Rudolf Nureyev as much if not more profoundly than the official biography. I was able to get to the intimate texture, the pulse of the moment, if you will.

Lackey: But there is a contradiction here. On the one hand, you say that novelists, through their latitude and freedom, can give readers a more textured biographical reality. On the other hand, you say in other interviews that you were not really that interested in Rudi Nureyev. That you were more interested in the nurses, the rent boys, the soldiers, and the shoemakers. Also, you just gave me an example of the way you get a better sense of your grandfather through Leopold Bloom, so there's something about this fictional figure that's different from a biographical subject. You are not really doing biography. You are doing fiction, and fiction gives us a sense of Rudi Nureyev. And yet, it also gives us a sense of the present and the future. Can you talk about this dual temporal component to the biographical novel?

McCann: It's very true that I wasn't really interested in Rudolf Nureyev. In fact, I knew nothing about him at first. And I really didn't care about the world of dance. But I cared about the fact that Rudolf Nureyev's story would only be told by those who were "officially engaged" with his life. By those whom he directly touched. Particularly by those in power, whether that be creative power or political or social. That the "biography" would default to those in power. And that the historian was sort of obliged, by the nature of how history is told, to go to those particular official stories of Rudi's life and rely on them and their form of truth in order to write the official account. But I was much more interested in the story of Jimmy Smallhorne, a working-class friend of mine from Dublin who was mesmerized when he saw Rudolf Nureyev on television. It was a story like Jimmy's that mattered, and that was my beginning of stepping into the biographical novel. The feeling that I wanted to be loyal to John Berger's notion that never again will a single story be told as if it were the only one.

Essentially, the job of the writer is to go into those anonymous corners of human experience, and kick up the intimate dust, maybe even reconstitute it. To say that one story belongs to all of us, and these stories can be written in a myriad of ways. I do, of course, use certain key people who are to help narrate the story. I use the mother; I use the father. But I use the supposedly anonymous figures too—the shoemaker, the rent boy, the maid. I know there is a massive responsibility here, especially if you are making things up and claiming it to be "true." And this raises questions about naming him Rudolf Nureyev or not. It was one of my editor's questions. But from the very beginning, I knew I had to call him Nureyev. Otherwise the novel itself would have no validity. Even though it was probably 90 percent imagined, I knew that it would not be valid if I invented his name.

Lackey: Why is that?

McCann: Just a gut feeling. Sorry, I wish I had a better answer, but it was pure gut. I felt that if I named him Ilya Denisovitch or something like that, I wouldn't really give a damn about the character. He wouldn't feel "real." And then I suppose I was proposing that these fictional characters that I created were actually as real as Nureyev himself. I was trying to go to the heart of what is actually true, and who gets to tell the truth, and who gets to own the truth, and who gets to shape the truth, and how do we know what is true anymore? Rudolph Nureyev's friends who read Julie's biography and then read my novel phoned me in London when the book first came out. They said they had been playing a parlor game among themselves to see who I had talked to because they found it very real, very honest. But, in fact, I didn't talk to any of them. I stayed away from anybody who knew Nureyev whatsoever. And so they invited me for lunch and they said, "So, well, how did you know this? And how did you know that?" Little intimate things about his body, for instance. Or his relationship with the shoemaker. They were shocked when I said that I had imagined it entirely. They said, "Well it's all true, and we love the novel." But do you know why—truly why—they liked the novel?

Lackey: Why?

McCann: Because they weren't in it. Because I wasn't intruding on their form of truth. And then they could project themselves imaginatively into any character they wanted to be. And they could tell the truth of what was imagined by negotiating their own experience. It was textural for them. It wasn't me dictating the truth. They didn't disagree with the novel, but they disagreed with the official biography! For instance, they said of Julie's book: "I was with Rudi that night. He was wasted, but he wasn't doing these other things she said he was doing." So the novel somehow seemed truer to them. This is not patting myself on the back, I hope. It says more about the reader than it does about me. The readers were able to go in there and reimagine themselves and affirm or even deny their own experience, in a way, through their own imaginative relationship to the text. They used fiction to make sense of reality.

Lackey: In 1957, Irving Stone gave an important lecture titled "The Biographical Novel." He authored a number of pop-culture biographical novels. In his lecture he said, "My focus is not so much on history; it's on character." In an interview, Julia Alvarez helped me understand this approach. Her biographical novel *In the Time of the Butterflies* focuses on the Mirabal sisters. When Julia was finished with the novel, she sent a draft of it to the surviving sister Dedé. When Dedé read the novel, she asked Julia:

how did you know that my sister kept a diary? Julia said that she didn't know that, but she made the inference on the basis of the logic of character. From what I can tell, biographical novelists do not privilege facts or history when constructing their narratives. They privilege character, and they believe that through character they can give readers a truth that is significant and important and can be used to illuminate so much more about the culture. For them, historical and biographical facts miss something of crucial importance that fiction can access. How would you respond to that?

McCann: I essentially agree. Character is important, but even more so is the language. Language is the fulcrum of it all. Plot, to me, is juvenile. It doesn't matter all that much. This is not saying that I want to invent everything. I want some of the facts to be correct, and I want the history to be texturally correct. I don't want to pervert the idea of what happened. If I'm going to mess with the facts, I want them to be as close as possible to what's true. Or to ground the truth somehow. So that the reader says, "Ah yes, that seems correct."

For example, I'm writing this novel set in Israel and Palestine right now. One of the characters has a daughter who gets shot. It's based on a true story in the West Bank in 2005—she gets shot with a rubber bullet. She had just bought candy, and I knew she paid a shekel for the candy. I asked an Arab friend what sort of candy was available at that time, and she gave me a whole load of different types, but one of the candies that you can buy is a string of hard sweets that form a bracelet. That's wonderful, I thought, a detail that the reader will absolutely remember: a candy bracelet on her wrist when she was shot. So I went and interviewed the father, and I asked him: "What sort of candy did Abir have?" And he said, "Well, she'd bought this little sleeve of hard candies that she had in the bottom of her schoolbag." I am now torn between the image of the bracelet of candies or the little plastic tube at the bottom of her bag. Which one am I going to use? I don't know yet. I am in a dilemma as to what things I should change, especially since I'm writing about a nonpublic figure. With Rudi it was easier. Rudi was a celebrity. The world already presented many versions of what was "true" about him. It seems to me that a measure of celebrity and a measure of public appearance give the writer more license to fudge the truth than if the person, or the character, is unknown. I'm well aware that there's a contradiction in that, but I am large, as Whitman says, and I contain multitudes.

Lackey: Joyce Carol Oates did a wonderful biographical novel about Marilyn Monroe called *Blonde*, and she said that she smudged Marilyn Monroe's character. I asked her why she did that, and she said because she didn't want people to think her character was just Marilyn Monroe, that her character was actually connected to the reader, and that there are certain features and dimensions of her Marilyn Monroe that become symbolic of all people, even men. Because this person in your current novel is unknown, you feel a need to respect his story. But does this mean that this person's story will have less symbolic or metaphorical significance than, let us say, your Rudi Nureyev character or your Frederick Douglass character?

McCann: No. And that's where it comes back to your point about facts and history and all of these things colliding. You know what's most important? I say language is a premium in everything. Language, feeling, music. The music of how a story gets told. The way it makes you, the reader, feel. The way it makes you come alive in a different body, in a different time, and allows you imaginative access to be somebody other than yourself. That is achieved through language. Yes, character is enormously important, but it's secondary to language because language makes the character.

Facts should be used properly and carefully, but they are not supreme. Language is supreme. You have to treat this mighty weapon with respect, because in the wrong hands it can really do bad things. And in relation to the biographical novel, especially if you're toying with notions of truth, you better be really careful. There is a big moral responsibility here. The moral responsibility of the writer becomes more acute when he or she is dealing with a situation or a character who happened to have actually existed. And the less known that person happens to be, the more acute the responsibility actually becomes. I have the chance to tell Bassam Aramin's story. He has told his story in other places, but there is probably not going to be an official biography on the shelves anytime soon. So I have a real responsibility to get his story right. I talked with him about this, and he said, "The only responsibility you truly have is the responsibility to my grief." How beautiful is that? And how perplexing? And how intimidating? It is a real minefield for me. I had a similar dilemma with George Mitchell in *TransAtlantic*. Senator Mitchell lives six blocks down the street from me in New York. I knew I wanted to write about peace, and the novel wasn't even so much about George Mitchell, but I wanted people to feel what it was like to be a man dedicating his life to the notion of peace. And I thought, "I'm going to have to do this, but it's a real story, he has a wife, children, and how am I going to do this?" So I wrote a letter, and his wife, Heather, wrote back to me. She loved *Dancer*, and she said, "If anybody can do it, you can. When do you want to interview the Senator?" And I said, "Well, I don't want to interview the Senator. I'm going to go away, and if you give me four months, I'm going to try to imagine what it was like for him." And so I did. And when I got the first draft done, I sent the manuscript to her, to get her take. And she called me up and she said,

"How did you know this stuff?" She said, "I only talked to my husband about where he might want to be buried two weeks ago. I'd never talked to him about this before." But I had posited that he'd want to be buried on a certain cliff in Maine. That was just my intuition. There's nothing really mystical or crazy about that. It's just you knowing your subject well enough and feeling your subject out, imagining him deeply enough. But she also told me certain things that I got wrong: "You know what? He would never wear brown shoes. Not on my watch." And so I had to change that. So I was doing the exact opposite of what a journalist would do. The *exact* opposite. I approached my subject and said, "Will you let me write about you?" They said yes. I went away and imagined it. When I had written it, I gave it to them to look at, and there were certain things that she thought were wrong, certain things that they couldn't believe were right, but in general they liked it. I went through three drafts with her until she then showed it to him. *Then* I interviewed him. And *then* I went walking with him, and subsequently he became a friend. But a journalist would never do that. And so it was a different approach. I don't think even the guys who were doing the New Journalism in the early 70s ever took that sort of approach. With this new Israel-Palestine novel, I'm going to show it to these two men beforehand and let them tell me exactly what it is that I'm getting wrong. It's important to me to get it right, or as right as possible.

Lackey: But this begs the question what it is that you are getting right. Let me give an example. In 1967, William Styron published *The Confessions of Nat Turner*. The actual Nat Turner dies in 1831, and we have no evidence that he ever had a homosexual experience. But he does in the novel. A lot of writers were furious with Styron, especially black writers. But Styron was very close friends with James Baldwin, and Baldwin encouraged him to write from a first-person perspective. Baldwin was actually living with Styron at this particular time. Baldwin was gay, and I would suggest that the homosexual experience was included in this novel, in part, to get to a certain kind of truth. What was the mental orientation that enabled people to violate blacks with impunity in the year 1831? And how is that same mental orientation operational in 1967 in order to justify violence against both blacks and gays? Styron included the gay scene in order to illustrate how those same structures are at work in both times against two separate groups of people.

McCann: You think he was conscious of that?

Lackey: I'm pretty certain because he says that his novel is as much about his time period as it is about 1831. But the truth he is giving readers is not biographical truth—Turner was probably not homosexual. Styron gives us a truth about social, political, and mental structures of oppression. I wonder if you could specify or define the kind of truth you give your readers. I know you don't like to be defined because you feel straitjacketed and boxed in. But I do think it is useful for us, especially in this time when Fox "News" is manipulating and controlling and disseminating false "truths," if we can be a little bit more precise about the kinds of truth biographical novelists give readers. And when it comes to truth, I see a tension in your writing. On the one hand, you are reluctant to be didactic. On the other hand, there's a real commitment to social justice in your writing. I would even say a kind of anger about the horrors of history. So I wonder if you could talk about this tension in your writing, but also the kinds of truth you are trying to access and represent in your work?

McCann: What I hope I'm going for is what Faulkner describes as an emotional truth. The human heart in conflict with itself. And I want a reader to suddenly recognize the complexity of the situation that the character or the characters happen to be in. And for them, for whatever brief moment, to be flared alive into the spirit of contradiction. And have them pose questions of themselves. The purpose of good art is not to give answers but to pose the proper questions. The priority of language is to embody the world rather than make it tell something absolute about the world. To embody us in wakefulness. So I believe that Styron was trying to wake people up. What you try to do is to knock people's comfortable balance off, just a little bit. Certainly in relation to this new novel that I'm working on, I'm really interested in knocking people's balance off. What's true, what's not true? I'm inventing things left, right, and center, even in the center of "historical truths." To me it is the apex of the fictional project for me. I'm taking it to its nth degree. I have pushed it fairly hard, even to those places where I refused to go in the past. God forbid, I might even be a character in this new novel!

We are being pushed toward these questions of what is true and what is not. But why? Why is this happening? It seems to me that these questions are politically important. Recall Colin Powell holding up a photograph of those infamous chemical tankers. Because we are told that this is X latitude and X longitude, we acknowledge the reality of the fact that there are tankers on the ground. And we trust Powell because he is in uniform, and he says, "This is a fact." But then he spun a fiction out of this fact. That particular "fact" contributed to many hundreds of thousands of Iraqi deaths. This manipulation of what is true and not true is what the contemporary novelist is flaring up against. So lives are at stake. And you have to work out of a reckless inner need to challenge and interrogate this notion of what is true, what you can trust. And so, my responsibility within a novel is to be honest to the texture of the time. Be honest to myself. Not to be didactic, not to tell people how to think or what to think, but *allow* people to feel. Allow people then to go in and question it themselves. To open up the moment for a little while so that others can peek inside and see what we don't want or refuse to see.

Lackey: With biographical novelists, there seems to be two separate approaches. For instance, when many critiqued Styron and his novel, he said, "Look, I'm not giving you history. I'm not giving you biography. What I'm giving you is a metaphorical diagram that you can use to illuminate what happened in 1831 but also what happened in 1967." Oscar Wilde has a different approach. In his play *Salomé*, which is based on the figure from the New Testament, he was using her in order to create an unapologetically sexual female. So like Styron, he is basically saying: "I'm not giving you history and I'm not giving you biography." Rather, he is using history and biography to invent something new. So there are two separate approaches: one is a biographical novel that creates a metaphorical diagram so that readers can illuminate the past and the present. The other biographical novel actually tries to bring into existence a new reality. Would you put yourself in the Styron camp of using biographical figures to create a metaphorical diagram so we have a new way of understanding both the past and the present, or would you say that you are trying to create a new reality through your fiction?

McCann: I'd be more in the former, though I'd like to be in both. In relation to *Dancer*, one of the things that I wanted to do was to stress this simple notion that every story matters. So no matter what rung you are on the supposed social ladder, you have a deep engagement with the world and your story is valuable, whether you are a rent boy down on 13th Street, or whether you are a soldier in the fierce cold of the Siberian forest. That somehow, all of these "anonymous" lives have an effect on history as we know it. An unacknowledged effect on history. To say: we matter. And one of the other things I was trying to do was to expand the notion of Irishness. I felt that I had a responsibility to my background, to my culture, and to my own history, and to remain an Irish novelist even though I live in the United States. One of my goals was to write a novel that would inevitably be an Irish novel that doesn't even actually once mention Ireland. And what I mean by that is that if I could go home with my novel, that we wouldn't be continually looking inward as a culture, wouldn't be continually critiquing our Catholicism, continually critiquing our nationalism, continually critiquing our engagement with the church and the hierarchy, but that we are somehow opening ourselves up and moving in new directions. What I wanted to do was to say that this culture is ours too—this Russian culture, this gay culture, this celebrity culture—and these other stories that seem to sit outside our immediate experience are actually available for us, and we can live them too. That seems to fit into the metaphorical diagram that you're talking about.

Lackey: Let's be more specific. In *TransAtlantic*, Douglass undergoes a transformation. When he first starts lecturing in Ireland in the 1840s, he has a limited understanding of universal freedom. He can't imagine that the Irish could be enslaved. But he has a transformation, and by the time we meet Douglass in the 1880s or 1890s, he focuses on female emancipation. But there is an even later transformation, which we get from the postcolonial scholar David Manyaki, who says that Douglass bought himself out of slavery while in Ireland, but that he went back to the United States "unslaved." So there is an evolution in the character of Douglass, which enables readers to understand complexities. What readers get is a truth about the nature of our condition. Many of us want to use simple binaries to categorize our situation: you are either slave or free. But you do not let us get away with that. By the end of the novel, you are asking us, "Look, I want you to think more deeply about what constitutes our condition. Are we really free?" My interpretation of your novel is, well, no we are not. The most we can say is we are unslaved. And this helps us understand Douglass in a new way. Can you talk about the Manyaki character and how he relates to the evolution of the Douglass character, especially in relation to Ireland and the Irish.

McCann: If I opened up my computer right now and went back to the very earliest versions of *TransAtlantic*, I would show you that the first two pages belong to David Manyaki. I originally wanted to write the story from his point of view. He was going to be in a university in Northern Ireland. And I wasn't quite sure what was going to happen to him, but I was going to create this fictional character who was important to me. He was Kenyan, and there were all sorts of overtones in relation to Obama and present-day scholarship. So yes, I definitely wanted to address colonialism and postcolonialism. I wanted to have an African scholar coming to Northern Ireland of all places, engaging with the process of peace, but also talking about Frederick Douglass from 150 years before. At that stage, the transatlantic flight was not included, and I worked for months trying to capture that voice of Manyaki, but I didn't have the voice in me, at least not yet. So I went about it in a different way. I thought it would be a wonderful tension at the end of the novel to have this African man come in, from a wealthy Kenyan background, married to a white Irishwoman. And it was incredibly important for me that he owned the house at the end of the novel because originally he owned the beginning of the novel. That he is the one who now has that territory. And he would be using it as a summer house of all things. There's the suggestion that maybe Hannah is allowed to go back there at times. There's a little prologue at the start of the novel that contains clues to everything the book is about.

Lackey: I want to come to this in terms of the Irish context. The years 2003 and 2004 are really important for the Irish and the biographical novel. You published *Dancer*, Colm Tóibín published *The Master*, and Emma Donoghue published *Life Mask*. These are three spectacular biographical novels. What I also find fascinating is that they all deal with the homosexual lifestyle. They resonate, because these are stories that, as you say, really matter. And to be quite honest with you, the homosexual lifestyle did not matter in the 1940s, 50s, or 60s. I have two questions for you. One, why the Irish? Why are the Irish doing this in 2003 and 2004? And why are you specifically writing biographical novels? And I don't think that it is an accident that Ireland would legalize gay marriage about ten years after the publication of these three novels. To my mind, great writers are the unacknowledged legislators of the universe. They forge the uncreated conscience of the race, as Joyce says. I believe that writers can do that. So I want you to reflect, just a little bit, about the role of the biographical novel in forging a new consciousness?

McCann: I don't really know what led us all to write about this at the same time. We all grew out of an education system that was brand new and *very* democratic. We were all more or less in our forties then. There were debates in Ireland about the homosexual culture. It was a topic of the times, or it was about to be. In Ireland we still had sodomy laws on the books and vile things like that. And I don't know what it was about the Irish imagination that felt that it could open this debate up a little bit. I love the notion that we could be the unacknowledged legislators or the unacknowledged or alternative historians of human experience. But I don't know what was in the air. I leave that for you to come up with. I can't think of any particular reason that we would all sort of go to that zeitgeist.

Lackey: I wonder if it has something to do with the political situation of the Irish under English rule. Mario Vargas Llosa and Sabina Murray recently published biographical novels about the Irish revolutionary Roger Casement. What I find extraordinary about that story is the degree to which the English were able to use Casement's homosexuality to demonize him, to control him, to dominate him, and to eventually destroy him. This was all part of a process to discredit and debunk his searing critique of English colonialism, specifically the English in Ireland. So why are the Irish producing such smart and insightful biographical novels in the early twenty-first century? I think part of the answer has something to do with the Irish recognizing how these structures of oppression function, and the biographical novel is one of the best aesthetic forms to expose these structures, because the Irish are highly attuned to issues of agency.

McCann: I was thinking of Joyce.

Lackey: Exactly, they are all thinking about forging their own reality.

McCann: I think there's definitely something there. We all grew up in the South and we were all relatively middle class. We were a product of that new education system that came about in the 1950s. And of course there was the issue of Northern Ireland and growing up during the Troubles. And being able to look at Northern Ireland was certainly important for me. My mum was from Derry, my dad from Dublin. I spent a lot of my summers up north. I've always been interested in those notions of oppression and the suppression of stories. Also, the feeling that this story wasn't *really* getting told in Ireland, and that it was time for us to sort of break out and open new turf.

Lackey: Biographical novelists seem to be focusing on the interiority, and they're not as committed to objectivity. In fact, they tend to think about mystery. Colm Tóibín addresses this idea wonderfully in *The Master*, the idea that art liberates the subject into mystery, that the novel is not trying to define who we are but is trying to set life into motion.

McCann: To recreate life out of life, as Joyce said.

Lackey: That's right. But there's a real commitment to mystery too. And I think this is inevitable when authors focus on a biographical interior?

McCann: Yes, mystery joining things together. The classic example, for me anyway, was approaching the story of Senator Mitchell. I said, "I want to write about you. I'm going to imagine you. You are going to get access to it, and we will layer the facts on later." And that's often what I do—I go into the realm of the imagination. The facts come later, and the fact-checking comes later. That's another thing that's very important to me that's perhaps incidental to the conversation. I meticulously try to get things absolutely right. So when I wrote *Dancer*, the novel went to dancers, it went to historians, it went to gay activists, it went to all sorts of experts. I probably got opinions from at least twenty-five specialists.

But let me return to my current novel *Apeirogon*, the title of which means a shape with a countably infinite number of sides. So many books—including my own previous attempts perhaps—try to explain what's going on in a logical, handcuffed manner rather than embracing the incredible chaos of being. Allowing people to understand that we have to embrace confusion has become increasingly important to me. We need to hold contradictory notions in the palms of our hands at the exact same time. But increasingly there is this move toward the simplistic, and people with just one idea becoming part of the central cultural landscape. You are a Democrat. Or you are a Republican. And your political party wants you to be as stupid as they need you to be. There is an overwhelming feeling that you can't embrace nuance quite as agilely as we used to. There's this refusal to accept opposing ideas, an ability to recognize that our own ideas can potentially stand in perfect opposition to one another. And maybe not just two ideas, but maybe eight, ten, twelve ideas are all helixed together in this complicated stew. So my engagement with Israel-Palestine is to confront my own complete ignorance about it. And then to perhaps say to the reader, "Your ignorance is valuable, you know? Your confusion is valuable. Here, I'm going to go ahead and confuse you in the weirdest way."

And I suppose that's part of my own engagement with the novel, be it biographical or otherwise. As I get older I want to throw as many colors as I can at the canvas. I want to "Pollock" my own work. I want to wake myself and confuse myself and even frustrate myself in the hope that I can discover something—maybe even something simpler—that I've overlooked about the human project.

10

The Biographical Novelist as Cultural Diagnostician

Anchee Min, interviewed by Michael Lackey

Lackey: Let me start by asking you a general question about all of your biographical novels. You have written biographical novels about Tzu Hsi, Jiang Ching, and Pearl S. Buck, but you make use of the fictional more in *The Pearl of China*, which is about Buck, than you do in your first three biographical novels—the character Willow from *The Pearl of China* is an invention. This stands in stark contrast to *Becoming Madame Mao*. At the beginning of that novel, you say that "every character in this book existed in real life." What are the virtues and potential dangers of including a fictional character in a biographical novel?

Min: I'd think that virtues or dangers would depend on how an author handles his/her material. There is no right or wrong, except whether or not it would fit. It also has to do with what an author's ultimate goal is. I love entertaining my readers, but my ultimate goal is that readers walk away with solid knowledge of China. If the original stories are loose and the narrative unfocused, as was the case with my early draft for *Pearl of China*, then I had to fix the problem. I ended up combining characters in order to give the story a clear focus. To me the process was like making clothes—it has to fit the body. If in real life the story comes naturally dramatic with leading characters in place, like Empress Tzu Hsi (Orchid), my treatment becomes different: handling the story would be like handling an antique—the less I touch and patch, the more valuable it is.

Lackey: Does that mean that Pearl S. Buck needs some extra touches?

Min: The character "Pearl S. Buck" did not, but the Chinese character "Willow" did. Bringing out the essence of the character was a big deal for me. I love the challenge. In the case of *Pearl of China*, if I had followed the original characters and wrote them as is, I'd have to spend a lot of time explaining where each character came from and their relationships with Pearl. I'd lose my readers on the way. So I created "Willow" to fix that problem. I claimed *Pearl of China* as a fiction so readers would not be confused about what they were getting. Readers told me that they were more satisfied because they found my story "real." Many readers come in quite well-informed. To me that's terrifying and exciting at the same time. I wanted to deliver a story that'd meet the readers', as well as my own, expectations, and in the meantime serve justice to history.

My experiences in China helped me create "Willow." She was a fictional character but she was real to me. I grew up with "Willows." My childhood was spent alongside the great Yangtze River in the town of Nantong, Jiangsu province. Pearl Buck also grew up in Jiangsu province (town of Zhen-jiang). The cultures and traditions were similar. I was familiar with the people and place. "Willow" was based on three women whose lives Pearl Buck touched, and they her. The Chinese characters played the supporting roles in *Pearl of China*, but "Pearl" was the main character.

Lackey: Can I ask a question about Hsu Chih-mo, who is considered one of the most renowned Chinese poets of the twentieth century? It seems like you were suggesting that there was a romantic relationship between Buck and Chih-mo. How much evidence is there to support that? And did you take any liberties? In other words, did you fictionalize some of that relationship?

Min: Well, allow me to first refer to an interview in your *Truthful Fictions* book. One author says: "We are not cameras; we are not recorders." To me, where I come from, mainland China—even with cameras, recorders, and reporters, you won't always find the truth, or get to know a person. That was especially the case in the 1980s and 1990s. While I was unable to dig out truth, or evidence of truth from interviewing people, I was able to connect the dots. For example, Pearl Buck described Hsu Chih-mo's hands in her own words. Her emotion was a telltale sign. She depicted the way he sat in her house for hours on end. They were enjoying a long conversation. I could feel the sky getting darker, the moisture in the air, the fragrance of the fields, the smell of southern China. She went on to paint the picture of the way he looked, and his hands, "like a piano player's, long fingers, beautiful as a woman's." Her adulation and affection were more than obvious. And he kept visiting her, sitting in her house, chatting into the night. What do you think they were doing? At the time, she had difficulties with her husband, who was not around. Hsu Chih-mo was known in China. He was a literary icon by today's standards, a talented, romantic, sophisticated, and handsome man in his thirties. As a poet, he was a publishing phenomenon. She was unpublished, and she struggled to get her foot in the literary door. It's only natural for her to enjoy his attention and friendship. Educated in England, Hsu Chih-mo recognized Pearl's talent and made an effort to befriend her. He encouraged her to keep writing. He visited her to satisfy his own needs, I'd believe—there must be a hunger in his mind no traditional Chinese woman could fill. (I identify with such hunger, or anxiety. I returned to China after living in America where all of a sudden I no longer felt I belonged. I suffered a nameless loneliness.) It would take a similar mind, a mind that combines Western and Eastern worlds and cultures to ease that anxiety. If Pearl S. Buck didn't have much to offer, she was equipped to offer that ease. And it would be an intimate exchange. A spiritual connection. That was my "evidence" to support "the romantic tension" between the two.

Lackey: So do you think that biofiction is basically trying to give us more speculative forms of biography? That it is ultimately about getting the biography of a life right? Is that what it is really doing?

Min: To me, it was a necessity to be able to speculate. For example, people say that Mao and Jiang Ching didn't have a love affair. Biography had eyewitness records that Mao and Jiang Ching were outside a cave "warming up to each other." Then the couple went into the cave, and shut the door behind them. Since there were no eyewitnesses, biographical accounts had to stop at the door. Did that mean "nothing happened"? To what extent could we speculate and at what depth? When the couple came out, Jiang Ching was pregnant, and Mao married her. What doesn't make sense to me was that historians chose to ignore Madam Mao Jiang Ching's own account—her shout at the Chinese court when she was sentenced to death. It was played out in front of China's national TV. Jiang Ching cried at the top of her lungs, "I was the only woman who followed Mao through rains of bullets and cannons! I was his wife for 38 years!"

Lackey: Let me ask you something about the nature of fictional characters. David Ebershoff has written a great biographical novel about Einar Wegener, the first person to have a sex reassignment surgery—Einar became Lili Elbe. Even though *The Danish Girl* is about Einar and Lili, Ebershoff says that "there is universality to Einar's question of identity." Would you say the same about Jiang Ching? Is there something universal in her story? Something that could enable people today to better understand the nature of their condition or their struggle to create self? This is something you do so well in your novel. On the one hand, Jiang Ching is a wicked person; she does some really horrible things. But she is also this person who is struggling mightily, as a woman, to try to gain a foothold within a culture that is denying her any kind of power simply because she is a woman. So I'm curious. Do you see her as more than just a biographical figure that you're narrating? Do you see her as a symbolic figure that can represent a larger struggle? And if so, what is the nature of that symbolism?

Min: I actually do not go that far. I was just taking care of my immediate task to give the characters flesh and blood. You talk about the biographical and biography. I felt truth is limited if the only legitimate way to collect evidence or express truthfulness was to follow where the cameras and tape recorders go. In reality even eyewitnesses often offer different versions of the same event. For example, the moment the Maos met. I kept all four eyewitness accounts in the book, because I couldn't pin down the one version that was 100 percent accurate and correct. I decided to "leave it to the readers." It was a bit distracting, but I'd like to remind readers that historical moments were viewed through different lenses. Characters could be dressed up or dressed down. It's good for the readers to know the difference.

I think biographical fictions add dimension to history. It gives a necessary tool to enter the doors that were closed. For example, with Hitler, we have the dates when he started his Nazi movement. With Mao, we have no dates when he started the Cultural Revolution. No dates or any interview revealing how the idea came to Mao and the moment he decided to act on his idea. There was no paper trail. With biographical fiction as a format, I was able to connect the dots. I began by first establishing what's going on in China with Mao as its president. Mao took over China in 1949. Ten years later millions of Chinese died of starvation, and the dying continued on a large scale. This told me that Mao conquered China but failed to manage it. His political rivals, the vice president and ministers were called to take over. This told me that the people of China were losing faith in Mao's leadership. I concluded: Mao was in fear, fear of losing his power. For Mao to start a "Cultural Revolution" calling "to return power to the grassroots" was an excuse and a disguise. Based on the outcome of Mao's action, the fact that he succeeded in getting rid of his vice president and his circle, Mao's intention could easily be figured out. What interested me the most was Madam Mao Jiang Ching's role on this real-life stage. She became Mao's political partner after decades of living as the backyard concubine. "I am Mao's dog, Mao asked me to bite, I bit!" She shouted at her sentencing, "I have the guts to tell my stories with Mao, do you have the guts to listen?!" These are fantastic lines I didn't have to invent.

One liberty I took was creating a conversation between Madam Mao and her daughter Na. I invented the scene. It was after Mao died and Madam Mao was in prison. She asked her daughter to help smuggle her memoir to be published in the west. Her daughter refused. She was trying to protect her father's legacy. So disappointed was Madam Mao that she ended up committing suicide. I could understand the mother-daughter relationship. Based on what I knew about the character of Jiang Ching, a woman of extreme passions, I speculated/imagined what she would say to her daughter. Years later in a Shanghai bookstore I ran into a memoir written by Jiang Ching's former secretary. His eyewitness account of the mother-daughter fight/conversation was a page as if lifted out of what I wrote. I was thrilled and pleased.

Lackey: Let me shift to a different topic. In *Becoming Madame Mao*, Jiang Ching plays the role of Nora from Henrik Ibsen's *A Doll's House*. This chapter reveals a lot about the function of art in exposing the subtle structures of oppression. As Jiang Ching says to Zhang Min, Nora lives in "an invisible cage," and Jiang Ching goes on to say that she knows "what it's like to be a prisoner." Can you talk about the way your novel illuminates the invisible cages that imprison Jiang Ching and women more generally?

Min: My grandmother had bound feet and she said to me, "Women are grass, born to be stepped on." Born a female, and you are already a loser was instilled in Chinese woman by the culture. Mao and his Communist Party won China by promising Chinese women equal rights. Madam Mao Jiang Ching became "Mao's Flag-carrier" based on her own background, the girl who tore off her feet-binding cloths.

Lackey: But the bound feet is a visible cage. What your novel does, in my estimation, so brilliantly is to explore and expose invisible cages. Jiang Ching feels confident that she is going to be able to do something powerful. She has a deep belief in herself. She sees herself as a peacock instead of grass. But she slowly realizes that no matter how skillful she is, no matter how intelligent, no matter how gifted, the men ultimately are going to crush her. At one point she realizes, "I'm either a prostitute or a concubine in this world." She sees these invisible cages that are really holding her in. So there's a difference between the visible cages of the bound feet of your grandmother to the invisible cages that hold Jiang Ching captive, who sees herself as having the ability and right to be more liberated.

Min: The invisible cage started with the visible cage. My grandmother taught me, "Learn to hide your broken arm inside your sleeve." It was her loving advice that a female must learn to surrender herself, and understand her place in life in order to survive. The tradition was an invisible cage. It was a "torture-chamber." I felt I was shut in as soon as I learned how to walk. As I grew I realized that the invisible cage, the unjust, was not so much from men and society. It was from myself. A sense of worthlessness had been molded into my cultural DNA. When I write about Madame Mao, I might not have sympathy for her, but I have absolute compassion. For one reason, I saw that Jiang Ching and women who were like her were deprived of understanding. It was my opinion that lack of education caused Madame Mao to turn out the way she was. By fate she was given a platform and great power. She had the microphone. She was under one man but above the nation. Yet she ill-used that microphone and ended up a villain in the eyes of history. The fact that she was proud to be "Mao's dog" was her true tragedy.

Lackey: There seems to be a stark contrast in your novel about Madame Mao. Jiang Ching lacks education, but there is Fairlynn, who is based on Ding Ling, and she is really well-educated. Ding Ling wrote the brilliant short story "Miss Sophia's Diary." Why did you change Ling's name to Fairlynn? And also, Fairlynn tells Madame Mao that she is working on a novel titled *The New Nora*. Can you briefly talk about the significance of that title insofar as it functions within the context of your novel?

Min: I changed the name from "Ding Ling" to "Fairlynn" for two reasons. Firstly I felt that this is an important character, and I wanted my reader to be able to remember her name. I kept the sound "Ling." I had readers tell me that they can't remember Chinese-spelling names. Fairlynn was Western-educated. Having an English name for convenience would be acceptable. Secondly I wanted to create a contrast. Fairlynn was the opposite of Jiang Ching. Fairlynn has something Jiang Ching did not have. The two women competed for Mao's affection. Fairlynn challenged Mao to explore her mind. To me this added a dimension to Mao as a character who was curious and had an appetite for excitement and inspiration. The fact that Fairlynn and Jiang Ching were at each other's throats makes interesting drama. Jiang Ching was the prettier one, so Mao went to bed with her. Ding Ling (Fairlynn) was an avant-garde type. She believed that in conquering "the emperor" she'd conquer the world. For a while she thought of herself as Mao's equal. But Mao turned out to be a beast, the man-beast that Fairlynn couldn't control. I was especially interested and fascinated by the fact that she frightened Mao. The way Fairlynn could see through Mao, projecting and delivering his thoughts before he did, frightened him. Mao hated to be figured out.

Lackey: But why have her working on a novel called *The New Nora*? And why have her tell that to Jiang Ching?

Min: That's Fairlynn's way of showing her feathers. She looked down on Jiang Ching and didn't bother to hide her feelings. She got punished during the Cultural Revolution when Jiang Ching ascended to power. It's not unlike an Imperial backyard concubine story. Fairlynn said to Jiang Ching: "I'm not Madame Mao, you are. But I'm better, freer and richer in spirit. I am a professional writer . . ." But was she? better? The educated women and a large portion of China's intellectual community, Ding Ling among them, supported Mao's Cultural Revolution at the beginning. They were the ones who ran Mao's propaganda machine and as a result harmed the nation and eventually themselves. The "New Noras" escaped their "doll houses" only to serve Mao who became their ultimate master. The character Fairlynn was my vehicle to convey this message.

Lackey: All of your biographical novels focus on women. To what degree are your biographical novels an attempt to reimagine the lives of demonized women and/or to correct the historical record about specific women and women more generally?

Min: I am not conscious about to what degree. I just wanted to give readers a balanced view of China rather than what was offered by the market. I was shocked by the Western establishment on the history of China. For example, the account by Sir Edmund Backhouse, coauthor of *China Under the Empress Dowager* (1910) and *Annals and Memoirs of the Court of Peking* (1914). Backhouse wrote: "My intercourse with Tzu Hsi started in 1902 and continued until her death. I had kept an unusually close record of my secret association with the Empress and others, possessing notes and messages written to me by Her Majesty, but I had the misfortune to lose all these manuscripts and papers."

There was no way the empress of China could possibly receive a non-Chinese man. She was watched by hundreds of maids, eunuchs, and Imperial guards. Edmund Backhouse's biography and memoirs were an assault on China and its history. Yet his lies were considered credible scholarly works and they shaped and influenced Western views of China.

Lackey: By this logic, are you saying that art is a weapon? It could be used as a weapon in a positive but also a very negative way. If so, this raises a really important question. Could somebody say that your novel *Becoming Madame Mao* is a dangerous book, that it does something really socially unjust? I imagine that you would say that your novel is socially just. But why? Why would it be a socially just novel? What is it about you that differentiates your work from, let us say, what Madame Mao was doing?

Min: Some Chinese scholars have a very different view of Madame Mao. They believe that she was one hundred percent evil. That's fine. People are entitled to their views. My view is: Madame Mao first and foremost was a human being, and must be interpreted as such. I was interested in understanding the circumstances under which Jiang Ching existed. Older generations of Chinese still hold on to the mindset that every downfall of a dynasty was the fault of a concubine. This was how Chinese history was written for thousands of years. I offer a different perspective.

Lackey: So do you think that the Chinese scholars would denounce your book as irresponsible or unjust?

Min: I have already been challenged many times. I don't mind. I enjoy the debate and discussion.

Lackey: But you don't think the book is unjust or irresponsible. You think that biofiction can contribute to diagnosing cultural ailments, to actually improving the culture at large. How does your novel do that?

Min: I do think biofiction can contribute to diagnosing cultural ailments. The perspective I offer was a wife of thirty-eight years of marriage to Mao. Her triumph was also her tragedy. It was an anatomical study for me. I dissected Madam Mao, her complexity. I tried to explore her strong will, her bravery, and her wickedness and greed. She loved to call herself "Mao's most faithful student." One thing she learned from Mao was "ruthlessness." Put out your enemies before they get you. It didn't bother her that millions died in Mao's fight to hold on to his power. The story of Madam Mao Jiang Ching is a package mixed with good and evil. I am interested in women's journey, especially the interior journey. I rejected altering core characters and events. I understood my book could sell better if I did that. I had claimed my books as fiction after all. But I fear misleading and misguiding, given the current ill-understanding of China. I let go of the temptations to make use of my artistic license, for example, to make Empress Orchid, Tzu Hsi, and her beloved general, Yung Lu, consummate their affair. I had my line to draw in terms of how far I'd stretch my material.

Lackey: That's right. There's that tension throughout the whole novel, and as a reader you are actually hoping that they will get together.

Min: I just couldn't do it. I was so tempted. Obviously, they were in love. It moved me during my research when I discovered that everything he did was to help her. And everything she did was to protect him. They were spiritually married. Soul mates.

Lackey: And this gets to a real key point. The issue is intellectual honesty. One of your narrative techniques in *Becoming Madame Mao* is this: Madame Mao says something, and then the novel shifts into the third-person narrative. And the third-person narrative oftentimes corrects Madame Mao. If I understand you, what you are saying is that what makes your novel more responsible and more just is that you have an abiding interest in accurate representation, to give us a more fact-based truth rather than some sort of subjective truth that is going to serve a political agenda. Is this the kind of distinction you are after?

Min: Yes, I'd say so. In my first draft, I started with Madame Mao's own voice, just first-person narrative. It was based on a lengthy article she wrote about her life in Shanghai. It was published by a left-wing magazine in which she described herself as a "revolutionary," and the Shanghai art circle as "hypocrites" and "arm-chair revolutionaries." Her voice was so convincing that I, and as well as my readers I was sure, wouldn't be able to help but buy her story and regard her as a heroine. The problem was that it was not an honest account.

I learned the true story behind her claims by accident. To make a long story short, I must burden you with a bit of the history of my own life: When I was nineteen, while hoeing weeds in a cotton field in a labor collective near East China Sea, I was picked by Madam Mao's trusted lieutenant in charge of propaganda films. A production was set into motion to pave the way for Madam Mao's takeover of the presidency after Mao's death. I was chosen only because I had a "correct face and figure," which fit the ideal image of Madam Mao's "Proletarian heroine." In the middle of my screen test, Mao died. The date was September 9, 1976. Two months later Madam Mao was overthrown, and I was denounced as her "trash." As a punishment I was ordered to sit in the audience to listen to crimes Madam Mao had committed. Horrible stories were told by newly released prisoners, who were former Chinese elite writers, producers, directors, and actors. They depicted the dark side of Madam Mao. They explained why they were jailed by her orders. They each described personal relationships with her. Eyewitness accounts. Tremendous details, materials which later served me well as I wrote *Becoming Madam Mao*. The accounts contradicted what Madam Mao Jiang Ching had written about herself. She was a grudge-holding, C-rate actress who saw no chance of winning as a movie actress. Denouncing the Shanghai art circle was her ticket into Mao's arms. She joined the underground Communist Party and ran to Yanna where Mao's Red Army headquarters was. Jiang Ching proved to be a brilliant actress on the real-life stage. She delivered a great performance ending with her becoming China's first lady. She didn't stop there. Her ambition was to become Mao's successor. She went out of her way to silence and wipe out the witnesses who knew "too much" of her history. She was nervous about the exposure of an incident when she was arrested as an underground Communist and released after she denounced the Communist Party. It was a "stain" she must erase. Recreating her personal history to fit the role as a future leader of China was the goal. Her "political purity" was her pass to power.

If I'd go with Madam Mao's own voice, she could take over the story. What would be lost would be the real story. So I decided that the format has to be dual, the third-person voice has to come back to correct the first-person voice.

Lackey: It is in that technique that you are able to give readers a responsible truth, and it is through that responsible truth that you can promote a more just world. Am I getting the logic right then?

Min: Yes, it is like the title of your book *Truthful Fictions*.

Lackey: A key moment for you, which you describe in your memoir *Red Azalea*, is when you were manipulated into denouncing an American teacher named Autumn Leaves as an enemy of the people, despite your personal feelings to the contrary. Throughout *Becoming Madame Mao*, you picture how Jiang Ching feels it necessary to eliminate those who know that she denounced communism when she was a young woman. In both cases, political ideology leads people to betrayal and violation. Can you briefly talk about the way literature exposes the power political structures and ideologies have in justifying the violation of people? And, to be more specific, how political ideologies can brainwash people to believe that what they are doing is right, even when it ultimately damages oneself and others?

Min: I was eleven years old when I denounced my favorite elementary school teacher. It was in the middle of the Cultural Revolution. People around me denounced their parents, their grandparents, neighbors, and colleagues. If I were not American-educated, I would not choose to expose my shame. If you ask a mainland Chinese about his/her role in the Cultural Revolution, the mostly likely answer would be that he/she was a victim. Nobody would take the responsibility and admit that he/she was a participant as well. People seem to conveniently forget, or have chosen to forget that we were the water that floated Mao's boat. I wanted to show how a child was transformed into a monster by political influences and brainwashing.

Lackey: I knew a little bit about the Cultural Revolution before I came to your books, but I didn't know it the way I now know it. And what's fascinating is I've been talking to some of my friends, and I have been explaining to them that what's happening in America today with Fox "News," the way it demonizes intellectuals and universities and is firing up a lot of the uneducated masses against intellectuals and the universities, parallels what happened with the Cultural Revolution in China between 1966 and 1976. So, to my mind, one of the most gratifying parts of reading both *Becoming Madame Mao* and *Red Azalea* was that I was able to say, "Not only did I learn all this about China, but you gave me new ways of thinking about what's happening in the United States today." Could you briefly talk about how literature enables us to see these structures so that we can fight them in ways that were not fought in China during its Cultural Revolution?

Min: China embraced communism precisely because the majority were poor and illiterate. We created chaos and destruction against our own best interest. We tore China apart and the country went backward for decades. America perhaps is going through its own Cultural Revolution. What was similar was the tremendous faith the uneducated masses had in their leader. Mao was a people-game player. He knew how to rock his base. A billion people were fooled.

Instead of "Make China great again," Mao said, "Men of humanity should refuse to preserve his life at the cost of that humanity."

Lackey: We have time for one more question. The historical novel came to fruition in the nineteenth century. This aesthetic form underscores how major historical events shape and determine human interiors. By the late nineteenth and early twentieth centuries, there was a revolt against the idea that history totally controls and determines human interiors, so some writers started to reject the historical novel and started to turn to biography in order to foreground human agency. This is when the biographical novel came into being. Can you briefly talk about your motivation for writing biographical novels within the context of the need for and the limits of human agency?

Min: It's about delivering a picture of complicity with whichever tool you end up using. Also it depends on the material writers have, how much material, the quality and quantity of it all, the degree to which the authors understand the material, and the depth of their knowledge, their knowing (or not knowing) and understanding. Secondly is their own experience and maturity as an independent thinker. I would not be able to create what I have without these components, and plus talent of course. Sadly in many cases, in the creative writing world, hard work doesn't necessarily translate into winning.

For twenty-seven years in China I was not an observer; I lived the events. I did not, like a writer/observer, live to chronicle the events. I was the event. The life experience enabled me to grasp the essence of China. My American education and thirty years living as an American have given me the understanding and perspective that there are different ways of portraying/reflecting on one thing. The goal was to get close enough to the picture of the truth and deliver knowledge and understanding. In terms of "aesthetics," I'd interpret it as the name of the vehicle/tool. I'd like to give a reply borrowing a line from former Chinese president Deng Xiao-ping (on achieving China's economy), "White cat (socialism) or black cat (capitalism), whichever cat catches the mouse is a good cat."

11

Speculative Subjectivities and the Biofictional Surge

Rosa Montero, interviewed by Virginia Rademacher

Rademacher: This book follows the path of an earlier book of interviews with US authors, who have written biographical novels. By representing the life of a real person with the aim of turning it into a fiction, the biographical novel distances itself from purely biographical aims, and instead plays with multiple possibilities of invention. The intention of the editor of that book, Michael Lackey, was to better understand why the biographical novel had come to be, why it has grown so substantially, and why it held appeal for so many writers at that moment. Lackey noted that earlier there had been only a handful of really good biographical novels written by authors such as Arna Bontemps, Zora Neale Hurston, William Styron, and Gore Vidal, to name some standouts. But, beginning around the 1980s, this genre suddenly became—almost overnight—very popular with both writers and readers. He wanted to better understand the reasons for this change, and to see if it was possible to define the essential characteristics of this genre or movement. This collection of interviews with US authors generated so much interest that it seemed a good idea to the editors at Bloomsbury to expand the conversation further with an additional book of interviews, this time with biographical novelists globally.

From your perspective as writer, cultural commentator, and journalist, have you observed this surge in the biographical novel, and if the answer is yes, is this equally the case in Spain? If so, what might be some examples that come to mind?

Montero: Personally, I love biographies. I have written two biographical collections: *Stories of Women* (*Historias de mujeres*) and *Passions* (*Pasiones*). I love the novel, too, but the novel is a different thing. The problem is that I'm not a fan of most of the biographical novels that are being published right now. I think this is primarily because of their commercialism, something that sort of cheapens them. For me, this success seems largely superficial.

Since we're living in a world marked by so much acceleration, and we're all so rushed and pressed for time, lots of people think that reading a biographical novel, and the same could be said of the historical novel, is an easy way to learn things. I think this is one of the reasons why the biographical novel has been so commercially successful, and these sales are part of the reason why many writers are writing books of this type.

One doesn't write a novel to simply illuminate through images or illustrations, let's say, the biography of another person, but to try to better understand the world, to search for the meaning of existence. And many biographical novels don't do this. They illustrate a person's life by shedding light on that person's life, nothing more. As a result, many biographical novels fall short both as novels and as biographies. You don't have any sense of what's been invented or not. Of course all biographies, like all histories, are in some sense subjective, but there still needs to be a documentary element which you can decide whether or not to believe. There have always been exceptionally great novels that have included real people as characters, but they have used these real figures as a means to this broader search for the meaning of existence. One that I love and that is really recent is *The Widow of the Van Goghs* (*La viuda de los Van Gogh*). It's by an Argentine author, Camilo Sánchez. I just read it a few months ago. It seems exemplary to me in the way that the author uses the life of Van Gogh, the character, to tell a greater story about the nature of existence.

When you write a novel that aspires, as I've indicated, to better understand the world and you use a real-life character whose life becomes embedded within the story, and who is not only there to illustrate the life of this person, then yes—you can produce really great novels. In fact, what I am especially fond of is when a novel is not constructed around the life of a particular real-life character, but when all of a sudden real-life characters appear in the book who are not the protagonist but who traverse the novel. There are a number of examples of this type of novel which are superb. For example, the Cuban-Puerto Rican author, Mayra Montero has a number of wonderful novels of this type. There is one called *The Messenger* (*Como un mensajero tuyo*) in which Enrico Caruso appears. The novel draws from the experiences of Enrico Caruso when he went to perform in Havana in 1920. But it's not at all a faithful representation of Enrico Caruso's life. It's a novel that's meant to be a novel. Or, another of her novels in this vein is *The Gentleman from St. Petersburg* (*El Caballero de San Petersburgo*), in which the ex-revolutionary Saint Francisco de Miranda has a prominent role. In my own book, *The Story of the Transparent King* (*La historia del rey transparente*), I include the real-life figure of Leonor de Aquitaine, but she is just one more character in the book, and she has to appear because I'm telling a broader story that involves her. But if I simply wanted to read about Leonor of Aquitaine in order to learn about her life, I am going to read a biography by Jean Markale, or something by another historian, so that I know that what I'm reading about her is true, or at least documented. What tends to be categorized as biographical novels in the bookstore are the types of books I don't really care to read.

Rademacher: Yes. This is what I was saying before about biofiction, about the biographical novel—that really what distinguishes this trend is that these works aren't trying to be biographies but very clearly novels. The best of these works incorporate real people in order to illustrate certain things, to question, revise, or illuminate certain aspects of a reality. They're not at all intended to be read as biographies, but rather as something that very clearly examines the real or the historical "truth" from a point of greater freedom and often suspicion.

To clarify somewhat what distinguishes biofiction from biography and from novels that refrain from including real-life characters, I'd like to explore more what you've said in a number of your novels about the recent surge in literature of this mixture of the real and the fictional. For example, you've written before (in *The Crazy Woman in the House*) that "literature today is experiencing a period of profound hybridity in which what stands out is the confusion of genres." Could you talk a bit more about what you mean by this hybridity and confusion of genres, and in particular with respect to the coexistence of the real and the fictional with which biofiction is experimenting?

Montero: Well, the fictions we create, the novel—these are in reality an expression of the dreams of humanity. And dreams represent our unconscious; they surge from our subconscious, right? And the subconscious of humanity is undergoing changes, just as obviously the society is changing—and so our myths, our ghosts, our obsessions, all of this is also changing. Our vision of the world affects our subconscious. So, obviously, today one can't write those great novels of the nineteenth century, as much as I adore them and think they're marvelous—because they don't represent the way we experience the world in the twenty-first century. Today, if you go out into the street, for example, and you ask the first person you see—regardless of where they're from—and you ask them, do you think there are many versions of yourself, of your identity, and they'll absolutely say yes. We already start from the assumption that within us are multiple selves; we don't believe in the self as a cohesive identity anymore. Before, we understood identity as something holistic and largely unchanging across a trajectory: you had childhood, then adolescence, and everything was scheduled along a certain path. But now, everything is chaos.

Rademacher: Life is uncertain for sure.

Montero: Yes, totally uncertain. And it always has been, but now we are much more conscious of this uncertainty. The twentieth century has been the demolition of the real, hasn't it? The century began by focusing on the relativity of time and space, then we were told the act of observing alters that reality and Freud spoke to us about the subconscious. . . . We all live this chaotic world and of course literature reflects this world and in turn our subconscious, and in turn our dreams, and in turn the type of fiction that emerges from this context is murky, turbulent, fragmented, completely mixed-up in all sorts of ways. What we end up with is literature whose identity is completely a hybrid of influences or genres. If in the past, there appeared to be a world of difference between reality and fiction, today the border between fiction and reality is completely blurred; fiction and reality are so tightly interwoven that all novels in some sense can be read as autobiographies, and all autobiographies are uncertain. And out of this what has emerged is a more formalized subgenre called auto-fiction in which the author himself or herself appears within the novel, an author who can purport to represent the real person or who can be completely fictional. And here we see reinforced what we discussed earlier, that if not even the self is trustworthy, certain, then of course one way to represent this reality in fiction is through the multiple selves of the author, all of which can just as easily be fictional as anything else.

I have done this quite often because I play a great deal with the borders of fiction and reality. In my most recent novel, for example, I appear as a character. I appear as my real self in a chapter but this also works to undermine this certainty because I explain to my character that life is also imaginary and I think that this helps my character within the novel; in this same novel, there is another character named Ana Santos Aramburu, who within the novel is the director of the National Library and who is in reality a person with that same role, and the poor thing—she's a friend of mine—had no idea that I was writing a novel with her as a character, so when I finished it I sent her the first draft so that she could let me know what she thought of her character. Luckily, she was happy with how it turned out.

Likewise, I did this a great deal in *The Crazy Woman in the House*, playing intentionally at misleading the reader. In truth, *The Crazy Woman in the House* is the most interactive book that I have written in my life because I included so much complicity in the game that I play with the reader. I created it in a way that the reader engages with the book thinking that it is autobiographical, but of course I am lying the whole time. There I am in the pages of the book, and in reality I appear to be this same person, but the me in the book is not me at all. In *The Crazy Woman in the House* the reader is made to believe that I have a twin sister, something that is not at all true in reality. In fact, the book is dedicated to this made-up twin sister. Moreover, the central chapter in the book, the one exactly at the center of the narrative and that seems to be the most important, is supposed to be about the childhood disappearance of my twin over a period of three days and the silence surrounding this event, but of course all of this is also imaginary, totally fictional.

And I think that this reflects very accurately the perception that I have of the world, a world that is unstable, confusing, a reality that could fall to pieces at any moment and leave everything in shards. For me, the relationship between reality and fiction is so porous and slippery that there are lots of occasions in which I'll be recalling something that happened ten, twenty years ago let's say, a while back, and when I'm remembering it, I'll ask myself, "Did that really happen?" Maybe I dreamed it, or perhaps I have written it, or maybe just imagined it. I don't know. Because for me, moreover, all of the four possibilities have the same weight of veracity. This memory of something is the same whether or not I lived it, or simply imagined it, written or not.

Rademacher: Perfect. You've already answered one of the questions I had about *The Crazy Woman in the House,* but continuing along these lines, in this work you refer at multiple points to the experience you have just mentioned in which one becomes lost—whether among real, geographic streets and places, or amid other intellectual and psychological spaces—this sensation that you evoke so well with the sudden disappearance of your imaginary twin sister, Martina, or as you describe using the metaphor of a whale in *The Crazy Woman in the House* as the "vestiges of vastness that submerge and the world is left silent and soundless and so very empty." Does this sensation of becoming "lost" in your view connect in some way to the mixture of biography/autobiography and reality/fiction that you experiment with in this book? Or, put another way, how might one best express this existential and ontological uncertainty through a specific genre or literary form?

Montero: Well, this is what I was saying before, I have the sensation that life is very tenuous, in essence that you can become lost at any moment. The truth is you can always wander astray, become lost to yourself; I experienced this for example in my twenties, attacks of anguish in which I really felt like I was losing contact with reality and with rationality, something I don't think is all that uncommon. It's not by accident that the majority of us writers started writing in childhood. And I think that one of the reasons perhaps that we are novelists is because we are more conscious of our deception. We talked earlier about how each of us is really many selves, right? But perhaps we are more conscious of this disassociation, or more open to it. Thus, you have this sensation that one can always become lost, including to oneself. Yet, being a novelist is still wonderful. I have always said that it gives you permission to be schizophrenic, because you are free to live your life in other lives, and at the same time it allows you to live your life in a more controlled fashion because you enter into these other lives and these help you to imagine other ways of seeing and understanding the world. And this same outlook of the novelist that enters into the life of a character, and this character tells him or her their story, is the same approach that I use with my biographies. My biographies are not conventional in the sense that although I stick firmly to the documentary facts, what I do is to build up these factual details with a type of character map, and so I immerse myself in the life of the biographical subject the same way I would with the imaginary characters that I invent. And while in biography you are obligated to respect the factual details, of course once you enter into a life, you try to see the world from that character's perspective and from that vantage point you grasp things that more orthodox, more externally focused biographers would likely not have captured.

For example, in the case of Marie Curie, I have read tons of biographies and other information about her, but no one else has observed something that I think is there. There is a general agreement about the first class scientific work Marie Curie made in the first part of her life. She was in the vanguard in the sciences, a groundbreaker, and nevertheless that in the second part of her life all of this was no longer the case. She wasn't any longer a scientist of the first order; she wasn't in the vanguard; she wasn't a groundbreaker. In the beginning some people said—in an altogether sexist way—that these changes happened with the death of Pierre, that he was the brains. But this has been shown not to be the case because in addition to her journals, we have the work that she did. So, what really happened? There is an explanation. When Marie Curie is able to isolate the radium, she sends a letter to her father and tells him about it. Her father, who was a professor of chemistry and lived in Warsaw, answers her "well . . ." with this patronizing tone, "Well, that's good that at last you've isolated it. Given all of the time you've spent, that's good that you achieved it." And he adds, "What a shame that it won't amount to anything." And five days after sending this letter, her father died, so in essence these were the last words she received from him, the last ones after the success of isolating the radium. And what did Marie Curie do during the rest of her life? She looked for practical applications for radium. Doesn't it seem like these two things are connected? Well that's what Marie Curie "herself" communicated to me once I began to immerse myself in the facts of her life. But this is not included in any biography. Because the traditional biographer would remain at more of a distance. This, then, is part of the enjoyment of creating biographies in this way. I don't fictionalize the facts. It is simply the effort to enter into the head of another person in order to see the world from that other subjectivity.

Rademacher: It seems to me that what you express coincides interestingly with what Julia Alvarez has said in an interview about *In the Time of the Butterflies*. She spoke about her decision to write the story of the Mirabal sisters as a biographical novel and to fictionalize their stories. She describes a type of truth "that is more than historical truth," that includes those facts, but that also aspires to what she hopes to achieve with a novel, "the emotive, the *lived* reality of a certain moment and its drama, and the intimate experience of the character living it." As well, she has said that the biographer also has to delimit the character, and that there is as much risk in distorting the life of a person in this form as there is in fiction, except that fiction offers the opportunity of competitive truths. This makes me think, too, of what Jay Parini refers to as a kaleidoscopic perspective, in which one can show multiple facets; there is not one singular perspective that overtakes the others. I'm wondering about the relationship between this concept of a kaleidoscopic story with what you have described as the capacity to play with the "what-ifs" through which the novelist "experiments with these potential lives."

Montero: Well, you've said a number of interesting things I'd like to comment on, but I'm not sure I agree completely with the words that Julia Alvarez has used, because, as I've suggested already, if I want to know about the Mirabal sisters, I want to read a well-written biography. If I read a novel in which the Mirabal sisters appear it is to know something more, not only about their lives. I can be fascinated by novels in which real individuals appear as characters, but only when these characters are used to try to better understand the world in its greater complexity.

Rademacher: Yes. Maybe the term for the biographical novel in Spanish doesn't translate or conform exactly to the concept of biofiction that I am trying to communicate. The idea of biofiction really has to do more with what you have been discussing. It is not simply an intent to depict a real life via a character, but to utilize this character to question a monolithic or dominant version of reality, and to open it to other possibilities. It is the effort to better understand the human experience.

Montero: Okay. I see what you're saying.

Rademacher: Returning to this consciousness of "playing with the what-ifs" as you express it, I am thinking also of an aspect that Michael Lackey has discussed as central to the new aesthetic of the biographical novel—inductive imagination. Lackey observes that in contrast with the novelists of so-called nonfiction, who negate a more global vision, the writers of the biographical novel immerse themselves within the life of a historical figure—as you describe doing with Marie Curie—in an effort to offer understandings that better cross cultures, and that from a dual temporal perspective, give us access to a more critical vision. I am wondering about the relationship of this approach to your comments in *Stories of Women*, in which you suggest that the dominant versions of history reflect the absences of a "collective amnesia" that has—through its "totalizing effects" (referencing your words) "obscured the lives of a diverse collection of extraordinary women, some admirable, others infamous." You note that the selection of only women is based on the desire to reflect the value of other representations, "unexpected social perspectives, as if real life . . . had gone in different directions from the official version, recognized with all its prejudices in the annals."

All of this is background to ask what role do you think the biographical novel, the biofictional work, plays or could play in opening up the reading of history to other critical representations, and how do these works differ from the role played by traditional biography, with its efforts to cordon itself off from fiction?

Montero: What you are aspiring to here is the capacity to talk about the human condition. And for this, there are so many fascinating examples. When Robert Graves wrote *I Claudius*, what was he talking about? He wasn't telling us the story of Emperor Claudius, but rather making an impressive fresco of the human condition. Of course, placing a biographical character with a panoply of invented characters in a story that could have happened that way but didn't, this, yes, is wonderful. This creates an opportunity for novelistic play, real literary play in the most significant of ways.

Rademacher: Absolutely.

Montero: What's more, this biofictional approach provides the uncertainty that, as we were discussing before, reveals the incredibly murky frontier between fiction and reality, or rather, it makes us conscious of reassessing our reality. And this is a really good thing. There is an excellent novel from last year, for example, by a Spanish writer, Vanessa Montfort. The novel is called *The Legend of the Island Without a Voice*. The novel explores a possible visit of Charles Dickens to an island off New York. In fact, the novel isn´t telling the story of Dickens. It´s more interested in the effect: the price of insecurity. We live in a world that's so insecure, and so the narrative has to be uncertain as well. In this way, then, the effect of the real that mixes with the fictional, from the point of view always of the novel, effectively makes us more aware of the existential uncertainty of the world in which we write. I like this very much, and I too use this strategy frequently.

Rademacher: You've already answered part of this question, but just to take it further—Why did you feel it was important to clarify that everything that you wrote about other people in *The Crazy Woman in the House* was real, but that you weren't sure you could assure the same about what you said about your own life? That is to say, is there an ethic that exists with respect to writing about the lives of others but that doesn't exist in relation to what we write about own lives?

Montero: I was playing with the reader, simply playing. Of course, with the lives of others one has to have an ethic. I like to make clear that the facts that I include about real people are documented. There is what we could call the real-real and then the real-imaginary, that is the truth of the lies in the novel—something that can often convey a more profound truth than the real-real. There were readers of *The Crazy Woman in the House* who were confident in the facts because they thought that they were reading my autobiography, but it was all fictional. I think that this structure enriches the book, enlivens once again the constant debate among what we invent and the "real-real." Memory is a complete invention. It's a story that we tell ourselves and that we constantly go about revising. Because what I remember from my childhood today is not what I will remember a few years from now. I have a brother, five years older than I am (and the fact about having a brother is true) and sometimes we get to talking about memories from our childhood and experiences we have had together, and his parents are not my parents. That is, his parents don't have anything to do with my parents—nothing. In fact, he has invented his childhood as much as I have invented mine. And if memory is an invention, then identity is also an invention because it is based on memory. And so our idea of reality is an invention. In these books it is evident that the real and the imaginary are so interrelated because it is a way of representing our world.

Rademacher: Changing topic a bit, I'd like to turn attention to another of your books, *The Ridiculous Idea of Never Seeing You Again*, in which your reading of Marie Curie's diary after the death of her husband forms the basis for exploring your own subjectivity following the death of your husband, Pablo. I wanted to begin by asking why Marie Curie interested you so much, and why you decided to write about her and to interweave portions of her biography with your own.

Montero: The issue is that I didn't try to write a book about Marie Curie to write a book about loss and grief. Because my husband had died two years earlier, I had already gone through the most intense moments of grief. When Pablo died, my friends said to me, "You should write a book about grief." There are plenty of books about loss that are marvelous and that I like very much, but I wasn't interested in doing that. At that moment, I had begun another novel, and when my editor sent me the thin little diary of Marie Curie—it's about twenty-eight pages, nothing more—for me to write a prologue, I read it. I thought I more or less knew about Marie Curie. But when I read those twenty-eight pages I was surprised at how differently I found her. What came through was how passionate she was, how different from the cold, scientific image with which she has been portrayed. And I was really interested in how this woman who was tremendous in everything also had this side of her. She had craziness, too. I was at that point in my own life when you begin to reflect upon a ton of essential questions—how to live better, to achieve more plenitude in life, to better capture the moment, how to live with less anxiety, how to free oneself from the mother/father stranglehold that can destroy your life as it threatened to do poor Marie Curie, who spent half of her life trying to prove to her dead father that radium had an important purpose. And also how to deal with loss. To learn how to live more fully and with serenity you have to achieve a certain understanding with death. It seemed to me that was also something else that connected us. This amazing woman could also provide me with a certain connection, to play out through her life, in a way, these questions that were nagging at me, like a conversation with her that in many ways are questions for all of us.

And that is how the novel came about, and also, something that I think you asked about as well, the reason for the hashtags. These emerged really naturally because *The Ridículous Idea,* as we talked about earlier, is a supremely mixed product, a hybrid. It is an autobiography of me that is not an autobiography; it is a biography of Marie Curie that is not a biography; it is an essay that is not an essay. So, there is a little bit of everything. From the start, in an essay—of course you know this—you have the thesis, the development of the argument, the concluding points. But here, I wanted to talk about twelve or thirteen essential themes, and I wanted to talk about them at different points, or rather, intermingling them, developing themes, pausing, and then expanding them again much later. So what occurred to me, very naturally really, was to insert these themes with hashtags in front of them. Because one of the great abilities we have as humans, and that we don't appreciate, is our capacity for symbolic understanding, our understanding of signs and symbols. And for the reader, even if they didn't understand it right away, the hashtag provided a clue to the idea being expressed and how it connected to the next. These hashtags helped to indicate that these were themes and ideas in construction throughout the book, and they seemed to me to be very useful signs for this reason.

Rademacher: This makes me think of how you have described biography as a type of "emergency map to navigate a confusing world." But what you have just expressed also communicates this need, this process by which one can't communicate or be understood directly, but rather through signs and symbols with the aim, at best, of arriving at an approximation of someone else's experience.

Montero: This concept of biography as an emergency map, as an existential map, reflects this question: How do we learn from the world? We have two basic ways to learn about life and how to live it. One is our own experience and rigorous introspection or self-analysis. And the other is knowledge about other people. In this way, then, biographies are effectively life maps, maps of where there may be signposts and shoals in life, because you can see where others have stumbled or failed, how they found love or fell out of it, the ways one might become lost. In this way, I have used Marie Curie as an enormous screen on which to project these possibilities.

Rademacher: I liked it very much too in *Stories of Women* when you told the story of Agatha Christie in which she took off in her car and went lost, spending days in a hotel without knowing where exactly she was nor who she was. And here again we have the example of someone who outwardly appeared so controlled, but who within also carried this disordered existence, this chaos.

Continuing with the discussion of this book, then, you note that your friend commented that Pablo is another subject present but absent from your book. In turn, you have stated that "in literature, in art in general, you can't arrive at this interiority of a life, that the memories that are most closely held are the hardest to express." I am wondering if you can talk a bit more, then, about why you decided to explore this absent life of Pablo, the presence of your loss, through the biography of Marie Curie? You've already touched upon part of this question. But since you've just described biographies as "existential maps," I'm wondering if you might elaborate a bit more on this point?

Montero: When I wrote this book, I had already gone through the hardest period of grief, and this also wasn't intended to be a grief book, but exactly the opposite—a book about living. And as I said earlier, if you want to learn to live more fully, you have to reach an agreement with death, with one's own death but also the death of those you love. So, when I talk in *The Ridiculous Idea* about Pablo I think I am being pretty discrete, and with the awareness that I am not talking not only about my own pain but also that of everyone. And I think that my friend was mistaken. Pablo is present a great deal in this book, and also through his absence, and this absence is the absence of the most important things.

Rademacher: It may seem an odd leap, but referring to the appeal of reality TV, for example, Annabel Lyon has commented on the capacity to create artificial order out of the chaos of existence. She says, "It feels good to see life coherently shaped into high points and low points . . . lifted out of the fog to a place where, for better or worse, we can see clearly at last." In a similar way, perhaps, you've talked about how many biographers have the "unfortunate custom of forcing the narrative into artificial highs and lows." Do you think that biofiction, when it's done well, by opening a narrow version of history to multiple possibilities, has the potential to contest this over-determination of the real?

Montero: Well, it all depends. This depends on the type of novel that one writes. All novels give order to the world in some way, even the most chaotic, because the world is much more chaotic than any novel. The world is an absolute chaos; life is an absolute chaos. Why do we create memories? Why do we turn our memories into stories? To give meaning to life. If we didn't, life would be pure noise and fury. We live in this overwhelming chaos and of course we have to give it all a certain order. And art gives it this semblance of sensemaking, all types of art. The act of mixing reality with fiction suggests this sort of ordered disorder. As I mentioned earlier, making evident that reality and fiction are connected makes the world a little bit more unpredictable, allows the chaos to make its way a little bit into our books, but only a little. The aim is still to try to make sense of life. If not, we wouldn't have a reason to make art at all.

Interview conducted in Spanish and translated from Spanish by Virginia Rademacher.

12

Stitching up the Auto/Biographical Seam

Stephanus Muller, interviewed by Willemien Froneman

Froneman: Authors of biofiction generally agree that the distinction between fact and fiction is anything but clear-cut and that the truth is sometimes best revealed through fabrication. Nevertheless, they are usually adamant that what they write is not biography but fiction. You take a different approach. What did you set out to write in *Nagmusiek* (*Night Music*)—an experimental novel or an experimental biography of Arnold van Wyk?

Muller: I set out to write a biography. The "experimental" only came later, when the impossibility of biography drove the project toward the experimental as an index of intellectual and creative contortionism, including the position occupied and signified by the novel. The impossibility lay, I think, on the level of truth claims, historical weight, narrative collapse, ethical scholarship—all problems relating to this kind of project as a post-Apartheid project—and also on the level of musicology's deeply irresolvable challenge of tracing sound in language by enlisting life and texts to suggest some kind of meaning.

Froneman: Do you think the impossibility of biography is more pronounced in post-Apartheid South Africa than elsewhere?

Muller: All I know is how difficult it is to write in post-Apartheid South Africa, and that includes the impossibility of writing biography. The latter comes with its own special problems that I suppose biographical writing everywhere shares, but in South Africa also includes the dystopian historical legacy of Apartheid, the lack of sociopolitical consensus, the amnesia, the moral torpor that lingers in the wake of a fascist police state that is not recognized as having been just that. As South Africans we cannot even agree what happened to us during the last fifty years, and this makes the writing of any South African historical narrative—including a biographical narrative—a quixotic endeavor.

Froneman: Where does your biographical subject, Arnold van Wyk, fit into the historical legacy you describe?

Muller: He was, like many white South Africans, one of those silent collaborators who was neither exceptionally racist and pro-Nationalist, nor particularly outspoken or brave in taking a stand against the system. Complicit. Entitled. Content to benefit from whiteness while pondering the higher things in life. Seemingly oblivious and largely indifferent to the blackness that made it all possible.

Froneman: But he was also in many ways an outsider and a displaced man?

Muller: Yes. He was a composer in a state and a community that did not particularly value music; he was a gay man in a heteronormative environment; he was a cosmopolitan thinker amid the parochiality of nationalism; he was a musical romantic in the age of the postwar avant-garde; he was a man of culture and letters in the land of braaivleis (barbecue), rugby, sunny skies, and chevrolet—as the jingle used to go; he was an artist in a university.

Froneman: Did you experience it as a burden—writing about a white, twentieth-century South African man post-Apartheid?

Muller: Not at all. I am also that man. It is a huge boon of whiteness, and part of its perversity, that the dissection of its mechanisms and composition, however critically, is an aesthetic pleasure.

Froneman: OK, let me put it differently. Is there an ethical imperative to account for the tradition of Afrikaans nonfiction when attempting to write the biography of someone like Van Wyk?

Muller: Absolutely. I would say that a vast majority of Afrikaans nonfiction writing—especially biography—has tended to feed into and from the nationalist narratives of the Apartheid-contaminated Afrikaner project in the twentieth century. Allowing redemptive claims of that project and its special interest in Western art music (which inform the importance of Van Wyk as a composer) was a real danger. So when I talk about the possibilities or impossibilities of writing biography in South Africa, these considerations form part of the responsibility of the writer, or the ethical imperative—as you put it—to confront head-on the complicity of "neutral" approaches based on "facts." Those two words reverberate with lies and human rights abuses. I shudder as I write them.

Froneman: Writing a composer's biography traditionally implies an attempt at canonizing a body of music. How does one redefine—or confront—the idea of canonicity in these circumstances?

Muller: By keeping the text open, by making the canon conditional, by making the conditions for canonicity explicit. But also by viewing the biography as a starting point for an exploration of the music, and not as the result of an a priori bestowed greatness that then imprints itself on all subsequent curation and staging of the music. Because Van Wyk's music is so unknown, locally and internationally, there is a wonderful opportunity to make it into a special kind of contemporary music, heard with twenty-first-century ears through recording technology that has the potential to create the Van Wyk sound, more than forty years after his death. The move toward inclusion into the canon, for Van Wyk, then runs through creative rediscovery of the man and his music—not the recognition of things we think we ought to find or hear.

Froneman: You mentioned earlier the position occupied and signified by the novel as one of the platforms for *Nagmusiek*'s experiment. Could you expand on this idea?

Muller: The novel is not, of course, a *solution* to the impossibility of biography per se, but part of a historical repertoire of narrative structure and canonized inter-texts that can be enlisted in the creation of meaning through any kind of writing. The historical integrity of the thing called "the novel" (extending to its contemporary position in particular ways) allows us to work with stories and verisimilitude and forms (signification) but in my view only as the fuel for the explosion of fictional directions that have departed from it in the twentieth century and exist today. In *Nagmusiek*, the novel became part of the tinder for the (auto)biographical conflagration.

Froneman: Yes, let's discuss this conflagration. In *Nagmusiek* you enlist as narrator a semi-fictional musicologist and biographer. Who is Werner Ansbach?

Muller: Asking the question in that way, we might as well call the conflagration an auto-da-fé. Werner Ansbach is of course a heretic of sorts, and he does come to a sticky end.

Froneman: Would you prefer a different formulation?

Muller: What I would prefer is not important. And I don't mean this as a rebuke; he is no longer mine to describe. Perhaps I would not have enlisted that word with all its intensity and color to describe Ansbach with his conservative habits, his love of routine, his less than ecstatic climaxes. But

I can see why the image is also exactly right for him. Ansbach the crucible in which the self and the other unite in spontaneous combustion with sometimes comic, sometimes tragic consequences. Another image might be to describe his first-person narration as a seam between the autobiographical and the biographical, and to view his character as an enabler of transgressions and movement between the subjectivity of the writer and the subject of the biography. Who is he, you ask? We meet him in the text as a highly strung loner in constant battle with the moles that disturb his lawn, a regular passive-aggressive visitor to his demented mother and an ambivalent object of desire in violent male and female sexual encounters.

Froneman: I like your metaphor of the first person narration as an auto/biographical seam.

Muller: It does work beautifully as a word in the way you write it above—I mean visually—doesn't it? The whole text, I think, is composed of seams. In the narrating instance it is perhaps less immediately obvious, but elsewhere the seam really emerges as the design principle. One can imagine a label for the book: hand-stitched in Stellenbosch, stitched-up in Bellville.

Froneman: I think we've found our title! In a way, *Nagmusiek* fictionally embroiders neither on the biographer nor the subject, but on this seam between them.

Muller: I think this is a very perceptive observation, and it speaks to the pleasure afforded by white writing, even—or especially—if it takes seriously the act of writing as a political act. But of course it is the peculiar thing about the seam that it can only hold the kind of attention and elaboration that we are attributing to it if it remains a seam and doesn't become a subject. Writing about the seam will be the death of writing; craftily, lovingly, mischievously embroidering the seam while writing about Van Wyk and Ansbach and Muller is the strange double strategy that imbues the seam with more than technical significance.

Froneman: This seems to me like a radically original take on the notion of biofiction. Those of us who know you recognize traces of you in Ansbach. But could we discuss some of the specific ways in which Ansbach increasingly comes to resemble Van Wyk as the narrative unfolds?

Muller: Ansbach's institutional alienation echoes that of Arnold van Wyk, his dreams and lectures become enmeshed with those of Van Wyk and his carefully planned and responsible academic project unravels before our eyes into the purgatory of incompleteness and frustrated ambition. His ambivalent sexuality and awkwardness make him unable to form lasting relationships, to connect to the world in a meaningful way except through that which he does as an academic and writer, and ultimately fails to do. He becomes progressively more alone, more disappointed and less and less convinced that one can adequately write about music.

Froneman: You also employ a number of character foils.

Muller: Most important among them is the "Groot Biograaf," or Great Biographer. I modeled him on the remarkable South African literary scholar of Afrikaans literature, J. C. Kannemeyer, who passed away in 2011 and who I was privileged to know. He is everything that Ansbach is not, and yet he is a source of stability and comfort for the younger man. But there is also the female muse, Cecile, and a number of smaller characters that, through Ansbach's encounters with them, help me to work out theoretical problems, show things that are difficult to say, pack out history in ways that affirm its provenance in subjective experiences.

Froneman: You mentioned earlier Ansbach's mole problem, his visits to his demented mother, and his sexual, how shall we put it, awakening. What role does allegory play in this crafty, loving, mischievous embroidering of the seam?

Muller: Something of this process resonates with the idea that truth or meaning is relational, and that it emerges by holding on for dear life to the tension that exists between the integrity or autonomy of entities and their interaction. Border thinking is what I think Walter Mignolo calls this thinking that happens on the seam, and allegory has its role to play in working out this tension. In a way it is part of a very conventional concern of literature: the layering of text that allows multiple interpretations, perplexing openness, revelatory exegesis.

Froneman: Would you say your decision to write the book in Afrikaans was another such attempt at border thinking?

Muller: Absolutely. I believe Afrikaans is a richly indigenized index of sounds and experiences and texts that allow for unravellings and breaches different to English. Because Afrikaans is not the language of global intellectual and economic exchange, and now also no longer the language of political power, it is also more obviously and delightfully resistant to instrumentalist delusions of the need to communicate everything to everyone. It is a border language, an aesthetic compellingly autonomous of its lumpen speakers and readers and coded with radical and experimental energy. Historically, I think of novelist Etienne le Roux's work as being powered by this energy; today the poetry of Nathan Trantraal comes to mind. Scholarly writing should not turn its back on Afrikaans.

Froneman: Ansbach's narrative about Van Wyk unfolds through a series of responses to archival documents: an obituary read at his funeral service, letters to and from friends and lovers, records of dental problems, radio talks, a set of photographs of his hands, to name but a few. Collecting, categorizing, and ordering Van Wyk's archive formed an important part of your project. What did you learn from this unusually close engagement with unsorted primary materials and how did it influence your ideas on biographical writing?

Muller: Primary materials—especially if encountered in unsorted, chaotic states—are not primarily carriers of information. Rather, they suggest an aesthetic and a direction. They demand a kind of tightrope-walking that requires a constant shifting and adjusting of balance. I never had very fixed ideas about biographical writing, and encountering the Van Wyk materials in boxes and suitcases imbued the biographical enterprise with a sense of discovery, mystery, even danger. Did I learn anything from this close engagement with unsorted primary materials? I don't know. Was I changed by it? Yes.

Froneman: Changed as a writer? As an academic?

Muller: As a writer, as an academic, as a person. Long before I had an idea where the writing was going, and even longer before I jumped off the cliff as an academic by taking the kind of risk which *Nagmusiek* became, I was enraptured by my discovery of treasure and dismayed by the realization that I could never bring it all to the surface. These were not the emotions primarily of a writer and an academic, but of an adventurer. And eventually one discovers personal limits, and the writing and academic positioning become little more than techniques to grapple with these newly discovered limits and the changes they induce in the newly limited.

Froneman: So the metafictional narrative also functions in a traditionally postmodern way (if one could call it that): bringing into the open issues of completeness, significance, and the accuracy of historical understanding.

Muller: Yes. Although my sense is that my decision to write in this way evolved less as an intellectual strategy than a practical one. In other words: I didn't think about the impossibility of biography only as an intellectual position; I experienced it as a reality of writing in the particular circumstances I found myself in as an academic in South Africa. Writing, in such circumstances, becomes an act of resistance, even heroism. And explicitly, messily grappling with issues of completeness, significance, and accuracy of historical writing seems to me to be inevitable and a condition for writing that matters in this time and place.

Froneman: Linda Hutcheon calls postmodern metafiction "narcissistic narrative," but in the context of postcolonial literature there is nothing self-evident about seeing oneself with one's own eyes. In a sense, then, you transform the playful deconstructive intellectualism of postmodern fiction into a more existential form of self-reflection.

Muller: You put it beautifully. But perhaps I *am transformed* by the postcolonial condition into this existential form of self-reflection. And literature and the sensibility of postmodern fiction responds to this transformation which, as you say, pushes beyond mere play, mere intellectualism, mere narcissism. Ever since my "discovery" of various strands of postcolonial discourse in the nineties, I was struck by the political direction it added to the postmodern sensibility. A direction that pointed toward rupturing the decorum of theory, of lancing play with the deadly serious, of running close deconstruction to political conditions that were less interested in metafiction than in the collapse of all intellectual categories into political imperatives. And constantly hovering on that edge.

Froneman: This heightened existential political agenda of which you speak becomes particularly evident when reading Werner Ansbach's narrative alongside that of another fictional biographer—Julian Barnes's Geoffrey Braithwaite in *Flaubert's Parrot*. It's hard to pinpoint exactly how and why, but the difference in grain is palpable. Perhaps it has something to do with the brutality of Ansbach's death wish. Or perhaps it is the pervasive sense that in writing *Nagmusiek* you were putting a lot on the line.

Muller: *Flaubert's Parrot* was a very important book to me when I was working out what kind of book *Nagmusiek* wanted to become. It convinced me that a sustainable writing strategy could be shaped around the aporia. I know what you mean, though, when you speak about the difference in grain. This could just be, of course, the result of a comparison to a writer of such measured elegance as Barnes. But you are also right about the timbre of risk that shimmers on the pages of *Nagmusiek*. It is a book that bends under the pressure of the constraints imposed by the silences of slow violence, and the need to break those silences.

Froneman: Was there the sense of being forced into fiction by the increasingly repressive atmosphere of the modern South African bureaucratic university?

Muller: When I started working on the project, that repressive atmosphere was primarily imposed by the orthodoxies of post-Apartheid historical compromises and the continued culture of moralism and hypocrisy that pervaded discourse on white South African musical culture. Later on—remember that the entire project lasted fourteen years—it became clear to me that the discourse of ethics that was being brought to bear on humanities research was in ominous ways playing a part in making critical work suspect and restricting the possibilities of freethinking critique. Whether the use of fiction was a solution to this problem or a provocation of the ethics machine, I don't know. I have resorted to fiction in other scholarly texts in response to the repressive assertiveness of which you write. And as we talk, hundreds of dissident students have been arrested at university campuses across South Africa, which have become heavily militarized zones. It is becoming clearer by the day that the unfinished business of the past will not be denied. We are witnessing the return of the repressed.

Froneman: I want to go back to unpacking this idea of biofiction in relation to *Nagmusiek*. Michael Lackey argues that biographical fiction "fictionalizes rather than represents the biographical subject" and that comparing biographical fiction to biography would be "a grave mistake because the two genres have radically different methods and objectives, and as such, they are premised on very different truth contracts." How would you respond to this? Are you saying that these distinctions are meaningless?

Muller: My work on Arnold van Wyk thematizes the madness-inducing activity of categorization, and to my mind statements such as the one you quote by Lackey hinge on defining terms in ways that I find far from obvious. I am ill-equipped to comment on a comparison of genres premised on assumptions about methods and objectives. If I were able to do so, *Nagmusiek* would not have been possible. And this is not to say that mine was an intellectually naive project; just that yielding to the intellectual category as a writer is restrictive in terms of allowing the experiment to become what it can be. The distinctions are certainly not meaningless for anyone concerned with categorization for whatever discursive or disciplinary reason that requires the delineation of the category. As a writer, however, I would argue that it is of limited use.

Froneman: This raises an interesting tension. Volume I contains the result of your painstaking labor cataloging (and categorizing) all of Van Wyk's works and sketches, including program notes and reviews—presumably, following a set of discursive or disciplinary imperatives.

Muller: Indeed. So the question arises: Does Volume I actually contain the conditions of possibility for Volume III (the biographical narrative proper)? Is Volume I a work by Ansbach or by Muller? Certainly the disciplinary ritual performed in Volume I is difficult to explain in the context of the work as a whole unless it is read as a performance of the problem, precisely by taking the category and the order of things so outrageously seriously. But in a sense this explanation is an ex-post facto dishonesty, for the reality is that in order to fragment narrative in a way that holds on to a sense of contour and structure, the categories and catalogs are rich points of departure. And Muller was running scared of the chaos that surrounded him.

Froneman: Couldn't this idea of categorization as a performance of the problem apply to the other items on Lackey's list of oppositions between biography and fiction too? What I mean is this: does *Nagmusiek* not also perform the problem of fictionalization vs. representation, of differing methodological expectations, and of clashing epistemological paradigms?

Muller: True. But of course the burden for adherence (as performance) is transferred to the catalog (Volume I) and the pleasures of play (as performance) are taken up in Volumes III and II (containing the index and notes), subsuming the kind of performance which occurs in Volume I into the larger staging of the text where adherence itself becomes an elaborate spoof. There is also a sense in which these concerns perform much larger ones. At this very moment in South Africa the inherited legacies of Western modernity are politically challenged in the biggest student protests the country's universities have ever experienced. In thinking about the performance of the problematic posed by categories, we also have to understand that in South Africa there is a radical reassessment of the structures and images and words that have strained (and failed in many respects) to deliver a post-Apartheid society. Werner Ansbach uses the word "bunker" to describe his workspace and his sense of the precariousness of his project. I think there is a sense in which *Nagmusiek* is already working out the impossibility of categories as we inherited them, and grappling with what remains when these are no longer available except as so much rubble and debris.

Froneman: Or, as Ansbach says at one point, following Paul Ricoeur: "Narrative does not solve aporias, but only resolves them poetically (and not theoretically)."

Muller: If the book manages to be such a poetic gesture that achieves however small a resolution of aporia in this sense, it would make me very happy.

Froneman: And how about the nature of your truth contract with your readers?

Muller: Despite the answer above, I believe that the truth contract with readers is compromised by the categorization game where the text is assigned a label (as opposed to labels being assigned to things in the text). For me, the truth contract hinges on the reader entering into the pleasure of the text, where truth emerges through the writing game.

Froneman: Yes, but in *Nagmusiek* the pleasure of the text also hinges strongly on the ambivalence created by the refusal to classify it, at the broadest level, as either fiction or nonfiction. I'm interested in the immense power of the absence of a fictitious disclaimer, and how this (mischievously again) enforces for its own agenda the binary it seeks to abolish. The reader is cajoled into the text not solely through novelistic jouissance, but also through Ansbach's heretical catachesis. Like all heretics, Ansbach stakes his life on the truth of his own doctrine. In a way the reader is converted, not "cruised." How else would you explain the extraordinary fact that *Nagmusiek* has been awarded literary prizes in both the fiction and nonfiction categories?

Muller: *Nagmusiek* accepts, I think, that there is not one reader, but many. And that, if allowed, readers will bring to texts that resist declaring themselves, surprising and contradictory responses. The literary prizes have been a source of great delight to me, precisely because I get the feeling that the book is not "claimed" by this recognition. The book is a literary stray, but a well-recognized one. At least within its small reception context. I cannot pretend to understand how this has happened, or what it means, any more than I fully understand the implications of the absence you speak of. But I read in your description of the book a recognition of something akin to a sexual seduction that results from a strategy of excitation and refusal, of heightening desire and yearning through the very absence of consummation. I like that:

Nagmusiek as an elaborate and sensual courting dance to the South African, Afrikaans, intellectual, familial, and disciplinary communities within which I exist and that I love. Perhaps those prizes show that some guilty pleasures have been indulged, and encounters have taken place.

Froneman: *Nagmusiek* is a beautiful and lavishly produced artifact. Did you conceive of the apparatus of the book as conveying some kind of meaning?

Muller: I was very fortunate to entrust my manuscript to Fourthwall Books in Johannesburg, where Bronwyn Law-Viljoen (editor) and Oliver Barstow (designer) were (and are still) making extraordinary books. Aesthetic objects, yes, but also embracing content that defies commercial publishing imperatives. And I was working closely with my friend, the filmmaker-artist Aryan Kaganof, who was very influential in pushing the implications of the intellectual project to include the artifact as an apparatus of meaning, as you so beautifully put it. So when you ask whether I conceived of this happening, the question is really when this happened. And the answer has to do with a gradual awareness of what kind of a thing this book wanted to be, and being fortunate enough to be surrounded by the right kinds of people at the right times; people who understood what books as artifacts could be and mean.

Froneman: The image of the seam comes to mind again.

Muller: Perhaps it is not surprising that in a country where the social fabric has been ripped apart over hundreds of years through waves of empire, colonization, and Apartheid, the seam should assume such totemic importance. And that it should extend beyond categories to media, and beyond media to artistic sensibilities, and beyond artistic sensibilities to people.

13

Complex Psychologies in the Biographical Novel

Sabina Murray, interviewed by Michael Lackey

Lackey: It seems that different types of writers have different types of truth contracts with their audience. For instance, an Oxford University history professor criticized you for not having an accurate grasp of the facts in your novel about Roger Casement. But you are a novelist, so you are more interested in human interiors than the historian's established facts. Can you briefly discuss the kind of truth that you seek to portray in your novel *Valiant Gentlemen*, and can you briefly clarify how the truth contract you establish with your reader is different from the truth contract that historians establish with their readers?

Murray: I came at *Valiant Gentlemen* from so many different directions, and I sat on that book for five years before I could even figure out what the book was. At the heart of that struggle was figuring out what truth was I trying to tell, and why I was the right person to tell it. What complicates using historical figures as subjects for writing fiction is that they have a ready group of people who are drawn to that person. With Casement, these are people interested in Irish history, gay studies, and humanitarian issues—all these people attach themselves to him. Casement has a larger-than-life life. But when you experience life, you experience it in very ordinary ways. Each of us in the fullness of our experiences is stuck living our life, and it fills the register of human experience. So the relevant question here is how does an individual, somebody who will be seen as a player in all these different fronts and fields and causes, as they move through history, experience that? How is that personal experience of history? What I was trying to do is create an almost moment to moment account of what it might have been like to be inside Casement's head as these larger things were unfolding, and to exist in the reality of not knowing what was going to be important until the dust had settled on it. History happens at a distance, at a remove. That's how we know what it is. But in the immediate experience of it, you don't know how your actions are going to set off other actions. And that was really what intrigued me, which is why the whole book is in the present tense, and there is no summary in it. It moves forward, and occasionally people will think back on things but in a very organic way. The truth that I was trying to get at is what was Casement feeling as he created this line through history, which historians now look back at and say, "Oh look, that was a major player, and it's because he did this." But what were his quiet moments? What were his private moments, too, that make a real life rather than what was significant that he did that can be arranged by subject matter into an understanding of historical merit?

Lackey: I like this idea of the present tense. There has been some debate among scholars regarding the differences between the historical novel and the biographical novel. The traditional view is that the historical novel is looking at the objective political and economic forces that shape and determine characters from the past, and we can use the historical novel to understand how we have come to be as we are in the present. But other people say the biographical novel is less interested in what has shaped and determined us from the past and is more interested in who we are in the present or what we can be in the future. So instead of accurately representing a biographical figure from the past, biographical novelists actually go back to the past and appropriate these figures because they can be used to illuminate not just who we are in the present, but who we can become in the future. Do you see yourself as trying to do recovery work to get to the real Casement? Or, do you see yourself as using Casement in order to say something about who we are in the present and what we can be in the future?

Murray: That's a good question. I think that it's important to look at a character like Casement who reshaped history as a human being rather than as a vehicle for communicating politicized ideas in order to soften a didactic agenda. Perhaps the biographical novel's embracing of personal psychologies offers an alternative to the historical novel's performance of understood notions. Why this interest in biographical novels now? Perhaps as we deal with the onslaught of technology, we forget that life is determined by people. There is not a moment in time where one doesn't interact with some dehumanizing element of technology. In the midst of all this, we wonder what it is to be a person. I wanted to look at colonialism, the Belgian Congo, the First World War, and to question what it is to be alive in the present of those situations. Decisions are made by people. I said to myself: "This is what's important here, human psychology. Important here are interactions." And I was lucky to find someone like Casement, who was dealing with massive historical movements: the opening up of Africa, the First World War, the Barings Bank Crisis, emerging gay identities. And that brings it to the now, this sliver of present that functions as a bullet into the future. Despite differing historical circumstance, people remain essentially the same. That's the big joy of going back to classical works and reading translations of writers as far back as Catullus. We discover that people are essentially the same. In the present, we do have to know more. We walk around with the weight of history and an expanding geographical knowledge with its cultural implications. In the classical era, one would have only had to know what had happened up until that point in time, and that knowledge would additionally be limited by lack of range of communication. Our lives have become incredibly complicated. We have to know about the different world wars. We have to know about the existence of all these countries that we wouldn't have had to know about at a different point in time. But through all of that, the psychology of people has not essentially changed. Biographical novels allow us to process history while suspending the knowledge of all that we know now.

Lackey: And the psychology of the people is what you are after in your novel.

Murray: Yes.

Lackey: Let's use a specific example to get some clarity about your approach. In 1936, Arna Bontemps wrote a really interesting biographical novel called *Black Thunder* about Gabriel Prosser. In 1800, Prosser led a slave rebellion in Virginia. In the novel, Bontemps uses the word "proletariat." But that word did not come into being for another forty or fifty years, so it is an anachronism. Some would criticize Bontemps for that aesthetic choice. But biographical novelists have a very different response. They say: "Look, these are strategic anachronisms. A novel is successful because it is able to simultaneously say there was a mindset at work in 1800 that is comparable to the mindset today." And so what is seen as a flaw by some people is seen as an aesthetic virtue by others, because the anachronism indicates that psychologies at work in the past are still at work in the present. You feel free to do this because you are not a biographer or historian. You are a novelist. How would you respond to that?

Murray: I would not use the word "proletariat" in dialogue, but I think it would absolutely be necessary to include in the narrative, because you are writing to a contemporary reader. You are not trying to recreate the past. It's not a *tableau vivant*. That's not what the biographical novels are trying to do. That's certainly not what I am trying to do. I am always translating for the contemporary reader. For instance, my character Herbert Ward frequently interacts with his children. In the reality of their existences, they called him "Bobby." That was their name for their dad. So it was originally in my novel as Bobby. But my agent said, "I keep stopping on Bobby." And I said, "Right. It's accurate, but it's wrong because it takes you out of the moment." I did some digging around and learned that sometimes they called him Dad. So I put Dad in there. And then when I was reading it, I thought, "That doesn't feel right either because that feels too contemporary." It's accurate but in its accuracy becomes inaccurate, because it violates the comfortable distance necessary for an authentic reading. So I came up with Father. That's not what they called their father. In fact, people didn't call their father "father." It would be as ridiculous then as it would be now if I started calling my dad *father*. But I needed to get it into the right register for the contemporary reader. To get the tone where it needed to be, I needed to manipulate the language. The narrative may be set in the past, but needs to be presented sensibly for a contemporary reader. The use of "proletariat" illustrates this, and so does the use of "father."

Lackey: The issue is one of effectively crossing cultures and times, which is crucial for you given your background. You are an American, but you have lived in Australia and the Philippines. I've noticed that there are many biographical novels dealing with transnational and cross-cultural ways of thinking. There's some real value in this. For instance, Casement went to the Belgian Congo, and through that experience he finally started to understand what happened to him as an Irishman under British rule. To what degree did your experience in Australia help you better understand somebody like Casement? To what degree did your experiences as an Australian or even an American help you understand the nature and structures of global political oppression, including some of America's overseas misdeeds? How does your novel illuminate cross-cultural political structures?

Murray: I don't really have a clear nationality, and consequently I don't really believe in national identity. My mother was Filipino, and I lived in the Philippines for a long time. Recently *Vice* sent me to Manila to write an article on Duterte because I function as local, and I've worked as a screenwriter for an Australian film company, since it's easy for me to make sense of that culture. But being biracial was just weird in Perth in the 70s. It really put me in the position of outsider, and I have a certain comfort occupying that role. Casement was always approaching from the position of outsider, while still negotiating the complications of being Irish, Northern Irish, and British. The key to my understanding of Casement is to extend my notions of national identity to Casement. How did Casement suddenly embrace Republican Irish ideas after functioning as British for many years? Because he could, because a mutable sense of national identity was not a stretch for him. When I was in Ireland, many of the Irish would say to me: "You don't seem very American." Well, I grew up in Australia, and that to some Irish people is a closer form of Irishness than being American, but some of it just stems from my not being very anything. As for understanding global oppression, in the Philippines I'm in the awkward position, dictated by my appearance, of being an obvious product of colonialism, while still sporting an adamant anti-colonial stance. The Philippines is a good place to find some of America's most flamboyant misdeeds. One of the strengths of the biographical novel is that you can represent all of this confusion that exists in a psyche and as long as it is articulate, you've done your job. I find it highly unlikely that Casement had a clear understanding of his identity, nationality or otherwise, and the biographical novel allows for this accurate, nuanced portrayal.

Lackey: What do you mean by a form of Irishness?

Murray: When I was growing up in Australia, much of what I was exposed to was dominated by Irish culture. I grew up with people whose parents and grandparents had come from Ireland and who spoke with Irish accents. And the kind of Catholic structures that I grew up with weren't Filipino-Catholic structures, they were Old World Irish-Catholic structures. This all contributes to my identity and is palpable in my engagements with the Irish.

Lackey: So we have these past conflicts in the Belgian Congo, the Amazon, and Ireland. But how do they help us today? Do those conflicts enable us to see something in the present and how certain structures operate in a similar way today?

Murray: It's so hard to make sense of the present. But, ultimately, every time you write about the past, you are writing about the present. You are writing about an insecurity in your current moment that you've yet to be able to determine because you don't have any distance from it. Otherwise, you would be writing about the present.

Lackey: To clarify my question, let's take the Oxford professor who criticized you. As a historian, when he's writing about Casement and his time period, he's not writing consciously and strategically about the present. He's saying: "I'm trying to get back to the past, and I want to get that person and period exactly right." But you are doing something very different, because as a novelist you are more interested in how the structures and conditions of oppression function in multiple places and at multiple times. So while you might be writing about the past, you are more comfortable getting some things wrong so that you can get other things right. But what is that other thing that you are trying to get right?

Murray: I like to write about people in a state of not knowing and the insecurities in the present of that state; I think that's an important way to understand a person's experience. So my big conflict with the Oxford professor is that politically, he being very English, thinks of Casement as a criminal because he was an Irish revolutionary, and he was ribbing me about that in a way that I thought was kind of hilarious. The Oxford professor is saying that Casement was wrong to believe the things he did, and my response is that regardless of the correctness of Casement's beliefs, my duty, as a fiction writer, is to present a set of beliefs that are accurate to the personality of my character. Casement was likely a conflicted individual and as a fiction writer I can portray that without judgment.

Lackey: This raises an important epistemological question. Casement has a conflicted identity. Was he British? Was he Irish? At a certain point, when he becomes critical of Britain, he says: "I'm not British. I'm Irish." At exactly this same time, there are major shifts in our theories of knowledge. We are moving away from ontology and becoming more phenomenological. We are less interested in what things and people are and more interested in how things are perceived. You seem to be working within the phenomenological tradition, because you say that you are less interested in history and more interested in the way Casement understood the world. But once we make that phenomenological shift, doesn't this totally undermine the whole enterprise of the historical novel in the traditional sense? To my mind, your shift to consciousness raises a different set of questions than the traditional historical novel does. The historical novel is trying to get facts right and show how they shape us, but you are saying, "Look, this is an epistemological problem." Once we center the novel within consciousness, we have a much different kind of aesthetic game going on. Can you talk about that aesthetic game?

Murray: I thought a lot about Casement's identity. I said, "How am I going to handle the problem of his identity? Because I don't think he knew who he was. In fact, that's why I want to write about him." How do you write about someone who really doesn't know who they are except in relation to what they are dealing with at that specific moment? Everybody's just more tolerant of these gray areas. And people responded very well to the fact that it raised interesting questions and didn't try to answer them all. It's a different way of reading; it's a different way of engaging. So that might have something to do with it. Also the fact that traditional historical novels are just so sealed off. They don't move into the present. If you are dealing with human psychologies, it does seem to just kind of seamlessly march into the current day. It doesn't seem like it's walled off, but more accessible.

Lackey: Can you think of a biographical novel that you admire?

Murray: First to mind is Colm Tóibín's *Nora Webster*, which is not particularly historical as it's set in the 1960s, and is also not written about a historically significant figure. While this may seem to diverge from our general discussion, looking at this book does help to illuminate my approach to writing about Casement. When I read *Nora Webster*, I was thinking, "Tóibín is taking a very ordinary life, and by just paying attention to the grandeur of human experience, he's making this profound statement on existence and joy and having a soul." He accomplishes through writerly patience, through careful observation of simple actions, for example a woman painting a ceiling. But because the thoughts are given such respect, you develop a transcendental compassion for this fictional person. He takes this ordinary person, and, through this process, renders them amazing. I thought that I would use this same patient observation and apply it to Casement. The effect was very different. It was as if I were looking through the wrong end of a telescope. I thought, "I'm taking this amazing historical figure, and through this technique, I'm rendering him a very simple man." The same technique does two completely different things to the historically significant and to normal people, to your characters. I became very intrigued with that. This approach might explain why biographical novels tend to be very satisfying. You can create a narrative from what people choose to look at, from what they choose to pay attention to. When you write in that way, you actually allow people into what it was like to experience that moment. And instead of functioning as an escape, the novel makes a person more a participant. I'm not trying to give people escape; I'm trying to give them an electrified experience of what it might have been to be a player in these moments. As for biographical novels that I admire, I am a big fan of *Wolf Hall*, which doesn't worry about the readers understanding all the details of the history, and gave me permission to do the same. And Peter Carey's *True History of the Kelly Gang* and *Parrot and Olivier in America*.

Lackey: Let's turn to your story "Periplus." I'm assuming that the protagonist of this story is your father.

Murray: Yes.

Lackey: At some point in the story he makes a comment about the construction of history. This leads him to ask: is he composing reality from art? This taps into an interesting controversy in the late nineteenth/early twentieth century. In the late nineteenth century, a lot of historians said that history is a science. But Lytton Strachey, who was a member of the Bloomsbury group and a friend of Virginia Woolf's, said: "No, actually history is an art." When we talk about the rise of biofiction, a lot of people say that the Bloomsbury group, Virginia Woolf included, played a crucial role in laying down the conditions for what would eventually become biofiction. I wonder if this whole idea of history as art rather than science is part of the reason why biographical novels came into being. In your biofictional work, you are not saying, "Here is the objective history." You are actually saying, "History is, to some degree, an art, a matter of perspective." Your short story "Periplus," in particular, showcases a character struggling with historical documents in order to make sense of contemporary experience. Can you talk about the nature and role of history in "Periplus"?

Murray: That is such an odd story. I was dealing with actual documents. I was dealing with actual events. It is one of those stories that bleeds into real life. In "Periplus," the character, who is translating a Greek passage, asks himself why we engage the classical world. Why do we? This is one of those stories that asks a whole lot of questions, and explores the issues, but doesn't really worry about providing answers.

Lackey: Did your father read the story?

Murray: Oh yes.

Lackey: Does he like it?

Murray: He likes it a lot, and he has now replaced a blank memory with the facts that I included in my story. But that is how we engage with history. Why do we engage the past? Why do we find it so important to go back? And what comes forward in all the past's communicative beauty tends to be things like writing and art. Essentially, history ends up being weighted heavily in art. Even when we are looking at wars, it is usually accounts of war that you are looking at. The whole book *Tales of the New World* is really about people being able to construct the other through texts and bring it, in text form, into another world.

Lackey: So would you say, "If you want to know a key thing about my father, go read this story because this story tells you who my father is"? Or, would you say, "in this story I'm using my father and one of his experiences to make certain points about the nature of history and the way we engage history?"

Murray: The latter for sure, although after reading the story, you might not know my father that well, but you know something about him very, very well.

Lackey: And you use that story for what purpose? Why did you write that story?

Murray: It is the fiction instinct. You have to situate yourself in somebody else's psyche in order to narrow the vision; my vision of the world has to be narrowed through someone else's psyche in order for me to make narrative sense of it. How that story came into being is that my father knew I was writing about explorers and had this paper he'd written as a young man that focused on Hanno. Originally, I was trying to write from Hanno's perspective, but I couldn't get a handle on it, so I started trying different things. I ended up with my father as a character. If I'm just looking at art and thinking about art and history, there is a loose connection in the thought process. But if I think about my father thinking about these things, then I can actually get an angle on it. And even though I'm not talking about events in my father's life, these are the kinds of thoughts he would have. Now he thinks he actually had them. And the story takes him from that moment in his distant past to a much more recent moment, which is when he's in Thailand in the Golden Triangle with a bunch of students.

Lackey: Did that really happen?

Murray: Yes. I wasn't there, but I know. I've been with my dad; he's a very philosophical, mystical, religious guy. And he does occasionally make these large pronouncements, as he does at the end of the story. So it is very plausible. Maybe it didn't happen, but because my father could have said it, because you are hearing something that my father could have said, it is almost as good as hearing something that he did say.

Lackey: Let's just assume there was a diary being written at this time, and we can prove beyond a shadow of a doubt it didn't happen. So it's wrong. It's false. Could you still say that it is true in a certain sense, that there is a certain kind of truth to it? And if so, can you specify the nature of that truth?

Murray: The belief system is provable. My father's belief system would generate that thought, so it belongs with his thoughts. If you were to put things in groups: thoughts that my father would have and thoughts my father wouldn't have, and you sorted it in this way, apples and oranges. That would be an apple thought, that would be a thought that he could have, and that could coexist with his other thoughts without creating conflict. So that's how I would explain that process.

Lackey: Let's briefly talk about the Mary Kingsley story "Fish." Kingsley was an extraordinary nineteenth-century woman who went to Africa to explore. In your story, Kingsley has conversations with fairies. Is there any evidence she engaged in conversations with fairies? How do these fairies function? Are they historically accurate? And what is their fictional function and value?

Murray: I like the fairies. Mary Kingsley was one of these wildly interesting people who are very difficult to write about because they live largely solitary lives. If you write my kind of fiction, people need to engage. They need to engage with other voices to find out who they are. People are what they see and what they say. But some people don't say a whole lot. There are interior thoughts, but you have to engage with the world in order for these to be revealed. And Kingsley was a very weird, isolated person. I had no one to put in the room to engage with her. Then it occurred to me, "What if she had an imaginary friend? What if she had fairies?" And I thought about the fairies, who are these sinister, horrifying, scary little creatures. And this introduced a Victorian vibe. It was through the fairies that I could get her to talk. So the fairies are not accurate to Mary Kingsley. I never read about her having this obsessive fairy thing.

Lackey: What is the function of the invented character in biographical novels? Let's take an example from your novel. Early in *Valiant Gentlemen*, Casement goes to a gay bar in New York City where he first starts to get some clarity about his own homosexual desires and orientation. Is that scene made up or real? And if it is made up, why did you include it and what were you doing in it?

Murray: I didn't want to deal with Casement's homosexuality in a melodramatic way. I thought his experience would be like anyone else's. I wanted to make it ordinary. So I tried to think of a scene that might be how an ordinary gay man would have been functioning at that time. I did my research. I read George Chauncey's *Gay Life in New York*. And then I thought, "He's not going to be there by himself." It was just a way of trying to normalize his experience. I wanted to write something that had that sense of place and people moving in it, that gave you a sense of the society that he was interacting with, and that gave you an idea of New York at the time. But ultimately, it was to make his experience of gayness seem in line with what it would be like going to a club now.

Lackey: In your estimation, is there a political or social justice component to the biographical novel?

Murray: There absolutely is. I believe in a politically engaged fiction. Novels are a very powerful tool for understanding. I think that people really learn best through reading fiction. For instance, there are so many people who don't know anything about contemporary South Africa except through J. M. Coetzee's books or who haven't engaged with anyone from the Dominican Republic but know something of the culture from reading Junot Diaz. That's just how we get our information. Casement was a lion for the oppressed. He kept doing that, and he did that while being a gay man. One of the things I wanted to communicate is, "History is propelled by a number of people of different backgrounds. People are not determined by sexual orientation. That's just a factor. It's an irrelevant way of viewing a person as a whole." And I think that was important to me when I was writing that.

Lackey: How does Casement's story speak to us today? Why him? What was the value of choosing him in particular for now? You didn't write about the apostle Paul. You decided that Casement was the man, that there was something about his story that is really important for people now. What is that?

Murray: It's that he actually affected real change, and by his example, he still affects change. People think about him as an almost religious iconic figure. And that's usually what I saw for him. That's why I was trying to peel it away and to view him more simple and human because of the saint-like quality that attaches itself to him. There is still a lot of work to do with gay rights around the world. I think that's very important, and that's brought attention to him. But I also think there's the fact that he lived in so many different places, the fact that national boundaries were breaking down. And he was somebody who really lived as a citizen of endlessly changing identity because of the world, but still managed to stay true to his ideals. I think that's probably what we identify with Casement when we are reading about him, that the future was proliferating so quickly. The world was changing at such a rate that it was very hard to figure out what to do and what your role in life would be and how to make moral choices. That's what makes Casement so appealing. How was he going to navigate morality and the world in a time of such upheaval? And he was a man who had a real desire to do the right thing. And he was feeling this way when the right thing wasn't immediately apparent. I really think that that makes him intriguing now.

Lackey: Let's briefly talk about changes to the biographical or historical record. Let me give you an example to illustrate. Russell Banks wrote a brilliant biographical novel called *Cloudsplitter*. It is about the son of John Brown, Owen. Owen dies in 1889, but Russell ended up having that character live until 1903. During an interview, I asked him: "Why would you make that change?" And he said: "In that novel, I was exploring the terrorist mind, and I wanted to convert Owen into a symbol. I wanted to show that this terrorist way of thinking is not something that happened in the nineteenth century and it's gone. I wanted to show my reader that it extends into the twentieth century." Would you say: "Russell, you just made a mistake. You can't do that. That is inaccurate. Therefore, your novel is flawed."

Murray: No, I'd say that it was a very good decision to make, but it's a different decision from what I would make. Given Banks's rationale, it's a fantastic decision, the correct one. The character has to do the work. And especially if you're trafficking in novels of ideas, which, obviously Banks is, you have to be loyal to the truth of the idea above anything.

Lackey: I love this phrase: "Loyal to the truth of the idea." Can you give me a few of your thoughts about the truth of the idea in "Fish" and *Valiant Gentlemen*? Either/or or both. What is your idea?

Murray: I am not inclined to be free and easy with dates, despite my respect for Banks's decision, so dates are not where you will find my embracing of the concept, but the introduction of the fairies in "Fish" illustrates loyalty to the truth of an idea to some degree. I wanted to show Kingsley alone and plagued by doubt, but still committed to realizing her goals. When she's traveling in West Africa, the fairies don't plague her. Introducing this fantastical element—fairies—illustrates the necessary points I wanted to make. And in *Valiant Gentlemen*, the big conceit is that Casement is in love with Ward. Maybe he was. It's as hard to disprove as it is to prove, but whether or not it's true, it's absolutely necessary to the plot of the book. Without the ability to make leaps like this, a work of fiction will stagnate. If certain elements of the book are fixed—real characters—other elements must be loosened in order to have the narrative achieve the lifelike frisson that makes the novel a necessary form. I'd say this applied to *Cloudsplitter*. If I had wanted to shift a date, I would have.

Lackey: Let me go to the last question. If you would have been living in the 1940s and you were writing the same novel, you would have changed the name, as Robert Penn Warren did in *All the King's Men*. Instead of Huey Long, he calls his protagonist Willie Stark. Something shifted culturally that allowed writers to name their protagonists after actual figures and readers to accept this. What happened?

Murray: Why would you waste your time reading a book about Willie Stark when you could read a book about Huey Long? That is how people feel. You want to pretend that it's not invented. If I say I want to write a book about this invented Irish revolutionary who's not really based on anyone, and he has all of these adventures, I don't think that it would seem as weighty, as valuable to a jaded public who aren't used to engaging with art for art's sake. You pretend it's not art. I don't know if that's saying that's why I did it, but actually I don't know if I would have been able to publish this book and get it into the hands of readers if I hadn't said that Casement was Casement.

14

The Slant Truth of the Biographical Novel

Nuala O'Connor, interviewed by Julie A. Eckerle

Eckerle: Let me start by giving you a little context for this interview and the project of which it is a part. Our focus is the genre of the biographical novel, a popular subject right now with both scholars and novelists. *Miss Emily* was published in 2015, which is well within the current boom of biographical novels. Works within this genre are distinguished by the author's willingness to name the protagonist after a historical figure. I want to start by asking, first, if you set out to write a biographical novel, or if you even think of *Miss Emily* as a biographical novel? And, second, why you decided to name Emily Dickinson after the actual historical figure?

O'Connor: The term "biographical novel" is not one that I use at all. I would always say "historical fiction" or "literary fiction," though I had an agent once who warned me not to use the term "historical fiction." Never use it, he said, because he felt it had negative connotations. Always say "literary fiction," he would suggest. It wouldn't have occurred to me to change Emily's name to try and mask her identity in any way. But even if I did write about an American recluse and poet in the 1800s, people are going to know it is Emily Dickinson. And you're going to end up fessing up at interviews that it is based on her in some way. In a sense, I don't see the point in not naming the character after the real person, unless you are setting it in a different era or you are doing something very strange.

Eckerle: Changing the name gives you more freedom. For example, Curtis Sittenfeld's *American Wife* is about George W. Bush's wife, Laura Bush. Much in her story was Laura Bush's story, but she didn't name her Laura Bush. And yet, we all knew that it was her. Changing the name gives the author more creative license to do whatever she wants, but there are interesting implications for each choice. And so, what do you see as the advantages and/ or disadvantages of naming her Emily?

O'Connor: The advantages: we know where we are and who we're dealing with. You also get to do tons of research, which I love. You get to honor your subject. The disadvantages: in some ways, people want the whole life. They want the life from birth to death, whereas I chose one year and a fictional maid in order to write my story. There's a curious thing in American publishing that we don't do here; you always write "a novel" on the front of the book, just to make sure that the reader knows this is made up. I find that really interesting. If you look at the UK edition, which also covers Ireland, we don't do that. In a sense, it feels like spelling it out to the reader. But I guess it eliminates ambiguity. This is a novel. And I think when it says "a novel," that should be enough for the reader to realize this is invention. This is based on a real figure, but what you read here you should not take as truth. And then when you do Q&As once the novel is published, invariably people want to know what is real in the novel and what is not real and what's true. And they are very hung up on this. "So is it true that X, Y, and Z happened?" And I say "no" because I start with bare facts, and I build outwards. What's true and what's not is not what's important to you as a novelist—story is what's important, narrative payoff. Emily Dickinson's life is not a story so, for a novel to work, you need to invent a story, motivations, consequences. Sometimes, as time goes on, you forget yourself what is fact and what is fiction. The research becomes so entwined in your mind with the story you've fabricated. And it's only when you are revisiting research (for articles and events) that you realize you hadn't, in fact, invented something, it was a part of the real history.

In Emily's case, her life is a life of gaps, but we have a lot of stuff. So we have excellent biographies of Emily. We have books just about her poetry that also can relate back to the life. We have some biographies which are not as good, and there's a lot of conjecture in them: Did she have epilepsy? Was she in love with Charles Wadsworth? All this stuff that almost reads like fiction. We have some of Emily's letters. We don't have a lot of the letters that were written to her because she asked that they be burned. So you can piece things together and you can use a lot. For someone like Belle Bilton, who my new novel is about, there is so little. There is so little that invariably you are inventing practically everything. For Emily, you can build her personality from the letters, from what other people have said about her. Her niece wrote a biography of her aunt, for example. But with someone like Belle, we don't have anything. She was an obscure figure. So there are different ways of approaching the novel. I'm interested in the line between biography/hagiography/story. I love to bellow life into long dead lungs and make a living, breathing person of someone we only know vaguely.

Eckerle: One of the things biographical novelists frequently do is to include an afterword or a disclaimer that says: "This is what is true. These were my sources. This is all that is not true." You chose not to do that. Do you think that that is because of this distinction between the United States and the United Kingdom and Ireland you are talking about?

O'Connor: If you have "a novel" written on the front, it should be enough. But, yes, I did choose not to include a disclaimer, and I did have a conversation with my editor about it. She didn't push for it. And since she didn't push, I didn't feel the need for the disclaimer or the list of reference books. I thought, "Leave it at 'a novel' and let that be enough." Having said that, my new novel will be different, because there's so little actual information about Belle. There are some newspaper reports, and then the court case which she was central to, and there are a lot of photographs of her because she was a dancer and actress. So I could piece things together from those sources. And then, obviously, I have her biography; I know where and when she was born. So, at the end of *Becoming Belle*, I have an afterword. I did that because so many of the players in that novel ended tragically and tragically young; I felt it would be nice just to catch the reader up on what happened to everybody. For example, Belle died at thirty-nine of cancer, she lived in Ballinasloe, County Galway, Ireland, she had five children, she had a happy marriage. I felt because there are so few facts for people to go and google, that I would give them a few facts at the end so that they could have a better knowledge of what happened to the house and the estate and to Belle and to her husband William.

Eckerle: So both of these characters are women who have a lot of gaps in their stories. Is that what attracts you to them?

O'Connor: Absolutely. The freedom to fill those gaps fictionally. And I say freedom advisedly because you will always have people who criticize. The Dickinson academics are quite protective. And I have become that way too over the years. I did the research and wrote the book, and I attend the Emily Dickinson conferences as much as I can. You become very protective of her. You don't like glaring inaccuracies like, say, on Pinterest there's a photo that goes around that's not Emily. And you just want to point out that's not her for accuracy's sake. Whereas I think what I am doing is something very different. I am taking some facts and then I'm creating fiction around them. I did feel it was an audacious thing to do. And I pussyfooted around the project for a long time. I wanted to do it. I wrote a poem about Emily as a baker because I had studied her poetry in school. And then I heard later that she loved to bake, and I love to bake too, so I was baking her cakes, her recipes. I got them on the internet. And then this poem emerged of Emily as a baker, and then I just couldn't leave the subject alone. Then I was thinking, "Wouldn't it be great if she had Irish maids?" I found out she had, in fact, had at *least* three Irish maids that we know about. And then the whole narrative thing starts spinning in my head: what if I put a very fresh, young Irish maid into the house? Someone who was a willing immigrant. Somebody in contrast to Emily, a little bit extroverted. And who gets to go outside the Homestead, so that if Emily and the book are contained in Emily's house, we at least have this person who goes out and experiences the world. That was the rationale. But some scholars criticized what I did. At an Emily Dickinson conference I did a reading, and one woman asked: "Why bother?" I answered as well as I could. I told her I approached Emily out of love and respect and kept as faithful to her as one does in fiction. And then another scholar was given a proof copy to read with the hope that she would blurb it, and she was quite annoyed by things that to my agent, editor, and me actually seemed very minor. She objected to there being a Christmas tree in Emily's home or Emily wearing snowshoes and the geography of the house. I have Ada, the maid, live in the house, and at one point Emily sees her in the corridor, and this academic was arguing that she wouldn't have been in that corridor. But I would argue that she was a maid of all work and she would have been everywhere in the house. I guess you cannot write about someone who is so beloved and an icon without people's back being up in some way. Whereas with Belle, it didn't occur to me that she would have direct living relations because I didn't investigate the family tree right down to now. And I discovered at least two of her great-grandchildren, so I wrote to one of them. And he said he was trepidatious, but he just hoped that his relatives come off well while also acknowledging that that side of the family was quite eccentric. I'm going to send him the galleys in September/October and see how he gets along with it.

Eckerle: This poses questions about the ethics of the biographical novel. There is a difference when you are dealing with historical figures versus people who have descendants.

O'Connor: Yes. Not many people outside of Ballinasloe would have heard of Belle Bilton. She lived here and made a very good impression on people here for the time that she was here. So I'm plucking her from obscurity. But yes, you do have to ask the question: "Who has the right to tell this story?" Well, I feel I, as a novelist, do have that right in a sense, and sometimes families feel they should be telling the story, but maybe they don't write or wouldn't be able to tell it in a way that will lift a character from obscurity in a way that's helpful. Now I'm *all for* facts; I love facts. I'm like a forensic researcher.

I really enjoy the research. It thrills me, and that's why I don't research and then write. I do a bit of research to get my juices going, and then I research more as I write. And I do a lot of layering and a lot of patchwork so that my research is woven through. But yes, there is always that question about who owns the person in a sense, who is qualified to tell their story.

Eckerle: And do you feel that as a novelist you have creative license to do whatever you want? Thinking about that question of who has the right to tell someone's story, do you feel that being an Irish woman gives you a certain kind of access or authority over characters like Belle or even the fictional Ada?

O'Connor: Yes, I think it does. With Ada, I made her a cousin of Maggie Maher, one of the Dickinsons' real maids. I set the novel in 1866 because I knew the Dickinsons did not have a maid then, so I had a year to play with. Mrs. Dickinson had trained her daughters in the domestic arts and, between them, the three women managed the house, but this meant that Emily had little time to write. This was also around the time that Emily entered her white phase (where she chose to dress in a white wrapper, rather than in a standard gown) and she began her retreat from the outside world. So here I had a couple of moments of quiet drama with which to begin my fictional exploration of a part of her life. My invented maid—Ada from Dublin—fit nicely into this gap. I'd wanted Ada to be quite young and already at that stage I think Maggie would have been twenty-five. And Ada had to be a match for Emily because it's a dual narrative: one chapter in Emily's voice, one chapter in Ada's. So they had to have parity of esteem in the novel. I made Ada be from my home place, and Maggie Maher is from Tipperary; Ada's mother is a sister of Maggie's mother. I put her from my home place because my people go back quite far where we're from in Dublin. I thought I could tap into their knowledge. So I have Ada working in what is essentially Farmleigh, the Guinness House in Castleknock; my relatives, from both sides, worked there, in the kitchen and on the land. So I was creating links, and it's something you do in a sense to honor your own family and your own past, but also it is a link to yourself and to your people, and it's a way of using your own history and the social history of where you're from and bringing it into a novel that is ostensibly about Emily Dickinson.

Eckerle: Were you tempted to use Maggie or to use a real historical figure?

O'Connor: Not really. I did a little bit of research into Margaret O'Brien and Maggie. They didn't really fit with what I wanted. I needed someone fresh off the boat. I needed someone really at the start of her journey into adulthood.

So for fictional purposes, I needed somebody that I could truly invent. From scratch. Ada's history was mine to concoct. That way, I knew, while I happily invented a fictional Irish woman, I could also weave her fiction around Emily Dickinson's world and invent a fresh Emily at the same time. I had written a novel before, unpublished, about a German expressionist artist. And I had stuck so much to the facts that the whole thing just collapsed. Having spent two years researching and writing it, I learned that if you stick too much with the facts, you are not necessarily going to end up with something story-like or novel-like. So you are actually better off giving yourself a lot of room for invention. By inventing Ada, I gave myself more freedom. Even though it is brilliant to use a real person, particularly somebody as interesting as Emily, it is also good to give yourself fictional license.

Eckerle: You say that this is a dual narrative. I love these voices working in parallel. I have two questions: why give Ada so much narrative space so that she is almost equal to Emily? And, given that choice, why is the novel titled *Miss Emily*?

O'Connor: The title is curious. When I was choosing a title, I wanted something that pertained to Emily's poetry. Her poetry was the first thing I ever found out about her, naturally. So I had taken "Tell all the truth but tell it slant," and I had turned it. I wanted to title the novel *The Slant Truth*. The second I said that to my agent she said, "No." She thought it was too poeticy and airy-fairy, nothing to cling to. Mind you, there is an enormous fashion for titles like that. We ended up at *Miss Emily*, which I was not keen on at all. It sounded very bald to me. I felt it was unfair to Ada because this was also her book, and a lot of people say to me, "Oh, but it's really about Ada. It's really Ada's story. It's not really about Emily Dickinson at all." And I would argue, well, it's about both Ada and Emily. So we had a lot of back and forth about this. We had this very long conversation, and we came up with all sorts of titles. Gráinne Fox, my agent, suggested *The Poet and the Maid*, and I countered that with "What about *The Poet and Her Maid* or *The Poet's Maid*?" And I said, "I like that possessive, which is why *Miss Emily's Ada* appeals to me." You get the mistress-servant relationship. In the end, Gráinne decided to start submitting the novel with the title *Miss Emily*. I was not crazy about it. But she said, "Well, let's just see. It could change later." But it just stuck. And it's amazing how quickly you get used to something and end up liking it.

Eckerle: I have to say, I like *The Slant Truth*, for what that's worth. That title is actually relevant to my next question. Two forms are often confused with the biographical novel: one is the historical novel, and of course you mentioned thinking about your novel as historical fiction at first. The other is biography. Readers want to know what's true and what's not. So there's something about that *Slant Truth* title that I think taps into some of this. What can the biographical novel do that maybe biography or traditional historical fiction cannot?

O'Connor: I suppose in terms of the title, at the heart of the novel there's a very large lie and a crime covered up, and Emily and her brother are complicit in that. So the whole thing about truth is at the center of it. And at the end you are wondering, "Can terrible events really be covered up? Can they be recovered from? And how do people fare after that?" We don't know, and this is another thing people infuriatingly ask at Q&As, "What happened afterward?" And you are like, "I don't know. It's up to you to decide." And people just get quite grumpy about this, that you don't know or that you haven't decided. But they don't realize what it feels like to write a novel and to let characters go and move on to the next project, which is currently the one you're excited about. So I think the novel spoke really to the heart of the story and of course to Emily's poetry and more to Emily herself.

Eckerle: Can you talk about the kind of truth that you give readers? Let me be more specific.

You start with an individual like Emily, and then through that character's interiority, you look out. But what kind of truth is that? Is it a completely new truth that's being created? Is it the novelist's truth that the biographical novelist brings? Is it an effort to force the reader to engage something in his or her self? These are some of the questions scholars have, and obviously there's no one consistent approach. So where do you think you enter that conversation about truth, or not?

O'Connor: Every novel's chief responsibility is to itself: to make the best possible story out of the set of circumstances the characters find themselves in, whether they are based on real people from history or not. Like all fiction, there is a fair amount of dissembling that goes on in the writing of historical work; we write it *now*, but it is about *then*. My hope is that I can lift women's lives out of obscurity and into some kind of spotlight: to add sinew and lifeblood, emotion and, indeed, facts to the female side of the story. Some people think novels start out with themes, but I certainly don't. I'm much more interested in women's position in society, in social history, and how women fared (and fare) in male-dominated societies, and whether, long ago, they could push against what they needed to push against, or whether they couldn't. And I see Emily Dickinson as a maverick who did not conform to the norms of her time. She didn't choose marriage, motherhood, childbirth; she chose to marry herself to words. And she was very sure of herself. She knew this was what she wanted to do, and so she did it. Her family were gentry; they were very influential in the town. They were also eccentric, all of them, in their own way, her parents included. But she chose a radically eccentric route in that she stopped going to church. So using the known basics of a real person's life, I then set out the nuance behind the background facts and, also, I leave ample room for my imagination to do its work. I wanted to be responsible to Dickinson's life and true to her spirit but I wanted her to seem real and human, flawed, and genteel, as I found her. So, in a sense, yes, by giving your character a personality, you're saying something about her. You're not instructing the reader but you're trying to shine a light, to open out the character to new audiences. To bring an understanding about something that you love and admire. Also, because I'm not a Victorian woman writing about Victorian women at the time, I can put in the things that nineteenth-century writers left out. So my Emily Dickinson menstruates, for example. That's the freedom I have now; I can bring twenty-first-century things that we're not afraid to talk about now into these novels. And it's kind of curious; sometimes, my editors want me to take out that stuff. But I always say, "No, it's very important to me that stays in." Because I have the freedom to do that, whereas they didn't then.

Eckerle: And do you need an Ada to talk about a menstruating Emily? Because that would have been part of the servant's work.

O'Connor: Yes, to wash the rags, basically. I could have probably had the scene with Vinnie, Emily's sister, but realistically, Ada's the one who's going to be cleaning up the mess, and so she's there. And I think that's the brilliant thing about maids; they are privy to all of this stuff, all of this intimacy that we wouldn't see.

Eckerle: I love the way you say that Emily Dickinson is a maverick because of course she is if you don't buy the reclusive narrative about her.

O'Connor: That's what I wanted to do. I wanted to blow The White Myth out of the water. White-clad Emily suits our idea of a recluse, a nun-like, demure figure who sequesters herself in her bedroom. But when you read her letters, she's incredibly funny. She loves to riddle. She's loquacious; she's almost cryptic half of the time. You wonder what the recipients made of these crazy letters. She's quite an intense friend, very demanding of her friends. And a lot of them back away. She was too much. "Oh, I wrote to you yesterday, and you never wrote back." It is like, "Let me breathe! I have three kids and a husband to mind." So you get a very different Emily when you read the letters, very different from the wafty recluse at the window. Even different from the only real picture of her we have, which is the daguerreotype from when she was sixteen. She appears to be in a black dress. It's probably not black; the photograph was black and white. She looks very serene. But behind that, she's writing letters to her brother when he's teaching boys in Boston telling him to thrash them. And she would say things like, "Oh, there was a cart accident, but nobody was killed, worse luck." Because then it wasn't newsy enough for her. She was very giddy. And feisty. A lot of people read her poems and think, "Oh, she must have been really depressed or depressing." It's not that; she was just really insightful. And for whatever reason, she was just interested in the vagaries of mental health and death. She experienced a lot of deaths in her family. Terrible, tragic deaths like her young nephew who died at eight of typhoid fever. So of course it occupied her mind. The graveyard was behind their house too. So she probably was watching funeral processions from her window every day of the week. I think when they teach her to us, they pick out certain poems. We don't get a lot of the nature poems. We don't get a lot of the love poems. We get a lot of the deeper ones, about death and failing mental health. It's interesting how someone can be presented in a certain way. So I wanted to show the other side of Emily, the lighter side, the gregarious side. The one who loved company, even if it was inside her four walls. And she was very friendly to the servants. When they interviewed children, as adults, who knew her, they would say, "Oh, we loved going there because Emily would always give us cake. Now Vinnie wouldn't; she would just kind of shoo us away." So Emily was warm, she loved children.

Eckerle: So how did Ada in particular help you convey this version of Emily Dickinson?

O'Connor: I suppose by being her companion in the kitchen and being allied to her. And I wanted it that they learned from each other; that it wasn't a one-sided mistress-servant thing, "Oh I'm going to teach you all my wisdom." But that Ada comes with her freshness and is teaching Emily things. And Emily is watching young love develop between Ada and Daniel and appreciating it. Loving being the witness to this. So by putting them together and just making them talk.

Eckerle: This question almost feels too simple, but do you think Ada symbolizes anything in particular for Emily? As a reader, I often felt that

Ada was equated with Ireland. There's an early line about how she stinks of the Liffey, as if she brings this with her. And of course for Austin she's everything negative about the Irish as he understands them at the time. Is Ada a representative of something, is she a symbol of something, or is she simply just this fresh kind of vision?

O'Connor: I certainly don't approach novel writing with the idea of writing about symbols. And it's not really until afterward when you have to start thinking about your novel as an entity that you have to start asking yourself these questions. What was I doing, consciously or subconsciously? Mostly consciously, you're not dealing in the whole area of symbols or themes or anything like that. I don't, anyway. And I know a lot of my writer friends would say no, they don't think in that way at all. But inevitably, yes, Ada does end up as a symbol of Ireland. However, she's not the traditional hand-wringing immigrant that we think about, who's away and crying because they want to come home. I wanted to make her a willing immigrant, someone who was quite ready to open out her horizons. I wanted Ada to be that sort of "I'm here now and I want to really strive," which a lot of Irish immigrants do. They just put their heads down; I see it now here with the Polish community in Ireland. They put their heads down, they work really hard, and they start to build wealth. If Emily is a symbol, well, she is a symbol of that proto-feminist, maverick, Victorian woman who made different decisions than what were expected of her. I probably would have had my reasoning earlier about Emily and how I wanted her to be this fresh, funny person that I had found in the pages of her letters.

Eckerle: A couple other decisions you made I found interesting. I recently visited the Homestead in Amherst, and the guide said that there were no live-in servants at the Homestead as opposed to at Evergreens. And so I was thinking about that choice, that you made Ada a live-in maid, but also that you had her experience horrible violence *in that home*, under the Dickinson roof. And then, and I know that you said the Dickinson fans were bothered by some of your choices, I think it is just audacious that you had her as a kind of accomplice to murder or at least a witness to murder, which is not typical of our Emily Dickinson stories. So I'd love to know more about your decision to have the assault within the home? And then secondly, why you took the story to this kind of extreme moment?

O'Connor: When I teach creative writing to students, I always say to them: "Something must happen." And, "You can't keep your characters safe." I can't go around saying that to people and then have two nice people like Emily and

Ada and have nothing bad happen to them. So something bad had to happen. And I'm not a planner. I'm what George R. R. Martin calls a gardener: I plant seeds and see what will grow. I don't know the ending as I begin. And so I work my way through, and it just feels at a certain point something has to happen. And it has to be something bad because what happens to your characters is usually a one-off event in their life, whether it's in a short story or a novel, and it changes things. And that's the basic premise of any novel. And so this thing had to be big and it had to change people's lives. I can't remember the moment or decision where I decided that it had to happen under the Dickinson roof. And I knew that people would be annoyed about that. I'm sorry. But I did feel I had to get Emily out of the house. And not just in her yard, but beyond the yard. And that I slowed down that scene deliberately so that Emily could take in what it felt like to be running through streets again. And so I slowed it down, and they pass lumberyards or whatever, where people are working or just starting to work, and there's fog, and you just get a real sense of her moving through and away from the safety of the Homestead. And then Austin comes into it, and I painted Austin quite black. I do believe he was a very troubled individual, particularly in light of what happened later on. Some of the publishers' staff know about the Mabel and Austin affair, and they were trying to get me to somehow shoehorn it in. But it takes place years later; I absolutely knocked that straight on the head. And then book bloggers are the bane of my life. You know the ones who write these really not very literate reviews of your books. And one of them just totally objected to the rape scene. She tweeted about it, and this was the one tweet that must have been retweeted about 300 times. Her review was a complete spoiler. It's like this trigger warnings thing that is in now. It's like nobody wants to read anything bad. Well, I'm sorry, but fiction is usually about something bad happening in the midst of a life, and that's what it is. And if you can't handle that, don't read books.

Eckerle: You mentioned the biographical novel about the German expressionist artist. Do you think you'll return to that project?

O'Connor: I don't think so, I spent so long on that, and I went back and forth to Germany and to Paris where she (Paula Modersohn-Becker) had lived and worked as an artist in the early 1900s. I was totally drawn to her art. I love expressionist art, and she had these monumental figures of mothers, and babies, and nursing mothers. I just absolutely fell in love with this art. I went to research her, and it turns out her diaries had been published in German and translated into English. There was an absolute wealth of material. She had left her husband to go to Paris to try and make it as a painter and was living extremely frugally, barely eating. She became quite ill, and so he brought her back to Germany. The next thing, of course, she's pregnant. That's enough to put a stop to any artist, but she went back to Paris, and he came and brought her home again. The baby is born, and within weeks she was dead. She suffered an embolism. And you just think, "If he hadn't have brought her back." There seemed to be a story there. And she was friends with Rilke. She was friends with Clara Westhoff, who was Rilke's wife. So there was a great cast of characters, and they were quite bohemian. They lived in Worpswede, which is an artists' colony north of Bremen. I had been there. It should have all worked, but it just didn't. Sue Hubbard has written a novel about her. Sujata Bhatt has written a sequence of poems about her. I tried to make it like a novel in a poem. I tried it from the point of view of her stepdaughter. I tried it from Paula's own point of view. I tried it in the third person. I started to write it like a chorus of voices. I tried Otto, her husband. But I was just flogging a dead horse. My agent showed the book to Bloomsbury, and they were tentatively interested. But I couldn't finish it. The whole thing collapsed on me. I over-researched it. I was relying way too much on her diaries. And in the end, I just said to my agent, "You know what? I'm taking it back, and I'm going to do something else." So I took it back, and what I did was a long short story about Paula, and put it into one of my short story collections. But it's not even a great short story. I just loved her. I was almost in love with her. I was so passionate about her. So it may be why I tiptoed around the Emily project as well. I was terrified of that falling in love and then not being able to do the thing, which may be why I did more research as I went along instead of that immersion thing that Emma Donoghue says she does, before writing a line. She can research for up to two years and then start writing. And she knows the arc of her story, and she knows the ending. I'm completely not like that. I don't have that thought process.

I'm certainly warming to the term "biographical novel." I've noticed that when bookshops have a historical fiction section, invariably it is full of books about wars and countries—historical events and places, rather than historical people. It might be more useful for me to start using the term "biographical fiction" to describe what I do, because it's true of *Miss Emily* and *Becoming Belle,* and of short stories I have written about Elizabeth Bishop, Assia Wevill, and others. And it's true of the current project I'm working on too. "Biographical fiction" seems a better fit all-around.

15

Postmodernism and the Biographical Novel

Susan Sellers, interviewed by Bethany Layne

Layne: Toward the end of the twentieth century, we witness the transformation of roman-a-clef into biographical fiction, where historical subjects are introduced under their own names. What do you think happened around this period to give novelists this liberty?

Sellers: The roman-a-clef is still being written, in the sense that novelists continue to be inspired by real people without identifying who they are. But the recent—to me exciting and welcome—proliferation of biographical fiction has its roots in postmodernism, with its twin suspicions of truth and fiction. Specifically, I'd cite post-structuralism as an impetus, with its understanding that once we recognize the sign for what it is—a fictional signifier for its referent—we are in the realm of fiction as soon as we communicate.

This has fueled a different attitude to truth. We're more aware than we used to be how narratives of events can change depending on who is telling them and for what purpose. Take the First World War, whose centenary we are currently commemorating. This was a series of real events, and yet as historians have discovered many supposedly truthful accounts were neither factual nor accurate. Wartime writing in newspapers was heavily censored, while firsthand reports were inevitably skewed by partial view and the agenda and/or emotional involvement of the individual recorder. Truth is also incomplete due to omission. For instance it took time for women's role in the war to be recognized, and the contribution of colonial troops is still largely overlooked. The recent 2016 referendum as to whether the UK should leave the EU exposed glaring anomalies in our approach to truth. It is now clear the Brexit campaign contained false promises (perhaps the most blatant being the lie about the money that might be saved for the health service): yet instead of questioning the validity of the result and prosecuting those responsible, we appear not to care. We're going ahead and breaking with the most peaceful supranational alliance in history, not because as an electorate we were equipped with the facts necessary to make an informed decision, but because of fraudulent propaganda and emotive responses—including politicians' desires to advance their careers.

I see a second factor at work in the trend to name source figures, which is our changed relationship to privacy. Fifty years ago, most of us would have lived in complete anonymity beyond the sphere of family, location, and work. Technology and the internet have changed all this. Even if we're not active on social media, we've probably all had the experience of finding ourselves tagged in photographs or named in posts. At the beginning of my career any student wanting to record a lecture had to come to the front with a clunky recording device and request permission. Now, I don't even know if I'm being recorded and it wouldn't occur to anyone to ask. We live in a more public world.

The internet's own dealings with truth are intensely problematic. At an individual level, we can select what we post about ourselves (though as surveys show this is overwhelmingly a fabrication, with three-quarters of respondents admitting to modifying or even faking the content of their posts). It's why the internet can feel such an alienating place, as we measure our lives against all the photos and protestations of what wonderful/awful/boring times others are having. Unlike actual works of fiction, complexity and nuance are rare on the internet. But truth is also a casualty of the internet Tsars. Type the name of any famous person or place into Google Images and half those that appear will have only a tangential connection at best.

All this has permeated our culture, so I suspect authors and publishers no longer feel it necessary or appropriate to withhold names. In the case of my novel *Vanessa and Virginia*, I never refer to the sisters as Bell and Woolf and I resisted all requests for a dramatis personae. But it never occurred to me to call them "Judith and Elizabeth," say. What fired me to write was their exceptionally close bond as siblings—their loyalty and support for each other, as well as their rivalries and occasional desire to free themselves from the other's orbit. Not to have used their first names at least would have denied their importance as inspiration.

But let me come back to postmodernism, and say a little more about its take on truth and fiction. When Virginia Woolf wrote her essays on "modern fiction" in the 1920s, she took issue with the preceding generation of novelists for what she termed their materialistic approach. We see this in her imaginary encounter in a railway carriage with three acclaimed novelists of her day—Arnold Bennett, John Galsworthy, and H. G. Wells—as she details how they would set about writing a fourth traveler, "ordinary" Mrs. Brown. What Woolf finds erroneous in the methods of these famous men is not so much their lack of truthfulness (indeed, she demonstrates how Arnold Bennett for instance would go to great lengths to describe factory conditions for working women accurately), but their refusal—as she puts it—to "look within" and render the complexity of Mrs. Brown's mind, with all its thoughts, fleeting impressions, memories, and emotions.

Woolf's modernist notion of what truth in fiction should be derived from seismic changes in understanding the human psyche by scientists such as William James (Henry James's brother, who first coined the term "stream of consciousness" to describe the interior workings of the mind) and Sigmund Freud (whose ideas were familiar to Woolf through her husband, Leonard's, reviews of his work, their publication of its first English translation on their Hogarth Press, and later on her own reading).

Postmodernism, on the other hand, perceives the truth of the human subject differently, in part through adjustments to Freud's model of the self as split between the ego (or conscious self), the id (or unconscious) and the super-ego (our internalization of the rules that govern who and how we must be). Jacques Lacan (to cite one of the most notorious commentators), for example, argued that even the apparently unified self that is reflected back to us in a mirror is a linguistic illusion, composed from all we have been told about ourselves and our place within whatever social configuration we are born into. This insistence that we are ourselves a fiction—and that our thought is prestructured and determined—sets the novelist a very different challenge to the one Woolf outlined.

To my mind, one of the most interesting postmodern writers is Hélène Cixous, who right from the start (even in early texts such as "Sorties" in *The Newly Born Woman*) has been interested in decoding and uncoupling the hierarchical binaries which structure thought—the mechanism whereby man identifies himself in relation to his inferior woman, white in terms of black, culture as superior to nature, and so on. In what might be called her fictions (I use the term loosely, since these are not novels in any conventional sense, but hybrid works that embrace poetry, biography, memoir, travelogue, philosophical reflection, and much else), Cixous explores how such organizational binaries might be transmuted into relationships of equality, and how as individuals we are rarely static or single but continually traversed (a favorite Cixousian word) by a host of others. So a text might begin with the author recounting a discussion with her mother (a German-born Jew whose family was killed in concentration camps), followed by the memory of an incident from Cixous' own childhood in Algeria. This in turn could lead to the report of an event in a newspaper, a dream about Adolf Eichmann, an imagined conversation with an actual figure such as Beethoven, or an encounter with a fictitious one. The task of the narrating I is to remain open to all such traversings, which it endeavors to lay before the reader as faithfully as possible. As a consequence, there is no division in a Cixousian novel between the factual reportage of traditional biography and the inventions of fiction.

For Cixous, writing is not only a tool and an ally (which is how Woolf appears to perceive it), but an equal and active participant. Cixous is interested in what the process of writing itself generates—those words, phrases, quotations, memories, people, stories, and dreams the writer has not consciously thought of but which writing conjures. Cixous proposes that the way to avoid the dictator position in the hierarchical binary author/reader (whereby the author shapes and controls to construct their own superiority) is to allow all such others into the weave and play of the text. In such a context—where there is parity between what is real and what is imagined, and where the writer's task is to dynamite and refashion the strictures of inherited thought—it would be inadmissible for Cixous not to name Beethoven, Eichmann, or her own mother Eve.

Layne: In the last volume of interviews, Michael Lackey noted the need to define "what the biographical novel is uniquely capable of doing." What opportunities does the biographical novel offer, in contrast to traditional history or biography?

Sellers: For me, the important word there is "novel." In other words, I think what it potentially offers is everything we look to novels to offer—with the additional precision and promise that it is a novel drawn from real life. While history or biography aims to present as many facts as possible (including different theories and viewpoints), this is not the main objective of a historical or biographical novel. Of course, the definition of what a novel can be is open, multiple and evolving: Woolf's modernist perspective is not the same as a postmodern one, and a biographical novel by a popular contemporary writer like Robert Harris is radically different to Cixous' auto/biographical fictions. But at the risk of generalizing with its attendant dangers of simplicity and falsification, I would say that whereas history and biography teach us about a period and people, fiction takes us there. It aims to place us in the moment—so we experience what it is like to be alive at that time or to be that person, without the advantage and constraint of hindsight but as events happen and choices are made. And actually I think that definition holds true even for novelists as poles apart as Harris and Cixous!

What this means in practice is that while historians and biographers are concerned with presenting the wealth of their findings, novelists focus on telling a story. Novelists might do the same amount of research, but we use it to different ends. We might strive to present an authentic depiction of women's lives in Renaissance Italy as in Sarah Dunant's trilogy, but our primary concern is to help the reader experience what an arranged marriage or life in a convent (the available options for the daughters Dunant is writing about) might feel like.

Layne: Max Saunders notes the truism "that most writers spend too much time writing to have otherwise eventful lives." In light of this, can you explain the appeal for biographical novelists of writers in general and Woolf in particular? How, if at all, does this relate to the "Death of the Author"?

Sellers: Well, I profoundly disagree with that truism! It's actually a discussion I have with my postman. My study window looks out over my front garden and of course I'm always at work behind it whenever he arrives. He finds it incomprehensible that I should be so stationary and confined, while he visits every house in my village and presumably dozens of others each day. What he doesn't see are all the journeys I make in my head. I'm writing a novel at the moment that is partly set in Russia, so while my postman might have been to the local sorting office and then driven or walked within a radius of several miles, I've spent the morning inside the Winter Palace at the time of Tsar Nicholas II!

Why are biographical novelists drawn to writers? Actually, in the case of *Vanessa and Virginia*, it was not her life as a writer that was especially fruitful. Of course, it was my admiration for Woolf that led me to her, and as the novel progressed I found myself increasingly fascinated by connections between what was happening in her life and her writing. Some of these are well documented: how her parents Leslie and Julia Stephen provided models for Mr. and Mrs. Ramsay in *To the Lighthouse*, and her drawing on memories of her brother Thoby (who died at the age of twenty-six) for Jacob in *Jacob's Room* or Percival in *The Waves*. But other links were generated in the course of writing—for instance, having drawn the triangle between Vanessa, Virginia, and Thoby as children (contested as it was), it fascinated me that this triangle seemed repeatedly to reoccur in the sisters' subsequent relationships.

But while there are plenty of references to Woolf's fiction in *Vanessa and Virginia*, there isn't a great deal about her writing life. On the contrary, it's Vanessa's work as a painter that is described in detail. But perhaps that's the reason: it's not my own art so I could enjoy imagining what it would be like.

I think the appeal of Woolf for those of us who have woven her into creative work is multiple. There's her dazzlingly experimental writing, but there's also the fact that we know so much about her. In addition to the ten novels and her biography of Roger Fry, there's a rich literature of what she terms "the personal essay," the diary she kept almost daily, a considerable extant correspondence, autobiographical writings, notebooks, scrapbooks, photo albums. . . . The wonder is so much has survived, and found its way into print or onto online platforms. The figure that emerges from this cornucopia is inspiring, witty, moving, contradictory and not always likable (Maggie Gee captures this aspect well in her *Virginia Woolf in Manhattan*). Woolf's detailed, revealing, multifaceted diaries and letters make her a novelist's dream. It's what fiction still has to offer in the age of film and the internet. The novel can delve into consciousness in all its diversity and complication in a way no other form can.

"The Death of the Author" is an interesting question, because if anything we seem to be resurrecting her. In literary studies at least we are once again attentive to the contexts in which texts are written, and this includes the author's life. And we could devote an entire conference to the recent big-business phenomenon of the literary festival where readers pay to meet the authors. But yes, perhaps Barthes's insistence was an ingredient in prompting some of us to go back to the life—in our fiction if not our critical work.

Layne: Is the novel a uniquely appropriate form for fictional treatments of the sisters' lives? What was enabled by Elizabeth Wright's stage adaption of Vanessa and Virginia? Could you see your novel working as a biopic?

Sellers: I'd put it even more baldly. I think the novel is the form par excellence for exploring any life. Woolf herself puts her finger on why when she has her spoof biographer in *Orlando* grumble because all his subject does is sit and think: this he protests is not something he can record in his biography. Well, it may not be a fruitful subject for a biographer, but it is the manna of novelists. Fiction transports us inside the life of the mind in a way no other form can. It's what makes it perfect for exploring the motivations, proclivities, hopes, generosities, fears, passions, antipathies, and cruelties of individuals.

In addition to superb biographies about Virginia Woolf and Vanessa Bell by Hermione Lee and Frances Spalding respectively, there's an excellent joint biography of the sisters' relationship by Jane Dunn. So it's interesting to think about what fiction does differently. For a start, a novel doesn't have to proceed chronologically. *Vanessa and Virginia* mostly does in the sense that it begins in childhood and ends shortly after Virginia's suicide, but the chronology is complicated by the fact that the story is told by Vanessa as she struggles to come to terms with her sister's death. And even if it proceeds chronologically, a novel is selective. Not everything can be included. For instance, in the biographical fiction I'm writing at the moment my character spends a great deal of time in America, much of it on long-distance trains, crisscrossing the country with various traveling acts. In a biography, one could easily list all the destinations and performances in a few paragraphs, but this wouldn't work in a novel. I need to choose one—representative—journey and portray this, so the reader gets a sense of what it was like to be on a train, sometimes for days at a stretch, confined in a small space with people one didn't necessarily get on with, before arriving in an unknown town at an unknown theatre often without time to rehearse. As well as necessary selection, fiction might speed time up or slow it down in a way that would be unacceptable in straight history or biography. For instance, if the biographical fiction is focused around a love story, the novel might only refer to previous relationships in passing (if at all) so they don't detract from the main drama. But there's no hard rule, and it's equally possible past experiences might become a means of emphasizing the benefits of the current relationship, or of probing how mistakes are repeated.

Unlike standard biography, which is usually written in the omniscient third person and in the biographer's voice, *Vanessa and Virginia* is written by an imaginary Vanessa in the first person, and addressed to Virginia almost as an elegy. My task is to get inside my characters' heads, try to render their voices. Rebecca Stott, a fine historical novelist, suggests the difference between fiction and nonfiction is that the former is written with all the senses engaged. So while a biography might describe the color and bustle of a London market in the early 1800s, the novelist's concern is for the reader to experience those sights, sounds, smells, textures, and tastes for themselves. The rules of biography and fiction may be closer than we like to think, but their emphases are different. In biography, truth (by which I mean the version the preponderance of available sources points to) has to come first. In biographical fiction, what comes first is bringing the life you are writing about alive on the page.

Watching *Vanessa and Virginia* transformed into a stage play was fascinating. What struck me most was the reduced role words play. They are important, but only as one ingredient in a gamut of possibilities and effects, including the actors' bodies and voices, the set, costumes, props, sound, and lighting. So while the line spoken by the actor might indicate an emotion, all the extra information about that emotion is conveyed through modulations in voice, a gesture, perhaps a phrase of music, a subtle change in lighting.

I think the sisters' story could be a biopic, but it would have to copy what Elizabeth Wright did when she wrote the stage play and transpose the material so it works in film.

Layne: What truths did biographical fiction enable you to communicate about Woolf's historical period and our own? Do you think that there is a distinction between the biographical novel and historical fiction more generally?

Sellers: Perhaps I can take the second of these questions first. There is a distinction in that the biographical novel is usually thought of as focusing on the life of a character or group of characters who have their origins in real-life people who may still be alive, whereas historical fiction may start with real-life figures but probably involves plenty of composite or invented ones who are not still alive. Under these terms, Annie Proulx's novel *Barkskins* about the French colonization of parts of America and Canada would be regarded as a historical novel because the characters are inventions, while Gore Vidal's *Burr* about the American Founding Father Aaron Burr would be a biographical fiction. But of course, like all categories, there is crossover and bending and breaking of the genre paradigm. Many novels meld characters drawn from known figures with characters that are based on likely suppositions about the people of a given period—especially where history has not left adequate records, in the case of women for example, or those disadvantaged by the political, social, and cultural hierarchies. It's why when Virginia Woolf in *A Room of One's Own* traces women writers across history, she combines discussions of Sappho, Margaret Cavendish, and Jane Austen with inventions such as Shakespeare's sister. In Jennifer Wallace's first-rate *Digging up Milton*, we have John Milton (or more accurately the dead body of John Milton) as well as an enthralling miscellany of vivid 1790 Londoners. And then there are the novels that fuse past and present. Rosalind Brackenbury's *Becoming George Sand* contains a wonderfully atmospheric depiction of Sand's writing life and affair with Chopin, set alongside the narrator's story in the present day. Both parts of Brackenbury's fiction can be labeled biographical since they involve the writing of lives, but only one is historical. Polly Clark's evocative *Larchfield* interleaves the story of W. H. Auden with a contemporary poet suffering from postnatal depression—a character Clark has indicated is largely autobiographical.

Part of the fascination of fiction set in a different time is the way it illuminates our own. In *Becoming George Sand* and *Larchfield* this is mediated through a character living in the present day—but as readers we map the past onto the present even if no such character exists to direct us. One of the rewards of biography is that it sculpts lives into shapes we can measure against our own. A good biographical novel does this too but also utilizes the additional pleasures of fiction: scene-making, dramatic tension, the immediacy of dialogue; plus stylistic devices such as imagery, reiteration, and contrast. It's worth noting that biographers are now incorporating more of these elements into their work.

As for the historical period, fiction helps the reader picture whatever is being described as if we too are living it. One of the elements I hoped to highlight in *Vanessa and Virginia* was the extraordinary freedom Vanessa felt after their father Leslie Stephen died, when the sisters moved out of the family home to their own house in Bloomsbury. Vanessa had been responsible for the running of the Stephen household—a task that weighed heavily on her and made it difficult for her to paint. Fiction invites us to experience such constraint and release in a way reporting the facts does not.

With *Vanessa and Virginia*, I wanted to tell the sisters' story, but for me a powerful component in that story was their dedication to their art. Although Woolf's diary betrays doubts and fears such as how reviewers will react, what it mostly reveals is her absorption in and commitment to her writing. We see this in her account of her long struggle to compose *Mrs. Dalloway*, where it's only after "a year's groping" that she finally lights on a solution to her problem of how to convey the past lives of her characters. Postmodernism might have helped dismantle the old hierarchies built on birthright, nepotism, and wealth, but what's replaced them is a celebrity system based on winning the media race. We need look no further than the recent American presidential election. Bloomsbury as a group and an ideology was not without its problems, but it did not prize fame or money above integrity and skill. Though Bloomsbury could be off-putting and even antagonistic toward those who were not part of it, its members attached importance to investing in and maintaining personal relationships. That model—of creating a work for its own sake and valuing love and friendship—is one we would do well to reconsider.

Layne: Is there a limit to the freedoms of biographical fiction? Does the biographical novelist have the right to invent, to take liberties, to subordinate historical truth to dramatic truth? Could you point to an instance in your own creative practice where you made free with the historical record?

Sellers: Will Gompertz, in his book *Think Like an Artist,* offers a provocative distinction between copying and stealing in art. Copying, he argues, requires skill, but no imagination or creativity. Stealing, on the other hand, is an altogether different matter, because when you steal you take possession. You have a responsibility to what you've now made your own.

Historical and biographical novelists decide for themselves how much of the factual record to keep, how much to eject, and where to embroider and invent. Although I regard fiction as the more ethical arena in which to explore and speculate in the spaces left by the historical materials, I am always careful to ensure that whatever I add is at least plausible in terms of the consensus of what is known. Something I wanted to probe in *Vanessa and Virginia* was whether the traumatic incidents in Bell's life together with the information we have about her breakdowns had any bearing on her sister's heart-rending decision to drown herself in the River Ouse near her Sussex home. Such an investigation seemed to me justifiable within the parameters of fiction, because of the pact the novelist makes with the reader. By adopting the label "novel," we advertise that there will be imagination and conjecture. I also felt the available materials gave sufficient basis for my hypothesis to remain. I'd have found it harder to include a scenario we know did not happen, such as Woolf giving birth to the child she at times longed for (a notion Clare Morgan plays with in *A Book for All and None*). This is a personal choice, however, and not a prescription. After all, it's simple enough for readers to check whether Woolf actually had a child. Where I draw the line is if work claims to be true when it isn't.

There are times in writing biographical fiction when one has to invent. One of the joys of writing about Woolf and Bell is the existence of so many photographs. Both sisters were keen amateur photographers, as were a number of their friends. But of course almost all are in black and white. Sometimes it's possible to match a picture against a description where the colors are revealed—but this is rare. So while my depiction of rooms or clothes is often based on photographic evidence, the colors are almost always guessed at.

The question as to whether this matters is interesting. I'd say it doesn't matter very much in terms of historical accuracy, but it can matter a good deal in terms of the fiction. Let me give an example: at one point I imagine Vanessa working on a version of an actual abstract painting, in which there are two red bars, one of which is bang in the center, the other off to the side. I do this at a time when Vanessa's relationship to her sister was difficult, and in my portrayal her emotions and that dominant central red bar merge. So those two red bars from the painting become an integral component in my account of Vanessa's feelings about Virginia. In a subsequent section I describe Vanessa sewing a dress. By making the dress red I could remind the reader of that earlier scene, while simultaneously adding a new layer to the complicated sibling dynamic between the two.

Is there a limit to the freedoms of biographical fiction? Yes, I think there is. One can't overload a novel with fact. This can be frustrating, especially if it's a particularly fascinating detail one has uncovered. For example, in the novel I'm writing at the moment, my character arrives in Paris in 1910 only a few months after the great flood. Researching this sparked arresting images of Parisians crossing streets on precariously erected gangplanks, but none of the scenes I wrote fitted. I tried a version where my character hears about the flood but it felt contrived. I even had a stab at making my character's arrival coincide with the flood, but then the flood became too important and overshadowed what I needed to bring out.

Of course one has to keep the reader on board in any piece of writing, but I think less about this in a factual piece where it's possible to have digressions and repetitions which—in a novel—might threaten the story one is trying to tell. Probably because Bell and her art are so important to *Vanessa and Virginia*, I was conscious as I was working that I needed to create a coherent, painting-like structure, full of echoes, resonances, variety, and contrast.

Layne: Related to this, could you speak to your transition from writing criticism to writing fiction? How might your authority inform the credibility attached to your inventions?

Sellers: I've always been interested in critical writing that involves creative elements. Part of the reason for this is political, part personal. My influences as a critic were the pioneering generation of feminist scholars who included their own stories in their quest to rectify the widespread exclusion of women writers. And I always get further in understanding when instead of being told what to look for, I'm given the means to discover this for myself. So when I came to writing criticism I borrowed and adapted creative techniques.

But there is a difference, which is that in fiction I'm attempting to produce a piece of art so any authority I might have as author is ultimately transferred to the reader. Woolf has a brilliant essay about just this. It's called "Evening over Sussex: Reflections in a Motor Car" and in it she imagines driving through the Sussex landscape and the liberating effect this has—so she almost forgets who she is as sights and sensations crowd in and overwhelm her. What's fascinating is that Woolf describes turning all this into a work of art she images in the story as a small statue. Her figure shapes and distills her heterogeneous impressions into a form she can hand to her reader. In offering her reader the statue, Woolf signals it is now ours to bring to life, interpret, and draw conclusions from. Unlike the critic, whose task is typically to argue and prove, the creative writer's role is to fashion a form the reader is given the liberty to experience directly.

Although in a factual or critical piece I am thinking about the reader and formal considerations such as the development of the argument, balance of information, the supply of evidence, etc., I'm not primarily concerned with producing a work the reader can receive and make their own.

Layne: The majority of my students are coming to *Vanessa and Virginia* with limited prior acquaintance with Woolf and Bell. Do you see your novel as mediating future encounters with your subjects' works?

Sellers: It was important to me that *Vanessa and Virginia* should be first and foremost a story about two gifted sisters that could be read by people who knew nothing or very little about Bell and Woolf. As a consequence, I worked hard to ensure that everything a reader might need to follow that story was present in the novel itself. At the same time, I was conscious that some readers would know a great deal—indeed had chosen the novel because they admired Bell's art or had read Woolf. So at least one of the many layers of which a work of fiction is comprised involves references only a more knowledgeable reader will notice. For instance, there's a scene where a moth circles a lamp on the table as the sisters talk. Woolf held the image of moths in her head as she was plotting her novel *The Waves*, though I doubt most people reading will be aware of this. But it doesn't matter because in my version it becomes an image for how Virginia sees her sister and isn't overtly connected to her writing.

What's intriguing is how organic the composition process becomes. Despite all the copious plans for how a narrative might develop, there's always a point when the work starts to give something back. Sometimes authors talk about this in terms of their dramatis personae: how the person they are writing about led them to realize they were not in fact going to do X as the author initially envisaged, but Y instead. It's a good sign, because it means the character is starting to come to life. But it doesn't stop with character. Ali Smith's lectures on literature published as *Artful* remind us all words include a heritage and that their meanings are multiple. Her title demonstrates this—encapsulating the art-filled experiences she is describing, while also posing questions about how that art-fullness is produced and why it is so important in our lives. At the same time, it links to the Artful Dodger in Charles Dickens's *Oliver Twist* which Smith is concurrently reading, where it refers to his skill in thievery (an apt metaphor for what most writers do all the time, consciously or not). So whether we're recreating characters who've already lived, or creating ones who have not, we write them in the knowledge of all the other books we've read—borrowing, adapting, refining, and jettisoning ingredients as appropriate. This happens at every level: the way we organize the narrative, who tells it, the style it is written in, how much to tell and when to tell it. Individual passages such as a dinner party will have echoes of other dinner scenes we have read. Usually in fiction these allusions are subterranean, but in biographical fiction where the individuals are well known it's likely such resonances will be spotted by the reader.

I don't know if this is true of all biographical novelists, but for me an important impulse in writing was the prospect of being able to interest those who were unfamiliar with Bell and Woolf in viewing and reading their work. Perhaps especially, I was aware of a desire to complicate some of the circulating stereotypes about the pair. I began *Vanessa and Virginia* in the early 2000s, when I became heartily sick of hearing that Virginia Woolf was mad and committed suicide, while her sister—where known—was branded a second-rate painter. Woolf did struggle with mental illness, but it was episodic and she lived a remarkably full and productive life alongside it. She also committed suicide: but not until she was almost sixty, had reformed the English novel into the shape we still know it in today, set up her own printing press publishing several of the pioneering masterpieces of literary modernism, read and traveled widely, written the first essay in the English language on cinema, delighted in love affairs and friendships—and so much else besides. Vanessa Bell was one of only a handful of students admitted to the Painting School of the Royal Academy, and her featureless portraits of her sister (to refer to just one example of her art) were a bold innovation in portraiture.

Layne: Jonathan Dee dismisses the biographical novel as an attempt at "grabbing up the genuine cachet those geniuses still deliver." How would you respond to accusations of its derivativeness? What would Woolf have thought of the genre?

Sellers: Dee's comment is highly derogatory, and so of course I want to disagree with him! But if we unpick Dee's no doubt deliberately provocative phrasing, it does perhaps refer to a truth, which is the harsh economic realities of book publishing and bookselling. We tend to be blissfully ignorant of this in universities, and indeed something that surprised me when I switched from literary criticism to literary fiction was that unlike academic presses decisions about what novels get published are almost exclusively based on a sense of what will sell. In trade fiction particularly, it's all about how much money a book might make. It doesn't even seem to matter how good a book is, or how well it is written, as long as it sells in sufficient numbers to justify the publisher's investment and hopefully turn a profit. Most publishers like to have their cachet authors too—those who garner serious reviews and win prizes. But in this climate, it must make a difference when it comes to decisions about what to publish and what to reject if the book is about an already well-known subject. Far easier to sell a book about Thomas Cromwell, one of the most powerful men in England under Henry VIII, than a purely imaginary and consequently unknown character. And if you're a debut novelist whom no one has yet heard of, harder still.

But though publishers have to think like this, I doubt many authors do. Writing a book, whether it's fiction or nonfiction, is hard work. Let me continue with the case of Thomas Cromwell: whether you're producing a biography or a biographical novel, there's an enormous amount of research to be done, not only into your subject's life, but into the period in which your subject lived. I don't just mean the history and geography, but the cultural mores too. For Cromwell, this might include dress, diet, furniture, what the roads were like, court behavior, the king's daily routine. Then you've got to think your way into the mindset of the figures you're writing about: try to imagine what it might be like living at a time of such strong religious faith, for instance. All this is before you even start writing a word of your book, let alone all the many drafts and versions it will undergo. So it's inconceivable to me that anyone would embark on such an undertaking purely to get a book published. There are after all easier ways of earning money and establishing a reputation. I think you choose the topic of your book because it fascinates, perplexes, and obsesses you.

The other problem with Dee's comment is that it rules out the possibility that the work inspired by the "genius" whoever it is, might contain any genius itself. I would challenge this, because I think genius is more generous and democratic than Dee implies. I'd argue that Hilary Mantel's two novels about Thomas Cromwell are shot through with genius, as is Gabriel Josipovici's *Contre-Jour* about the painter Pierre Bonnard, and Janice Galloway's novel *Clara* about Clara Schumann. I could add other examples.

What would Woolf have made of this genre? Well, she wrote about real people all the time, sometimes naming them (as she does with Elizabeth Barrett Browning in her novel *Flush*), sometimes giving them pseudonyms as in the case of Vita Sackville-West in *Orlando*, and sometimes—as with her parents or brother—disguising them with fictional names.

Layne: How influenced was *Vanessa and Virginia* by Woolf and Bell's own artistic innovations? Was it difficult to express a painter's vision in language?

Sellers: It's my belief that all contemporary novelists—particularly women—are indebted to Virginia Woolf, whether they are aware of it or not. Woolf reshaped the novel in so many ways it would require several lectures to do justice to them all. She was not alone in this of course (she herself was influenced by an array of writers from the Greeks, Shakespeare, and Montaigne, to contemporaries such as Dostoyevsky, Proust, and Katherine Mansfield), but those of us writing today are her inheritors—even if we choose to ignore or overturn what she achieved. Despite this, I was determined to avoid pastiche in *Vanessa and Virginia*. Indeed I was terrified of producing a kind of sub Virginia Woolf speak. But certainly the wonderful fluidity of Woolf's prose as it moves across points in time and between characters, her consummate understanding of shape and rhythm right down to sentence level, and the opulence of her vocabulary, were all ingredients I aspired to emulate.

I looked at as much of Vanessa Bell's art as I could in preparation for writing, and a number of her paintings became important sources. I spent time with artist friends too, talking to them about painting and in particular familiarizing myself with the processes involved so I had a palette of language and basic understanding. My aim was to make my descriptions of Vanessa painting vivid and engaging to nonartists. Watching painters at work was a revelation in terms of how a blank canvas slowly transforms into a picture, and with hindsight I can see that this slow, brushstroke by brushstroke accretion influenced my own structure, which is a mosaic of vignettes.

Layne: In *Given the Choice*, you shift from biographical to "pure" fiction. Could you speak about the processes involved in that transition? How different were your restrictions and liberties with invented versus historical characters?

Sellers: I'd say it's a good deal easier to write purely made-up fiction! Though I did research for *Given the Choice*, I did so on a "need to use" basis. For instance, I wanted to give my central character an activity to illustrate her creative flair and demonstrate her consideration for others so I cast her as a great cook. Since I'm a so-so cook myself my research for this was to watch videos on YouTube. *Given the Choice* is set in the contemporary art world and I spent a very pleasurable day in London visiting galleries and talking to people. A turning point in the novel is the catastrophic stock market crashes of the early 2000s and I did read up on this. But unlike *Vanessa and Virginia* I never felt I had to become an expert in any of these areas: I simply needed enough to lend authenticity and color. This immediately halves the amount of time the book takes to write.

In a straight novel the research is always subservient to invention, whereas in a biographical fiction I am conscious at every step that whatever I write has to be in keeping with the world and lives of the people who inspired it.

But let me come back to Ali Smith and *Artful*. In one of the many trails she leads us on she recounts an anecdote from Charlie Chaplin's biography, in which Chaplin, playing with his sons, trains a telescope on a passer-by and offers a running commentary: he wonders why the man drags his feet, if he's on his way home and what his job might be. It's a perfect evocation of what novelists do all the time—we see something and start to imagine and speculate. For Smith, it's what art is: this mixture of thieving and empathy. And if we agree with her definition and connect it to fiction, then the question becomes whether the more ethical course for novelists is to name the inspiration for our adoptions and adaptions. I would argue that it is.

16

The Anchored Imagination of the Biographical Novel

Colm Tóibín, interviewed by Bethany Layne

Layne: The first question I wanted to ask was to do with the transformation of roman-a-clef into biographical fiction toward the end of the twentieth century. I wondered if you had any thoughts on what happened around this period to give novelists this liberty?

Tóibín: I wonder if for each writer the needs are different and the impulses are different. Take Penelope Fitzgerald writing *The Blue Flower*, Michael Cunningham writing *The Hours*, John Coetzee writing *The Master of Petersburg*. Each of them, I think, would insist that this came to them personally rather than as part of a movement or something that was in the air. I was fascinated by *The Blue Flower* because it was very subtle, dealing with whole areas of romanticism and feeling, and Fitzgerald was actually working with a very interesting set of ideas in some beautifully chosen sentences. And with Cunningham, he was playing a game between the idea of *Mrs. Dalloway*, Virginia Woolf, and the present, so that was a different sort of thing. I think with Coetzee, he was working out something quite personal, which was first of all his interest as a deep reader in Dostoyevsky, which really goes throughout his work. But also, I think he was dealing with personal matters to do with grief, to do with things that had happened to him that he wanted to find a metaphor for. And the death of Dostoyevsky's son offered him that metaphor, offered him a way for certain feelings to be described and dealt with, which he did not wish to deal with directly. Now, in the case of Henry James, I think if you give the immense amount of material available on him and his family to any number of people and you say "you must come up with eleven stories from this material," each person would come up with a different set of eleven stories, and that would in turn tell you something about the lives and the preoccupations of all of these people. So biographical fiction is, in a way, like all fiction, a sort of veiled autobiography, made of elaborated versions of the self that would otherwise remain hidden. Using the bare bones or a set of facts that are available to deliver on feelings that have not had a focus until then. This is precisely what Shakespeare and Marlowe were doing in the sixteenth and early seventeenth century, where they're getting bits and pieces of old stories and making plays out of them, *Tamburlaine the Great* or *Faust*, or the history plays, or, indeed, *Lear* or *Hamlet*. In other words, it's not something unusual; it's just that in the roots of the novel there are novelists who just don't do it. Jane Austen doesn't do it, and in general Henry James doesn't do it, although in some of his short stories he is writing about the lives of writers and painters that seem close to certain people whom he knew, or close to himself. And there's something odd about these stories, where you feel it would be much better if he'd stuck more closely to the facts of a single painter or a writer, rather than trying to invent somebody who seems slightly too far away. But I can't give you a zeitgeist, because I live in an imaginative country which is defined by the concrete. I live in the concrete; I can't abstract from anything in particular to say that there was something in the air at the end of the twentieth century meaning that a number of novelists just said "here it is, I'm not going to bother trying to pretend; I'm just going to say a real name." But *The Blue Flower* and *The Master of Petersburg* and *The Hours*, these three novels seem to be particularly good novels; they seem to have taken a great deal of imaginative energy to produce, and they do not seem to me like literary exercises, and that's therefore interesting.

Layne: Definitely, and this leads me to my next question. Michael Lackey mentions the need, as he puts it, to define "what the biographical novel is uniquely capable of doing." And so I wondered, for yourself and for the other authors you mentioned, if you care to speculate: what does the biographical novel offer that traditional history or straight biography might not?

Tóibín: Well, I think it's very far away from straight biography. The Leon Edel biography of Henry James tends to be chronological, analytical at times, informative at others, with footnotes. Straight biography always has an argument, and if you talk to someone that has known somebody whose biography has been written, they always say "it wasn't like that. They were not like that." And so the idea, which I think fascinates novelists in particular, is how much information is actually misleading, and how much information has been burned, destroyed. In the end, nonetheless, a partial portrait is offered as a full portrait. And so biography, despite its footnoting and its rigorousness, can be actually a falsification of something. However, since it is often just the amassing of the facts as they are available, it's not a dishonest form, but nonetheless, there's always a feeling that if those letters that are now burned were in there, it would make a difference. This is something Janet Malcolm has dealt with, for example, in her book about Sylvia Plath and biographers. To get back to your question, it seemed to me that I was working imaginatively, and that I was merely using these details about James in the same way that I would otherwise use memory, and that there really wasn't any difference in the process for me. I had imagined a character and I began to work with him. He's very, very close to the character in my second novel *The Heather Blazing*, which appeared in 1992. It's something that nobody noticed; but that's fine with me, I don't need people to notice things. The figure of James is quite close to the figure of Eamon Redmond in *The Heather Blazing*, who is a high court judge. I'm using judges, I'm using the court, I'm using certain years in the Irish court system, along with a middle-aged man who is alone a great deal, who has a certain sort of power, is haunted by certain memories, and is trying to function in a public world, or in some relationship between the private world and the public world. One is a judge; the other is a named writer. But the difference in the way I worked wasn't great. With *The Master*, when I was starting in the morning I could find something by James to read, but with the judge I could often go back to a judgment of the courts, and I had also spoken to great numbers of judges because I had written a short history of the Irish Supreme Court. So I had all that to come back to, where the rooms were, what the corridors were like, how those men spoke. I had all of that research done, and I was thus able to imagine really, putting flesh, putting blood or something, into the body where the bones were already there. So I was doing that both times.

Layne: That's interesting. And in your lecture for the Henry James Society, you mention that the character of James came to you in a similar way as the protagonist of that earlier novel.

Tóibín: Yes.

Layne: That's really interesting. So you see the biographical novel, I take it, more as a subgenre of literary fiction than a sister genre to the biography?

Tóibín: Oh, I don't even see it as a subgenre. The previous novel I had written was called *The Blackwater Lightship*. It's set in rural Ireland in the early nineties; it has six characters and it happens over seven days. It's got a lot of Irish memory, Irish weather, and intense family relationships, that lower-middle-class Irish environment. When it was done, I myself was done. It was a very intense book to write, and I didn't want to produce such a book again. Coming to the James material in the aftermath of that, I wanted something with greater amplitude, that looked at a character who had many more choices and chances than the characters in the previous novel. So, I think it has to be seen in the context of that novel written just before, rather than in a wider context. But it's not a subgenre—it's just another thing I did.

Layne: So it was the right time for you to write about James as much as anything?

Tóibín: Yes.

Layne: OK. I wonder if we could go on to an idea that Max Saunders puts forward about the truism that "most writers spend too much time writing to have otherwise eventful lives," which seems to be undermined by the number of biographical novels about writers. As you mentioned yourself, we have *The Hours*, *The Master of Petersburg*—I just wondered why writers might be appealing subjects, and why James in particular might have been so appealing?

Tóibín: I think Max Saunders's point is interesting because one of the problems writers have is that we don't actually have jobs. I know my colleague John Lanchester, for example, is good on the subject of hedge funds, but I'm not, and I've also not done a great deal of physical work like digging roads. Henry James is particularly bad at people having a job; he really isn't good on the subject of how they make their money. And it's not something one would read Virginia Woolf for either. In *The Good Soldier*, the Ford Madox Ford novel, one wonders what it is they do. When everybody else seems to go to work in the morning, so many characters in fiction don't seem to go to work in the morning, and when they do, it's often terribly interesting because we're getting something we're not quite used to. As I say, there are exceptions to this—someone like John Lanchester, or Don DeLillo's first novel *Americana*. There are novels about work, but it doesn't come automatically. It doesn't come as easily as novels about sitting at home doing nothing much. But the other thing is that, in the case of Henry James, it might seem that nothing much happened to him, but, in fact, one of his closest friends committed suicide and he was made to feel partly responsible. He knew a great deal of disappointment—books that obviously did not sell and all of that. But there was also, more importantly, the question of his secret sexuality, which makes its way into the books in that there are often secrets—sexual secrets—which if known would be explosive, which obviously come from the life he lived. So the fact that people are just writing doesn't mean that they are not also in love or worried about money, or desperate in some other way, and all these emotions make their way into fiction. But I think the question of work remains open: I'm not aware of many novels, other than Graham Greene's, about being a civil servant. William Carlos Williams wrote a book about being a doctor, but I'm not aware of a good novel about what it's like to be a nurse. Are you?

Layne: Well, there's a section in *Atonement*.

Tóibín: *Atonement* does deal with that. And in *Saturday*, we have a brain surgeon and McEwan has scientists. But in general, I think I would divine that writers are not especially concerned with work, but the emotions that a lot of people live with—worry, depression, exhilaration, lust, hunger—these things can actually make their way into novels directly from the writer's most shallow and deepest preoccupations.

Layne: I think that's a really useful and interesting distinction. I'd now like to come onto the idea of film and fiction. A great appetite was created by the nineties film adaptations of James—I'm thinking here of the Jane Campion *Portrait*, but also of the Merchant Ivory adaptations of *The Wings of the Dove* and *The Golden Bowl*. Could you see your way to a James biopic—perhaps even an adaptation of *The Master*—or is there something uniquely appropriate about the novel as a form?

Tóibín: Somebody bought the rights at one point to *The Master*, but it was never made. I think what you would have to do is take a single episode, such as the relationship with Constance Fenimore Woolson, and work with that single episode. And you would almost have to do it as a single story rather than as a biopic. People were talking about having Simon Russell Beale play the part of James, and that interested me because he's mainly a stage actor and really not as well known as he should be, and he's certainly somebody who would be new to you if he appeared on the screen playing the lead part in a film. So it didn't seem to be impossible, but it would require the right screenwriter—certainly not me, anyway.

Layne: Maybe there's something useful about a lesser-known actor, one who wouldn't necessarily trail a huge star persona?

Tóibín: Yes, so Simon Russell Beale seemed to me that he would make a real difference in that he would bring something almost from the nineteenth century, this idea of a pre-film world. But it's been a long time since anyone mentioned it, so I don't think it's on anyone's agenda.

Layne: That's a shame. I was very interested to learn about your working title for *The Master*, *The Turn of the Century*, which seemed to me to communicate an interest in James's period as much as in James himself. Perhaps you could say a little about whether that's true? And the biographical novel and the historical novel: would you want to see those as distinct?

Tóibín: Oh I do see them as distinct, and I'll give you an example of how they're distinct.

Sometime in about 1896, Henry James has his apartment in Kensington wired for electricity—now this is a huge moment, just imagine it, people coming in, setting up where the lights are going to be, the switches; the whole business with oil and gas lamps is going, and this new thing is coming. I think that belongs to a historical novel. If you're writing a historical novel this is a marvelous scene for you where you're actually getting a key moment in history and you're integrating it into lives and you're seeing what the next day will be like. All I knew was, it would ruin my novel. It would be the end of the novel. It would just take a few pages to do, and you would just sigh, because I cannot dramatize this. Instead, I must be in James's mind all the time, I must be living with his preoccupations, and I cannot start thinking about what age Queen Victoria is or the details of interiors. I just cannot get involved with that. On the other hand, I found out that James was with his brother William, his sister-in-law Alice, and his niece Peggy at the end of December 1899, and what was going to happen next was really extraordinary. In the first four years of the twentieth century Henry James produced three masterpieces: *The Wings of the Dove*, *The Ambassadors*, and *The Golden Bowl*. With the exception of Shakespeare in certain years like 1599 or 1606, when he wrote *Hamlet* and *Lear* but also two or three other works, we don't really have anything like that. James's books took, it seems, a year each to do, and they're long, they're complex, and they represent a flourishing of the novel's form, of what it is that James had been striving toward. There's the inwardness of the characters, the sense of them as complete, of the lives being completed by the author, and also all three novels have very intricate plots, which are actually quite gripping. Two of them have been made into films for the simple reason that there's a drama inherent, and *The Ambassadors* awaits its film. But this business of what the "turn of the century" meant for James was, without his knowing—because he really didn't think, especially with *The Golden Bowl*, that it was going to be such a big and complex book—that his whole life had been building up to this turn of the century, when he would be left alone in Lamb House. He moved to Lamb House in '97 and there he is, at the very end of my book, after William and his family have gone. Some readers will know, and some of them won't know, but it doesn't really matter, that this extraordinary energy is there in him and is now going to be harnessed. So that was my interest in the "turn of the century," rather than as the end of an era or an epoch; it was the beginning of something psychologically and artistically significant for James, rather than the death of Queen Victoria or the beginning of a new era in history.

Layne: And you lead up to that so well with those little germs you give him, like in the antique shop with Lady Wolseley.

Tóibín: What I was trying to do was that, if you knew those late books of his, such as *The Golden Bowl*, you'd get an extra pleasure by going "Oh my God! That's where he's getting that antique shop!" I was putting things like that in, but being really careful not to do it too much, almost as a sort of a joke I was having with a certain reader. It's almost like something I would put in from home, something very local, that only somebody from my town would fully understand the implications of. But aware also that people outside the town will read the book who will not get that joke, or will not get the implications of something. So it's the same idea of just stitching in little private things, little funny references. I think composers can do it, put a tiny bar that's taken from Haydn or Shostakovich, but only the composers in the audience will know what they've just been playing with. So, it's an odd aspect, where you get a funny little moment of mischief, or a private moment with two or three readers, but I try not to do it too much because it's self-indulgent.

Layne: Since you raised the question, I'd like to think a bit more about different readers, different readerships. I ask this question because I recently taught *The Master* on an undergraduate course about biographical fiction where the vast majority of students hadn't come across James, or, if they had, they had perhaps read one story. I just wondered how you saw the text working for those kinds of novice readers of James? Is there a sense of responsibility, of introducing them to James?

Tóibín: No, I didn't see it as a responsibility in that way, as being an introduction to James. I really don't care if anyone reads James or not. I mean it'd be nice for them if they did, if they'd like that sort of book. My responsibility was to the actual reader of my book, and was to say "my contract with you is that you can read this book without feeling undermined if you haven't read any other book in your life." And I've just done the same thing with *House of Names*, where you can read the story of the House of Atreus without ever having been to a play, or read any Greek history, or knowing anything whatsoever about these characters. In both cases that's quite important for me, that you could pick this book up as the first book you would read, or the only book you would read, and it would contain a world without you feeling "I'm not qualified to read this book" or "This book is only for a certain sort of person and I'm not that sort of person." I really wouldn't want that.

Layne: And how about the transition you made from writing *The Master* to writing criticism about James? I'm thinking of the essays that Susan Griffin collected in *All a Novelist Needs*. That must have been a really interesting process.

Tóibín: What happened was people started to think that I knew a great deal about James, that I should write introductions to books and essays and reviews. I was still living in the afterglow of the book and was absolutely fascinated—every time a new book came out about James, I would immediately read it in the same way as there must be people who read everything about Napoleon or who read everything about Mary, Queen of Scots. But I was just fascinated by James, so I kept saying yes, and I found that I built up opinions that I hadn't really had before I wrote the novel, about James, and about James's work, and I began to write criticism about James. That was nice, it was indoors work and it kept me out of harm's way.

Layne: Interesting way of putting it!

Tóibín: But one book I need to mention to you is coming out in September. It's called *Mrs Osmond*, by John Banville, and it's a sequel to *The Portrait of a Lady*. It's from Isabel leaving Gardencourt following the death of Ralph Touchett, the train journey from Gardencourt to London, and then what she's going to do when she goes back to Rome. I have to say, it's very well written and emotionally accurate. The things she's noticing and seeing in London, the hotel, her time in Paris and Florence, her memory, her relationship to her maid. All these are exquisitely rendered. I was reading it quite late last night actually, and I'm not finding it a pastiche; I'm not finding any false notes. It seems to me to be a genuine thing. I haven't come across that before, a serious artist doing a sequel. Sequels tend to have what Henry James talking about historical fiction says to be a "fatal cheapness," and then suddenly one comes along and it doesn't.

Layne: I'm looking at rewrites of *The Portrait of a Lady* in my book, including Kirsten Tranter's novel *The Legacy*, but I hadn't known of any sequels, so you've just made my day with that one. I now have a question about the freedom of biographical fiction and where that might end. Does the biographical novelist have the right to invent and take liberties? Maybe you could speak about an instance where you yourself have taken such liberties?

Tóibín: This is a really difficult question and, oddly enough, the fewer liberties you take with the main character the better. You can't just bring him to America at a time when he didn't go to America—it's better just to stick to the facts. But, in the case of *The Master*, Henry James did go to Dublin at that time, he did stay in that house, those people are there, that ball takes place, but the servant Hammond is made up because I needed something to happen to him in the night, and so I brought that in. James's response to Hammond then contributes to the character I'm building for him. I'm not sure the word is responsibility, because you can do anything you like, but I think from the reader's point of view there is a sort of contract that says "more or less, I'm sticking to the facts here. More or less, this is how I imagine this man lived in these years." What I'm doing then is trying to imagine what life might have been like from his side, his perspective, how he might have felt all this and lived all this. Now I noticed, for example, there was one review of the book that said Henry James was much funnier, much better company, people described him as being somebody that was really quite ironically witty, and this was somebody who was not much in the book. This is because what I'm working from is a deep interior, from a place within him, not his social self, but his private self. So I'm not then too worried about that, that doesn't really bother me. But I am following the facts more or less with him, so that I don't bring him to Italy when he didn't go to Italy, I don't have him buying a house when he didn't buy a house. So I don't take any liberties in that sense, because he's not a fictional character, he's already there. There are facts that you have to deal with, and the facts become nourishing as well as restricting. That he leased Lamb House in that particular year becomes a nourishing fact. If I make up that he stayed in London another year, it doesn't nourish me. It almost goes back to your very first point that I've been denying up until now, and saying that *The Master* is a work of pure imagination where I'm looking at particular obsessions of my own. Nonetheless, in the rules I set myself, I do, I think, have a duty—though duty is a funny word. Let me get this right: it's that the more I stick within the framework of the facts, the more I get from that, the more I feel that this is real and I have to make it more real, I have to make it seem to matter more on the page. You're anchored, you're getting an anchor from certain facts, and that anchor is not merely factual but emotional, and it brings a great deal with it, it carries you. And because it carries you, you can get a great deal of energy from it. Whereas if you're fabricating, something more dissolves than merely your relationship to the fact, a set of feelings dissolve or become diffuse. It's something like that.

Layne: It's fascinating. So any invention has to exist within that overall truth framework?

Tóibín: The inventions could be side characters and, obviously, dialogue. You have no dialogue, but you know that James was in Rome then, or he was in Venice then, or he got that letter from his brother then. And that somehow or other acts as an anchor, gives you some further anchor which is emotional as well as factual.

Layne: It seems a little churlish now to go to Jonathan Dee's very hostile view of the biographical novel that is taken from an essay called "The Reanimators." He calls it the "art of literary grave robbing." He describes the biographical novel very much as an attempt to cash-in, of "grabbing up the genuine cachet these geniuses still deliver." I wondered if you could respond to this idea that writing about historical figures is somehow derivative.

Tóibín: He does have a point—the problem with his point is that it's just not a very interesting one. All fiction takes its bearings from things that have happened in one way or another. It'd be very hard to think of a pure novel, and I think the real grave robbing, oddly enough, is often done from people who are alive, and in using things that belong to your life and belong to you, and offering them to the world as though they're fictional when they're actually true. I'll give you an example that I discovered in a biography of Saul Bellow: a great deal of *Herzog* happened, and his wife did indeed run away with a man with only one leg. I was horrified, I really was horrified. I'd thought he'd made all of that up. There's always a problematic relationship between a novel and life, and there's something often that only the novelist knows, little things and big things that only the novelist knows, and there's an element of ruthlessness in how novelists proceed in relation to that. I've never known any novelist to say "I can't write that because it will hurt the feelings of somebody else." People tend to write it and worry about it later, or deny it, or try and wriggle out of it. Well, it's not an easy thing to wriggle out of. However, Jonathan Dee's point is right when you look at Shakespeare making his plays about kings that were recognizable, or Goethe deciding he would write a version of *Faust*. So what are you going to go and see? Only a play by Goethe, which is some "pure" invention of his? Or are you just going to go and see *Faust* because it's already got a marketing campaign going on for a number of centuries called *Faust*? So too, if you're going to write a novel about Virginia Woolf, Dostoyevsky, Novalis, Henry James, Shakespeare, Marlowe, you don't have to explain to the reader, "Oh this is just some rural Irish event that occurred in my imagination," you've already got a campaign gone before you. There is an element of a publisher saying "hold on a minute, are you going to write me a novel about Tolstoy, or are you going to write me a novel about your bachelor uncle who lived on a farm?" The thing is, the bachelor uncle novel could end up being a better book, but it's a harder sell. So I think that, someone like Marilynne Robinson has proved to us that you can get the most provincial people and give them an extraordinary glow and aura, and on the other hand Michael Cunningham in that extraordinary opening of *The Hours* can actually dramatize the suicide of Virginia Woolf, with a great deal of deeply held feeling. Or indeed John Coetzee has Dostoyevsky arriving in the morgue to identify his son, which is not merely unforgettable, but oddly pure in its procedures. I think there's a difference between reading the thing and getting the feeling from it, and thinking about it later and whether or not it was morally right. This is probably the difference between where I am and where Jonathan Dee was. I suppose the point is really if it's done well, if you can make it work, just do it. Don't worry, just do it and get the next sentence right.

Layne: To come back to *The Master*, and to James's own narrative innovations, I wondered how far you felt your style in that text was influenced by James, was, in a way, Jamesian? And what you thought about the point Benjamin Markovits raises, that it would be "impossible to 'do' late James"?

Tóibín: I think Banville's book is involved with James's style and having fun with it, so I don't think anything's impossible. But what I was using more than anything else was the question of point of view, the question of consciousness. Everything in *The Master* is known or seen by James only, he's the only one who notices, remembers, sees, and feels in the book; everything is told through his eyes. You can call it third-person intimate; it's something that James refined and did a great deal with. And I was also attempting to write most of the book as though Hemingway had not lived, in other words as though the great advance that Hemingway made in prose, which was simplifying things, breaking sentences down to something very simple, hadn't occurred. I was using broader brush strokes. It would be as though a painter now was painting as though before impressionism, and certainly before cubism. I was attempting to give myself the freedom (or the restriction) of that. Once I started, once I got the first notes, I had a sort of sound for the book in my ear. But the main thing I got for the book was the single consciousness.

Layne: For the final question, I'd like to discuss *The Testament of Mary*. You say you're keen not to think of biographical fiction as a subgenre, so you may not want to think of biblical fiction in the same way, but I just wondered how, if at all, you might categorize *The Testament of Mary*. How different was the experience of writing about a biblical character, rather than a historical or purely invented one?

Tóibín: I think the point of *The Testament of Mary* is its form, that it's short and written in the first person. So it's a novel for a voice, it really has quite a strong connection to cantata, to aria or recitative, or, indeed, monologue in the theatre. It really is connected to voice in a way that—I hesitate to say this—you get in Molly Bloom's soliloquy, a woman suddenly, out of the blue, coming to speak. So I didn't see it in a biblical context, more of in a formal literary context.

Layne: I actually listened to the audiobook with Meryl Streep reading it and it felt a curiously appropriate form.

Tóibín: Yes, just the way she builds up the tone, the sort of hushed beginning, and the sounds she makes. Also, I've seen it performed in the theatre about five or six times with different actresses, and everyone brings something different to it. But I didn't see it in the context of any other biblical text as much as I saw it in the context of moments in Greek theatre, especially with Electra, Medea, Antigone, in which a sort of powerlessness becomes power, using a woman's voice. That was the idea.

17

I Believe in the Novel

Olga Tokarczuk, interviewed by Robert Kusek and Wojciech Szymański

Kusek, Szymański: *The Books of Jacob* is your first work of fiction which narrates the life of a historical figure—for some a major reinvention of the traditional Polish historical novel, for others a prime specimen of the contemporary biographical novel. But the release of this volume marks a more radical shift in your writing: an ostensible departure from the themes, styles and literary forms which you've been traditionally associated with. What are the origins of this "revolution" in your writing life? When and why did you come up with an idea of writing this novel?

Tokarczuk: I don't tend to think in terms of literary genres. I think more in themes, in whole ideas, about whether they interest me and whether they'll be powerful enough to galvanize the immense energy it takes to write a novel. Usually what happens is that an idea attracts me, and itself suggests—or imposes—the form most suitable for telling that particular story. I've long been fascinated by the subject of the Jewish presence in Polish (and, more broadly, European) culture, and above all in the interplay of Jewish and Polish culture that is visible over so many centuries and on so many levels. So when I came across the story of Jacob Frank and his acolytes as I was ferreting around in various sources, straight away I knew I really wanted to tell it. This was an idea for an extended essay or a play (and in fact I later found out that it is a theme that has come up in theatre plays on several occasions), but I felt that a novel would be a better vehicle for it—for its exoticism and many ambiguities, and also the vast amount of material, detail, and minutiae. I believe in the novel. I believe that the novel is one of the most sublime genres of literature: it has the power to enrapture the reader and take her into a kind of trance. So much can be communicated in a novel, not just information. The novel has the ambition to build up a kind of virtual world, in which the reader is immersed up to her ears, and must make herself at home for a while. It operates on several levels, because it forges an emotional bond with the reader, and stimulates the mechanisms which generate empathy. It's a form of total communication.

Kusek, Szymański: So what were the major challenges that you had to face while working on *The Books of Jacob*? What turned out to be the most difficult while tackling a novel so very much immersed in history?

Tokarczuk: The vast amount of research, of course. The subject of the Frankist movement has not been sufficiently studied in the academic literature. It was not until I was already part way through writing the novel, in 2011, that Paweł Maciejko's book *The Mixed Multitude* was published. And I think this is now the seminal work for all those studying Jacob Frank and the Frankists. I read it in the English original, even before the Polish translation came out. Before I got my hands on that, I used many, many other sources, some of them monographs, but most of them scattered, minor papers, which looked at the history of the Frankists and the issues that grew up around them from several different angles. From the outset, though, the single most important source for me was Aleksander Kraushar, a Polish historian of Jewish descent, and his book *Frank i frankiści polscy* (Frank and the Polish Frankists), which was written and published back in the nineteenth century and never reprinted, condemned to gather dust on library shelves. Other sources were also important, though—sources on Polish history, on everyday life in Podolia and the rest of Europe in the eighteenth century, on the contemporary politics, on multiculturality. . . . I was interested in details such as how people traveled in those days, where travelers stopped for the night, what they ate, and so on. I had no experience in such extensive research; I was totally unfamiliar with the methodology. I did it all by instinct, intuitively. And then there was the question of material sources, and traveling to them—to see the Dniester, Ivanye, the cathedral in Lviv, the market square in Brno, the castle in Offenbach, to look at landscapes and get a feeling for atmosphere. I love trips like that. Everywhere I went I found something small that eventually proved useful for the book.

Kusek, Szymański: It may sound trite but it was Aristotle who already noticed that historical narrative differs considerably from literary narrative. While the former describes what did indeed happen, the latter is not obliged to—and in many cases does not—follow the so-called historical facts. In this sense, it is entirely dependent on the writer's imagination. The biographical novel is a dimorphic genre, which is forced to combine two types of narrative: historical and literary. It also negotiates its position with reference to historical truth and fantasy. What is your stance on this issue? Did it affect the way you wrote *The Books of Jacob*?

Tokarczuk: It's somewhat presumptive to argue with Aristotle, but these days we think differently. We can never be sure that the historian who first did the describing did not make things up, add things of his own invention, take sides. We have to ask what historical facts actually are. Are we to treat the annals of Ioannus Longinus historically? At the root and source of every story there is a person; historical facts are abstract, true only at the macro level of generality. Establishing the details is extremely painstaking work, and the further back in time the historical event, the more difficult it is. It requires a reading of all kinds of written sources with the awareness that many have been lost forever, and it requires their supplementation with the fruits of archaeological, biological, cultural, and philological research. It also requires good will and a certain honesty, because the facts actually discovered may not conform to the researcher's expectations. I would make so bold a claim as to say that in this sense everything is literature, and individual historical narratives are often no more than points of view. Literary narration always tries to build up a convincing, even mimetic virtual world, but this does not mean that it is entirely random. It has to conform to something like a principle of reality. In the historical novel this moment of responsibility for reality is simply quantitatively greater. Imagination and poetic license still have to be subordinate to facts. Again and again in the course of my work on *The Books of Jacob* I came up against situations where I was working with historical facts. These were the fixed points of my story, which I had to take into account and could not ignore. And then there was the more or less empty space between those points—and it was in that space that the literature began, because I had to fill in those empty swathes and blank spaces with my imagination. I gave this method of working the name "the conjecture method." I took the term "conjecture" from the language of archivists and text critics working with early writings; conjecture—filling in the gaps where parts of a text have been lost or rendered illegible—is a vital practice in their line of work. If a text is incomplete we have to deduce what might have been in the missing sections, and in the best possible faith fill in the blanks in such a way that the reader has the impression of continuity and probability.

Kusek, Szymański: Have you been a regular reader of historical and biographical novels at all? Are there any specific novels that you could cite as having some kind of impact on *The Books of Jacob*? Would you say that your book is in dialogue with a particular tradition of historical or biographical fiction?

Tokarczuk: This might sound strange, but I'm not really a fan of historical novels, and I'm certainly not competent enough to make any pronouncements about them. The ones I've read have tended to put me off with their dry, male perspective, which prioritizes "historic events"—often reduced to wars, battles, truces, alliances, negotiations, treaties, and so on. These I prefer to call "historical political novels," because they are born out of the now rather anachronistic understanding of history as a series of wars, battles, and peace treaties fleshed out by the biographies of kings or other leaders. I was always more interested in the micro-history approach—telling the past in small, local spaces, using the context of everyday life lived by ordinary people often entirely unrecorded by history. Even in Tolstoy I would skip huge sections of text where he described army positions and regroupings. This usually patriarchal view of people and society irritated me; I think popular historical novels often used to reinforce such conservative schemata. When I was young I read quite a lot of Teodor Parnicki's work, and I think his vision of the past moved me: that history is a mystery which we have to discover by taking part in the story, as it were. I also liked Marguerite Yourcenar, who portrayed people from the past just like those contemporary to us, equally complex and "fragile, feckless, internally divided."

Kusek, Szymański: The classic form of the historical novel which should be traced back to Walter Scott is, one could say, politically charged. You can find evidence for this both in Scott and, for example, classic Polish historical fiction such as the works by Henryk Sienkiewicz. Those novels were always written with an intention of solidifying specific political or social beliefs and attitudes. They were written either for a given nation or in order to create an imagined national community, as Benedict Anderson would see it. Interestingly, the subtitle of your book states that the book has been dedicated to one's "fellow patriots for reflection." Was *The Books of Jacob* deliberately conceived as a political work—because its reception in Poland was very much political?

Tokarczuk: I suspect it is impossible to write an apolitical historical novel. History has become (or perhaps always was) a very delicate space in political terms. "Who controls the past . . . controls the future: who controls the present controls the past," Orwell wrote in *1984*, and politicians—today as never before—are fully aware of that fact. This is abundantly clear in the history war that is being waged in Poland. So I was aware of the political connotations of this story, and I understood what times I was writing it in—times of renascent nationalism, of a return to xenophobia and even racism, and above all to antisemitism, which was never properly processed in Poland. I also knew that there were several seminal moments in the book which would be difficult both for me as a writer, and for the reader. Authors have a tendency to become attached to their characters, and instinctively start to defend them. And here I had to describe extremely grim events, such as the fact that the Frankists themselves acted against their coreligionists, or their use of rather controversial methods (concealing the truth, manipulation, and ultimately invoking the myth of "Christian blood" allegedly needed by the Jews for their magic practices) to defend their interests against both the Catholic Church and Orthodox Jewry. This is not a story about angels. For this reason, wherever I found myself on sensitive ground I tried to keep to the facts as far as possible, and the facts helped me to get through the difficult moments. *The Books of Jacob* is a novel founded on facts and sources, and as such was much easier for me to write than sketching out the structure and plot strands of my previous novels had been—we already have the time frame of the story, its scope, and even the characters already partly formed. And of course we have the ending!

Kusek, Szymański: *The Books of Jacob* has been dedicated to Jacob Frank, an eighteenth-century Jewish mystic, a leader of one religious sect and a heretic, as well as the self-appointed Messiah. What attracted you to his life story? Why should he become the character in your novel?

Tokarczuk: He fascinated me as a figure above all in the context of the age in which he lived. His was a time when Enlightenment ideas were gaining momentum in Europe and new visions of society were being born. As I read the sources I realized at one point that Frank was a kind of pre-Zionist, a sign that the Jews were becoming aware of their place in Europe. At the same time, it is undeniably the case that the system of beliefs attributed to Frank was (and is) a rather chaotic, very fluid, explosive, syncretic melange of various types of heresies from the more or less distant past, sourced not only from the borderline regions of Christianity and Judaism. Their horizons are far broader, and their roots lie primarily in Gnosticism. These are still very under-researched regions which harbor much that is unclear. As I have been interested in this subject myself for a long time, this part of my research gave me a great deal of pleasure. And being able to make use of my own hypotheses and musings was more satisfying still. Another aspect of equal importance is that Frank was an immensely interesting figure in psychological terms, though he ultimately proved unfathomable. He was too complicated and ambiguous to tell him properly, from beginning to end. Today I am sure it is impossible to tell the life of another person in the belief that any kind of whole, cohesive truth about them can be uncovered or a finite, complete picture obtained. Perhaps we should only ever look at people from the dynamic perspective—as a process, constant becoming, change.

Kusek, Szymański: The classic theory of historical fiction—the one originated by Georg Lukács—sees the biographical novel as an antagonist of or even a threat to the historical novel. Since it does not address big History and refuses to testify to the spirit of the times, the writer of biofiction is seen as a victim of biographical gossiping—entirely irrelevant from the point of view of Hegel-influenced Lukács who would like to trace the changes in consciousness in the historical context and not an individual's life. What was your priority while writing *The Books of Jacob*? Was it to narrate the life of Frank or—with the help of Frank's individual life—show some major changes taking place in this part of Europe in the eighteenth century? Is there any big History in Frank's small history?

Tokarczuk: I believe the exact opposite: that big History is nothing but the reflected light of many small histories, a kind of Phantom composed of hypothetical generalizations. Human life is all that is real. The rest is a system of generalizations and projections. I don't think we have any cognitive means other than seeing the world through the relations of individuals with others, with nature, and with themselves. I am not aware of any sense that we have which might help us to understand the vast processes of history. We test, we touch, we deduce, we make hypotheses—many of which are nothing but projections.

Kusek, Szymański: Recently Edmund White admitted to having reservations with regard to biographical novels which take for their major characters the people who do not yet have proper biographies. He claimed that one of the objectives of biofiction was to fill in the gaps that had been left by historical narratives. So far not a single biography has been dedicated to Jacob, your titular character—in this sense your novel precedes history. What was your attitude to historical sources and documents? Is the narrative that you tell in *The Books of Jacob* historically accurate?

Tokarczuk: I myself find it hard to understand why there is still no decent biography of Jacob Frank (not counting Kraushar's monograph on the Frankist movement, but he is not the central figure in that work). As I was writing the novel I wondered why it is that he as a figure is not a subject of research. What are historians doing? What are they researching? Why has such a signal, colorful, important movement as Frankism not been the subject of any major study in Poland (or anywhere else in the world, for that matter)? Is it taboo? Or—dare I say it—laziness? Or maybe it's an example of the fact that history really is not objective, on the contrary: that it is at the mercy of historians' individual whims and idiosyncrasies, their political views, or the basic human preference for passing over uncomfortable subjects in silence. The same has been true of the Jewish community: no one has tackled Frank's biography there either. He has always been rather distasteful. This is wonderfully clear in Gershom Scholem's *Major Trends in Jewish Mysticism*, in the section on Sabbatianism, where, on realizing that he cannot leave Frank out, his tone switches abruptly and his normally controlled language is flooded with emotion. As a writer I have the privilege of having to be loyal only to myself. The only things that disciplined me in this work were the sources, and I tried to be as faithful to them as I possibly could. Wherever I had to describe events which were ambiguous or controversial, or which I myself did not understand fully, I kept to the original texts. That was the case with the Lviv dispute—the whole of that scene is based on documents, as it was recorded (we can but hope that it was recorded truthfully). And it was recorded in great detail by Church secretaries. Naturally, every reading of a text necessitates a degree of interpretation. As I was reading the notes from the Lviv dispute, for instance, I tried to imagine who those secretaries were, what they privately thought, and above all whether and to what extent they were objective.

Kusek, Szymański: And what about the novel's biographical accuracy? Which characters belong to history and which belong to fiction? And why?

Tokarczuk: Most of the characters in the book are historical figures, above all the second narrator, Nachman of Busko, the teacher and close friend of Jacob Frank, his spin doctor and brain. Sadly, little has been written about him, and I had to create him and give him a voice. From the various narratives about him recorded in the sources I was able to deduce who he was and how he worked—and above all what his relationship with Frank was. I made him in such a way that he saw as much as possible and offered a kind of explanation of Jacob's charisma. Another interesting figure is Moliwda, the Frankists' translator and protector. In this case I found Andrzej Żuławski's book *Moliwda* extremely useful. Żuławski, who was as fascinated by the subject of the Frankists as I was, tried to build up a very sensitive, profound portrait of the man. In a novel by Julian Brinken which I found in manuscript form in the National Library, Moliwda is depicted entirely differently—as a searing, caustic aristocrat. My Moliwda is slightly different—he is a broken man who is still searching and lacks confidence. In the sources I found a single sentence regarding his youth: about a miller's daughter, whom he married in a "mésalliance" which carried with it a very harsh penalty. I assumed that the severity of the punishment might have been due to the miller's daughter being Jewish; society tended not to tolerate such transgressions. This was my reasoning for his ambivalent and curious attitude toward Jews, and for the fact that he afforded them so much assistance. Jacob Frank's companions are historically documented, though for the most part rather laconically. Naturally, the various clerics are also historical—both the strange, ignominious figure of Bishop Kajetan Sołtyk and the divided, genuinely benevolent Bishop Dembowski, and even the minor chroniclers of events. Every figure I found in the documents I attempted to slot into my book somehow, to make use of their existence. The time I spent with Father Chmielowski and Elżbieta Drużbacka was also a delight, of course. Both figures had faded somewhat into oblivion, and Father Chmielowski was actually rejected by the younger generation of his enlightened successors. I have been reading Benedykt Chmielowski for years and I consider him a highly significant Polish writer, chronicler of the mentality of the provincial Polish noble class. I, at any rate, have learned a lot from him about how our ancestors perceived the world, and about their sensitivities. Elżbieta Drużbacka, in turn, continues to defend herself, not only as a great Polish poet of the late Baroque. The power of her poems remains undiminished, and her life, lived with remarkable awareness, presages the emancipation of women in Polish culture. Something similar is true of Katarzyna Kossakowska—I came across her letters and she made a huge impression on me. I started to admire her: this uncowed, valiant female politician, entirely unlike the women portrayed by Kraszewski or Sienkiewicz. These latter, deliberately or not, pursued a policy of tailoring their female characters to their own expectations and to the mores of their time, always building them in the roles attributed to them by a society of self-confident, dominant men. However, the main narrator in this novel, Yente, and many of the other women in Frank's circles are born out of my imagination. It is a sad fact that history is keener to record men than women, and better at doing so. I decided that I had to individualize all these people, mentioned solely as "wives," "lovers," "waiting women" and "mothers," give them a voice, furnish them with personal features, and put them to work. History without women is undeniably falsified history.

Kusek, Szymański: So many characters populating the pages of *The Books of Jacob* and fighting for the reader's attention testify to your book being a very special type of biofiction, the kind that one could call poly biographical or simply polyphonic. Why did you decide to choose such a method of telling Frank's life story? Why this polyvocality?

Tokarczuk: Other novels of mine are also polyphonic. Sometimes I think about this type of writing as panoptic. I like to create a scene, and characters, and let them live. I like to look down on relationships from above; I believe that reality is not a series of individual, isolated subjects and objects but the infinite quantity of relations between them. I see reality as the stage for these relationships—not only those between the subjects, but also their relationships with objects, and with nature. It would be hard to give an account of any kind of social process without incorporating this multiplicity of points of view, this interaction of so many energies.

Kusek, Szymański: But such a panoply of characters poses considerable difficulties for the narrative techniques that are most commonly employed in the biographical novel, namely first- and third-person narratives. In *The Books of Jacob* various types of narratives are intertwined with each other while the narrator appears to be in a complicated relationship with her "omniscience." What is more, you have decided to introduce the character of Yente whom you called "fourth-person narrator." In fact, she has the greatest insight into the fictional world. Could you explain the reason behind bringing so many diverse narrative strategies to one book?

Tokarczuk: The most important question that comes up at the very beginning of the process of writing a novel is: Who's talking? Who's telling it? Through whose eyes are we looking at the represented world? The volume of material, of temporal planes, of points of view was too huge to be borne by a single narrator. Yente grew out of my doubt that I could fit everything into one book. The reason for her appearance was technical, but sometimes I see something metaphysical about her jack-in-the-box entrance. She just appeared, her entire story intact, ready to speak. And she saved the book. With every book I have a problem with the narrator, with the Voice That Tells The Story. It's very hard to invent, fit, discover. It's this voice that is the spirit of the story, and it sometimes takes me years to find it, even though I might have a plot and characters all ready and waiting to go. If there is anything metaphysical about writing novels, for me it's searching for that Voice. The moment I find it, the work all falls into place—you might even say it "writes itself." I define the Voice as the part of the mind which offers the vantage point from which the story will be possible to tell in the form most ideally suited to it. I also worked in different tenses with my three narrators (Narrator, Yente, and Nachman). The first two use the present tense, the time of the here-and-now; their stories are unfolding before the eyes of the reader unintermediated, and we do not know how each situation will end. This is the dynamic, immediate, burning element. Nachman uses the past tense, the tense we use to look back on our lives. Nachman tells of his life with Jacob and tries to be honest and truthful insofar as he is aware of what happened. This is his confession, and in it he reveals secrets from the perspective of hindsight.

Kusek, Szymański: Yes, it appears that every single character in your book has a distinctive voice—apart from Jacob, the main protagonist! Weren't you tempted to look at the world through his eyes and, in the manner of Marguerite Yourcenar or Hilary Mantel, "enter" the consciousness of your character?

Tokarczuk: Yes, I tried. I tried many times, desperately, but the figure of Jacob Frank is so alien to me that I was completely unable to identify with him psychologically. And here I should point out that even Frank's contemporaries were unable to fathom him out. Accounts of him are so diverse that they vary even in their descriptions of his physiognomy; this was a man who provoked the full gamut of thoughts and emotions. I suspect that, like so many other leaders of religious movements, he had a psychopathic personality and constantly needed strong stimuli. This is essentially the opposite of my own temperament. I have usually had little trouble creating my characters and identifying with them; indeed, on many occasions this has been a greatly inspiring learning process for me, to be able to create an extension of my own personality, but this time that didn't happen. To use contemporary psychological nomenclature, Frank had a low fear quotient, huge aspirations, immense conviction of his own power, and something else that I would call an "undemocratic character structure." All the while he was calling for equality, fighting for the right to autonomy, and assimilating "his people," he never lost his utmost belief in his own superiority. I intuitively resisted "getting into the skin" of the main character, bearing in mind the old adage that no one is great until others make him so. In this book Jacob Frank is merely the pretext on which the stage is set. I also believe there is something slightly amoral about trying to get inside the mind of a person who once existed historically and tangibly. It's a bit like forcing your way into their intimacy, their privacy, their autonomy, and taking possession of it, and they can't defend themselves against this form of abuse.

Kusek, Szymański: So what is the role of the writer of biofiction? Does she freely create the characters and their inner worlds or is she a voice/translator/medium by means of which the reanimated historical figures speak to us. We're asking about this for a reason, taking into account your interest in spiritualism which featured prominently in your 1995 novel *E.E.* and *Prowadź swój pług przez kości umarłych* (Drive Your Plough Through the Bones of the Dead) of 2009. Even the subtitle of *The Books of Jacob* states that the story is "narrated by the dead and supplemented by the author through conjecture." Could you explain this method to us?

Tokarczuk: That is a metaphor, of course; I'm not a necromancer! But human contact with the past and with our ancestors is something more than participation in celebrations of their memory. It's a kind of intuitive sense, which is often more highly developed in artists and which allows them to perceive the world synthetically, as a whole. I don't think it has anything to do with spiritism, which seems a rather primitive approach to me. The way I understand this synthetic sense is as a way of seeing the world on several levels at once—the physical, the emotional, the intellectual, and the intuitive. And I quite consciously try to tell my stories in this synthetic way, to whatever degree I succeed. Sometimes this perception is close to insight. And sometimes that happens as I'm writing—suddenly something will resolve itself, effortlessly and naturally, and I have the impression that I'm seeing it happen through a veil. That kind of experience really bonds you to the text you're working on, and you begin to get the feeling that it's actually crying out to be written.

Kusek, Szymański: In this year's series of Reith Lectures, Hilary Mantel—the writer with whom you appear to have a lot in common—said that working on the Thomas Cromwell trilogy has been a kind of calling up spirits. Such a formulation of biofiction turns the writer into a medium, writing into a séance, novel into raising from the dead, into life-after-life of the resurrected characters. Wouldn't you agree, despite your mistrust toward spiritualism, that *The Books of Jacob* is a work of spiritualist writing, while writing a biographical novel is a way of calling up ghosts?

Tokarczuk: No, I think that would be oversimplifying it, and using the wrong terms. With an open, synthetic approach to the world that looks beyond various types of arbitrary divisions and stereotypical perspectives you can sometimes see things that might surprise others. A link, perhaps, or a sort of symmetry of meanings. . . . And quite apart from that, writing a large, demanding novel is a completely separate psychological process which releases considerable mental energy, and sometimes you can just see more broadly and more fully. In my case, identifying with characters, with a historical period, and with its part-imagined, part-recreated sensuality puts me into a state of mind in which my attention is highly focused, and picks up details which I would never normally be able to comprehend. At that level of concentration the imagined world can often be as intense as the real world. For a few years all I was interested in was the eighteenth century; I listened to the music of that period, studied the art, and delved into the details of the everyday life. It's like a trance.

Kusek, Szymański: Biofiction scholars often pay attention to the fact that biographical novels tend to verge toward disguised autobiographies, that while writing about the life of the other we actually write about the self. Would you agree with such a view? If so, do you consider *The Books of Jacob* to be autobiographical in any sense?

Tokarczuk: I wouldn't exaggerate. That was an individualistic perspective inspired by psychoanalysis that was fashionable a while ago. I see it completely differently: when I write, I put my own ego away in a drawer, and my biography on hold. Writers who write like I do usually don't actually have a biography. We are at the service of the stories we tell, we are their "hired hands," if you like, in the same way as patrons of the arts once hired artists to create works for them. It's the story first, then me.

Kusek, Szymański: So what about your future plans? Was *The Books of Jacob* a one-time adventure with biographical fiction? Is there any other historical figure that you find fascinating enough to turn him or her into a fictional character?

Tokarczuk: On the whole I have good memories of my work on it. After a vast amount of effort on many levels I have a great sense of the satisfaction of the discoverer, and the feeling that it was worthwhile. But there's something else. That immense outlay of years of effort and probing work to restore the existence of something that was close to fading into oblivion gave me a sense of community with my characters. This was a novel that enriched me and made me more aware. I would love to go back to history. Perhaps not now, because I have other things to write. But at author evenings when I've been asked similar questions, I've mentioned the Arians—they are a little-known subject that is rarely taken up in art. All we have is some very general information, but no reflection about them. There are masses of cobwebby stories like these. And the more broadly we come to know and experience our history, the wiser and better we will be as a society.

Interview conducted by Robert Kusek and Wojciech Szymański and translated from Polish by Kusek, Szymański, and Jessica Taylor-Kucia.

18

Biographical Fiction and the Creation of Possible Lives

Chika Unigwe, interviewed by Michael Lackey

Lackey: Let me start by asking you a question about your Equiano biographical novel. Do you see that work as more biography or fiction?

Unigwe: When I started writing it, I think I saw it as a cross between biography and fiction. But the longer I stayed with it, and the longer I thought of it, for many reasons I think it is more fiction than biography.

Lackey: Can you tell me a few of those reasons?

Unigwe: Equiano did a really good job of writing his autobiography. And second, I don't think you can do a biography without, at least at some point, being able to interview the subject, and of course with Equiano I couldn't do that at all. Also is the issue of ascribing to Equiano motives and emotions that I can only guess. I give him motives that would make him a much more personable character, a much more likable character. As a creative writer, I have the audience in mind. The first time I tried to write Equiano's story was supposed to be for Macmillan books and was supposed to be for children. But when I started writing, I realized I couldn't do this, because, if I did, there were parts of his life that I had to completely ignore. For instance, how do you explain to children that he was an overseer? That he used to be a slave and then he became an overseer and then he leaves and then goes on to become an abolitionist? Adults can understand the nuances. They get that people sometimes are pragmatic. But with kids, it is very difficult. So even in the novel when I'm trying to ascribe motives to Equiano, these are motives that I can only guess at, but also motives that make him less mercenary, less repulsive. Equiano is a very iconic figure; I don't want to embellish, but I don't want to destroy his reputation in any way. Biographies can't have falsehoods.

Lackey: But fiction can.

Unigwe: Yes, fiction can, certainly.

Lackey: But what kind of falsehoods? What are legitimate falsehoods and what are illegitimate falsehoods?

Unigwe: I can only talk for myself, but I think the kind of falsehoods that fiction deals with help tell the story. As a writer, you always start with a bias. You have a motivation. The falsehoods that propel your biases and motivations are allowed. With Equiano, for example, I'm writing for a twenty-first-century reader. I was very aware of that when I was writing. I was aware of some of the things that he might have done or that he did that, to a twenty-first-century eye would be considered inexcusable. So I have to provide falsehoods in a way to clarify the nature of his motivation. So falsehoods that help explain motivation are allowed.

Lackey: Let me briefly address what I considered one falsehood. I read Equiano when I was in graduate school, and I remember him being a deeply spiritual man. But in your novel, I was struck by his spiritual crisis, a crisis that almost resulted in suicide. Let's imagine that we found a diary of Equiano that was written three days before his death, and he says: "Despite all my trials and tribulations, I never considered suicide, so if anybody ever writes about me and has a suicide in that story, they are wrong." Is it possible that you could be totally wrong about Equiano's biography, but still be right in another sense? And, if so, in what sense could you still be right? In other words, what kind of truth are you trying to give your reader?

Unigwe: Yes, it could still be true, because my novel is not a biography of Equiano. It starts with the story, using Equiano as the skeleton. But the flesh that comes onto Equiano, well, I'm not expecting the readers to take that flesh as the truth. I'm expecting them to take it as something to explain Equiano, to bring Equiano into the twenty-first century.

Lackey: So the spiritual crisis in the novel is not supposed to be Equiano's spiritual crisis as much as a more universal experience of a spiritual crisis. Is that right?

Unigwe: To a certain extent, yes. It is not the spiritual crisis of Equiano the man, but of Equiano the character in the novel. One of the reasons why I found Equiano an easier subject to write about is that his autobiography is much more political than personal. He leaves a lot of holes in the narrative, and it was in those holes I was able to insert my own truths.

Lackey: Can you explain the function of the frame narrator? You don't really give this person much of a voice. It is about six or seven pages and then the majority is Equiano's narrative. Can you tell me why there was no dialogue?

Unigwe: The novel is set right after Equiano loses his wife, so it is an introspective time in the character's life. There wouldn't have been as much introspection if there was a dialogue between Equiano and the doctor, who introduces us to Equiano's story. The novel is primarily about the nature of grief, and it is in the nature of grief to be a monologue rather than a dialogue. Also, I wanted to use Equiano's story not only to explore Equiano the man, the character of Equiano and his spiritual crisis, but also to explore the much more universal nature of grief. I don't think that it is possible to explore grief in a dialogue.

Lackey: Why did you decide to dedicate the novel to Susannah, Equiano's wife?

Unigwe: Because Susannah is hardly ever mentioned in Equiano's autobiography. He writes this whole book where he talks about himself, how he's made it, the evils of slavery, but Susannah is just a footnote. But she's more than a footnote. I thought that was an injustice to Susannah, and in a way, I felt like I was righting a wrong done to Susannah, because she belongs in this tale. In Equiano's narrative, we hear more about Joanna, his daughter, and Susannah is almost completely erased, almost as if she didn't exist.

Lackey: So you are righting a wrong. To what degree do you see your writing as engaging in a form of social justice or bringing about social justice?

Unigwe: Almost every fiction does that. All writing is political, whether you are aware of that or not, because that is what fiction does. It entertains, but it is also a form of activism.

Lackey: Is the biographical novel particularly suited to function as a form of activism? What is it about this particular genre that can have this kind of impact?

Unigwe: The biographical novel gives us room to expand on real lives in a way that imagined fiction does not. Of course, this is imagined fiction, but it is based on real people, so it gives us room to expand on that life and the societies in which they lived as well as other times.

Lackey: Scholars have expressed some concern that the biographical novel is treated like the historical novel. The traditional view of the historical novel is that authors reach into the past in order to give readers an objective perspective of what happened so that readers can understand how they came to be as they are in the present. With biographical novelists, the emphasis seems to be more on the present and the future rather than the past. Biographical novelists do not just go to the past to represent how we got to where we are. They are actually thinking about how they could use the biographical subject in order to bring into existence a new reality in the present and for the future. How would you respond to that?

Unigwe: I think that definition is correct. One of the challenges I had in writing Equiano was to clarify the extent to which the story explains the past but also gives us not guidelines for the future but a projection into the future.

Lackey: What do you mean by a projection into the future?

Unigwe: To answer this, let me focus on my current biographical novel, which is about Joanna, who was Equiano's surviving daughter. She died in 1857. There is very little known of her beyond the fact that she married a white man, Harry Bromley, and that the last years of her life she lived alone. So she didn't live with Harry. Harry was a clergyman. And I find her story fascinating. She was a privileged, biracial woman. She has some money from her father when she turns twenty-one, and she marries relatively late for her times and ends up not living with this man by the time she dies. There's very little known of Joanna beyond where she was born, whom she married, and the fact that sometimes she signed her husband's accounts, that she signed "J. Bromley," so she was educated. Writing Joanna today, it would be a disservice to create a woman who doesn't go beyond what society laid out for her. I could not write Joanna without writing a woman who is strong, who is very feminist, who provides an alternative for women, not just in the past but also in the future and now as well.

Lackey: Is that because Equiano himself did exactly that same thing? There were roles assigned for black men, and he transcended all those roles. There was something quite extraordinary in the nature of his life.

Unigwe: Yes.

Lackey: And so she's carrying on the legacy of her father, to some degree.

Unigwe: She's carrying on the legacy of her father, but I also want a Joanna who not just carries on the legacy of her father but who goes beyond that, someone who is a role model for women now as well as the future.

Lackey: This raises a really important question. I have noticed that there are two separate ways of thinking about biographical novels. William Styron authored a great biographical novel about Nat Turner. In the novel, his Turner has a gay experience, which is odd, since there is no historical record of this happening. So why would Styron include that scene? Styron was close friends with James Baldwin, who was gay. When Styron was writing the novel, he was talking to Baldwin nightly about it. My suspicion is that Baldwin was the basis for the Nat Turner character, and what Styron did in the novel was to show how the structures of oppression in 1831 that were used against blacks were the same structures in 1967 that were used against gay people. So in his novel, readers do not get the real Turner. Rather, Styron invented and then used Turner to give readers what he refers to as a "metaphorical diagram" to describe a certain way of thinking that was operational in two different times. Another type of novel is David Ebershoff's *The Danish Girl*, which is about the first man to have sex confirmation surgery. Einar Wegener became Lili Elbe. Ebershoff is doing something different. He's not just using a metaphorical diagram to describe something that happened in the past. He's actually trying to bring into existence a new reality, a new way of being toward trans people. How do you see your novels? Are they giving readers a metaphorical diagram to understand structures that worked in the past and that continue to operate in the present? Or, do you see yourself as bringing into existence a new reality, a new way of being?

Unigwe: I think that both of those things are linked. As a writer, I use these historical figures in order to make their stories relevant in the twenty-first century. Since they are already known, they exist within a recognizable framework. When writing, I ask myself, "Why would a twenty-first-century reader want to read this? What would make it impressionable? What would make it relevant to a twenty-first-century reader?" Having a Joanna who is completely restricted by the realities of her times doesn't say anything about how we have moved beyond those times and doesn't say anything about how we can move beyond the position of women in the twenty-first century. So Joanna has to be bigger than her time. She even has to be bigger than now.

Lackey: But there are two separate ways of thinking about being bigger than a certain time period. Joanna lived primarily in the nineteenth century, when women were supposed to be submissive, passive, and demure. You want Joanna to be relevant to today. But what it means to be a twenty-first-century woman is very different from what it means to be a nineteenth-century woman. Is your focus more on the content of a woman's role at a particular time? Or, is your focus more on the abstract ability to transcend one's environmental conditioning?

Unigwe: That's correct. I think a Joanna who is a nineteenth-century hero but still restricted by nineteenth-century rules and structures is less interesting to me than a Joanna who is a twenty-first-century woman in the nineteenth century.

Lackey: So how do you cue your reader that this is what you're doing? How do you indicate that you are really taking a look at this woman with such strength of character and personality that she can transcend the codes of her time, thus making her relevant to readers today?

Unigwe: That is where the dramatic tension comes in. The Joanna I imagined is a character who is very much aware. She isn't unaware of the fact that she is living in the nineteenth century. She is very much aware of the injustices of her times. She is a woman who knows that she is supposed to sit at home, that her education is limited to playing the piano and speaking some French, and then waiting for a man to whisk her off at nineteen. She is aware of all these things, but she is also aware that there is a certain injustice there. Also is the fact that, as a black woman, she goes to the balls with her friends, and she notices that there are additional restrictions against her. For example, in one scene, her friends are talking about getting married and who is at whose ball, and Joanna is aware that because she is biracial, she is seen as less, almost inferior to her friends. She realizes that no matter how much milk she bathes in, she is never going to have a white skin color. So my Joanna is conscious and politically aware. I wanted a character who, as a strong woman, would fit into the nineteenth century, but who would be a strong woman now. That is much more interesting for me than creating a woman who is aware of the limits, of the limitations of her times, but who stays within those limits. I want a Joanna who is a feminist.

Lackey: This raises an important question about the particular and the universal. You have lived in Africa, but you have also lived in Belgium, and now you live in the United States. While you locate your characters in a concrete place and time, eighteenth or nineteenth-century England, you also take your readers beyond the nineteenth century and England. Can you talk about your experiences living in Nigeria, Belgium, and the United States, and how that's impacted your writing?

Unigwe: I think that at the beginning I was very much an advocate of Obioma Nnaemeka's nego-feminism, which basically states that you are aware of the patriarchal systems in place, but instead of fighting patriarchy, you manipulate your way into power. So, for example, one of the initial stories I wrote is about a woman who is in a really terrible marriage. But marriage is important in her culture, so she can't leave. But then she has to find a way to fight her husband, and the husband wants a son. So she goes and has her tubes tied without her husband's knowledge. But she's still within the patriarchal system. She hasn't really changed anything. She hasn't fought the system; she's just fought one person, which is what nego-feminism does. And one of the manuscripts that is now with my agent has a woman who is in an abusive relationship. She breaks out of it. There is that evolution about which I was not conscious. I can see it in my writing. I can see it in the way my writing has progressed. From this woman who stays in, and instead, rather than fight the system, she fights the one person. But she still supports the system that oppresses her and that is oppressive to other women. This is different from the woman who says, "You know what? Bugger this, I'm going to leave, and I don't care if the whole world crumbles." So it's not a conscious evolution, it's an evolution that has happened over the years.

Lackey: Let me ask you a question about the scene in which Equiano covers the mirrors. At this point, he has a mental breakdown, which terrifies the children and leads the housekeeper to say, "You are scaring the children." Was that made up?

Unigwe: Everything in the Equiano novel apart from his name and the timeline of things are made up. I was just using Equiano as a framework.

Lackey: A framework for what?

Unigwe: A framework for the novel that I wanted to write, and a framework for the topics that I wanted to explore. And so everything else had to be made up.

Lackey: I just interviewed Sabina Murray a couple days ago. She wrote a biographical short story about her father, and she said there are all kinds of invented scenes in it. But she said that she was faithful to the idea that she was after. I asked her, "What is that idea?" And I'm curious, what is the idea that was behind the novel? What were you really after in the Equiano novel?

Unigwe: In the first instance I wanted to explore grief. But after writing it, and now in hindsight, I would say I also wanted to explore the continuation of the slave trade and identity.

Lackey: So the slave trade is really important. But there is no legal slavery today. So if your novel is about the past and the present, are you thinking of slavery in a more subtle and nuanced way?

Unigwe: A twenty-first-century person reads it and sees that the powers that encouraged slavery to abide are still present now as well. Take labor, for example. Equiano was told to provide cheap labor. And now you have them in the factories of Bangladesh and India and whatever. So now we have more conversations about slavery, because those same powers or motivations that encourage slavery are still there. I keep coming back to this idea of Equiano working as an overseer. Slavery could not have lasted as long except that the people who were oppressed became people who oppressed and used to keep slaves down as well. Here I'm thinking of the Nat Turner movie as well where Nat is used as a preacher to tell the other slaves why they have to be obedient. I'm also thinking of when I did my research and when I wrote my novel about prostitution. It is not the white customers or the white agents that are used to keep Nigerian women in "slavery." It is fellow women. It is women who used to be prostitutes who come out and become madams. They are the ones that are used to keep these girls in bondage.

Lackey: Let me ask you a technical question about your Joanna novel. We know a lot about Equiano. We have a framework for understanding specific events within his life. So that's a real clear instance of somebody taking a figure from the past, recognizing it has tremendous symbolic power, and then creating a narrative that is relevant for today. Joanna is different because we know so little about her. This raises the question whether your Joanna novel is going to be a biographical novel. Maybe it is just pure fiction. Is your novel pure fiction or is it a biographical novel?

Unigwe: I think it's a biographical novel to the extent that Joanna existed as a real human being; to the extent that the conditions that affected Joanna and the systems that she lived in and that she has to fight against in the novel were real; to the extent that we know that Joanna married late at a time when people married really young. Why did Joanna marry so late? Could it be because she was black? Could it be because she was headstrong? Could it be because she was too choosy? And we also know that she didn't live with her husband during the final years of her life. Why did she live alone in London? And what was she doing there those years that she lived in London? We know that she used to sign her husband's accounts sometimes. Was that symptomatic of her feminist spirit?

Lackey: But I do wonder if this might actually qualify more as a historical novel. The historical novel takes an invented figure as the protagonist and then lays out the history of the time period and fills that protagonist with all kinds of symbolic meaning. Whereas the biographical novel is taking an actual historical figure and showing how this figure is going beyond the historical events. There is a parallel case with what you are doing. In 1979, Barbara Chase-Riboud published a groundbreaking biographical novel; it was called *Sally Hemings*, who was Thomas Jefferson's slave "wife." That novel was groundbreaking for many reasons. One of them is that Chase-Riboud speculated that Jefferson had a loving relationship with Hemings for thirty-seven years and fathered many children with her. That is considered a biographical novel, and what's fascinating about it is almost everything that Chase-Riboud speculated about and posited has turned out to be true. But then Chase-Riboud wrote a follow-up novel about one of the daughters. We have almost no information about that daughter except that Jefferson fathered her, that she ran away, and that she was light enough to pass. So is that a biographical novel? I have spoken to Barbara about this, and she says, "I think it is." But I said, "But what is the basis for your character?" To my mind, it is really a historical novel because she does all the research about the time period, she fills the character with all this research. In like manner, I wonder if your Joanna novel actually would qualify more as a historical novel than a biographical novel. Your thoughts?

Unigwe: The way I understand the historical novel is that it has a lot less space for fiction in it. It has to stay as close as possible to the facts in a way that biographical fiction doesn't have to. In a historical novel, the author is invested in being true to the realities of that time, so there is little space to create characters that transcend their time in a very radical way, which you can do with biofiction. So in that way I think that Joanna is certainly more biofiction than historical fiction. There are things that Joanna does that I doubt that she would have been able to do if I were writing historical fiction. So I think in biofiction you are able to dream a lot more, a lot wider. Your dreams are more expansive, as a writer, than in historical fiction. Readers don't come to biographical fiction for truth. They come to biographical fiction for possibilities.

Lackey: Would you say inspiration?

Unigwe: Yes, inspiration, but also for possibilities. I think you can go to historical figures for inspiration but not necessarily for new possibilities, for alternate possibilities. And I think that's much more important than inspiration.

Lackey: That is such a great idea. Can you expand on that?

Unigwe: What makes it possible is the fact that biofiction authors allow themselves the freedom to invent in a way that historical fiction authors don't. I've tried to write stories based on real life, and I have failed woefully. The more faithful I am to real life, the more I realize that the characters are very prohibited, or inhibited in what they can do. With Equiano, for example, I had to give myself permission to invade Equiano's emotions and to invade his memory and to change things. I had to give myself permission to make him have completely different reactions from the actual Equiano. For instance, in his autobiography, Equiano got to a mental place where he was almost at peace with slavery to the extent that he was aware of all the positives that slavery had given him. At the point when he quit being an overseer, he didn't quit being an overseer because he felt a moral crisis. He quit being an overseer because it wasn't working for him anymore. He wanted to do something else. But I find the moral crisis that he would have or he should have faced much more interesting and much more relevant than a mercantile crisis. And I had to get to that point where I wasn't looking to Equiano's real life for inspiration for the novel as much as his invented life.

Lackey: Where is the creation in biofiction? Can you talk about the nature of the creative process and where creation happens with this form of fiction?

Unigwe: With Equiano, I have kept true to some of his life, to the main, broad brush strokes, like the place of birth, the things that made him Equiano. But the invention comes in when ascribing motivations. The same way as I would ascribe motivations to any fictional character I was writing because that is what makes fiction fiction. You are ascribing motivations to people, and I'm ascribing emotions to this man that I didn't know at all. And so every aspect of his life which his autobiography doesn't cover, which is basically everything to do with Equiano as a person and not Equiano as an abolitionist, I've invented that.

Lackey: Will the Joanna novel follow the same format as the Equiano novel? Is it going to be basically an extended monologue?

Unigwe: No, it's not. The Joanna novel is going to be completely different. It's not a monologue. It starts toward the end of her life, but that's also probably going to change. She will delve into her past, which will give her the opportunity to reflect on her life.

Lackey: How did you do your research for this book?

Unigwe: There's just one book on Joanna, and it doesn't say much more than who she married and when she was born and when she died.

Lackey: Any surviving children?

Unigwe: No, they didn't have any children at all, so there's absolutely nothing about her. But this opens up space for me as a writer. Why didn't they have children? Did she have miscarriages? But I'm also reading books about lives of women. So the other books have been more historical than biographical. I look at the lives of women in Joanna's time, what it was like to be a country parson's wife because her husband was a parson at some point.

Lackey: Here I want to make a link between Equiano and his daughter. I know very little about her, except what you have told me. What engaged me most in your Equiano novel was the spiritual crisis. That was very powerful and moving. But your Equiano eventually triumphs over that crisis, which is consistent with the actual Equiano. But I do wonder if he would have been even more grief-stricken, even more devastated had he discovered that one of his daughters dies very young and that the other daughter is going to marry, but is never going to have children. Would Equiano have come through that spiritual crisis?

Unigwe: Probably not.

Lackey: Because it would have been so devastating. So will you extend the grief theme into the next generation through Joanna? Is she going to be going through that same kind of spiritual crisis?

Unigwe: I don't think so.

Lackey: And why not?

Unigwe: Because Joanna is a very strong character. Her role models are not the traditional ones. So even though she enjoyed playing the piano and singing and speaking some French in the novel, her role model is her aunt who would, in the twenty-first century, be seen as a feminist victim of her time. Her aunt, her mother's sister, never wants to marry, so Joanna grows up having her grandmother complain about Joanna's aunt.

Lackey: Wasn't she arrested and then sent to Australia? That's what happens to her at the end of the Equiano novel.

Unigwe: Yes. But in the Equiano novel she's just this petty thief who steals stuff and then is sent to Australia.

Lackey: Is this true? Is this a real character?

Unigwe: No. In the Joanna novel, her crimes are more crimes of a woman who refuses to be tied down by her roles and gender, a time when she's expected to marry and have kids. She doesn't do any of those things. And she is sent out of the house, and she has to survive any way. And part of that survival is to steal, and then she gets sent off to Australia. Sometimes, I forget which parts of the book are fictional and which not. I hesitated before answering that question because I wasn't sure anymore whether she was real or made up.

Lackey: And you ended the Equiano novel with the Joanna material. Were you tempted to expand it even there?

Unigwe: I think I ended it because I wanted a reminder that I wanted to do a Joanna novel. But I also find Joanna's story much more interesting and probably much more relevant to the twenty-first century than Equiano's story.

Lackey: What made you turn to biofiction?

Unigwe: I came to biofiction, both the reading of it and the writing of it, pretty late. The first time I heard of Equiano was in high school. I think it was maybe middle school, so maybe seventh grade. And we just read a paragraph on Equiano, and that was it. And I remember being struck by it because, before then, I always thought of the transatlantic slave trade as something that happened to Kunta Kinte. It had no bearing on my life. And suddenly we're reading about this kid who was taken into slavery at the age of ten. And I never forgot that, and I always wanted to delve deeper into history. It wasn't until I moved to Europe that I read the story of Equiano, and then its relevancy became much more striking to me because I had made a transcontinental journey. I was sure that there was little known of Equiano outside of the academic world. And I came to biofiction precisely because I wanted to write the Equiano story, but I didn't want to write a biography of Equiano because I am not well equipped to write a biography. And the only way I could do that was to write Equiano's story and to bring more people to Equiano by writing him in fiction.

List of Biofiction Authors

Kevin Barry was born in Limerick, Ireland. He is the author of the novel *City of Bohane* and two short-story collections, *Dark Lies the Island* and *There are Little Kingdoms*. He has won the IMPAC Dublin Literary Award, the *Sunday Times* EFG Short Story Award, the European Union Prize for Literature, and many other prizes. Barry published *Beatlebone* (2015), a biographical novel about John Lennon and his ownership of Dorinish Island. In *Beatlebone* we meet Lennon at a time of creative strife on a madcap adventure off the West Coast of Ireland.

Laurent Binet was born in Paris in 1972. He is the acclaimed author of the international best seller *HHhH* (acronym for *Himmlers Hirn heißt Heydrich*, "Himmler's brain is called Heydrich"), for which he was awarded the 2010 *Prix Goncourt du premier roman* and the 2011 *Prix des Lecteurs du Livre de Poche*. The novel was named one of the fifty best books of 2015 by *The New York Times* and has been translated and published in almost forty countries. It has also been adapted to the cinema. Binet's second novel, *The Seventh Function of Language*, published in 2015, was awarded two prestigious French prizes, the *Prix Fnac* and the *Prix Interallié*.

Javier Cercas (born 1962 in Ibahernando, Spain) is a critically acclaimed writer and professor of Spanish literature at the University of Girona, Spain. His most recognized novel, *Soldiers of Salamis* (2001), earned the Independent Foreign Fiction prize in 2004 and was made into a film by director David Trueba. His novel *Anatomy of an Instant* received the Spanish National Award for Narrative Literature in 2009. Since 1987, he has published ten novels, most recently *The Monarch of the Shadows* (2017). Outside of Spain, his work has been translated into more than thirty languages and has received numerous awards in other countries (e.g., France, Italy, Great Britain, Portugal, China, and Chile).

Writer and sculptor Barbara Chase-Riboud divides her time between Paris, Rome, and Milan, and is the author of the best-selling classic *Sally Hemings* (1979), which changed American history and won the Janet Heidinger Kafka Prize; *Valide: A Novel of the Harem* (1986); *Echo of Lions* (1989); *The President's Daughter* (1994); and *Hottentot Venus* (2003), winner of the Black Caucus American Library Association Award for Fiction. She is the prizewinning poet of multiple collections: *From Memphis & Peking* (1974); *Portrait of a Nude Woman as Cleopatra* (1987), winner of the 1988

Carl Sandburg Poetry Award; and *Everytime a Knot is Undone a God is Released* (2014). Her sculptures are exhibited internationally and included in museum collections such as the Smithsonian, MOMA, the Metropolitan Museum, and the Philadelphia Museum of Art.

Born in Dublin in 1969, Emma Donoghue did a PhD (on eighteenth-century literature) at Cambridge University before moving to Canada. She is best known for her contemporary novel *Room*, but many of her books of short and full-length fiction are historical in setting (fourteenth to twentieth centuries, San Francisco to London) and fact-inspired. *Life Mask*, *The Sealed Letter*, and *Frog Music*, in particular, are biographical novels closely based on the surviving records of the lives of real historical figures.

David Ebershoff is the author of four books, including *The Danish Girl* and the #1 best seller *The 19th Wife*. *The Danish Girl* was adapted into an Oscar-winning film starring Academy Award-winners Eddie Redmayne and Alicia Vikander. It was nominated for four Academy Awards, three Golden Globes, two Screen Actors Guild awards, and five BAFTAs. In 2017 the *New York Times* named *The Danish Girl* one of the twenty-five books that have shaped LGBTQ literature in the past twenty years. Ebershoff's books have been translated into more than twenty-five languages to critical acclaim and twice *Out* magazine has named him to its annual *Out* 100 list of influential LGBT people. Ebershoff was formerly Vice President and Executive Editor at Random House. Originally from Pasadena, California, he now lives in New York City.

Hannah Kent's first novel, the international best seller, *Burial Rites* (Pan Macmillan, 2013), was translated into thirty languages and shortlisted for the Baileys Women's Prize for Fiction and the Guardian First Book Award. It won many awards, including the ABIA Literary Fiction Book of the Year, the Indie Awards Debut Fiction Book of the Year, and the Victorian Premier's People's Choice Award, and was shortlisted for the International IMPAC Dublin Literary Award. Her second novel, *The Good People* (Pan Macmillan Australia, 2016; Little, Brown US, 2017), was shortlisted for the Walter Scott Award for Historical Fiction, the Indie Books Award for Literary Fiction, and the ABIA Literary Fiction Book of The Year Award 2017. Kent is also the cofounder and publishing director of the Australian literary journal, *Kill Your Darlings*.

David Lodge CBE is a literary critic and the author of sixteen works of fiction, including *Small World* and *Nice Work*, both of which were finalists for the Man Booker Prize. He has published two biographical novels: *Author, Author* (about Henry James) and *A Man of Parts* (about H. G. Wells). He was Professor of English Literature at the University of Birmingham until 1987. He has also adapted his own and others' work for stage and screen.

Colum McCann is an internationally best-selling author whose novels have been published in thirty-five languages. He has received many honors, including the National Book Award, the International IMPAC Dublin Literary Award, a Chevalier des Arts et Lettres from the French government, and the Ireland Fund of Monaco Literary Award in Memory of Princess Grace. He has published two biographical novels, *Dancer* and *TransAtlantic*. He currently teaches at Hunter College MFA Creative Writing Program.

Anchee Min was born in Shanghai, China, where she lived until she was twenty-seven years old. Min came to the United States in 1984 on a student visa, and she became an American citizen seven years later. While in China, Min worked as a laborer at a collective farm near the East China Sea. While hoeing in a cotton field, Min was discovered by Madam Mao's talent scouts from the Shanghai Film Studio. Min was selected for her "proletarian good looks" for Madam Mao's propaganda film. Min was punished after Mao's death and Madame Mao's subsequent fall in 1977. Min's first book, the memoir *Red Azalea*, was published in 1993 and was translated into thirty-four languages. Since then, Min has published best-selling novels, including four biographical novels: *Becoming Madame Mao*, *Empress Orchid*, *The Last Empress*, and *Pearl of China*.

Rosa Montero is an acclaimed novelist and an award-winning journalist for the Spanish newspaper, *El País*. A native of Madrid and the daughter of a professional bullfighter, Montero published her first novel at age twenty-eight. She has won Spain's top book award, the Qué Leer Prize, twice—for *The Crazy Woman in the House* in 2003 and *The Story of the Transparent King* in 2005. A prolific author of more than twenty-six books, her other titles include *The Delta Function*, *The Ridiculous Idea of Never Seeing You Again*, *Stories of Women*, and *The Cannibal's Daughter*, among many others. In 2017, Montero was awarded the National Writing Award in Spain. The ongoing impact of Montero's work has motivated at least ten individual books about her as an author, and myriad studies of her works. Her books have been translated into more than twenty languages.

Stephanus Muller is a professor of music at Stellenbosch University, where he founded in 2015 a music archive, the Documentation Centre for Music (DOMUS), and in 2016, an interdisciplinary institute for music research (Africa Open—Institute for Music, Research and Innovation) of which he is currently the director. He has published academic articles and fiction (in English and Afrikaans) and has worked on artistic projects with various artists in different media. Some of these include the films *An Inconsolable Memory* (2013) and *Say it with Flowers* (2017) with filmmaker Aryan Kaganof and the publication *Jong Afrikaner: an Autobiography* (2012) with photographer Roelof van Wyk.

Sabina Murray is the author of six works of fiction. The short-story collection *The Caprices* was awarded the 2002 PEN/Faulkner Award. Fellowships include awards from the National Endowment for the Arts, the Guggenheim Foundation, and the Radcliffe Institute. She teaches in the MFA Program at the University of Massachusetts at Amherst. The short-story collection, *Tales of the New World*, a work of biographical fiction, engaged with historical figures including Mary Kingsley, Ferdinand Magellan, and Jim Jones. The biographical novel *Valiant Gentlemen* was a *New York Times* Notable Book.

Nuala O'Connor (AKA Nuala Ní Chonchúir) was born in Dublin, Ireland, and she lives in East Galway. Her fifth short-story collection *Joyride to Jupiter* was published by New Island in June 2017. Penguin USA, Penguin Canada, and Sandstone (UK) published O'Connor's third novel, *Miss Emily*, about the poet Emily Dickinson and her Irish maid. *Miss Emily* was shortlisted for the Bord Gáis Energy Eason Book Club Novel of the Year 2015 and longlisted for the 2017 International DUBLIN Literary Award. O'Connor's fourth novel, *Becoming Belle*, will be published in 2018. www.nualaoconnor.com.

Susan Sellers' scholarly publications include *Language and Sexual Difference*, *Myth and Fairy Tale in Contemporary Women's Fiction* and *Hélène Cixous: Authorship, Autobiography and Love*, the latter emerging from close work with Cixous during time spent in Paris. She is the coeditor, with Jane Goldman and Bryony Randall, of the Cambridge University Press edition of Virginia Woolf's writing, and volume editor, with Michael Herbert, of *The Waves*. As a creative writer, Sellers has published novels, stories, and reflections on the practice of writing, including the biographical fiction *Vanessa and Virginia* (2008), which is translated into sixteen languages and has also been adapted for the stage, and *Given the Choice* (2013). As Professor of English and Related Literature at the University of St Andrews in Scotland, Sellers's teaching spans modern and contemporary literature and creative writing.

Colm Tóibín was born in Enniscorthy, County Wexford, in 1955, and was educated at University College Dublin. His body of work, which includes journalism, literary criticism, and travel writing in addition to novels and short fiction, has been translated into over thirty languages, and has earned him honorary doctorates from the University of Ulster, University College Dublin, the University of East Anglia, and the Open University. He is Mellon Professor in the Department of English and Comparative Literature at Columbia University and Chancellor of Liverpool University. Numbered among Tóibín's nine novels are two works of biofiction: *The Master*, published in 2004, about Henry James, and *The Testament of Mary*, published in 2012, about the mother of Jesus.

Olga Tokarczuk is one of the most popular and critically acclaimed Polish writers whose works have been translated into more than twenty-five languages. She is a two-time recipient of the Nike Literary Award (and a five-time winner of the Readers' Prize) and many other international awards and recognitions such as the Usedomer Literaturpreis, the Kulturhuset Stadsteatern International Literary Prize, and the Vilenica International Literary Award. In 2018 she won the Man Booker International Prize for her book *Flights*. Her works in English include *Flights* (2017), *House of Day, House of Night* (2003) and *Primeval and Other Times* (2010). Her 2014 best-selling novel *The Books of Jacob* is almost a thousand-page-long biographical novel about Jacob Frank set in eighteenth-century Central and Eastern Europe. In 2016, Agnieszka Holland directed the movie *Spoor* based on Tokarczuk's 2009 "metaphysical crime novel" *Prowadź swój pług przez kości umarłych* (Drive Your Plough Through the Bones of the Dead). She lives in Wrocław, Lower Silesia, Poland.

Chika Unigwe was born and raised in Enugu, Nigeria. She is the author of, among others, *Zwarte Messias* (a biographical novel based on the life of Olaudah Equiano), *On Black Sisters Street* and *Night Dancer*. She is currently working on a novel based on the life of Equiano's daughter, Joanna (a chapter of which appeared in the anthology, *Africa 39*). She was listed in 2013 as one of the best African writers under thirty-nine and was shortlisted for the 2004 Caine Prize award for the best fiction by an African writer. Her other awards include the 2012 Nigeria Literature Award, a BBC Short Story Award, and a Commonwealth short-story award. Her works have appeared in *Guernica*, *The New York Times*, the *UK Guardian*, *Transition Magazine*, and *Wasafiri*.

List of Interviewers

Julie A. Eckerle, Professor of English literature at the University of Minnesota, Morris, is author of *Romancing the Self in Early Modern Englishwomen's Life Writing* (2013) and coeditor of *Genre and Women's Life Writing in Early Modern England* (2007) and *Women's Life Writing and Early Modern Ireland* (forthcoming). She is currently working on an edition of seventeenth-century Englishwoman Dorothy Calthorpe's private manuscript and a book on early modern women's life writing in the Irish context.

Willemien Froneman is extraordinary associate professor of music at Africa Open, Stellenbosch University. She has published mainly about *boeremusiek*—a marginal and much-stigmatized genre of South African popular music. Her work has appeared in *Popular Music and Society, RMA Research Chronicle, Cultural Geographies, Ethnomusicology Forum*, and *Critical Arts.* She coedits the journal *SAMUS: South African Music Studies.*

Kelly Gardiner's latest novel is *1917: Australia's Great War*, shortlisted for the NSW Premier's History Awards. Gardiner's previous books include the young adult novels *Act of Faith* and *The Sultan's Eyes*, both of which were shortlisted for the NSW Premier's Literary Awards; the *Swashbuckler* trilogy; and *Goddess*, a work of biofiction about the seventeenth-century French swordswoman, cross-dresser, and opera singer, Mademoiselle de Maupin. She is a lecturer in creative writing at La Trobe University, Australia, and her academic writing has appeared in international and local journals and books. Gardiner is also the cohost of Unladylike, a podcast about women and writing.

Stuart Kane holds an MA in creative writing from the University of Birmingham, England. He is a school teacher by day and an avid reader and researcher of biographical fiction by night. Kane is currently at work on his first novel, a biographical fiction about a legendary footballer from the 1970s.

Robert Kusek is an assistant professor in the Department of Comparative Studies in Literature and Culture at the Institute of English Studies, Jagiellonian University, in Kraków. His research interests include life-writing genres, the contemporary novel in English, and poetics of memory and loss, as well as a comparative approach to literary studies. He is the author of two monographs, including *Through the Looking Glass: Writers' Memoirs at the Turn of the 21st Century* (2017), and several dozen articles published in books, academic journals, and magazines, as well as coeditor of ten volumes of articles.

Distinguished McKnight University Professor at the University of Minnesota, Morris, Michael Lackey is the author and editor of eight books, including *Truthful Fictions: Conversations with American Biographical Novelists*; *The American Biographical Novel*; and *The Modernist God State: A Literary Study of the Nazis' Christian Reich*. He is also the editor of *Biographical Fiction: A Reader*.

Monica Latham is a professor of British literature at the English Department of the Université de Lorraine in Nancy, France, and a specialist in Virginia Woolf and genetic criticism. She has published numerous articles on modernist and postmodernist authors. She is the author of *A Poetics of Postmodernism and Neomodernism: Rewriting* Mrs Dalloway (2015). She is also the coeditor of the annual series *Book Practices and Textual Itineraries*.

Bethany Layne is Senior Lecturer in English Literature at De Montfort University, Leicester. She has published widely on biographical fiction, with a particular focus on Henry James, Virginia Woolf, and Sylvia Plath, and her monograph *Henry James in Contemporary Fiction* is under contract with Palgrave Macmillan. While a teaching fellow at the University of Reading in 2017, she pioneered the first specialist biofiction module in the UK, and organized a related conference, Postmodernist Biofictions.

Virginia Rademacher is Associate Professor of Hispanic and Cultural Studies at Babson College. She has published in *Persona Studies, Journal of Spanish Cultural Studies, a/b: Auto/Biography Studies, Ciberletras, Hispanic Issues*, and *Monographic Review*, among others. She is the author of varied articles and book chapters that examine new narrative formats, including the contemporary surge in biofiction. Her current book project relates trends in biographical fiction to approaches to uncertainty, speculation, and risk. She holds a PhD from the University of Virginia, an MA in international affairs and economics from Johns Hopkins University (SAIS), and an AB from Harvard University.

Melanie Masterton Sherazi is a postdoctoral instructor of American literature at the California Institute of Technology and a former University of California President's Postdoctoral Fellow of English at UCLA. She received her PhD in English from the University of California, Riverside. She is currently writing a book that explores the genre-bending literature, visual culture, and performance produced by African American cultural workers in Cold War Rome during the 1950s and 1960s and traces their collaborations with leftist Italian artists and filmmakers. Her work has appeared in

MELUS and *Mississippi Quarterly*. She edited and wrote the introduction to William Demby's posthumous novel *King Comus* (2017, Ishmael Reed Publishing Company).

Wojciech Szymański is an assistant professor in the Department of the History of Modern Art and Culture, Institute of Art History, University of Warsaw, Poland. He is an independent curator and art critic; member of the International Association of Art Critics (AICA); and author of the book *The Argonauts: Postminimalism and Art after Modernism: Eva Hesse, Felix Gonzalez-Torres, Roni Horn, Derek Jarman* (2015) and numerous academic and critical texts. His research interests include visual and literary memory of the Great War, queer visual archives, and performativity of historical records and artifacts, as well as shifting paradigms of cultural memory from the nineteenth to twenty-first century.

Further Reading

Biofiction from interviewees

Barry, Kevin (2015), *Beatlebone*. New York: Doubleday.
Binet, Laurent (2013), *HHhH*. London: Vintage Books.
Binet, Laurent (2017), *The Seventh Function of Language*. New York: Farar, Straus and Giroux.
Cercas, Javier (2001), *Soldados de Salamina*. Barcelona: Tusquets, 2001. Print.
Cercas, Javier (2003), *Soldiers of Salamis*. Trans. Anne McLean. New York & London: Bloomsbury.
Cercas, Javier (2014), *El imposter*. Barcelona: Literatura Random House.
Cercas, Javier (2017), *El monarca de las sombras*. Barcelona: Literatura Random House.
Chase-Riboud, Barbara (1979), *Sally Hemings: A Novel*. New York: St. Martin's Press.
Chase-Riboud, Barbara (1986), *Valide*. New York: Morrow.
Chase-Riboud, Barbara (1989), *Echo of Lions*. New York: Morrow.
Chase-Riboud, Barbara (1994), *The President's Daughter: A Novel*. Chicago: Chicago Review Press.
Chase-Riboud, Barbara (2003), *Hottentot Venus: A Novel*. New York: Anchor Books.
Donoghue, Emma (2004), *Life Mask*. London: Virago.
Donoghue, Emma (2008), *The Sealed Letter*. Orlando: Harcourt.
Donoghue, Emma (2014), *Frog Music*. New York: Little, Brown and Company.
Ebershoff, David (2000), *The Danish Girl*. New York: Penguin Books.
Ebershoff, David (2008), *The Nineteenth Wife*. New York: Random House.
Kent, Hannah (2013), *Burial Rites*. London: Picador.
Kent, Hannah (2016), *The Good People*. New York: Little, Brown and Company.
Lodge, David (2004), *Author, Author*. New York: Viking.
Lodge, David (2011), *A Man of Parts*. New York: Viking.
McCann, Colum (2003), *Dancer*. New York: Picador.
McCann, Colum (2013), *TransAtlantic*. New York: Random House.
Min, Anchee (2001), *Becoming Madame Mao*. New York: Mariner Books.
Min, Anchee (2004), *Empress Orchid*. New York: Mariner Books.
Min, Anchee (2007), *The Last Empress*. New York: Mariner Books.
Min, Anchee (2010), *Pearl of China*. New York and London: Bloomsbury.
Montero, Rosa (2003), *La loca de la casa*. Madrid: Alfaguara.
Montero, Rosa (2013), *La ridícula idea de no volver a verte*. Madrid: Seix Barral.
Muller, Stephanus (2014), *Nagmusiek*. Johannesburg, South Africa: Fourthwall Books.

Murray, Sabina (2011), *Tales of the New World*. New York: Black Cat.
Murray, Sabina (2016), *Valiant Gentlemen*. New York: Grove Press.
O'Connor, Nuala (2005), *To the World of Men, Welcome*. Dublin: Arlen House.
O'Connor, Nuala (2009), *Nude*. London: Salt.
O'Connor, Nuala (2009), *The Wind Across the Grass*. Dublin: Arlen House.
O'Connor, Nuala (2012), *Mother America*. Dublin: New Island.
O'Connor, Nuala (2015), *Miss Emily*. New York: Penguin Books.
O'Connor, Nuala (2017), *Joyride to Jupiter*. Dublin: New Island.
O'Connor, Nuala (2018), *Becoming Belle*. New York: G.P. Putnam's Sons.
Sellers, Susan (2009), *Vanessa and Virginia*. New York: Houghton Mifflin Harcourt.
Tóibín, Colm (2004), *The Master: A Novel*. New York: Picador.
Tóibín, Colm (2012), *The Testament of Mary*. New York: Scribner.
Tokarczuk, Olga (2014), *Księgi Jakubowe*. Kraków: Wydawnictwo Literackie.
Unigwe, Chika (2013), *De Zwarte Messias: Roman*. Antwerpen: De Bezige Bij Antwerpen.
Unigwe, Chika (2014), "Soham's Mulatto," in *Africa 39: New Writing from Africa South of the Sahara*. Ed. Ellah Wakatama Allfrey. London and New York: Bloomsbury, pp. 328–35.

Biofiction scholarship from interviewees and interviewers and biofiction from interviewers

Froneman, Willemien (2017), "Ex-Centric Hermeneutics in Stephanus Muller's *Nagmusiek*," *Royal Musical Association Research Chronicle*. https://doi.org/10.1080/14723808.2017.1328013
Gardiner, Kelly (2014), *Goddess*. Sydney: Fourth Estate.
Kusek, Robert (2015), "Provincial, yet Major? Damon Galgut's *Arctic Summer* and Transnationalism of Biographical Fiction," *Journal of Commonwealth and Postcolonial Studies*. 3(1): 3–20.
Lackey, Michael (2014), "Introduction," in Jay Parini's *Conversations with Jay Parini*. Ed. Michael Lackey. Jackson: University Press of Mississippi, pp. ix–xxi.
Lackey, Michael (2014), *Truthful Fictions: Conversations with American Biographical Novelists*. Ed. and Interviewer Michael Lackey. New York and London: Bloomsbury.
Lackey, Michael (2014), "The Uses of History in the Biographical Novel: A Conversation with Jay Parini, Bruce Duffy, and Lance Olsen," in *Conversations with Jay Parini*. Ed. Michael Lackey. Jackson: University Press of Mississippi, 125–48.
Lackey, Michael (2016), *The American Biographical Novel*. New York and London: Bloomsbury.

Lackey, Michael (2016), "Locating and Defining the Bio in Biofiction," *a/b: Auto/Biography Studies*. 31(1) (Winter): 3–10.
Lackey, Michael (2016), "The Rise of the Biographical Novel and the Fall of the Historical Novel," *a/b: Auto/Biography Studies*. 31(1) (Winter): 33–58.
Lackey, Michael (2017), Biographical Fiction: *A Reader*. Ed. Michael Lackey. New York and London: Bloomsbury.
Lackey, Michael (2017), "The Futures of Biofiction Studies," *a/b: Auto/Biography Studies*. 32(2) (Spring): 343–46.
Lackey, Michael, and Katya Lackey (2018), "The Ethical Benefits and Challenges of Biofiction for Children." This contains my essay about an interview with Jane Yolen and Robert J. Harris, *a/b: Auto/Biography Studies*. 33(2) (Winter): 5–21.
Latham, Monica (2008), "Virginia Woolf's Suicide Notes: Michael Cunningham's Art of Transposing a Life's Epilogue into a Fictitious Prologue." *Last Letters*. Ed. Sylvie Crinquand. Newcastle: Cambridge Scholars Publishing, 37–55.
Latham, Monica (2011), "*On the Rocks*: Women (and Men) in (and out of) Love," in *Études Lawrenciennes* 42. Paris: Presses Universitaires Paris Ouest, 281–317.
Latham, Monica (2012), "'Serv[ing] Under Two Masters': Virginia Woolf's Afterlives in Contemporary Biofictions," *a/b: Auto/Biography Studies*. 27(2) (Winter): 354–73.
Latham, Monica (2014), "Thieving Facts and Reconstructing Katherine Mansfield's Life in Janice Kulyk Keefer's *Thieves*," *European Journal of Life Writing*. 3: 103–20.
Latham, Monica (2015), *A Poetics of Postmodernism and Neomodernism: Rewriting Mrs. Dalloway*. New York: Palgrave Macmillan.
Layne, Bethany (2014), "'Henry Would Never Know He Hadn't Written it Himself': The Implications of 'Dictation' (2008) for Jamesian Style," *The Henry James Review*. 35: 248–56.
Layne, Bethany (2014), "'I did it, I': The Afterlife of Sylvia Plath's Journals, 1956-2003," *Adaptation*. 7: 82–90.
Layne, Bethany (2014), "'Simultaneously Anticipatory and Retrospective': (Re) reading Henry James Through Colm Tóibín's *The Master*," *The Henry James Review*. 35: 87–94.
Layne, Bethany (2014), "'They Leave Out the Person to Whom Things Happened': Re-reading the Biographical Subject in Sigrid Nunez's *Mitz: The Marmoset of Bloomsbury* (1998)," *Bloomsbury Influences Papers from the Bloomsbury Adaptations Conference, Bath Spa University, 5-6 May 2011*. Ed. Elizabeth Wright. Newcastle: Cambridge Scholars, 30–45.
Layne, Bethany (2015), "The 'Supreme Portrait Artist' and the 'Mistress of the Phrase': Contesting Oppositional Portrayals of Woolf and Bell, Life and Art, in Susan Sellers's *Vanessa and Virginia* (2008)," *Woolf Studies Annual*. 21: 78–106.

Layne, Bethany (2016), "Reinstating 'The Person to Whom Things Happened': Review of Priya Parmar, *Vanessa and Her Sister*, Norah Vincent, *Adeline: A Novel of Virginia Woolf*, and Maggie Gee, *Virginia Woolf in Manhattan*," *The Virginia Woolf Miscellany*. 89 (Spring): 39–41.

Layne, Bethany (Forthcoming), "Her Own Words Describe Her Best?: Reconstructing Plath's Original *Ariel* in *Sylvia* (2003) and *Wintering* (2003)," *Plath Profiles*.

Layne, Bethany (Forthcoming), "The Turn of the Century: Henry James in Millennial Fiction." *The Henry James Review*.

Lodge, David (2006), *The Year of Henry James or, Timing is All: the Story of a Novel*. London: Harvill Secker.

Rademacher, Virginia (2012), "The Art of Seduction: Truth or Fanfiction in the World of Online 'Friends' and the Blogosphere." *Hybrid Storyspaces: Redefining the Critical Enterprise in Twenty-First Century Hispanic Literature*. Eds. Christine Henseler and Debra A. Castillo. *Hispanic Issues:* 9 (Spring), 97–122.

Rademacher, Virginia (2017), "Truth and Circumstantiality in Javier Cercas' Biofictions," *American Book Review*. 39(1) (November/December).

Sellers, Susan (2017), "Writing *Vanessa and Virginia*," in *Biographical Fiction: A Reader*. London and New York: Bloomsbury, 81–84.

Szymański, Wojciech (2014), "Aretino's Eyes: Looking at Paintings in Hilary Mantel's *Wolf Hall*," in *The Art of Literature, Art in Literature*. Eds. Magdalena Bleinert, Izabela Curyłło-Klag, and Bożena Kucała. Kraków: Jagiellonian University Press, 65–75.

Tóibín, Colm (2010), *All a Novelist Needs: Colm Tóibín on Henry James*. Ed. Susan M. Griffin, Baltimore: Johns Hopkins University Press.

Index